MORE THAN BREAD

J S Langley

"Their pains we felt not at all
Their lives we did not lead
nor their rise, their loves, their fall
when they bled, we did not bleed
Instead, we slept, throughout their time
deaf to care and tumult of the mind
until that which makes us what we are
together came and in our body bind
So, if to learn from our past's store
our own minds do turn, as they must
we ought, as we enter through the door
accept that we do but seek to filter dust
looking for diamonds and not for rust!"

Titus Lucretius Carus (circa 65BC)

Paraphrased "Keep the people fed on Bread and Circuses and they will (be sufficiently satisfied and) not have the passion to revolt."

**Roman satirical poet Juvenal
(1st-2nd Century AD) Satire X**

"The human soul needs actual beauty even more than bread."

**D. H. Lawrence, Nottingham
& the Mining Country, 1929**

"Living dangerously is what we all do, although sometimes we don't realise it. Life is fragile and we walk on eggshells, feeling immortal. The best thing, and maybe the only thing, is to make the most of every moment as if it were the last and try to leave the world a better place rather than a worse one…

G.L (Discovered Manuscript) n.d.

INTRODUCTION

1. How it all started

It is hot and humid. The rain has just stopped. Water is falling from the fingers of fronds 100 feet in the air that wave amongst the tree-sized horsetails, club-mosses, tree-ferns, and seed ferns, competing for height and light, and standing above an undergrowth of their green genetic cousins.

Down through this entanglement of species the water makes its way before dripping into the stagnant pools at their feet and creating a series of concentric ripples that spread and interfere with their neighbours, producing a unique, though transient, natural artwork. Swamp gases bubble to the surface, into the humid and sulphorous-smelling atmosphere.

It is 320 million years ago, and we are in one of the vast swampy rainforests that covered much of the land. It will be another 90 million years before the first dinosaurs tread the Earth. In this time, a far different group of animals reign supreme. Dragonflies, with a wingspan of 30 inches, hawk through the clearing air, their diaphanous wings shimmering rainbows of sunlight, their complex eyes hunting out their prey. An 8 foot long millipede, over 18 inches wide, undulates its armour-plated, segmented, body forward, its 60 legs working in rhythm as it searches out and feeds on the abundant plant matter littered on the forest floor. A scorpion-like creature over 2 feet in length lurks in the shade awaiting the rustling approach of its unsuspecting prey. Amphibians poke their eyes above the green pooled-water and between the fallen trees small reptiles scurry, hiding away in crevices.

It is a world that we have never seen, it is more time ago than our minds can easily comprehend.

And in this world Carbon, Hydrogen and Oxygen bind together in polymer structures; lignin and cellulose, strong enough to build and support the rainforest flora, and, on the surface of these, the miracle of photosynthesis is taking place. Carbon dioxide is absorbed from the atmosphere, an atmosphere thicker than the one we breathe today and 60% richer in oxygen. Water is absorbed through roots and transported by internal phloem and xylem circulatory systems. And sunlight, shining through a blue sky, powers the transformation, producing carbohydrate building blocks, releasing the redundant oxygen into the air.

Winds or time topples these trees and they wither amongst the undergrowth. The crack and fall of the highest breaks through the buzzing background noise of insects, the scuttling of feet, and the trunks crash through to splash into the standing water.

Anaerobic conditions and the lack of decomposing bacteria and fungi leave these bodies to accumulate, layer on layer, layer on layer... as there seems no end to theses floral life cycles, that seed, grow, topple, seed, grow, topple, shallow roots taking purchase on dead comrades. And so it goes on, for millions of years, each upon each, increasing the weight, increasing the pressure on the lowest and, little by little, death by death, hundreds of tons accumulate, then thousands, then millions.

But this world is not everlasting.

Carbon dioxide levels in the atmosphere decrease, temperatures drop by 8°C, and glaciation causes a significant drop in sea levels. In these cooler, drier conditions the rainforests do not fare well and their remnants are wiped out by further climatic change.

The demise of their habitat causes the extinction of many of the rainforest's inhabitants and creates a biological vacuum into which reptiles will come to thrive.

And so, the buried ancestral seams of lost life are compressed, and the temperature rises, pushing out water, the hydrogen and oxygen in the carbohydrates, enriching the seam in carbon. In time the seam sinks lower and is further compressed, further enriched, until it is 70-90% carbon, a new black rock is formed, and held, suspended, with energy to burn.

Over the millennia, land is laid on land and the remains of one age sinks beneath another until, wracked by greater forces, there is disruption to this regularity; compaction, expansion, upheaval, sinking, twisting, rising, fracturing and intrusion, a slow enfolding, a rippling that becomes a new temporary permanence of valleys and hills, rivers and seas, mountains and caverns, and within all of this, as a small aside, a black rock, softer than most, pokes its nose above the green… a geological clue to what lies beneath.

2. Coal and Us
(319.7 million years later)

The land that we plant our feet upon feels solid beneath our soles, but it is not.

The past is like a foreign land, distant in time but not in geography. Once parted from living memory it can only be recalled through the artefacts left behind. Just like the world today, the past cannot be told through generalities and conjecture. The texture of life then was no less complex than it is now. If we struggle to understand our own times, what chance do we stand of trying to understand a vanished one?

Our nature dictates that we continually seek to answer the same questions: 'Who are we?', 'Where do we come from?', 'Where are we going?' and in our quest for answers where do we have to look but backwards?

And so we look at parts of past, fossilised, worlds and simplify them for modern appraisal, like returned time-travelers who have lost their journals and whose recollections disagree.

A black rock, comparatively soft, breaks the surface, on the side of a hill or the banks of a brook.

New forests carpet the land, different woods, their roots planted well above the ancient remains of ancient forests.

Who knows when we began burning this black rock? It was easy to discover, this rock that kept on burning after a forest fire had subsided. Perhaps it failed to prove its worth at first, and so had to bide its time, almost worthless after so long in preparation.

In the time of flint axes and tools surface gathering or shallow mining were possible. But why would they do it? What advantage would it give them over the collection and the burning of the abundant supply of wood?

But when the vast forests declined and the human population increased, with its need to cook, to heat, to smelt metals, when the demand for fuel increased whilst it's traditional source decreased then, probably some 5-6,000 years ago, wood and wood charcoal were no longer enough and this strange black rock was utilised, perhaps through sheer necessity rather than efficiency, and our exploration and exploitation of this strange material began in earnest.

As there are different qualities of ore, so there were different qualities of this black rock, better or worse suited to need, and the best was dug, and stored, and traded, and used.

By now a single species has become predominant, brushing hindrances aside by the use of superior weaponry until the main threat that remains is itself. The land is no longer a partner but a possession. Everything is there for the taking, all things are impersonalised commodities, articles for trade in markets that assign values, values that vary based on location, supply, demand and fashion.

And at this time there is a new invention that holds sway. Gone is the trade of goods for goods, the bartering of value one to the other. Now begins **the age of Money**, first introduced to use up metals that cannot hold an edge, that had little practical use other than to ornament or hold drink or put food upon. This smoother of transactions fast becomes a monster of our own creation and, although it cannot be eaten nor drunk, cannot clothe nor house, build nor destroy, it takes control and becomes a facilitator of progress, an impediment to betterment, a basis for belief and order, a producer of disillusionment and tyranny. It smooths the path to a better life; it fuels conflict and greed.

It is plausible that the Romans used this fuel on Hadrian's Wall; there is some evidence of shallow workings and in the deposits left behind in the ruins of forts, although there would have been no shortage, at this time and in this area, of wood and wood charcoal.

As time flows on we can be more certain and a name is ascribed, 'coal', a word probably derived from the Old English 'col' or 'glowing ember'.

We are now only 1500 years away and can begin to accumulate clearer evidence.

In the 9th century the Anglo-Saxons have left us written evidence of coal being used in the household and for metalworking, and the Anglo-Normans give reference to their blacksmiths using coal.

In 1259 Henry III granted a Charter to the Freemen of Newcastle-upon-Tyne for liberty to dig coal. But the amount of smoke produced was deemed injurious to health and, with so much wood and charcoal still to hand, its use faltered.

In the 14th and 15th centuries, as need for alternatives to wood increased, coal was extracted from surface workings and increasing numbers of pits were dug, following the seams down into the earth.

In the reigns of Queen Elizabeth I and King Charles I, burdened as they were by taxes and monopolies, the coal industry flourished. As the pits went deeper the difficulties increased, exposing the need for ventilation and light to work by. Men, women, children and animals were all employed in conditions largely out of view of those who invested and prospered on the back of their labours.

As the pits became deeper and more widespread, new problems emerged; flooding, tunnel collapse, noxious gases, suffocation, and explosions were common and engineers and scientists bent their inventiveness towards these problems, developing new machinery powered by horses, standardising their strength to provide a measure of power in this new age.

But let us turn a blind eye to the worst of it and instead remember that James Watt patented his steam engine in 1784, Davy his miner's safety lamp in 1815, Stephenson his locomotive in 1829, and that their combined application in mining, railways, factories, shipyards, iron and steel works were seminal amongst an explosion of other inventions.

As need and new uses escalated, so the extraction of coal accelerated, in quantity and in efficiency, and there was an accompanying increase in both the numbers employed and the fatalities. By the middle of the 19th century every 50,000 tons of coal extracted cost a life, a yearly average of 5 fatalities for every 1000 people employed.

Mines extended and deepened and more rules and regulations were introduced, many for the better. The importance of coal rose to the level of a necessity, so much so that people began to worry that it may soon run out. Geologists searched for new deposits and were unanimous in their reassurances that there was no need to be 'feared of it's being all used up...'

3. Early 1900's Northern England

Why would intelligent, grown men voluntarily spend 10-12 hours a day in a hole in the ground? Why would their wives let them? Why would their sons follow them?

Throughout England, Scotland and Wales, the early 1900's saw mainly adult men and boys, aged 12 and upwards, routinely leave the surface world behind them and rattle downwards into darkness packed together like we are now on the London Underground at rush hour.

How can we begin to imagine, sitting in our centrally heated rooms, what their lives were like, the taste and smell of it, the touch and the sounds that held sway when sight was dulled?

But do it they did, and daily.

Nearly 1 million people out of a total population of around 38 million heaved over 200 million tons of coal out of the ground each year with the quantity of coal still remaining in the North Eastern deposits alone estimated at over 10,000 million tons, lying in a shallow basin-shaped coalfield 1,000 feet down that rested beneath a blanket of millstone grit, limestone and sandstone. The majority was 'good coal' and it lay waiting in seams that were, on average, 2-4ft thick.

These are just numbers, what is harder to see in our 21st century minds are the families, the homes heated by the very coal they dug, the shops, the cinemas, the railways that made up their world, the newspapers that fed their minds, the pit owners and shareholders that fed themselves well and managed the maths.

A tenth of the total population was involved in supporting the mining industry with quarries and brickworks, railways and seaways, shops and supplies. In the collieries, 1 in 4 of the employees worked above ground; cleaning, sorting, transporting, accounting, managing, paying, organising, buying, selling, ensuring that the men that went down into the pit were furnished with what they needed to do their jobs and that what came up, that ultimately paid everyone's salary, could be managed and dispatched promptly.

In this world electricity was a new and emerging utility, competing with steam and compressed air as a power source underground and in the wider world the internal combustion engine was on the rise, creating a need for oil, and, in the homes of the 'better off', natural gas is providing lighting and powering cookers.

The first powered flight was less than 10 years ago and the world is bubbling with the results of new explorations, new discoveries and old conflicts that are reported and read at lightning speed, the news filtered through the reporter's lens, the information as unbiased as Huckleberry Finn or Oliver Twist.

It was an age of increasing wealth, where everything was about looking ahead, and not about looking behind. It was an age of perpetual progress, it was an age of growing discontent at the uneven spreading of wealth, while everyone wanted more.

In the North East of England there was ample employment and this fueled a flow of immigration and the need for colliery houses, shops, pubs and schools.

These were lives of their place and time, far different from those who lived in the Amazon rainforest, or the African savanna, the Pacific Islands, or the 'untouchables' of India. Occupied fully by their own world, they came to accept their lot as 'normal', operating unconsciously within its bounds and conventions. The daily task of dealing with their own trials and tribulations, their own tragedies and joys, was more than enough to occupy their hearts and minds.

Average life expectancy was around 50, there was no NHS, no antibiotics, no vaccination programs. Doctors and Vets alike were expensive and could be unconscious vectors of infection. Pharmacies could mix a potion or ointment, a paste, an oil, some pills, powders or balms, all concocted from their shelves of mainly natural ingredients whose uses and doses had been learned and passed down over the centuries, patient by patient, through success and through failure.

The life expectancy of a miner was less than the average, with diseases like pneumoconiosis, also known as 'black lung' or 'miner's lung', and silicosis being the result of the repeated inhalation of coal dust. The symptoms of these diseases were evident every day in the mining communities through the laboured breathing and raucous coughs of the sufferers. Such ailments were accepted as an endemic condition, a condition that, if you were lucky, happened to others; until it happened to you.

The metal latticework of the pit head winding gear towered over each of the multitude of collieries, looming over the ant-like movements below, the red glow of the fires and furnaces, the belching of white, grey, black exhausts of steam and smoke. And, fanning out from the pits, lay regimented rows of terraced houses, and passing through and around these new villages, the tubs, rumbling empty and full, the rails, the traps and the carts, the roads and the pathways.

The men, the women, the children, the vehicles and the horses were all in independent, though interconnected, movement, harnessed to a common purpose, fulfilling their individual roles that collectively brought in the means to eat, to drink, to live, to love, to die, all under that same watchful eye, that turned and raised, raised and lowered, with the regularity of a ticking clock.

PREFACE

The window is open.

I can see the washed green of the open fields, hear the musical fluting of birdsong, smell the after-rain freshness. In my mind memories are rekindled of evermore dimly remembered times. I try to catch them before they disappear, they ripple through my fingers like melting snow.

Today is the kind of day that poets write about, but not me! I am inside, glued to my desk with a job to do. Even though I am alone, my imagination people's the space around me with a throng, jostling for attention.

Sunlight and shadows play in black and white patches that tremble, ever-changing, over the walls of the room, the floor, the ceiling, the stacked shelves of books where Jane Austen is squeezed in between Joseph Heller and Margaret Atwood.

If I could see my own reflection, look at myself from the outside, then I would see that I am hunched over, sitting uncomfortably, staring at a computer screen. I am trying to concentrate. I have a book to write. The curser pulses over a vacant line.

I think about how to begin.

How do you tell a story of a time that is not long gone but is far enough away to be a lost part of our collective recall, less easy to imagine than the Stone Age?

It is barely more than a century ago that the people I am trying to conjure up lived their ordinary lives, breathed as we breathe, sensed as we sense, and were heated by the same sun. But it is as if it were not just a different time but a different place entirely, a time deprived of colour and drenched in drudgery and hardship.

Drudgery. That's how we see the past. A world of hard work and short lives. Full of darkness and pain, the antithesis of the world that the human spirit hankers after. Yet Artistotle equated work with happiness, meaningful toil as a means of self-fulfillment.

And what of the evidence? Surely working deep underground in the sweaty, dusty dark for 10 hours at a time cannot be fun! But what of the fortitude, what of the friendships forged, the mutual dependence that superseded any difference in accent, colour or creed? Why would families relocate to pit villages if there were better on offer elsewhere? Our vision is blurred by our parochial present but what of other parts of the world that are currently at war? What of those countries where crops are failing, forests are burning? Ask those in the midst of these things whether they would rather be part of a pit village community… and then we may get a less jaundiced view, perhaps a better perspective.

Complete drudgery! I cannot believe it!

Were there no flowers in the Springtime, did no one ever laugh or sing?

It feels like I am embarking on a voyage into a dystopian past where there was no respite, a primitive time compared to our own sophisticated world, a time when people lived, and accepted to live, in conditions we would sneer at. There is no doubt that their lives, on average, were shorter than ours, but were they less fulfilled?

Since the early 1900s so much has changed but have we, as humans, evolved any further? Don't we share the same needs, harbour the same fears, and don't we retain the same predisposition to repeat the same mistakes?

In my mind I try to reconcile the many hours of research and reading that I have done in preparation for this task, during which I've tried to see what lies in the spaces between the black on white lettering that purports to tell our history. I've attempted to peek beneath the cleansed vocabulary and seek out the sounds and smells, the sights and saltiness of the places where people moved, worked, were born, loved, and died. Somewhere within this melange of fact and fiction I hope that I have heard some chattering echoes, though they be as fleeting as birdsong, of some of those who navigated their way through their allotted days, manacled to their times, just as we are manacled to ours.

So let us try to travel beyond the horizon of our own living memory to where imagination must take the place of flawed or limited recollection. Unavoidably we will carry with us, preloaded in our minds, the baggage of current perceptions of right and wrong, of good and bad. Knowing this, let us, through force of will, temporarily lay aside these 'truths' and take a backward glance at lives that we can never properly understand but upon whose endeavours our own lives have been built, directing our gaze towards the Noth East of England, flying over hills and streams, towns and rivers, swooping across a tract of land that is bordered on the east by a natural coastline and on the remaining three sides by invisible lines, drawn on maps and agreed by history and committee, lines that cut through fields, divide rivers, separate valleys and tickle the heather on the high moors.

Within these confines we find towns and villages that are connected by a spider's web of roadways, railways and rivers. Over these we pass as we descend towards one of the many small coal-mining communities that lie within reach of Newcastle upon Tyne, that has farms within walking distance, and that belches out its own smoke. As we get closer, we see there is a quarry and alongside this a small woodland that stands green on this sunny day, green, despite the coal mine that drifts grey smoke only a few hundred yards away, far enough downstream for the waters of a small stream to gurgle and crackle clear over scattered stones, whipping up small patches of white foam that sparkle bright in the captured sunshine.

It is a wood criss-crossed with tracks, a wood with open glades and today, on this warm, late, Summer's day, a wood with a small boy playing by the stream, a small boy called Jack…

Chapter 1

The afternoon sun was warm in the valley; wildflowers lifted their showy heads above the green grass blanket and nodded in yellows and reds and blues. Poppies rose the highest in the disturbed ground, dancing red, their black hearts beating to the rhythm of the gentle breeze.

By the chuckling water, upstream of the pit and running clear, Jack Lawley stood to attention. His raggedy trousers were almost long enough to touch the tops of his itchy grey woollen socks that buried themselves in a pair of scraped and worn hob-nailed boots that used to belong to his brother. A broad smile spread across his face as, oblivious to the real world around him, he inhabited his imagination. In his young hands he held a half-rotten branch, tightly clenched.

It was bigger than him.

But to Jack it was not a branch, it was a Martini Henry rifle, breech-loading and rifle bored, the pride and joy of any old soldier. He stroked the stock, he knew from his Grandpa that real soldiers looked after their rifle, fed and cleaned it with the care a mother would give her newborn child. This rifle, Jack's rifle, had been well-used over the last blue-sky hour and so the barrel was scorching hot and had to be handled with care.

Jack lifted the gun to his shoulder, a familiar, smooth movement that his Grandpa had taught him as they re-lived together the old man's war stories; stories that spoke of the African heat, a dust that caked the back of your throat, a khaki uniform that had replaced the red and matched the colour of the burnt land in which he had fought.

When his Grandpa was in full flow, Jack would stare at the scars on the old man's arm; the badge of a real soldier his Grandpa had said, the sign of a man. Sometimes the old man would let Jack run his fingers slowly along the hairless ridges and feel the slick unevenness. Jack would do this reverently, as if the old scars might suddenly re-open if he were too careless. With their imaginations joined they would fight the unseen hoards until Jenny, Jack's mother, called them in to tea, complaining that her father was filling Jack's head 'with all kinds of rubbish'. But Grandpa would wink at Jack behind his daughter's back, and Jack would smile away the criticism. Jenny's bark was always worse than her bite.

Now though, he was on his own in the woods and Jack was determined to show how well he'd learnt his lessons as he fought on, despite the searing heat of the sun that blazed under the lower rim of his light, imaginary, soldier's helmet and burnt the back of his neck a painful red. Jack ignored this imagined pain, knowing that such scarring was the honourable badge of a seasoned 'redneck'.

In front of him the black bodies of defeated warriors were piled high, some still moaning and groaning in their death throes. The onslaught of the ruthless Zulu Impi had been repulsed by the fearless stand of Jack and his imaginary friend, Rupert, who had passed him his ammunition and mopped the sweat from his fevered brow. But such a victory had only been won by the skin of their teeth and now that the fight was over Jack gasped for breath and tried to recover himself. After a moment, he straightened his back, stood up straight and erect to his full height, shoulders back, chest out, his face serious in what he hoped was a look of grim pride as he muttered to himself and to the world in general,

'For Queen, for country, and for the Empire.'

'Jack, what the hell are you doing?'

Jack turned towards the call. It was Edward, his older brother, and it broke the spell.

The soldier's pith helmet of tea-stained tan dissolved into a head of matted, tousled fair hair encased in a flat cap. The soldier's coat, khaki threaded beneath a brown covering of African dust, melted back into an off-white flannel shirt that was a hand-me-down from his brother.

Edward, who was already taller than his father, Frank, had broad shoulders and muscles hardened by his already two years working underground. He was much larger and more powerful than Jack by grace of his extra years and build and was still shouting.

'Ma sent me to look for you. She's worried sick about you as usual. God knows why. I've been looking all over the bloody place.'

Jenny did not allow swearing in the house, so Edward, old enough to be working down the pit and drinking with the local men in the pub, sometimes made up for it when he was out.

Jack stared at him, then at his surroundings. He was standing on the far side of the stone-chattering stream. Between the two brothers and across the stream lay a conveniently laid tree trunk, struck by lightning in some earlier, forgotten time and now used as a convenient crossing.

Jack looked at the stream, then at the bridge and then at his brother, he would not be brought back to reality so easily.

His fertile imagination worked up a new scheme.

His clothes turned to a shade of Lincoln green, although he didn't really know what colour Lincoln green was, and he lifted his face to look at his brother, his back stretched to the very limits of his tallness.

'Do not attempt to cross this bridge Little John for I, Robin Hood, am your superior and have the right of way.'

'What the f…?'

Taken off-guard Edward hesitated, then grinned.

His younger brother's imagination never ceased to amaze him and looking quickly around to ensure that they were not observed, he rubbed his coal-grimed chin, felt the reassuring rasp of fine, unshaven stubble, and decided it might be fun to join his brother in this latest round of fantasy.

Picking up a large stick, a foot and a half longer than Jack's, he turned his flat cap peak-to-back and stepped forward.

'I challenge you, Robin Hood,' he shouted, 'for no-one gets the better of me. I am Little John, the toughest guy around here.'

'So, we must fight,' shouted back Jack, a white smile splitting his soiled features, 'there is no choice. This is war, and our war is our duel.'

A cloudless blue heaven peeped through the tangled canopy of branches and leaves; shadows shifted about their feet driven by the gentle breeze. The stream sparkled.

Edward and Jack stepped onto the opposing ends of the tree-trunk bridge. The chattering water and the occasional twittering of invisible woodland birds bore witness to the approaching conflict.

The bridge was part carbon-charred black, evidence of its violent past, and was slowly decomposing. The surface was slippery and streaked with the browns, yellows and greens of encroaching moss and fungi. Bracts stood from its sides like ears, listening but not hearing.

'Come on then Jack, let's be having you,' said Edward, stepping onto his end of the fallen tree.

'I know not this Jack of whom you speak,' said Jack, 'make way Little John, make way for Robin Hood.'

Jack stepped forward, his boy-pitched voice reverberating through the still, clear, Sunday morning air of childhood.

'You must be bloody joking,' snarled Edward, as he swung his staff in a wide, experimental, aggressive arc. The stream below sighed with the swish of this haymaker of a blow.

In the story Jack had read, Robin Hood and Little John duelled to an exhausted standstill.

In this more real-world encounter Edward's stick caught Jack "smack!" on the side of his head and knocked him off-balance. His staff somersaulted from his grasp, and he scrambled desperately for a purchase but found nothing but fresh air.

As he lost control, his world began to operate in slow motion. He seemed to watch himself, a helpless observer of his own downfall, as he spiralled lazily through the air, reaching out his arms, grasping with his fingers, stretching, and falling agonisingly short of a safe hold, frantically he reached out for something, anything, to grab hold of and halt, or at least slow this agonizing decent.

But it was not to be, and time fast-forwarded to normal speed as he crashed heavily into the cold, stony bed of the stream.

Briefly he felt a sharp, knife-like pain accompanied by a dull thud as his head hit a subsurface rock.

And then blackness shrouded and enveloped him.

Slowly a thin red line unfolded onto the surface of the cleansing cool waters of the stream and began to wind its way downstream.

Edward laughed in his triumph.

'Take that Robin Hood,' he cried, adrenaline still pumping through his victorious veins, 'that was too easy.'

He looked down at Jack lying prostrate in the stream and thought that he was acting again, trying some new trick or to be dramatic in order to negate his defeat.

'Get up!' he called.

But Jack did not move.

'Come on, Jack, get bloody up.'

But there was still no movement.

'Jack, stop messing about, I beat you fair and square.'

Met with only stillness and silence, two characteristics foreign to Jack's nature, Edward peered more closely and saw the red on the water.

Victory turned to panic.

Edward threw aside his now-offensive weapon and jumped into the stream. It was only ankle deep and he splashed over to Jack and grabbed at him, pulling his face out of the water, and shaking him back to a dazed semi-consciousness.

'Shit, shit, shit! What will Ma say now… and what will father do?'

Only blurred images and muffled sounds, as if coming to him through a blanket, were discernible to Jack. He groaned.

'Oh, thank god, thank god,' said Edward, 'At least you're not dead.'

As Jack partially emerged from the warm, comfortable blackness of unconsciousness he felt an excruciating pain that pounded in his head, as if someone were beating a drum in his brain. He moaned and Edward lifted his arm around his shoulders and dragged him effortlessly out of the water.

'Listen Jack, just tell Ma you fell, OK. You fell over. Got it. OK?'

Taking the weight of Jack's body, Edward threw him over his shoulder and started off, half-walking, half-jogging, in the direction of the smoking rows of colliery houses.

Chapter 2

And to what kind of home was Jack carried back, and to what kind of world?

His was a time when the natural balance was shifting.

The land was being vacated and taken for granted, the perception of its importance was diminishing, whilst towns and cities were growing.

The race was on to exploit new machines; inspired by invention, fuelled by coal and gas, driven by steam and electricity.

The ripping from the earth of long-buried resources ever more quickly and in higher volume was both lucrative and imperative.

At this time such underground resources were easily located and apparently of infinite supply. It was as if they had been purposely laid down millions of years ago in anticipation of this moment, lying buried and largely undisturbed, awaiting the advent of man and his reaching of this pinnacle of social development, of discovery, of exploration, of invention, of industry, of ambition and of intent.

People moved with the work. New mines were dug and new communities created from amalgamations of immigrant workers from all parts of the British Isles.

At this time there were more jobs than miners.

These workers and their families needed homes, so the mine owners constructed them, making the roof they put over their worker's heads a part of their employment contract.

New towns and villages sprang into existence and grew. Streets of terraced houses with small front gardens and back yards that held a coal store and a dry privy.

Inside, the houses had two downstairs rooms and two up. The most important room in the house was the back room with its coal fired cooking range. This room was multi-functional, it was the kitchen, the dining room, the bathroom, the laundry, and sometimes a bedroom.

But Jack knew nothing of such wider context, why should he? What he did know, and that intimately, was that his village had three identical streets of houses, creatively named First, Second and Third Street and that the matriarchs of each house fought a perpetual battle with water, soap, mop and bucket against the black dust that blew over from the mine workings when the wind was in the wrong direction.

Jack lived in Second Street, at number 21.

As they approached the outskirts of the colliery village the air smelled of smoke.

Edward stumbled forward, still half-carrying, half-dragging his semi-conscious brother. At the bottom of Second Street, they were spotted by a young girl.

It was Sarah Hudson one of their neighbours. She was a little younger than Jack and was skipping and chanting, throwing up dust with her feet.

She called over,

'What's up Jack, Edward, you playing wounded soldiers? Can I be nurse?'

'It's not a game, Sarah,' gasped Edward, breathless from his exertions, 'run to our house. Tell our Ma. Jack's hurt. Hurt for real.'

Sarah was shocked, but she understood immediately, and without another word she turned and started running up the street. Like everyone else, Sarah was no stranger to the realities of accident, injury or even death that were all facts of life in the colliery village, and she ran as fast as her legs would carry her, clattering up to the open door of number 21, and not stopping, but rushing straight in, yelling,

'Quick, come quick, come quick, Jack's been hurt!'

Jack's mother was at the kitchen table. Her youngest son, George, was tugging at her apron for support, unsteady on his legs.

Before Edward reached the front step, Jenny was outside and so were a small but growing number of interested, curious or concerned neighbours that had heard the noise.

Jenny wiped her hands on her blue checked apron; a neighbour took hold of George and moved him away with offers of a piece of bread and butter. Edward was already taller than his mother whose wiry frame belied her strength. She pushed him aside to get a better look at Jack.

'What's happened? Let me have a look.'

Jenny's fingers parted the matted hair that lay lank on Jack's forehead, feeling for damage. There was a deep cut just above Jack's right eye from which the blood flowed. Jack winced as she touched it.

Edward started to gabble an explanation.

'So, he hit his head?' asked his mother.

'It was a game. It can't have hurt. It must have been when he fell in the stream.'

Jenny turned to look at Edward. She reached out to touch a slick red patch on his shirt, took in the sweat streaming down his forehead, the worried look on his face.

'But you're bleeding too.'

'No, Ma, that's Jack's blood. I carried him back.'

Jenny turned her attention back to Jack.

'So, he fell in the stream?'

'Yes, off that old tree that's there, the one across the water.'

'And he hit his head?'

'I didn't see,' said Edward, grim-faced, sheepish, holding back.

'Alright, stand away now Edward, leave Jack to me. Go and find George for me.'

'But…'

Jack blinked and caught a blurred glimpse of his mother's concerned face.

'Jack! Jack! What have you been up to?'

His head buzzed.

He felt pain, it throbbed like a living thing, he could hear it in his ears and thought that it must be the only sound in the whole world. Surely everybody must be hearing it. He closed his eyes tightly, trying to escape into a quieter, less painful world. As he reached back, he could feel the blackness returning, it felt warm, welcoming, comforting. The last sounds he heard as he drifted away were in his mother's voice. She was talking to the assembled neighbours.

'Liz, can you go get Elsie Walton,' she said to a neighbour, 'I think we'll be needing some stitches,' and then, turning to the rest, 'Doesn't look too bad. I can cope with it from here, thanks.'

The small crowd dispersed, some disappointed that the drama was seemingly over. Sarah Hudson was the last to move away.

Vets and doctors were costly, even assuming you knew one that would respond to your call in good time, so the option of using someone from within the community who had a reputation for 'knowledge and experience' was often the preferred option. In several respects farm animals, especially the big shire work horses, got more care and attention than people.

Elsie Walton was related to the family that ran the Pharmacy in the local town. It had not gone down well when Elsie announced that she was going to marry a miner although, from the evident change in the shape of her body, there was general acceptance that the matter was of some urgency.

Now firmly established in the mining community, Elsie lived at number 1, First Street, and maintained a large store of medical supplies. Although procured primarily for her own and her family's use she was happy to share both her supplies and her expertise with anyone who asked for it, and, as word had spread of her knowledge, this was now most of her neighbours and friends. She was particularly known for her ability to stitch up both animals and people and she took equal care with both. If a job was too big for her, or outside of her capabilities, then she would say so. She would never pretend to be more than she was or to know more than she did.

She was a large woman, straight talking, scrupulously clean, with a big heart and a ready smile.

Jenny was on the lookout and was relieved to see Elsie, with her recognisable gait, waddling quickly up the road, bag in hand.

'What seems to be the trouble?' she asked, as she settled down onto her knees alongside Jenny and Jack, breathing deeply to try to catch her breath after such a brisk walk.

Jenny showed her the cut and explained what had happened. Edward watched on but kept quiet. Jack groaned.

'Alright, let's lift him into the house and I'll see what I can do.'

Edward stepped forward and lifted and carried his brother through the open front door, through the front parlour, past the potted aspidistra that looked on with bowed head, and into the back room. Here he laid Jack gently on the kitchen table and stood back, waiting for further instructions.

Elsie wouldn't have known the statistics, but she knew that infections were often worse than the original wound, that they were common and that they often led to a fever and even death. She probably wouldn't have called it blood poisoning or sepsis, but she was a stickler for cleanliness and believed that by keeping everything; the home, the body, and any cuts or other wounds clean, that the risk of infection was kept down.

In fact, infections were the most common cause of death across almost all age groups and, although research was progressing into the causes and means of prevention, the breakthroughs that were to come had not come yet and the average lifespan across the United Kingdom was close to 50.

A number of the infections and diseases, like dysentery, cholera, and typhoid, were waterborne and historically there were two defences against the poor quality of the drinking water; one was fermentation and the other was boiling the water.

The process of fermentation was a form of water purification and sterilisation and as the climate in the North East of England was not conducive to the growing of grapes and the consequent production of wine, it was beer that had become the trusted staple.

Brewing was not a modern invention; it was probably established by the Celts well before the arrival of the Romans. It certainly took place whilst they were here though, and there is archaeological evidence of Roman soldiers imbibing quantities of 'Celtic ale', an ale made from malt and flavoured with herbs or honey. It would have been very different to the beer the Lawley family were familiar with, as hops were only introduced to England in the 15th century.

The boiling of water was the second method of sterilisation and the introduction and spread of tea drinking, which by the 19th century was available in quantity and at a cheaper cost than beer, had spread to all classes and communities across the United Kingdom. The advent of tea coincided with the growth of towns and cities. Such a concentration of population, initially coupled with the poor sanitation, increased the transmission of infections and disease. Tea drinking, which became a national obsession, was a significant weapon in combating this.

As well as the boiling of the water, the tea itself contained a range of ingredients including antioxidents that provided a stimulant effect, enhanced blood circulation and protection against disease. In Jack's household, amongst most others, tea drinking was considered an everyday necessity, and the kettle was never far from the range.

The addition of milk and sugar to personal taste served to increase its popularity and as it still tasted good cold, it was a universal part of a working man's 'packed lunch' or bait, although a hot drink was always welcome on a cold or rainy day, as a break from chores or after hard toil. It was no coincidence that tea was one of the first products that the Co-operative Society first provided when they emerged to combat the 'Company Shop' with its elevated margins.

With Jack laid on the kitchen table in front of her, Elsie Walton rolled up her sleeves and got down to work.

'Boil a kettle for me, Jenny, would you please, somebody bring me a bowl, a jug of cold water and a clean flannel.'

'Do you need any soap?' asked Jenny.

'Don't worry, pet, I've brought my own.'

If Elsie's job was hygiene, then one of her essential tools was her soap. And it was not just any soap. Elsie believed in the advertising liberally spread about by William Hesketh Lever and his company, Lever Brothers. Sunlight soap was best for general cleaning, Starlight soap for the complexion and, crucially, Lifebuoy Disinfectant soap, "a carbolic disinfectant for use in the prevention of sickness and the preservation of health, guaranteed perfectly pure and free from injurious chemicals", for cleaning wounds.

There were other soaps, lots of them, but Elsie believed in the purity, the efficacy and the consistent quality that Lever Brothers claimed for their products. Yes, they did cost more and yes, she did not have much money on which to keep her household afloat, but even so she felt it was money well-spent. She knew in her bones that it was the right thing to do and although they lived very different lives, came from very different classes of society and there was very little prospect of them ever meeting, she felt that in William Hesketh Lever she had found a kindred spirit when it came to a belief in the importance of hygiene.

Elsie lifted a bar of Lifebuoy Disinfectant soap, with its characteristic red colour, out of her bag and laid it reverentially on the table.

Jenny brought over the whistling kettle from the range and Edward brought the rest.

Elsie let the water cool a little as she examined the wound more closely,

'Hmm, that's quite a cut you've got there, my lad,' she said.

Edward, listening, wished that the ground would open up and swallow him.

'Do you think it'll need stiches?' asked Jenny, peering over Elsie's shoulder.

'Almost certainly, but maybe just two or three. Let's get him cleaned up first and then we'll see.'

Elsie poured some of the water into an enamel bowl and tested the temperature with her elbow. She added a little cold from a jug and, when she was satisfied, she dropped in a couple of crystals from her range of medicines, wet the clean flannel, stroked it across the red bar of soap and started to clean Jack's wound, gently at first.

Jack winced and tried to pull away.

'Just you keep still my lad, it's for your own good,' said Elsie.

'She's right, Jack,' said Jenny, 'just do as Mrs Walton tells you.'

Jack wasn't in any position to argue so he bit his lip and tried to keep his dazed and throbbing head as steady as he could.

Elsie Walton cleaned the wound fastidiously, using clean areas of flannel as other parts became soiled, dipping it into the bowl to refresh the water and the soap when necessary. She fought her constant battle against infection with a concentrated earnestness knowing that even lesser wounds than this could become deadly if they were not cleaned and treated properly. When she was finally satisfied, she dug out a pot of yellow, greasy, evil-smelling ointment of her own making from her bag and smeared it liberally onto Jack's wound. It stung like blazes! Jack's eyes watered but he gritted his teeth and held himself as steady as he could.

'Just three stiches I think,' said Elsie, 'can you clean this bowl for me Jenny, and re-boil the kettle if you would.'

'Will he be alright?' muttered Edward.

'What's that?' said Mrs Walton, turning around to look at Edward, her face flushed from her efforts.

'Will he be alright?'

'I think so, but he'll need an eye keeping on him for a few days and if he develops a fever or dizziness I'll need to know.'

With freshly boiled water Elsie sterilised her implements and then bent forward and put in three neat stitches. Then she smeared on some more of the ointment, covered the area with a square of lint and wrapped a white cotton bandage around Jack's head. He looked like a wounded soldier.

Jack's eyes were fully open now and he was looking around, dazed but present.

'There, that should do it,' said Elsie, 'if he starts slurring his words or anything like that, then you'll have to get the doctor, otherwise just keep an eye on him like I said, and I'll come back to take out the stitches in about a week. He's already got quite a bump, but the cut looks as though it's clean. Good job he's got a hard head!'

Elsie Walton smiled reassuringly.

'Thank you, Elsie,' said Jenny, 'I'll watch him.'

'I'm feeling much better,' muttered Jack, and he tried to sit up to prove his point. As he did so he felt a shaft of pain as if his head had just been struck by lightning and he laid back down again with a groan.

'I'd move slowly if I were you,' said Elsie.

'That's foreign to his nature,' said Jenny, starting to relax a little.

Jack did as he was instructed, and, more slowly this time, tried again to sit up and slide himself off the kitchen table and onto his feet. Edward was standing by to catch him.

'Well, he's a trier that's for sure,' said Elsie, watching Jack's determined struggles.

'Go sit in Grandpa's seat by the fire in the other room,' said Jenny, 'I'll bring you a cup of tea.'

'And me?' asked Edward.

'You get washed, change that shirt, I'll be putting the supper out soon.'

Edward turned away; shoulders slumped.

'Oh, and Edward.'

'Yes, Ma?'

'Over supper the two of you can tell me and your dad what actually happened.'

'Alright, Ma,' said Edward gloomily. He wasn't sure how his father was going to react and, all of a sudden, he felt like he was five years old again, afraid of being scolded.

Elsie cleaned and packed away her things. As she was leaving Jenny said, 'Thanks, Elsie, I'll come round tomorrow and see about that blouse you wanted.'

'There's no need.'

'It'll be mid-afternoon, mind.'

'I'll have the kettle on.'

Edward gave up the whole bed to Jack that night, in a guilty effort to try and help him get some recuperative sleep. He slept downstairs in a chair, waking up with a stiff neck and aching shoulders. Jack, on the other hand, despite the luxury of having the bed to himself, still didn't sleep well. When he finally dropped off, he dreamt that he was standing on the top of a mountain, right on the pinnacle, balancing himself precariously, surrounded on all sides by cold air and the prospect of a precipitous fall. Here he wavered, trying desperately to keep his balance, a strong wind buffeting him, a wind that constantly changed direction, always blowing his hair into his eyes. It didn't matter how hard he tried, how hard he looked, there was no way down and he knew that he could not remain there forever, at some point his balance would give way and he would fall to a certain death. He tried to scream but the wind blew the sound back down his throat.

Finally, his foot slipped, his arms flailed as he fought for balance, but it was no good, the battle was lost, and he began to fall. He closed his eyes, felt the air rushing past him, felt his body turning, spinning out of control, felt the fear… and then he opened his eyes.

He was in bed, lying on his back, his whole body was slick with sweat, his head was pounding, his hands gripping the bedsheets. White knuckled he held on, seeking stability, wanting the world to slow down and settle. But the bed rose up, tossed and turned as if it were alive on a raging sea and Jack held on, body rigid, eyes open. As he watched, the bed pivoted and his head rose and as he looked down over his chest and past his feet, he could see a hole open up in the floor, a circular hole, spinning around its circumference like a whirlpool, and in the middle, in the middle, was only blackness.

Beyond endurance he held on, beyond his remaining strength he held on. The pounding in his head became the sound of the sea, of waves crashing onto jagged rocks, of a small voice that called out 'Jack!'.

And then he could hold on no longer, he began to slide down the bed towards the waiting blackness, a blackness that seemed to pull at his feet. Slowly at first, he began to slip, then faster, and faster, his feet disappearing into the hole, then his legs, his chest… the blackness must have him, he could fight it no more.

Just as he had given up hope, he felt a strong hand on his shoulder, a strong grip that held him and shook him.

'Jack, Jack, wake up, you're shouting, you're having a bad dream! Jack!'

Jack opened his eyes. He felt his familiar bed, the sheet drenched in sweat. He felt his head pounding, pounding like the beat of a drum, like hearing his own heartbeat. He saw the ceiling of his bedroom, sloped but steady. He felt the bed beneath him, stable, settled. And he felt the strong hand on his shoulder.

Slowly he twisted his neck, focussed his eyes. His mother was leaning over him, concern in her eyes,

'Sorry, Ma,' he murmured.

The mining village was built next to the pit itself, the pit head winding gear rising high above, wheels turning, steel ropes passing like sinews through its iron skeleton. The houses were laid out in terraced rows, like a military barracks, and the coal dust and the smoke gave a blackened appearance to the whole. To town dwellers these conditions might appear squalid and artists and writers from outside the community did little to dispel these views and everything to reinforce them.

But scratch the surface and there lay a vibrant and proud community.

There was no bugler, but instead the pit buzzer sounded out, calling the workers to their shifts, and for those that might learn to sleep through that clarion call, there was the 'thud, thud' of the 'knocker upper', who walked the streets and responded to the times chalked on the slates at each door. For each household their rhythms and routines revolved around the colliery shift system.

The next morning Jenny took off the bandage to have a look. Elsie Walton's ointment had kept the wound moist and made the bandage easier to remove without the problem of it sticking to the wound. Nevertheless, Jack winced as the cold air hit the tenderness of the newly exposed skin.

The area was a rainbow of colours; a red line crossed by black stiches surrounded by a swollen blueness that tended towards purple and yellow in places.

'Probably best if we leave the bandage off, let the wound dry off,' said Jenny, 'just be careful you don't knock it while you're at school.'

Jack was expecting this. He knew that his mother's mantra was that if you can walk, if you can talk, then you were fit enough to go to school. He could walk, he could talk, so no day off school for him. He didn't mind. He liked school. He looked at his mother with doleful eyes.

'Couldn't I have a bandage for just one day?' he said.

His mother looked at him.

'To protect it from getting dirty,' he said, although the real reason he wanted a bandage was to maximise the effect his injury would have on his classmates. He wasn't expecting sympathy but was already conjuring up suitably heroic answers to questions he was bound to be asked.

He held his mother's gaze with his sheepdog eyes.

'Oh, alright then, I'll get a clean bandage, but it comes off as soon as you're home mind.'

Jack nodded. This would provide a second opportunity, maybe some of his playmates would want to touch his wound when the bandage was off and maybe he could barter a marble or two for the privilege?

Chapter 3

This was not the first time Jack had worried his mother.

Jack Lawley was born screaming into the world in the Spring of 1895. Queen Victoria was in her 76th year, the 58th year of her reign, and it had been a harsh winter, the snow falling thickly and enough ice floating in the Tyne to be a problem for shipping.

Jack, at first, proved himself to be up to the task of infant survival. He took to the breast well, much better than his elder brother, Edward, and, as his mother would tell the neighbours, he was an easy sleeper. In fact, he slept so peacefully that Jenny would sometimes wake him, just to make sure he was alright.

At the age of 9 months, he was already pulling himself upright, at 18 months he was running around and attempting to form words.

At 21 months he was struck down with whooping cough and nearly died.

It started as what appeared to be just another cold, a runny nose, sneezing. It was when his temperature rose, and the coughing got more violent that Jenny began to worry. She'd seen these symptoms before in other people's children and knew it could be serious; even fatal.

When Jack had an episode of coughing that lasted until his lips turned blue, his eyes ran and every breath was a gasp, Jenny became desperate.

She clasped Jack to her to try and comfort him and settle his panic.

She talked to him gently and calmly although he was too young to understand what she was saying.

He, in turn, could not articulate how he was feeling and simply held tightly on to his mother who stayed awake all night with him, watching his breathing, keeping him going.

The next morning Jenny asked for help from Elsie Walton. She provided an ointment to rub onto Jack's chest and feet and also prepared a mixture of herbs and camphor oil, instructing Jenny to add a few drops into some boiling water and place it so that Jack could inhale the goodness in the moist tendrils of steam that rose into the stifling air.

Frank, Jack's father, together with his Grandpa, offered assistance but were shooed away. Edward kept his distance.

But despite all the care and attention the coughing persisted, and Jack grew weaker, unable to eat properly. Jenny began to fear the worst. She again talked to Elsie, asking her whether there was anything else she could do. She felt helpless as a mother, simply standing by and watching her son suffer like this.

Without consulting Frank about the expense, and on Elsie's advice, she called in the doctor, who visited the house.

Doctor Milne examined Jack and told Jenny to keep doing what she was doing and that, 'God willing', things would improve in the coming days. Jenny asked what she should do if there were no improvement, and the doctor declined to answer.

It was almost 3 weeks after the doctor's visit, the longest 3 weeks of Jenny's life, a 3 weeks in which Jack never left her side, cocooned in warmth, a 3 weeks in which Jenny continued, somehow, to carry on with the essential household chores; the cooking and the cleaning and the laundering, that things finally began to change.

Grandpa had tried to comfort his daughter and brought in fresh food from the allotment. Frank had done what he could to lighten the load, but he had to continue to do his shifts underground to keep the money coming in and, as far as the multitude of household tasks were concerned, he was hopeless. In fact, his ineffectiveness was one of the few things that brought a fleeting smile to Jenny's face.

At first the change in Jack seemed to be for the worse.

He became more uncomfortable and unable to settle. His temperature remained high. He had lost weight and strength and retreated into himself, curling into his blanket like an embryo in his attempts to find sleep. Jenny was half afraid to let him, worried that he may simply drift away and not wake up.

But sleep he did, and more often, each time for longer. Now when he coughed it sounded looser and his breathing less laboured. Jenny held her own breath and when others said that he seemed a little better she told them to shush, not wanting to tempt fate.

In the long days that followed it became obvious that Jack had weathered the storm, his appetite returned with a vengeance and agonisingly inch by inch, step by step, he regained his health.

Jenny was a combination of delighted, afraid, thankful, and exhausted.

In later years Jack would not even be able to recall ever having suffered from whooping cough, but his mother would always remember it… every second.

But this was not the end of it. There was Chicken Pox, Measles, Mumps, Scarlet Fever and a broken arm awaiting young Jack as he made his precarious way through his infant years.

'Best the boys get sick when they're young,' his father would say in response to Jenny's worries, 'they're more resilient when they're young and it's no good if they go down the pit and start catching things then. They'll not be popular if they're full of infection when they're down there or if they're always sickly and taking time off and losing their money.'

It was a harsh doctrine and not always the right one. Infant mortality was high, and these accidents and diseases could be fatal.

Jenny held her tongue however and soldiered on, helping her boys as best she could. She knew that it wasn't that Frank didn't care for 'his boys', in fact it was all he lived and worked for, to keep a roof over their heads and food on the table, but he couldn't equal the emotional depth of their mother. It was one of the things he loved about Jenny.

Jack, it seems, took his father's words to heart.

The Chicken Pox initially presented itself as a slight feverishness before confirming its presence by a rash of red spots that started on Jack's back and then spread itching and ugly over his face, chest, arms and legs. Within a day or two the spots had turned to pustules, and it was all Jack could do to stop himself scratching himself raw.

'Try not to scratch them,' said his mother, a task easier said than done, 'if you scratch them, they can leave a scar, but if you leave them alone they'll go away by themselves.'

She saw the disbelief in Jack's eyes; saw into the uncomfortableness of the world he was currently inhabiting. Each second was an irritation; there was no position he could lean into or rest in that would bring any comfort for more than a moment. In his young mind this illness was his whole life, and the suffering endless.

Jenny rubbed his irritated skin gently with Vaseline that brought little whimpers of temporary relief. She fed him on milk and barley water and from Elsie Walton got a concoction of nitrate of potash that Jack drank sparingly to relieve the fever.

The pustules eventually dried up and health flowed back into Jack's young limbs as easily as it had flowed out. It was an astonishingly fast recovery, and Jack seemed to instantly forget what he'd been through and get back to behaving like the young, energetic, mischievous boy that he was.

'Told you,' said Frank, as he and Jenny watched Jack running about in the yard.

'That's easy for you to say,' said Jenny.

The Measles was worse.

It again began like a common cold and then morphed into fever, and a cough and a headache. Then came the rash, appearing first on Jack's face, making his skin feel rough to the touch. Half-moon in shape, raised from the skin and dull red in colour, the rash galloped downwards to cover the rest of Jack's body within the next 24 hours. Vomiting and inflammation of the eyes added to Jenny's concern, and she again sought advice from Elsie, who came round and examined Jack from top to bottom.

'I know it looks dreadful,' she said, 'but it's a good thing the rash is out, it's much more dangerous if it isn't.'

Jenny tried to look reassured, but failed.

'Keep him in bed, keep him warm and quiet. Feed him on barley water and milk. It's important he doesn't lose too much liquid. Even if he doesn't want it, do what you can to get him to drink. If he gets worse then get the doctor, there's only so much I can do. Keep him warm and watch that his breathing doesn't worsen. That's the worst thing with measles, the chest and the lungs, just keep a close eye on him, even through the night. I'll bring over a drink for the fever. Boil his clothes and sheets, use Lifebuoy soap to keep things clean.'

These were hard rules to follow when Jenny had the rest of the household still to look after. Frank, Edward, and Grandpa mucked in where they could. Meals were reduced to bread, butter, cheese, jam and tea, always tea. But there were no complaints.

Jack was moved downstairs to be close to the fire, and the fire was kept fed with coal so that it burned through the night as well as the day.

It was impossible to maintain 'ideal' conditions in such a cramped and busy house, but Jenny did the best that she could. Elsie brought along a quinine tonic with the instruction that Jack be given a tablespoonful three times a day and that he should be encouraged to eat what he could as well as drink.

The strain on the household was immense, and Jenny was getting exhausted.

Grandpa, who normally slept in the kitchen but had been moved onto the couch in the front parlour, tried to help where he could. The kitchen and backyard were a sea of waving washing, even more so than usual, as Jenny tried to keep everything clean and replace Jack's bedding and clothing regularly. Grandpa would ask Jack if he wanted to hear a story and Jack would nod, he loved to hear stories. For Jenny it was a welcome distraction and a temporary respite.

Grandpa liked to fill his far-fetched stories with witches and gremlins, goblins and trolls, and would have a twinkle in his eye as he rolled out the words. Jenny was convinced he made them up as he went along.

'OK,' he said, 'I'll tell you a story.'

He put down his empty pipe, sat down on one of the kitchen chairs, and made himself comfortable. Jenny picked up her sewing, it was what she did to relax, it was what she enjoyed doing. She also liked hearing her father telling his stories, though she seldom admitted it. She knew he was proud enough of his talent without any encouragement from her.

'This story doesn't have a beginning, it starts in the middle,' said Grandpa, 'It's a story about a little boy and the little boy is in a witch's kitchen. The door is locked and barred but there is a window. The witch has forgotten to lock that and, you never know,' Grandpa winked, 'but that might be important later on. I don't know how the little boy got there,' he continued, 'but I do know that he was in terrible trouble. I don't know if you've ever been in a witch's kitchen,' Jack, who was trying his best to listen without wriggling all the time, shook his head slightly, 'but it's not a very nice place to be, you need to get out of it as quickly as you can, it's full of strange things and strange smells, like bat's wings and frog's tongues and boiled cabbages. You don't want to stay in there if you can help it.'

Jack crinkled his nose in disgust; he didn't like cabbages. His eyes glistened red in the flickering light from the coal fire, it matched the colour of his rash.

'Now then, the witch peels some carrots and puts them into a big black metal pot with some potatoes and other vegetables. She heats the pot over a roaring fire. When everything's in she dips one of her bony fingers into the pot.

"Not quite hot enough yet," she says to herself, and then turns to the little boy and says, "Another few minutes and then you can jump right in. I'm hungry, you know." And right at that moment her stomach rumbles, making an empty kind of noise.'

'You see, the witch was going to boil the little boy into a stew,' Jack's mouth fell open, 'but luckily the little boy was a clever little boy, and he had other ideas,

"I'm not going to jump into that pot until I know that you're a real witch," he said, "you might just be an old woman pretending to be a witch."

"Oh, but I am a real witch," said the witch.

"Then prove it!" said the little boy.

The witch scratched her nose with a long, dry, dirty fingernail.

"Well," she said, "I'm not doing much else this evening, so I suppose there's no harm."

'So, she took off her hat, held it upside down in one hand and clicked the fingers of her other hand over the top of it. There was a little shower of sparks, and a mouse jumped out from the hat, landed on the kitchen table, rolled onto the floor, and ran off to hide in one of the corners. The witch put her hat back onto her head.'

"There," said the witch, "is that proof enough for you?"

The little boy thought quickly, "No," he said, "anybody could have done that, that mouse could have been in your hat all along, and it just jumped out when you scared it with those sparks. Anybody could have done that."

"What do you mean, anybody could have done that?" said the witch, "no they couldn't, that was magic!"

"Well," said the little boy, "I don't believe it. You'll have to do something else to prove to me that you're a real witch and not just a clever trickster."

"You're a very awkward little boy aren't you," said the witch, "and I'm beginning to think you're going to be quite chewy when I eat you."

'The little boy gulped, but he stuck to his guns,

"If you want me to jump into that pot then you'll have to prove to me that you're a real witch, otherwise I'll run around this kitchen, and you'll have to catch me. Go on, do something else!"

'The witch really couldn't be bothered to chase people around her kitchen, especially as the little boy looked as though he could run quite fast, so she said,

"OK, watch this."

'And she took a little stick out of one of the many pockets in her long raggedy black dress and she waved it over a pie that was on the table. There was a little puff of smoke… and the pie grew legs! It grew legs, and it got up and it jumped off the table and it ran away into another corner of the room, a different corner to where the mouse was. The pie wasn't daft, and it didn't want to risk the mouse having a nibble at it.

"There," said the witch, "only a witch could do that!"

'The little boy thought quickly, and then he said,

"How do I know that that pie didn't just have its legs tucked underneath itself all the time and was just waiting for you to wave that stick? And when you did, it just unfolded its legs, stood up and ran off! I'm not sure there was any magic in that, it was just a trick like you see people do at the fair."

'The witch was getting angry now, and hungry, she wanted this sorted out so that the boy would jump into the pot and start bubbling away. She was pretty sure the water would be hot enough by now.

"OK," she said, "you tell me what I have to do to prove to you that I am a witch."

"Well," said the little boy, "that's an interesting question. You know, if you were a real witch, you would be able to change your size."

"Change my size! That's easier than giving a pie some legs or creating a mouse out of my hat," said the witch contemptuously.

"Well," said the little boy, moving across to the kitchen table where there was a bottle with a stopper in it. He lifted up the bottle and took the stopper out.

"If you were a real witch," he said, "you would be able to shrink yourself so small that you could fit inside this bottle."

"Think of something else," said the witch, "that's too easy."

"No, no," said the little boy, "if you can shrink yourself small enough to get into this bottle then that would prove to me that you were a real witch after all."

"OK," said the witch, and she raised her bony arms above her head and moved them around in circles. Then there was a kind of whooshing noise and the next thing the little boy saw was that the witch was inside the bottle!

'As fast as lightning the little boy pushed the stopper back on top of the bottle and jammed it there as tightly as he could.

'The witch was very angry and banged on the sides of the bottle with her bony fists.

"Let me out!" she yelled, "Let me out at once!"

"Let you out?" said the little boy, "so that you can put me in a pot and boil me up for your supper, and maybe a cold lunch tomorrow with the leftovers, you must be joking!"

'The witch changed her tune.

"If you let me out," she said in a soft voice, "I promise I won't eat you and what's more I'll give you a bag of gold to take away with you."

'The little boy laughed. He knew enough to know that you can't trust anything a witch says.

'So then he took the bottle and threw it into the pot that was bubbling away on the fire. Then he ran to the window… do you remember that even though the door was locked and bolted the window was open, I told you that might be important… and he opened it wide, and he climbed through it, and he jumped out the other side, and he ran off as fast as he could, and he kept on running until he got home. Oh, my goodness, what a story he had to tell everyone. The only thing is, I'm not sure if anybody would have believed him?'

'Was that a true story?' asked Jack, uncomfortable yet comforted.

'As true as there are witches,' said his Grandpa.

Jenny put down her sewing, 'Time for some more of that tonic now, Jack,' she said, then she turned and whispered to her father, 'Thanks, dad, I needed that.'

But these respites were few and far between and Jenny was showing increasing signs of tiredness. With Frank she was irritable, with anyone else she was subdued, and she proceeded from one task to another in a daze.

Then an invisible point was passed and, just when Jenny thought she could not carry on, Jack began to improve.

The first thing that happened was that the rash subsided, and then the skin dried and flaked and shed, and then, thanks be, the fever left. Only the cough persisted, stubbornly hanging on for a few more weeks before it too became a thing of the past.

'That was a bad dose,' said Elsie sometime later, 'I was a bit worried.'

'It was much worse than when Edward had it,' said Jenny, 'I was pleased of your help and doubly pleased you didn't tell me you were worried too. That wouldn't have helped at all.'

'I know,' said Elsie.

Compared to the Measles, Jack breezed through the Mumps, showing the customary swollen glands, a headache and a sore throat.

Scarlet Fever was another matter.

Although not as bad as the Measles the rash was red, ugly and angry and Jack's mouth and throat were very sore. Jenny saw to it that Jack drank his barley water, and she bathed him, using Lifebuoy soap as directed by Elsie, to ease his burning skin.

Soon the rash began to subside, and Jack cleared yet another infectious hurdle that had been placed across the course of his young life. Jenny was becoming expert at soothing, bathing, and warming and when her youngest son, George, came along soon after she felt she had more confidence in knowing what to look out for, how to deal with it and, crucially, when to call for help. She had not realised what a charmed life Edward had lived until she saw what Jack had had to endure.

The broken arm, achieved by Jack climbing too high and falling out of a tree, was straightforward compared to the infections. It was a clean break, healed quickly and left no lasting weakness or mark.

When not ill or injured, Jack was naturally inquisitive and showed a genuine curiosity about most things. His normal conversation was all questions; 'What?', 'When?', 'How?', but most often 'Why?'. This became an annoyance to most and his elder brother repeatedly told him to 'Not ask stupid questions!'

His Mother, Father and Grandfather tried to humour him and his mother would ask, 'Jack, where do you get all these questions from?' in exasperation while being secretly proud of his inquisitiveness, that she was convinced was a sign of intelligence.

This verdict she often repeated to her husband, who responded by telling Jack anything interesting he'd read in the newspaper that day. Jack soaked up stories and answers like a sponge and was not shy to say, 'Didn't you tell me before that…?' in a corrective kind of way, when one of the answers he was given contradicted a previous one.

It was a relief to all when he was in school.

Chapter 4

The head teacher of the village school was called Wilkinson Hughes.

There were two classes. His wife, Enid, taught the younger children, and Wilkinson taught the older ones. Short in stature his voice boomed and bounced off the classroom walls, the trace of a Welsh accent still recognisable to those in the know.

Both deep and resonant, the sound rose from his chest as if each word was eager to express itself clearly before it was trampled over by those coming after.

At 5 feet 5 inches tall and of muscular build he was the ideal stature for a miner; strong in limb and able to negotiate most of the underground tunnels without the risk of developing a permanent curvature of the spine. And indeed, Wilkinson Hughes had been a miner, an underground worker, rising to Putter and then on to do the job of a Hewer, shifting coal at the face.

For more than ten years he had worked down the pit and those that worked with him said that if you had Wilkinson Hughes as part of your crew then there would never be a shortage of conversation, even if, at times, no one was listening. They would also say that he was always ready to lend a hand and was liked for it, and that he was not shy to offer a word of advice, whether it was invited or not, and that this was less widely appreciated.

His ebullient, honest character overcame most reserves though and he was popular enough, always likely to smile or to raise the spirits of others. It was therefore seen as a real shame when he had his accident, trapped between unforgiving metal and stone, his leg damaged, his shoulder broken, an accident that had left him with a slight limp and a weakness down one arm.

Unable to work underground and with little money to his name he was offered the opportunity to train as a teacher and he leapt at it. With his wide interests and engaging character, he took to it like a fish to water and was now looked upon, along with his wife, with respect by those in the village who had children, and that was the majority. This esteemed position was not to be underestimated as, in a mining village, it was normally jobs that involved manual labour that were judged the higher calling.

The school day began at 9.00 am, the longed-for lunch-time break was from 12 until 2pm, and home-time was at 4pm.

Most children brought a slice of bread and butter to eat in the playground at morning break, but they went back home for lunch. There were no school meals.

Each of the two classes contained over 60 pupils, but the teachers could easily see the pupils at the very back of the class as they taught from a slightly raised platform. Even the teacher's desk, that sat on the teaching platform, was set especially high, with its own high-chair, so that the teacher could look out over the whole of the class even when seated. Both Mr and Mrs Hughes were eagle-eyed. The chances of bad behaviour escaping their notice was small.

Mrs Hughes seldom walked around the class, preferring to teach from the front. Mr Hughes, on the other hand, was a prowler, unable to keep still for long, and would walk between the lines of desks and benches waving his arms around expressively to punctuate his pronouncements. His wife would regularly chastise him about this, but he would only reply that if God had intended him to be still, He would not have invested him with so much restless energy.

When the teacher wanted to show something to the class, like letters to copy or sums to do, then they would write it on a large blackboard in white chalk. The blackboard was itself on a wooden easel so that it could be repositioned or moved around, if necessary, although this was rarely the case.

When the teacher had finished with the blackboard or needed more space, one of the children would be told to clean it with a duster. It cleaned easily but with a lot of writing or a dirty duster, and with over vigorous strokes, there could be quite a cloud of white chalk dust produced which got up the noses of the children seated near the front and made them sneeze. The white dust was in stark contrast to the black dust outside, that the wind constantly carried in from the pit head.

Each of the two classrooms had its own coal fire. Coal was supplied free from the pit so there was no shortage. The school caretaker cleaned out the fireplaces and re-set them with paper, sticks and coal at the end of each school day and refilled the coal scuttles ready for the following morning.

Entering the school was like entering a church. There were two entrances, one at each end of the building, one for 'Boys' and the other for 'Girls'. Each had a large, arched, red stone doorway and the pupils were called to lessons by the ringing, actually the loud clanging, of a handbell, shaken vigorously by Wilkinson Hughes, in his good hand.

The face he wore for his pupils was schoolmaster-stern and indeed it was a foolish student who went against him, especially when a beating at school was often followed by a beating at home if news of a misdemeanour was relayed. Most times though Mr Hughes' look was somewhat softened by an irrepressible twinkle in his eye.

The first area encountered, after the children had passed over the threshold of the building, was the cloakroom, a separate one after each entrance. Here they divested themselves of any heavy outdoor clothing and made their way quickly along a short corridor to one of the classroom doors.

If they were interested, and generally they were not, there was a paper pasted on the corridor wall outlining the "School Rules". This was largely superfluous however as a number of the children had not yet learned to read and anyway they all knew the most important rule; if you misbehave, you get whacked, if you fight in the playground, you get whacked, if you talk in class, you get whacked, if you spill ink, break something, trail mud into the classroom… then you get whacked and, most importantly, it is the teacher who decides if you deserve to get whacked or not and it is he or she who will dispense this justice, usually through the use of a rattan cane specifically procured for the purpose. What's more, as the imposed sentence was normally meted out in front of the whole class, so as to act as a deterrent to others, it was something best avoided if at all possible.

Once you understood this rule and the consequences of pushing the boundaries too far, then any other 'rules' were unnecessary.

It was the boys that got whacked most often; either because they misbehaved more than the girls or, more likely, they were caught more often. It was of no defence for a boy to say that someone else had put him up to it, in fact it was a sure sign of weakness and low moral fibre and may result in a harsher punishment.

In reality Wilkinson Hughes used the rod sparingly, but the threat was always there and when he did use it, he did it with the intent of teaching the offender a painful lesson.

Between the two classrooms was a partially glazed partition wall so that, if necessary, Mr or Mrs Hughes could attract the other's attention without the need to leave the classroom and their pupils unattended.

Each student was allocated their own space somewhere along the rows of wooden bench-desks, each space having its own white ceramic inkwell and, alongside that, a shallow trough designed to hold pens and pieces of chalk to stop them rolling about. Each student also had their own small wood-framed slate chalkboard.

Jack got his wish and was able to show off his bandaged head at school.

The teachers were little impressed as with so many children in such an environment, Jack's escapade was just one among many.

The children, on the other hand, were more interested and Jack exaggerated his story sufficiently to appear both brave and unlucky. He didn't tell anybody about his dream however as that was too scary and he wished he didn't remember any of it himself. Sarah Hudson was particularly sympathetic and, in the school yard, tried to push away those who wanted to touch the wound and find out how much it hurt.

Elsie Walton came back as promised, and carefully examined her handiwork, cleansing the area before removing the stitches.

'There we go,' she said, 'good as new.'

Jenny thanked her and told Jack he should too.

'Thank you, Mrs Walton,' Jack said obediently.

'I know this is wasted advice,' she said, smiling, 'as you seem to catch everything and then damage yourself just for fun,' Jack thought about his previously broken arm, he really shouldn't have tested out his powers of flight like that, he lowered his eyes, 'but do try and be a bit more careful.'

She took one last look at the wound, it was nicely healed, she was always amazed at the healing power of children.

'You'll just have a small scar, I think,' she said, 'I don't think anyone will notice it.'

Jack didn't want a big scar, but he did want some kind of mark he could point to when the need arose. This sounded perfect.

'Thank you,' he said again.

Chapter 5

It was now some time after Jack's accident, the bandage was forgotten, the scar barely visible.

'Sit yourselves down now,' said Wilkinson Hughes, 'get your chalkboards ready to copy the letters I've written on the blackboard and sit quietly.'

He waved his hand towards the blackboard and then looked out at his class. There was silence. He smiled.

'Armstrong.'

A small boy sat bolt upright as if he'd just received an electric shock.

'Yes, sir?'

'Armstrong, what is the first letter on the board?'

The boy looked and considered carefully; it was never comfortable to be chosen first.

'It is a "cee", sir.'

'Is it indeed,' said his teacher, 'and what kind of "cee" is it?'

The boy swallowed.

'It is a capital "C", sir.'

'That's right, Armstrong. It is a capital "C". It is no good learning to write if you cannot tell which letters are capitals and which are not.'

Wilkinson Hughes proceeded to pick on other children at random to read out the other letters he had written on the board, as well as the "C" there was an "o", an "a", and an "l".

'Now write these letters on your slate, and you older ones help the youngsters if they need it,' he paused, letting his eyes sweep from one side of the classroom to the other, 'but do it quietly.'

As they worked Wilkinson Hughes prowled around the desks, helping some, asking for more neatness from others, or simply nodding and moving on.

When he felt that sufficient time had been given to the task he moved back to the front of the class.

'Now, Elliot,' he said, turning to a girl of about 8, 'what have you written?'

'I've written a capital "C", a small "o", a small "a" and a small "l",' she answered diligently, before adding, 'sir.'

'Hmm,' said the teacher, 'Charlton what have you written?'

The answer was the same.

'And Lawley, what have you written?'

Jack looked at his slate, the letters were not as well formed or confidently written as he'd like them to be, his neighbour Sarah's were much better, and she was almost the same age.

'I've written the word coal, sir,' said Jack, 'with a capital "C".'

Wilkinson Hughes smiled.

'Indeed, you have my boy, indeed you have!'

The class let out an almost audible sigh of relief that the correct answer had been given.

'We have to learn our letters, but we also have to remember why we're learning them,' said Mr Hughes, 'they are our tools, like picks and shovels, spades and garden forks. If you don't put them to work, they are no good to you, no good at all.'

He paused for effect, then he carried on, getting into his stride.

'Letters need to be put to work,' he said, 'put into words, into sentences and so forth. And then they mean something. This word "Coal", for example, means a whole lot to us around here doesn't it. Its only four letters long but that word holds all our lives and our livelihoods, our food, our clothing, our housing, in its grasp. History is buried in its letters as well as beneath our feet,' Mr Hughes tapped the boarded and polished wooden floor beneath his feet and a few of the children couldn't stop themselves from glancing down at it, 'there is coal down there, I don't know how deep, but it is there, maybe at this very moment some of your own fathers or brothers, uncles or cousins are working down there, sweating in the darkness, heaving the coal from the face to the bottom of the shaft. And do you know what coal is?'

The class knew their teacher well enough to know that this was a question that they did not need to answer. No hands went up.

'Coal was once forests and swamps, trees, bushes, ferns, peat and so forth. Coal was once green and brown and yellow and red. It was part of a lush and plentiful vegetation that grew or fell and stewed in peat bogs on the surface of our Earth. Right here were we sit now there were forests.'

Some of the children's eyes were wide, how could coal be anything but a rock and anything but black?

'And then,' continued the teacher, he loved telling them things like this, educating them through engaging their minds, their imaginations, sharing his own enthusiasm, 'then these forests fell, the peat bogs were buried. Maybe they were crushed beneath enormously heavy sheets of ice that crept down from the North Pole. Maybe the sea flooded the forests and the swamps and the bogs, engulfing everything that had lived on fresh water in salt water and bringing them to an end. Maybe something else happened, but what we do know is that it did happen, and it happened a long, long time ago. Can you guess how long?'

A hand rose hesitatingly.

'Yes, Rutherford.'

'10,000 years ago, sir.'

There was a titter from some of the other children, nothing could be that old. They were all less than 12 years old, even their grandfathers and grandmothers were only 50 years old, if they were lucky, and that was very old indeed.

'Quiet,' said the teacher, 'thank you for your answer, Rutherford, anybody else?'

Jack's hand rose. He hadn't meant to do it, his body seemed to have become a law unto itself.

'Yes, Lawley.'

'Over three hundred million years ago, sir'

The class erupted in laughter. Wilkinson Hughes reached for his cane and rapped in on the blackboard. The laughter stopped immediately.

'Why do you say that, Lawley?'

'I read it in a book, sir.'

'And what book was that, Mr Lawley?' the use of "Mr" sounded threatening to Jack's ears, he answered cautiously, racking his memory to ensure he got it right.

'The Saint George's Magazine for Boys and Girls, sir.'

'That's a magazine not a book, Lawley.'

'Yes, sir, sorry, sir.'

'However,' said the teacher, 'you are correct. It was over 300 million years ago that the coal that we mine today was starting to be formed from dead and dying trees and vegetation.'

There was a murmur, 300 million years was a difficult thing to grasp. Wilkinson Hughes let the incredulous hum continue for a few moments. Jack breathed easier. Sarah nudged him.

'Well done, Jack,' she said.

'So, you see, all those millions of years ago this coal was laid down and covered by other layers of land, layers that were heaped one upon the other, and they were so heavy that they crushed, squashed and squeezed the coal so that all the water was driven out and it became solid, just like we know it today. And then it lay there, it just lay there waiting, waiting for the time when man would be clever enough to control fire, forge metals, invent engines and become ready to build the world we see around us today. Do you know what coal is?'

This time he did not wait for an answer, time was pushing on and he wanted to finish the lesson.

'After losing its water and going through other chemical processes over such a long time, what is left is mainly made up of only one element, and that element is carbon. There are different types of coal, some that are better for your kitchen fires, some for firing up steam trains, some for melting metal but all of them are carbon rich. And that's why it's black. If carbon of this kind of structure was red, like iron ore, we'd be burning red coal, your fathers would be coming home with red faces.'

He could see that the children had never thought about this, coal was coal and coal was black. But it didn't have to be, he just wanted to fire their minds while there was still time, before the pit, the home, marriage and family layered new responsibilities on top of them and buried their imagination.

Wilkinson Hughes was a believer in individual creativity, in always being interested in learning more, knowing more, applying that learning, passing it on to others. He wanted any passion they may have for learning not to die but to be encouraged. He hoped that someone in one of his classes would someday become a teacher and not a miner or a homemaker, a domestic servant or an accountant.

'…or what if it was yellow… or green,' he said, smiling at the children's incredulous faces. He was reaching the end of the lesson now, 'And this one thing, this coal, and our need for it to fire our new and developing world, is why we are all here today. It is why these houses, your homes are here, it is why your parents are here, it is why this school is here, it is why you are in my class today, it is why I am here to teach you. We are all built upon coal, remember that and let's hope there will always be coal and a need for coal, for if there weren't where would we all be then?'

He hadn't meant it as a question, but a hand shot up. It was Armstrong again.

'Yes, Armstrong?'

'We'd be in London, sir, that's where we'd be.'

Chapter 6

Jack had so far managed, perhaps by luck rather than good judgement, to navigate his way over a number of the life-threatening hurdles that were placed before each of the inhabitants of the colliery village. There were those who managed to completely avoid at least some of these perils but there were others whose journey's end was not a happy one. Even in fiction not all of the heroes and heroines survive to the end of the book.

With five, six or sometimes more children to look after the women ran their homes with military precision. The children were allotted chores, the older children looked after the younger and the mother controlled the family finances, ensuring that they stretched far enough to cover food, clothes, and cleaning and that there was, if possible, still a little left over 'for the pot'.

The doors of the houses were normally open and never locked. Neighbour knew neighbour intimately and the speed of word of mouth communication, of gossip, news and rumour, was faster than any newspaper could ever achieve and more embellished in detail, some of which was exaggerated or invented in the course of the repeated re-tellings.

Although the women would generally help each other out with half cups of sugar or flour in lieu of two eggs or half a pint of milk, and freely pass on advice, sometimes unwelcome, on the treatment of illnesses, or the correct method of food preparation, there was also a healthy, though largely unspoken, competition between households.

By some social alchemy an acknowledged pecking order was established with each matriarch intuitively knowing her own place and that of others.

Knowledge and wisdom would be passed from mother to daughter and some of the older women would also choose to mentor younger women that they particularly liked although there was also an undercurrent of tension as younger, newer, mothers strove to prove themselves against the tried experience of the older generation. Most of the time this provided spark and interest to their lives but on some occasions, it could become personal, and quite vicious, and could lead to unhealable wounds between the warring parties. Such contests may even escalate, with other women taking sides, and, over time, which could stretch to years, there could be real casualties.

The men would generally ignore the intricacies and dynamics of the female hierarchy and confine themselves to grumbling about the cost of food and clothing, and how little was left over for beer money.

Parents looked forward to a time when sufficient of their offspring survived to working age and the household income increased as a consequence. If a girl left to go 'into service' then it would be expected that she would send part of her income home.

This longed-for time of plenty presented the opportunity for a few luxuries or perhaps even for a few savings to be put aside before their children got married and moved out to take on their own responsibilities. At best this more affluent period was short-lived and families in this phase of their lives were looked on with a mixture of envy and hope.

It was Grandpa who brought the news, stroking his moustache and looking serious.

The Tindales lived on the same street as the Lawleys and Jenny could remember the arrival of the twin boys and how it had been welcomed as auspicious, both for the growth of the community and for the future of the Tindale family. Boys would bring in wages.

It was a common sight to see the boys running around together and being chastised by their mother for their mischief. They always seemed to be arguing but at the same time would stick up for each other against any and all outside threats. It was unusual to see either of them on their own, they came as a pair.

At Grandpa's request the Lawley family, all except Frank who was on shift underground, came together around the kitchen table. The coal fire crackled at their backs. Slowly he told his silent, attentive audience that the twins had gone off to play and had been seen disappearing towards the woods, which was one of their usual playgrounds.

On this occasion however they must have changed their minds and sneaked back unnoticed, making their way behind the rows, through the colliery grounds and towards the disused quarry.

Jack interrupted to say that it was well known in the school playground that there were lots of bird's nests and bird's eggs to be found in the low undergrowth that surrounded the quarry, and the twins might have gone looking for them. The best ones were the coloured ones with spots or splodges.

Grandpa continued. Jenny hung her head.

Unfortunately, because of the recent heavy rainfall, the old quarry, whose sides were steep and relatively bare, was deep with brown, murky water. It seemed most likely, according to the person Grandpa had spoken to, that one of the twins had climbed one of the trees that clung precariously to the quarry side and, on reaching out for a bird's nest, had simply overbalanced and fallen into the water. His brother, instead of running for help, had reached out to try and help him, even though neither of the two boys could swim, and followed his brother into the icy cold.

The slickness and steepness of the quarry wall, the panic which must have set in, the limited strength of the boys and the depth of the water all conspired against them and prevented the boys from gaining a suitable hold and hauling themselves out.

If they did call for help, which surely they must have done, the noise of the colliery workings, the rumble of coal as it was moved, tipped, and loaded would have drowned out their cries.

Whatever the case, the boys were unable to save themselves and, finally exhausted by their efforts, the water won, and they lost.

The faces around the kitchen table showed their understanding of what they were hearing.

'They were found this morning,' Grandpa concluded, 'after their parents had raised the alarm but darkness had hampered the search. They were floating on the surface of the water, face down, hand in hand.'

Although death was a constant companion to those who lived in the colliery village, disease or accident taking a regular toll, the death of such young twin boys was somehow particularly poignant.

The old clock chimed in the living room in the silence that followed.

'So, they won't be starting school?' said George, too young to grasp the full meaning.

'We'll pop in to pay our respects,' said Edward.

'I'll come with you,' said Jack.

'That'll be fitting,' said Jenny 'I'll tell your dad when he gets in from his shift and we'll go round tomorrow. I'll take them some bread and find out when the funeral is.'

Jack and Edward called at the Tindale's house, taking off their caps as they entered.

In the far corner of their kitchen, under the window, lay the two small corpses, swaddled in white sheets.

Mrs Tindale, a matron at thirty and heavily pregnant, welcomed them and directed one of her daughters to lift the edge of each of the sheets in turn.

'They've laid them out real nice already, and the coffins will be ready tomorrow.'

A younger child, a boy, crawled on the stone-flagged floor and Mrs Tindale gently directed him away from the kitchen fire with her foot.

'We're so sorry,' said Jack, 'If there's anything we can do…'

'Thanks,' said Mrs Tindale, wiping an eye with the corner of her apron, 'Your grandfather has already been round and left us a few eggs.'

Jack and Edward stayed only a few minutes, remembering the twins, swapping stories.

'Our mam will come round when she can,' said Edward as they were leaving.

There was a good turnout for the funeral. Some of the mothers had clubbed together to organise some food and the service took place at the village church.

The twins were not alone. Infant mortality was high as a result of the dampness in some of the older cottages, the poor water quality that always needed boiling before drinking, the variable nutrition and the lack of medical treatments.

For all that, conditions were better than they had been.

Jenny's grandmother, for example, had lost four children, her own mother had lost two. She knew as well as anyone that the feelings of helplessness and loss had to be put to one side as life, full of all its endless chores, did not stop.

The twins were buried together in a grave marked only with flowers.

Chapter 7

Outside of school and after his chores, Jack was given freedom to roam and made the most of it by regularly leaving the colliery village, painted black with coaldust, and emerge, after not too many steps, into rolling farmland that had been farmed for hundreds, if not thousands, of years.

During these adventures he'd met and become friends with Peter, the son of one of the local farmers and used to go out to see him when he could. His Grandpa had made the connection as he would do a bit of labouring on the farm when extra hands were needed and in return, as well as pay, a cartload of manure for the allotment would occasionally come his way.

Peter was a natural with the farm animals and would proudly show them off to Jack, especially the horses.

All Jack had to do, before he left, was to tell his mother where he was going and promise to be home before dark.

And then he was off, a boy under his own steam, running to get on to the familiar farm track, leaving the blackened streets behind, amazed at how quickly black became grey and grey became green. As he ran, he breathed in lungfulls of the crisp air. It felt cooler and smelt of animals.

As he skirted one of the hedged fields the farmer, Peter's father, spotted him and called him over.

The farmer's name was Jim Moore. Born and bred a farmer, he was tall and strong from the manual labour, browned and weathered by working outside. Like an old, gnarled oak he was rooted in his land. He had no wish to be anywhere else and no ambition to be doing anything else.

It was a warm day and the flies were out. Jack tried to swat them away, but Jim Moore stood completely unperturbed. Jack looked up at him,

'Don't they bother you, Mr Moore?' he asked, unconcerned about talking to an adult, used as he was to holding his own against his elder brother and joining in conversations about today's News with his father. As his mother would say, "Our Jack's not shy at coming forward, though I'm sure it'll get him into trouble someday.".

'Don't what bother me?' said the farmer.

'The flies,' said Jack, 'I don't mind them most of the time, but these cleggies, they suck your blood before you know it. Their bite hurts.'

'No point worrying, you get used to it when you're out and about all day. Though I do agree that them cleggies are the worst. They're silent in flight you know. It's the females that bite you, the males don't have the mouth parts, so they can't feed on blood, they feed on flowers instead.'

'Really?' said Jack.

'As real as I'm standing here young man, talking to someone who should not be questioning the wisdom of his elders,' Jack looked sheepish, 'And another thing, them females hide, waiting in the shade for their prey to pass by, using their brightly coloured eyes to spot it coming. And when it does, they sneak out, silent like, suck your blood and fly off before you feel the bite. I don't like them, but I've got to give them credit.'

'But don't they bother you?'

'My skin's too tough for them, tougher than a cow's hide I reckon. So, they go for easier prey like you, young man… you're a prime target.'

'But I don't want to be a prime target,' said Jack, 'I want tough skin like yours.'

Jim Moore gave a thin smile.

'Don't wish it too quick, lad, it's time and hard work as toughens the skin. It's years in the making and not without its scars.'

Jack tried to ignore the buzzing, wondering if he should tell the farmer about his own scar but decided against it. If you can hear the flies buzzing then they're not cleggies, he thought, and tried to ignore them as he looked out across the fields.

'Where are the young'uns, Mr Moore?' he asked.

'Not quite ready for the fields yet, lad,' said Jim, rubbing his stubbled chin, his hands resting on the rams-horn handle of his staff, his watery eyes on Jack's upturned face.

'They're in the barn,' he said, 'Peter's helping to look after them.'

Like most farmers, Mr Moore cared about his animals, their physical health and their well-being. Yes, it was what his father and his grandfather before that had done, yes, it was his sole source of income, a business that kept his family fed and a roof over their heads, but it was also something more. He wouldn't have liked to admit it, but Mr Moore loved what he did. He loved the fields, the yearly cycle of planting, tending and harvesting, and he loved his livestock. He knew he would be sending most of them off to the butcher at some stage and although he was careful not to let any of them became 'pets', he knew all of them individually, their different markings, their personality quirks. He wanted to give them the best life he could while they were in his care.

And Mr Moore loved being out in the open air, under the cathedral of the sky. It gave him a sense of space, a comforting feeling of knowing his own small place in the vastness of the world. Even when he was covered in mud or muck, even when the cathedral sky was full of dark clouds and dropping heavy raindrop sized lamentations upon him, he still loved it, though to hear him talk you would never have believed it.

With hands hardened early in life by work and weather, he had learnt to avoid making 'soft talk' when amongst other men and joined in the banter about the state of animal breeding, the best and the worst of it, the way to tell a better animal from the rest. He was happy to talk about these kinds of things for hours, around the kitchen table, in the fields, or over a pint at the pub. But in his heart... in his heart he had a fondness, and when he saw a spark of interest in Jack's young face he could not resist it.

'You can come and take a look if you want to,' he said gruffly.

There was no need for an answer. The farmer turned his back and began to plod slowly and methodically towards the ramshackle collection of farm buildings that were a kind of family album; the barn built by his father, the stables from his grandfather's time. Jack followed at his heels like one of his collies, obedient yet playful, skipping to control his pent-up excitement.

As they approached, the smell of farmyard manure got stronger and Jack had to be careful not to slip on the cobbled yard that was unevenly covered in patches of straw and cow dung.

Jack crinkled up his nose.

'There's a lot worse smells than this in the world,' said the farmer, noticing his reaction, 'You get used to it after a bit,' he said, 'that's the thing about smells, you get used to them… don't even notice them after a while.'

Jack couldn't believe that you could ever get used to the smell of the farmyard and he wasn't that sure that there were many smells that were worse. However, he held his tongue, and they continued on their way, boots scraping on cobbles.

Mr Moore shoo-ed away a couple of ginger hens with his stick, and together they made their way past the pig styes and into a large stone-walled barn.

As soon as they entered the barn, Jack was hit by a wave of warmth. He knew barns like this could be stone cold when they were empty but this one was full of the warmth of life, new life; shuffling, mooing, breathing out air that steamed in the confined space. The milky smell of young calves and cows was unmistakable, and Mr Moore smiled as Jack gazed around, his mouth falling open.

'Better close that mouth, lad' he said, 'don't want you catching any flies.'

Jack closed his mouth.

A central aisle ran down the concrete-floored building. In the middle of this there was a drainage gulley that helped in the collection and periodic clearing away of straw, poo and pee. To the left and right of the aisle there was wooden fencing that rose to a height of about 3 feet and behind that the space was segregated into stalls, each having fresh straw strewn on its floor.

For some reason it reminded Jack of a church, with the reverend Mr Moore and a congregation of cattle.

At regular distances, hung over the fencing, were troughs containing either water or cattle cake.

'Seems Peter's not about,' said Mr Moore, 'but go on, they won't bite you. They don't have their teeth as yet.'

Jack walked up the aisle looking at the young calves, their large eyes, feeling their eagerness. He picked out one that had distinct black and white patches and went over to it. It did not back away, and Jack leaned forward and started to scratch the top of its head.

'Nearly lost that one,' said Mr Moore, 'hell'uv'a job it was, and late into the night and all. Take up a bit a cake lad and see if it'll take it.'

Jack did as he was told, his mother would have been surprised, and scooped up and held out a few pellets of cake in the palm of his hand. The calf looked at him and then tilted its head to one side and stuck out a long, pink, prehensile tongue, scooping up the pellets of cake and eating them with relish.

'Seems like you've got a way with them,' said Mr Moore, 'just like Peter, not everybody can do what you just did.'

Jack repeated the trick a couple more times.

'Put your hand in its mouth,' said Mr Moore, 'don't worry, it'll not hurt you.'

Jack stuck out the middle three fingers of his right hand and moved them slowly towards the calf. The calf took them readily into its toothless mouth and started to suck, its large brown eyes staring up into Jack's face.

'That's how it'd suck on its mother's teets' said Mr Moore.

'It's got a strong suck,' said Jack, rescuing his fingers.

'Aye, it does that,' said Mr Moore, 'won't be long before it's got some teeth through, you'd not be wanting to put your hand in its mouth then, you'd lose your fingers.'

Jack shuddered at the thought and in his mind he saw himself counting his fingers and finding at least two of them missing, a calf standing nearby, looking at him and chewing lazily.

They stayed in the barn for a while and Mr Moore called over one of the cowhands and asked where Peter was.

'He's gone to that far meadow,' was the reply, 'wanted to see how the grass was.'

The answer more than satisfied Mr Moore, a good farmer must always know his land, and he was hoping Peter would become a good farmer, he was doing his best to teach him.

Together the two men showed Jack how to inspect the calves for health, what to look for, what to do if you spotted a problem. Jack was full of questions, and they responded patiently. It was good to have an enthusiastic audience.

'Not all of them make it,' said Mr Moore at the end.

Jack looked around the barn. It was full of bustle, and breath, and noise.

'That's a shame,' he said, 'but there's enough left isn't there?'

'Aye,' said Mr Moore stoically, 'there's always enough to be getting on with.'

Chapter 8

The farmhouse and many of the outbuildings were constructed of local stone, both new quarried and reused Roman leftovers. At 30 inches thick the walls were substantial, the roofs tiled and the doors solid and bar-able, built to defend against the Reiver raids that had plagued these English-Scottish border regions for over 300 years.

Occurring mainly at night these incendiary attacks were either to steal cattle, to fire a barn, or to further fuel a feud between families, each of whom thought that they were the wronged party, the original cause having been lost somewhere in the exaggerated retellings of accusations that were spread across the generations until only a feeling of deep-seated wrongdoing and a justifiable thirst for revenge was left, seared into the souls of the warring families.

Unification under the reign of King James I/VI brought a new order and windows were widened and more outbuildings were confidently erected, with functionality rather than security being uppermost in their design.

Now, the farmhouse occupied one side of the cobbled yard while other buildings; barn, shed, pigsty, dairy, radiated out from the adjacent two sides and the side facing the farmhouse was gated and fenced.

The yard, as Jack could confirm, was permanently pungent with the smells of animals and manure. Thankfully, as the stereospecific chemical sense receptors in the nose became saturated, any newcomer eventually became accustomed to the odours and, after a while, they would hardly notice them. Just as Mr Moore had said.

It was the farmer's wife, Mrs Ella Moore, who ruled in the farmhouse.

Ella ran the engine room of the whole complex and, with seeming ease, oiled the wheels and kept them turning. Her days were filled with the endless tasks of cleaning, laundering, cooking, baking and shopping, as well as caring for her combined flock of animals and people, including the cheekily clucking chickens and the daily collection of their eggs.

Some of her jobs were dictated by the seasons, the availability of produce, and there were always jars of jams and chutneys in her larder. And it wasn't just her immediate family she was concerned with. She put these first, of course, but she still took the time to keep in touch with the farm worker's wives and families and was often the first to know of pregnancies, births or deaths and she would pass on any important news or gossip to her husband, with a strong recommendation for action were she thought it was necessary.

There were so many chores that occasionally she would employ some of the women to help her out, those that didn't already work in the dairy and such like, and they would welcome the bit of extra cash, and a small share of the produce if the making of jams or chutneys was the task at hand.

The work was hard as was evidenced by her hands, the strength in her arms and the windblown complexion of her face, but the work was not without its smiles, and the women would find lots to talk about while they washed, boiled, sorted and chopped.

In the local town Ella was recognised for her generous nature but was also known to be a 'straight talker'. If you asked Mrs Moore a question you would get an answer and it was best you were prepared for it, as it would most likely be clear and unfiltered. For this reason, she was normally given a respectful amount of space to move around in, while those who met her were polite and she was polite back.

It was through Jack's visits to the farm that Ella had first got to know his mother, Jenny, and it was through her, sitting at the Lawley kitchen table drinking tea, that she kept up to date with the colliery village, the comings and goings, the doings and the not doings.

Whenever she visited Jenny, she would bring a 'little something' and Jenny would find something to give her in return. The main reason for the visits, apart from a genuine friendship that formed between them based on mutual hard work and the experience of being a mother, was that Jenny began to do some dressmaking for Mrs Moore and other pieces of sewing for the rest of her household; sewing being one of the few things that Mrs Moore would admit to never having got the hang of.

As Jim Moore and Jack left the cowshed, Ella was coming out of the farmhouse. She was carrying a bowl of peelings.

'Hey, you two,' she said, 'nice day for a walk, though some people haven't got the time.'

'Now, Ella,' said Jim, 'I was just showing Jack the calves as Peter wasn't about, he'd showed an interest.'

'And I've got an interest in you getting that fence fixed up on the big field, don't want them cows out again.'

'I've fixed it,' said Jim, 'Houdini couldn't get out of there now.'

'About time,' said Ella, softening.

Jack was very aware that her bark was worse than her bite.

'After I've given these peelings to the pigs, I'm going to collect the eggs and then I'm going to start on the cooking for tonight.'

'I'll take it to the pigs,' said Jack.

Ella looked at him, smiled, she had a bright smile when she chose to use it, which was more often than you'd think. She handed the bowl to Jack. It was piled high and quite heavy. Jack wrapped both arms around it.

'Just call her out and chuck it over the wall. Don't go in, that big sow can get nowty when she's got wee-uns.'

'Don't worry, Mrs Moore,' said Jack, 'I know what to do.'

Jim went back into the barn to 'finish up'. There was a calf he was a bit worried about he said, and he just wanted to take a look before moving on to another of his endless list of jobs.

When Jack got to the pigsty, he looked over the low wall and whistled. The inside was full of well-trodden mud and, in response to his call, there came a languid sound of squelching from within and then a large pink pig's head emerged and peered at him suspiciously, it's ears erect.

Jack tapped the metal bowl on the top of the wall and then reached over and slopped the contents into a low trough.

The sow waddled over.

Back in the shadowy interior, Jack could just make out some movement in the straw. The sow lowered her head and started to eat, slurping, crunching and dribbling.

'Your table manners are atrocious,' said Jack, aping the upper-class tones of an old aunt who had once come to visit them and had turned her nose up at almost everything they did.

Jack took the bowl back to the farmhouse and knocked at the door.

'Come in, Jack, door's always open.'

The door led directly into the kitchen. Ella Moore was elbow deep in flour.

'Just put it over there,' she said, nodding towards the wooden draining board.

Jack did as he was bid.

'There's four eggs for you in that bowl,' said Mrs Moore, 'the hens are laying well at the minute and I'm sure your Ma could do with them.'

Jack picked them up and put them carefully in his pockets. They were still warm.

'Thanks, Mrs Moore,' he said.

'That's not a problem, give your Ma my regards.'

'I will, Mrs Moore.'

'And Jack…'

'Yes, Mrs Moore?'

'Tell your Ma we might have a bit of work you could be doing if you're interested, mucking out and such like. After school or at weekends. Peter could show you the ropes.'

'Really!' said Jack.

'Now, Jack, don't get too excited,' said Ella smiling, 'your Ma mightn't like the idea, and besides, we're only talking about paying you a few pennies here and there. You might come along with your Grandpa sometimes.'

Working on the farm and getting paid! Jack couldn't believe it.

'I'll tell her,' he said, 'thanks Mrs Moore, thanks a lot!'

'Don't thank me,' she said, 'it was that daft husband of mine, it was his idea.'

At that moment, Peter appeared at the kitchen door. He was wiry, with tousled black hair and muddy boots.

'Hi Jack,' he said.

'Don't you bring that muck in here!' said his mother, 'now off you go, the two of you, and Peter…'

'Yes, Mam?'

'Be back by supper time, you hear.'

'Yes, Mam,' he said, and then in an urgent whisper to Jack, 'come on, quick, I want to show you something.'

The something he wanted to show him was a horse that was getting reshod. There was always something interesting happening on the farm.

'We don't need charity!' said Jenny, when Jack had got home and proudly put the four fresh eggs, still intact after jostling about in his pockets, on the kitchen table.

Jenny was totally familiar with the bartering that went on between households; a bit of butter for a few slices of bread, a cup of sugar in return for flour… but she didn't want something for nothing! She didn't ask for it, she didn't need it, and, if people found out that she'd taken it, it would give completely the wrong impression.

'It's only four eggs, Ma, and I didn't ask for them, they were freely given.'

'I'm sure they were,' said his mother bristling, 'but your Grandpa keeps a few chickens on the allotment, does she think we can't look after ourselves?'

Jack didn't know how to answer that, so he said,

'And, Ma…'

This probably wasn't the right time, but he was bubbling to say it.

'Yes?'

'Well, Mrs Moore said that if you wanted, then, well, then they could likely find me some work to do around the farm,' he paused, 'after school or at weekends, only for a few pennies mind, and only now and again.'

His mother thought for a moment.

'Were you given the eggs before or after she mentioned that?'

Jack tried to remember.

'Before, I think. Yes, it was before.'

His mother smiled.

'That's alright then,' she said.

Jack was none the wiser.

'She was buttering me up,' said his mother, 'a friendly offer of a few eggs, hoping for a favourable reply.'

Jack had no idea if there was a connection between the eggs and the suggestion of work. Mrs Moore had simply said the hens had been laying well and that seemed to make sense enough to him.

'So, Ma, what do you think?'

Jenny considered her reply.

'I think its very nice of them to offer,' she said, 'but I don't want you taking any money off the Moores.'

Jack looked crestfallen.

'On the other hand,' said his mother, 'seeing as you go around there to see Peter… and there will be work needing doing, there's always work needs doing on a farm then…'

'Yes?' said Jack, his hopes rising a little.

'Then you can tell them that I don't mind if they give you a bit of work to do. Peter will be working anyway so you'll be disturbing him if you don't join in,' she paused, 'but Jack...'

'Yes, Ma?'

'No money, you just remember we don't ever need any charity from anybody.'

'No, Ma,' said Jack, 'but would you want any more eggs?'

His mother smiled.

'No more eggs… but perhaps a bit of their cheese…'

She left the idea hanging between them, and Jack grabbed at it and understood.

'And the next time you go over there…'

'Yes, Ma?'

'You make sure you take one of my cakes. I'll make one with a bit of icing on the top.'

'Yes, Ma.'

Later, he told Edward about his adventures.

'Yes,' said Edward, 'Jim breeds good cows. If you get your meat from one of them, you know it'll taste good.'

Jack didn't like the idea of the calves being turned into meat, so he changed the subject.

Chapter 9

Mr Wilkinson Hughes allowed questions to be asked, but such freedom was never to be confused with a lessoning of class discipline. To ask a question you must raise your hand and only speak when you were asked to. To shout out was punishable by the cane.

Although concentrating on the 'three R's' (although only one of the subjects actually starts with that letter), other subjects were taught in school, including history. Mr Hughes had just finished his lesson on the Romans and Jack's hand shot up.

'Yes, Mr Lawley.'

'So, sir, were the Romans around here, in our village?'

'The Romans were definitely around here, there are still signs of a Roman Road not so far away, and you might imagine columns of Roman soldiers marching along it, or chariots, or carts or any of the people who needed to get about.'

These remarks were met with a soft communal intake of breath 'The Romans had been here!'

'They would not, of course, have been in our village,' the teacher continued, 'as our village did not exist in Roman times.'

There was an exhaled breath of disappointment.

Jack had one more try. His hand was up again.

'You're full of questions today, Mr Lawley, let this be the last.'

'Did the Romans work down the pit?'

This was greeted with barely suppressed laughter and Mr Hughes slapped his cane on his desk. There was immediate silence.

'The Romans did not work down the pit as you so eloquently put it young man, as there were no deep pit workings at that time, the modern wonders of the steam engine being many hundreds of years in the future,' he paused, 'it is possible however that they used coal, but that would have been from surface or shallow deposits.'

The idea of the Romans burning coal, the same coal as they dug, the same coal that fueled their fires and ranges at home, was a fascinating one. All of a sudden, the Romans didn't seem so very different to them.

That night, around the kitchen table, Jack talked about what he'd learnt of the Romans.

'Yes,' said his father, 'they built forts and towns and bridges and roads. The world must have been a very different place in those days, with the Romans in charge.'

'In charge?'

'Oh, yes, they ruled; they told you what to do, they carried weapons, they handed out punishments…'

'They sound like mine owners with swords,' said Edward.

They all laughed.

'How do you know so much?' Jenny asked her husband.

He looked sheepish.

'Fascinated me when I was a boy, don't laugh, but I wished I was a Roman.'

George sniggered. Jenny shushed him.

'Not a serf then?' said Edward.

'No, a Roman soldier, maybe one that lived on the Wall.'

'The Wall?' said Jack.

'Did it not come up in the lesson?' said his father.

Jack shook his head.

'Well, the Romans built a wall right across the country, all the way from Newcastle to Carlisle and beyond.'

'Why did they do that?'

'For defence, to exert control, who knows, one thing's for sure though and that is that it was an incredible achievement to build it, without explosives, without steam engines, with only hand tools, manpower, and horses and carts.'

'And woman-power,' said Jenny.

Frank smiled.

'That has to be indisputably true,' he said.

'Where is it now?' asked Jack.

'I've only ever seen bits of it,' said his father, 'it's in ruins now, of course, a lot of the stone has been robbed out to build farmhouses and such like, but there's still some remains can be seen. Parts of it are about 10 to 15 miles north of here I would guess. It's not an area that's heavily populated these days.'

Jack looked at his father wistfully.

'I'd like to see it,' he said.

'Well, Jack, maybe someday you will,' said his mother.

That night Jack's dreams were full of Romans speaking with a North-Eastern accent and about a stone wall that would keep the sheep in, and for days afterwards his daydreams were about the life of a Roman soldier; hard, strong, ruthless… his sword shining in its scabbard.

Chapter 10

On his next visit to the farm, Jack told Mrs Moore of his mother's decision, her husband overheard and said, 'Free labour! Well, we can all do with a bit of that and, you never know, you might learn something useful along the way.'

Peter was itching to go out.

'Come on, Jack,' he said, 'there's some work to do in the stables.'

His father laughed.

'Seems like your free labouring has started already. Here put these old boots on. I'm thinking the job might be messy and we don't want your mother thinking we're taking advantage,' he paused, 'free labour, who would have thought it, and in this day and age too.'

After Jack had changed his boots, the one's he'd been given were Peter's spare pair so they weren't a bad fit, he and Peter rushed outside.

Ella Moore watched their retreating backs through the open door that Peter was well known for not closing behind him.

'What do you think?' she said.

The farmer scratched his chin.

'Saves us having to work out how many pennies he's due, I suppose. I would have been happier giving him something, don't much like the idea of taking something for nothing, even if he's not that strong in the arm as yet.'

'What do you think we should say?'

'Say nowt, accept it just as it is. Him and Peter get along fine, let them sort themselves out.'

He thought for a moment.

'Actually,' he said, 'it's probably for the best, this way Peter and him can just do what they choose without me interfering. Peter knows what needs to be done and now he's got somebody who'll willingly help him out once in a while.'

He turned to his wife.

'Be a shame if he left with nothing though.'
Ella smiled back at him,
'I'll see what I can do,' she said.

The stables that the boys hurried towards housed the big draught horse, Samson, a couple of cart horses and a pony. Their job today was to clean out Samson's stall and put in some new bedding while he was out, working in the fields.

It was a hard job for a boy of Jack's size and age, and he was struggling to handle the pitchfork and shovel.

'Look here,' said the stableman, 'don't tickle the top of it, we're not moving it piece by piece. Dig your fork into it and lift it into the barrow, look like this… see, dig in, lever it up and into the barrow.'

Peter, who was watching, laughed. He loved everything to do with horses, even cleaning them out.

'He's not used to it,' he said to the stableman.

'I can see that,' was the reply.

'Look Jack, tell you what, you move the barrow, I won't fill it too full each time and then we can work as a team; I'll lift, you carry.'

'I'm going to leave you boys to it,' said the stableman, 'I've got plenty else to do and this looks like its going to keep you busy all day.'

And it did. But as Jack got more used to the conditions he switched with Peter and, without the stableman looking over his shoulder all the time, learnt the best way to use a fork and how much of a forkful his young muscles could successfully lever into the barrow. The two boys enjoyed working together and the time went quickly.

Mrs Moore tried not to disturb them, although she did call them in for lunch, only allowing them inside after they'd washed their hands in the freezing cold rainwater trough in the yard and had taken their boots off.

Putting in the new bedding was a joy in comparison to the mucking out and seeing the horse's reaction when he returned to his stall was reward in itself.

Peter loved all the farm animals, but his favourites were the horses.

'Look after your horses, Jack,' he said, mimicking his father, 'they're the power and the heart of the farm. For your big draught horse, choose one with a calm temperament, treat him well and he'll look after you. Without the horse there'd be no farm, gentle giants that's what they are…'

The Moore's heavy working horse was a Clydesdale, known as a breed to be powerful, steady, and patient. Samson was all of those things, his colouring was mainly chestnut with a white splash on his forehead and the characteristic white feathering to his lower legs. At 6 ft tall at the shoulder, and weighing 1,600lb he towered over the boys.

'He's massive,' said Jack, being brave enough to reach up and stroke his flank.

'He's a real beauty,' said Peter, as the horse lowered its head to take an apple out of his hand.

'He needs about 40lb of grain, hay or forage a day, and about 20 gallons of water to wash it down,' said the stableman, trying to hide his pride in the horse, and failing, 'Keeping a horse like this is a big expense, not just the feeding but the shoeing and the all-round care'.

'But without him there'd be no farm, he's the engine that drives at the heart of it,' said Peter.

'That's right,' said the stableman, 'he's expensive, but he's worth every penny I reckon,'

Samson was a docile giant, able to haul heavy loads, or pull the plough from morning till dusk, working most contentedly on his own but happy to team up with another horse, called Caesar, from a neighboring farm when necessary. He navigated the landscape with a steady pace, was intelligent, and seemed to enjoy the work. He was as content ploughing, harrowing, spreading compost, digging potatoes, raking hay, or hauling in the harvest, always treading lightly for such a large animal, avoiding compaction of the precious soil, and, through his composted manure, making his own contribution to the essential supply of organic fertilizer.

'The work done by the horses,' said Peter, 'the smells, the gentle sounds, the feet plodding on the ground. It's like a partnership between the worker, the horse, and the land. When you're out in the fields it gives you time to think, to appreciate the world around you,' he paused, 'but it's hard work and you've always got to keep at least half your mind on the job.'

'He's been out ploughing today,' said the stableman, 'turning over that top layer of soil, bringing all those fresh nutrients to the surface and folding them weeds and crop remains into the soil where they can best decay and add a bit of nutrients back. We'll leave it to settle and dry, and then he'll be back out doing the harrowing, breaking up them clods and providing us with a nice even soil we can get our seeds into.'

Jack was amazed how much everybody knew about a world that was largely a mystery to him.

At the end of the day, as Jack was preparing to leave, Ella Moore called him over,

'Here's a jar of chutney to take away with you,' she said, 'It's been sitting in the pantry a while so it should be nicely matured and good for eating now.'

Jack thanked her and tucked the jar inside his jacket to keep safe.

As he walked away from the fields and towards the colliery village Jack felt a kind of closing in of the world. The people who had moved there were a mixed bunch, pulled by the work. Some, from other terrace-streeted communities, seemed to settle quite easily, others who had migrated from seaside villages, centred on fishing, or from wide, stretching countryside, with woods and distant mountains, took some time to settle into this more claustrophobic way of living. For Jack though, this was all he knew and his after-school escapes into farmer's fields, dells, woods and streams had become a part of the balance of his life.

Later that evening, the Lawleys were sitting around the kitchen table eating a pot pie and some vegetables that Jenny had prepared. The jar of chutney was open, and Frank took it and ladled a good spoonful onto his plate. After a few mouthfuls he said,

'Oh, Ma, this chutney really goes well with the pie, it's one of your best, did you do anything different?'

Jack covered his face with his hands, everybody else just carried on eating, they didn't understand the situation.

Jenny sat calmly, looking directly at her husband.

'It's not my chutney,' she said, 'Jack brought it back from the farm, its Ella Moore's.'

The sound of eating stopped.

Jack's eyes swivelled first to his mother and then to his father. Edward, George and Grandpa looked on. They all knew how sensitive Jenny was about her cooking and about her chutneys and preserves. The tension rose as Frank took another mouthful of pie and chutney combined. He chewed it thoughtfully, swallowed and then took a swig of tea to wash it down.

'You know,' he said, 'that chutney has a bitter aftertaste that I hadn't noticed before. Have you still got any of your apple and tomato chutney left, Jenny, I think I'd like to switch to that,'

'I think I've got a little left,' said Jenny, 'if you're sure you want to change?'

'Oh, I'm sure,' said Frank.

Jenny got up and went over to her shelves.

When her back was turned there was a series of smiles and nods between all the members of the male contingent. Even George understood that somehow there had been a crisis, but it had been averted.

When Jenny returned there was a scramble for the chutney jar.

'I didn't realise this was so popular,' she said, 'I'd better make some more.'

Just before bed Frank took Jack to one side,
'I don't mind you bringing things back from the farm,' he said, 'but in future you better warn me what you've brought.'
'Yes, Dad, I will,' said Jack.
'That chutney was good though,' said Frank, smiling, 'but try and get some cheese next time, your mother doesn't make that.'

Chapter 11

Jack's enquiring mind was evident at school and instead of quashing it as an inconvenience, Wilkinson Hughes encouraged it. He was not one of those teachers who demanded only obedience and the achievement of mediocrity.

With his teacher's help Jack took to reading early and was well ahead of most of the other children in the class. To keep him quiet, Mrs Enid Hughes, who taught him in the early years, would give him a book, ask him to read it, and then tell her about it. From poor beginnings, but with encouragement, Jack gradually caught on and, one night, Enid warned her husband, 'Wilkinson, you'll have your hands full with this one'.

But far from having trouble, Wilkinson Hughes had welcomed the challenge, had been keen to follow his wife's lead and had encouraged Jack in his reading. Indeed, he came to believe that he could do more and took to loaning Jack one book at a time from the school's eclectic library collection, that was an accumulation of donations and second-hand purchases.

So, one afternoon, as the children were leaving school for the day, running out under grey skies, the streets tonally blackened in proportion to the distance they were from the pit head, heading home to chores and an evening meal, Wilkinson Hughes put his hand on Jack's shoulder and pulled him to one side. Jack wondered what he had done wrong.

'So, Lawley, I have another book for you.'

Wilkinson Hughes held out the book. Jack took it excitedly.

'Thank you, sir,' he said.

Wilkinson Hughes smiled, 'You don't need to thank me, I'm just loaning you this book, you're going to bring it back when you've finished it and tell me what you think. What you liked. What you didn't like. It's a work of imagination. I thought you might like it. Is it a deal?'

Jack took the book and looked at the title. It was called "The War of the Worlds" by somebody called H.G. Wells.

'It's a deal,' he said.

Jack took the book home and showed it to his mother.

'Go and get some water,' she said, 'I need to get it heated up before your dad gets back from the pit.'

Jack went to put the book in the front room. His grandpa was just coming in from the allotment carrying an armful of edible greenery.

'What you got there?' he said.

Jack opened his mouth to speak but a shout from the kitchen interrupted him.

'Jack! Are you getting that water or not, that bucket won't fill itself.'

'It's OK,' said his grandfather smiling, 'just leave it on the side there and I'll have a look at it while you're out. Best do what your mam says, it's always the best way to keep out of trouble.'

Jack knew the wisdom of his grandfather's words, set the book down and ran past his mother and out of the back door.

'And don't dawdle!' were the words that followed him out.

When Jack got to the water pump at the end of their row there was a queue. He was third in line. Sarah Hudson, the girl from next door, was in front of him and a rather large lady was at the front filling up two buckets. The water came out fast, splooshing into the bucket and splashing over her legs. She swore and stooped to fill the second bucket, more carefully this time.

'Never the same bloody pressure,' she said, 'every day it's different, was nowt but a trickle the other day.'

Sarah turned to Jack,

'It was clever of you to know about the age of coal,' she said.

'There was nothing clever about it, just reading and just remembering that's all,' said Jack.

'But it was brave to put your hand up with such an answer, everybody laughed,' she persisted.

'Wasn't brave, I knew I was right, there's nothing brave about telling the right answer.'

'Sarah, your turn now,' said the large lady, 'watch out for the pressure, don't want you wetting your clothes, your ma wouldn't like you coming home all soaked, would she.'

'Alright Mrs Russell I'll be careful,' said Sarah.

'Here,' said Jack, grabbing her bucket and putting it under the spout.

'I can do it,' said Sarah, and tried to push him out of the way.

'Sure, you can,' said Jack, 'but I may as well fill two buckets as one.'

He filled the bucket and handed it to her, the water was clear but icy cold, just like the look that Sarah gave him.

Jack smiled.

It made it worse.

Sarah turned on her heal and started to walk off. She walked carefully and with a stoop, both hands grasping the looped handle of the bucket, trying not to spill any.

'Men!' she muttered to herself.

When Jack got back home his mother took the bucket of water and started dividing the contents between kettle, pot and bowl and then put a few more lumps of coal on the fire that fuelled their black iron kitchen range.

His grandfather was at the kitchen table pulling the outside leaves from some cabbages.

'Jenny,' he said, 'I was thinking of throwing these leaves in with the hens, give them something to peck at.'

Jack's mother glanced up, she'd moved on now to sorting out soap, scrubbing brush and a clean shirt for her husband's return.

'Why not,' she said, 'them outer leaves are of no use to me, been got at by caterpillars and snails. You do what you want with them.'

His grandfather winked at Jack without his mother noticing.

'I'll take Jack,' he said, 'might be some eggs to fetch back.'

Jack's mother just nodded, and they took off.

Grandpa's allotment was one of a series that occupied land allocated for the purpose on the outskirts of the village. Some of the allotments were occupied by pigeon lofts, decorated in bright colours. Others were unkempt and overgrown with weeds. Most were like Grandpa's with a shed at one end for tools and shelter and well tilled and manured soil for potatoes, cabbages, carrots and other vegetables, like leeks. Not so common features of Grandpa's allotment was the space given over to a chicken coop and an area for soft fruits; blackcurrants, gooseberries, and raspberries.

When they arrived Grandpa threw the greens to the chickens who gave them immediate attention, clucking in their attempts to be first and secure the juiciest parts.

'Grab yourself a spade,' he said to Jack, 'I got some new manure from Jim Moore the other day, thanks to you I think, and it's got to be dug in.'

'Why is it thanks to me,' said Jack.

'Although he didn't say anything, my guess is that this is part payment for the work you've been doing.'

'I haven't done very much, I've learnt more than I've done.'

Grandpa smiled, impressed by Jack's honesty.

'I always seem to be shovelling this stuff,' said Jack, 'shovel it at the farm, shovel it here…'

'Don't be so reproachful, it's good stuff. It's what feeds the soil that feeds the seed that grows the food that you eat, so just you remember it's a critical link in the chain.'

'The smelliest link,' said Jack, shovelling as best as he could.

'Put some more over here… good lad, that's perfect.'

They worked on for half an hour and then the air started to cool as the sun lowered herself towards the western hills.

'I'll tell you one thing,' said Grandpa as they were walking home.

'What's that?' said Jack.

'It might be a bit smelly but that manure's a much better payment than that chutney you brought back.'

Jack looked at his Grandpa, and then they both started to laugh. Grandpa put his arm around Jack's shoulders.

'I had a quick look at that book you brought in,' he said, 'just like you, I've always loved stories, so you just keep reading, Jack, reading and learning, but always remember this one thing, books are stories and not real life… and real life is the most important thing.'

Jack listened but didn't really understand.

Jack used to talk to the family about some of the books he'd read, although he didn't always remember them entirely accurately. They'd liked hearing about "Huckleberry Finn" and "Oliver Twist" and it made Jack feel good to share his new knowledge.

Frank, Jenny, Grandpa, Edward, George and Jack were all in the kitchen. They were drinking tea.

'What?' said Frank, 'A man is shipwrecked on an island that's full of little people?'

'Ridiculous,' said Jenny, 'what's the use of a silly story like that? It's even worse than one of Grandpa's stories.'

Edward grinned. Grandpa didn't react. Jack soldiered on.

'Obviously the little people are scared of him, so they start off by being very nice…'

'I bet they do,' said Frank.

'…and they argue amongst themselves a lot.'

'What do they argue about?' asked George.

'Silly things,' said Jack, wishing he'd read a different book. It wasn't his fault that this was the story.

'Go on, Jack,' said Edward, 'tell us more.'

Jack sighed.

'Well actually, they have a big argument about which end of a boiled egg you should break into in order to eat it properly. You know, by dipping your bread in. Should it be the "pointy end" or the "round end"?'

Jenny looked confused.

'I've never even thought about that,' she said, 'which is right?'

'Sharp end,' said Edward.

'Round end,' said George.

They both laughed.

'Who cares?' said Edward.

'In the story,' said Jack, 'the little people care, they get so het up about it that they argue and then they split up into the "pointy enders" and the "round enders". There's about the same number of people on each side. The argument divides families and keeps growing until there could be a war about it.'

'Who would go to war over something so stupid?' said Jenny, 'like I said, it's ridiculous. You've got to read better stories than this, Jack, instead of wasting your time.'

'I don't know,' said Grandpa, 'people do go to war over stupid things.'

As an ex-soldier, Grandpa got respect when he talked about military matters.

'Oo, this is getting too serious for me,' said Jenny, 'I thought this would be fun.'

'What happened at the end?' asked George.

'Things go wrong, and the man has to escape from the island. Luckily, he does escape and finds his way back home.'

'At least there's a happy ending,' said Jenny.

'Erm,' said Jack but immediately decided not to tell them about the rest of the book.

'What's the man's name anyway?' asked Edward.

'Gulliver,' said Jack, 'and the book is about his travels.'

'May as well of stayed at home,' said Jenny, 'don't see the point of such silly stories.'

Jack made a mental note not to tell anyone about the new book he'd just been given, the one called "War of the Worlds", the one about Martians and their death-dealing heat-rays.

Chapter 12

It was common for the same family to farm the same land for several generations. Compared to the farmers, the miners were transient 'in-comers' and it was not unusual for the local farming families to be suspicious of them and the damage they were doing to the land, and so they tended to keep their distance.

These two separate worlds existed side by side, one black and one green, one concerned with the soil, one concerned with what was deep beneath it. The little interaction that there was between them tended to be transactional and polite. The miners and their families consumed the produce of the farms; the farms used the local coal on their fires and kitchen ranges.

Other than areas of common interest, like football, they talked a different language; the miners talked of tubs and tracks, lamps and explosives, the farmers talked of weather and wool, crops and cows.

Jack was abnormal in bridging these two worlds. His youth, his lust for wandering and his general enthusiastic inquisitiveness tended to dissolve barriers, and his friendship with Peter cemented his link to the Moore's farm.

Both worlds had their own sense of pride and balance, and 'charity' was not to be tolerated by either side. If something were received, then there needed to be some kind of return. If Jack did work on the farm, then there needed to be recognition. If Jenny did sewing for Mrs Moore, then there needed to be payment, in kind or in cash. Nothing was free in these worlds, everything was earned, and everything had a value.

Jack was a handy helper. Not that they couldn't have done without him but he and Peter enjoyed each other's company and the work that Jack did, if not done by him, would have to have been done by somebody else, maybe faster and better, but still…

Ella Moore was in the dairy making cheese. She had a dairy maid to help her, and they were both scrubbed up and clean. Jack was allowed to watch but was told not to get too close.

'We must keep everything hygienic,' said Mrs Moore, 'for every cheese of this type we make we use 8 pints of our full fat milk, and we always make at least four cheeses at a time. How many pints of milk is that, Jack?'

Jack scratched his head; it was more than he could do on his fingers.

'32,' he said eventually, '4 lots each needing 8 pints, that's 4 times 8 and 2 times 8 is 16 and 16 plus 16 is 32, so the answer's 32.'

Ella Moore smiled.

'That's a very long-winded way of doing it,' she said, 'but you got there in the end.'

The dairy maid was pouring steaming milk into a wooden tub.

'If you don't make enough, it loses its heat too quickly and the texture of the curd is too watery. We've gently warmed the milk to 95°F, not too hot, and the tub we're using is a nice size for 32 pints, it's not too big.'

When all the milk was safely poured, Mrs Moore took a bottle from a nearby shelf.

'It's easier to buy the rennet these days,' she said, 'it saves all the trouble of getting it from preparing a cow's stomach.'

Jack screwed up his face, that sounded horrible.

'Don't look like that, that's the way I used to have to do it when I was a girl,' she smiled, 'though I'm glad I don't have to do it now.'

She measured out 2 drams of rennet one after the other and dripped them carefully into a jug and then diluted it with 6 times the volume of water. She handed the jug on to the dairy maid who then stirred the mixture well before pouring it into the warm milk and stirring the whole thing slowly for three or four minutes.

The lid of the tub was then put in place. It was a snug fit.

'Right,' said Mrs Moore, 'that's it for at least an hour, you scurry off now Jack and we'll be getting the moulds ready.'

The moulds were of two pieces, both pieces were open bottomed rectangles of elm, about 7 inches long by 5 inches wide and 6 inches deep. Elm was a good choice as it resisted the wet well and had no flavour of its own. The two pieces of a mould sat on top of one another, the top one having a series of small holes drilled through its sides to help the whey escape.

Jack went off to help Peter with a pony. Peter showed him how to put on the halter and hitch her to a cart, and then they were off taking jugs of water, hay and tools to wherever they were needed. They even had a jug of beer that Mr Moore had given them to share between the labourers in the water meadows.

To finish off the cheese, a clean board was set on the main bench and a clean straw mat on top of that. The moulds were then put on the mat and, once the curd was firmly set, it was gently lifted with a skimming dish in 'leaves' that were laid into the moulds, filling them to the top and reserving a particularly complete 'leaf' for the topmost layer.

No pressure was applied, and the whey was allowed to simply drain away on its own. Once the level of the cheese had sunk below the top part of the mould this was taken away. The lower mould remained in place until the curd was firm enough to hold its shape, the top curling inwards all around the edge. It was then removed, the straw mat trimmed and retained to support this very delicate product. The cheese was then ready to be wrapped for market.

After their day's work in the fields, Jack was ready for home. He'd built up an appetite and was looking forward to his supper, whatever that might be.

Before he left Mrs Moore gave him a linen wrapped package.

'Here's a bit of our cheese for you,' she said, 'we finished this one yesterday so it should be ready to eat.'

Jack carried it home as if it were gold.

At the supper table, even before they began on the stew that Jenny had prepared, they sat with the linen wrapped block in the centre of the table and Jenny carefully peeled it open. There was fresh bread and some ripe tomatoes, and nobody needed asking twice to try the cheese.

It was Jenny who spoke first.

'This is what Ella takes to market, its good cheese.'

With such a mark of approval everybody felt free to express their own appreciation. Between the six of them the cheese was soon gone.

After the meal was over, and as Frank was about to head down to the pub with Edward, he took Jack aside.

'That's better,' he said, 'better cheese than chutney, Jack, better cheese than chutney.'

Chapter 13

Neville Hudson, husband to Alice, father to Sarah and neighbour to the Lawleys, was a bad drinker.

He was well known for it, and no matter what promises he might make at the start of an evening, by the end of it he was drunk.

And he was not a nice drunk.

The alcohol seemed to release some kind of pent-up anger in him and he would end the evening looking for a fight and eventually stagger home to a wife and daughter who waited in dread.

Although Alice did her best to protect her daughter, she did so at the expense of herself, regularly explaining away the bruises she couldn't hide by complaining about her own clumsiness.

But the walls of the colliery houses were thin and the Lawleys couldn't help but hear.

Alice was a frequent visitor to her neighbour's kitchen and one day Jenny summoned up the courage to talk to her about it,

'He's not a bad man,' said Alice, being careful to avoid eye contact, 'it's the drink that does for him.'

'It's true that my Frank says that down the pit he's a solid enough worker. They're part of the same team most shifts and they all rely on each other down there,' she paused, 'but we can't be having this, Alice, it's not right.'

Alice wiped her face, 'Don't worry yourself, Jenny,' she said, 'it's not as bad as you seem to think. He's a good father,' now it was her turn to pause, 'and he's promised to stay off the drink.'

'He's promised before, hasn't he?' said Jenny.

'Aye, but…' Alice's voice trailed away, the truth was that she didn't really believe it herself, 'anyway,' she said, straightening herself, 'I'd best be getting back, there's plenty to be doing.'

'Aye, there is that,' said Jenny seriously, 'there is that.'

Neville Hudson's drinking did nothing to help the family budget and Alice was regularly short of money. She patched and darned her own and her daughter's clothes as best she could, to make them last, but it wasn't a skill in which she excelled.

'Neville's always had a problem with drink,' said Alice to Jenny one afternoon, 'I thought I could change him but I can't. There was this one time he came home, it was before we moved here, all cuts and bruises he was and, as I was patching him up, I asked him what happened and he just told me to shut up.'

'I found out from one of the neighbours what had happened. She was having a good laugh about it. Neville had been drinking at out local, The Old Oak, and had apparently had a few and was beginning to shoot his mouth off. Looking round for a target he saw an old man sitting in the corner minding his own business, grey haired and quietly sipping his pint and reading a newspaper. For some reason Neville decided to poke fun at this man, asking him how many teeth he had left, wondering if he could still walk… that kind of nonsense. Those around him either laughed, which spurred him on, or told him to back away, which he ignored. The old man just looked at him, and said nothing, carried on sipping his pint and reading his paper. Neville took his silence as a sign of weakness and kept going, after each insult taking a step closer to the old man. Eventually he got close enough to grab the newspaper out of his hands, calling him a "silly old toothless bugger!" and saying that he wasn't even worth insulting. That was obviously the last straw, it would be for anybody wouldn't it? The old man jumped up with amazing speed and agility that belied his looks and gave Neville the thrashing that he probably deserved and which I was left to patch up. No one stepped in to help Neville, he'd brought it on himself and the man he'd picked on had been a Hewer for many years and a local boxing champion thereafter.'

'Oh, dear,' said Jenny.

'He couldn't have chosen a worse target. Apparently the man was of a placid nature, but once riled was not ashamed to defend himself. All the neighbours knew about it, and everybody thought it was very funny. Neville didn't, and it's probably one of the main reasons that, a couple of months later, we up sticks and moved here, although the pay was better here as well. I thought and hoped that something like that would teach him a lesson, that he would ease off the drink and realise nothing good comes of it. To be fair it did for a while and he never went back into that pub again. But time's not always a great healer…'

'And he forgot about it?'

'Or chose not to remember it,' said Alice, 'and if I ever tried to remind him he wouldn't like it. I don't know what the power of drink is to some, Jenny, but I do know that it keeps pulling my Neville back into its clutches.'

Later that night Jenny took Frank to one side and told him the story,

'Aye, we all know the effect that drink can have on some,' he said, 'all I can say, and I've told you before, is that he's a different man underground; he's a good worker, honest, reliable.'

'I don't care what he's like underground,' said Jenny, 'I care what he's like at home and I'm telling you this, and I've told you this before, you have to do something.'

Most girls were trained by their mothers from an early age on all the things needed to look after a household.

Cooking and cleaning were essential skills to look after a miner husband and a growing family. Girls were not considered as much of a future financial asset as boys, and, for girls, an early marriage was seen as one of the few ways to break out of the home and stand on your own two feet.

This is what had happened to Alice and as far as she was concerned, she'd made her own bed and now she had to lie in it, however uncomfortable that might be.

She did worry about her daughter's future though, conscious that her own marriage did little to encourage her daughter in that direction, and she knew that the only real alternative, other than dirty jobs like topside coal sorting at the pit that she wouldn't wish on anybody, was to try and find a suitable place 'in service' which had the dual benefit of her earning some money of her own and, crucially, enabling her to leave home, leave the village, and start a new life somewhere else.

When Alice thought about this, she wished that she had the same chance but knew that she didn't. There was nowhere for her to run to, much less with a young daughter in tow. If Sarah did leave then she worried about whether she would ever see her again and feared the increased loneliness that this would bring her way. She tried not to think about the future. It didn't look good.

To try and increase her opportunities, Alice, as well as teaching Sarah about household chores and upkeep, encouraged her in her schooling, thinking that that might give her a better start than she had had, and soon Sarah was demonstrating her ability to read, write and do her numbers as well as, if not better than, her mother.

At school, as Jack was one of the children Sarah knew best, she gravitated to him. Jack didn't mind, he was used to looking out for his younger brother, George, and so he also looked out for Sarah, ensuring that she was invited to join in with the playground games. She was very good a hopscotch.

He did notice however that Sarah's clothes were raggedy and in poor condition. Being a boy, he asked her about this,

'These are my school clothes,' said Sarah indignantly, 'my mummy tries very hard, but we don't have much money. These are the only clothes I have.'

When Jack got home, in amongst tales about the Maths he was learning, he told his mother about this.

'Oh,' said Jenny, 'I see.'

To Jack, his mother's answer was one of those confusing adult answers, and the 'I see' seemed to mean something more than he could understand.

'But they have a wage coming in, don't they?' he persisted, 'and less mouths to feed than we have, how can they be short?'

'Shush now,' said his mother.

A few days later Sarah was wearing a new smock, made from a hardwearing fabric. Sarah showed it off proudly,

'Your mother made it,' she said to Jack.

Jack asked his mother about this when he got home, and she admitted it.

'Shush, Jack,' she said, 'now don't you go telling that to anyone else, including your father, you hear.' Jack nodded, 'Sarah really shouldn't have told you.'

'I hope it wasn't very expensive.'

'No, Jack, it wasn't expensive,' said Jenny, who had actually done the work herself from left over fabric she had from another job and had gifted the finished article to Sarah's mother. That's what you did if you were a good neighbour.

A few days later Alice was round, talking to Jenny in her kitchen,

'Thanks for Sarah's smock,' she said, 'it's made a big difference.'

Jenny smiled.

'That's no problem.'

'But,' continued Alice, 'could you not do it again, please.'

Jenny was surprised and, seeing the look of consternation on her face, Alice burst into an explanation. As she spoke, she refused to make eye contact.

'It's just that Neville wondered where I got the money from to buy new things for Sarah. He wouldn't believe that I'd got it for nothing.'

'Oh,' said Jenny, instinctively reaching forward and touching Alice's arm.

Alice winced.

'Alice!?'

'It's OK, I've just bumped into something. I'm so clumsy. I'm always doing it.

Jenny knew better of course.

Alice always wore long sleeves and long dresses, but even so there were times when bruising showed on her neck and face, and this wasn't the first time that she'd been pained at a touch. But if Alice wanted to keep her problems to herself, then it was difficult for anyone to help.

'If…' said Jenny.

Alice interrupted.

'He's a good man really,' she said, 'and I do my best.'

Later that day Jenny spoke to Frank.

'How long can we let this go on?' she said.

Chapter 14

It was a weekend, and Jack was sitting on the couch in the front parlour reading a book. Sunlight was streaming through the open front door and adjacent window and covered him in light and warmth. His grandfather was in the room with him. His face was lined and wrinkled with age and marked and tarnished from the life he had led. His moustache, of which he was immensely proud, bushed from his upper lip. Wiry and rough it still sported the odd strand of black amongst the grey and displayed the evident care with which it was tended and tamed into shape.

Shirt sleeves folded back to the elbow, the old man smelled of the tobacco that he used to fill his pipe. The staining on his fingers and the wear and yellowing of some of his teeth gave testament to its frequent use. Although Jenny would tell him to sit by an open window or go outside to 'save the rest of the house from that stink' today he was sitting in his seat by the fire with the pipe in his hand.

The seat had a hardwood frame and was softened with cushions. It was from this chair that he and Jack, who was a keen audience for his stories, some true, some embellished, some complete fantasy, would travel the world together.

The old man's face was set in concentration as he looked over at Jack, his watery eyes trying to focus. Suddenly the family clock that was the focal point of the room, chimed an hour. It was set five minutes fast and disturbed Jack's concentration. As his body moved, he seemed to ripple amongst the shadows cast over him by the pointy leaves of the aspidistra. The plant was almost like a member of the family and sat proudly in its pot, on the floor below the window, where it thrived on rainwater, cold tea and neglect.

'Do you think stories can teach you anything, my boy?'

Jack squinted into the light, 'I just enjoy reading,' he said.

The old man smiled.

'Would you like to hear a story?'

Jack nodded and moved himself into a comfortable position, ready to listen.

'Alright then, this story is about King Arthur, let me just get comfy before we start.'

The old man adjusted the cushions on his chair and scraped it closer to where Jack was sitting, and more into the warm sunlight.

As his grandfather drew nearer Jack saw the scars on his arm. Jack had a scar of his own now and unconsciously raised a hand to touch it. It was completely healed and almost invisible, but he could still feel it. The unwelcome memory of his fall flashed through his mind.

'If that is what it takes to get a scar then I don't want any more,' he thought as he settled back to listen to another of his grandfather's stories.

'This story involves somewhere quite close to here,' said Grandpa, 'this whole area is steeped in folk tales you know, and one of them involves King Arthur, who together with his knights always fought to defend these shores and is said to have promised to return to help us in our hour of greatest need.'

'But how does that work?' asked Jack, 'where is he and how would he know?'

'Well now, that's exactly what this story is about, so shall I tell you?'

Jack nodded.

'The legend is that King Arthur, his queen Guinevere and his knights of the round table were all enticed into a cave somewhere below Sewingshields Crags, which is not too far north of here, by a wizard who put a spell on them, a spell that put them to sleep, a spell that could only be broken when the country was in direst need and someone found them and woke them with a blow on a bugle horn and the cutting of a ribbon with the enchanted sword, Excalibur. Doing that would set them all free.'

'That's very complicated,' said Jack.

'That's the thing about wizards,' said Grandpa, 'they don't make things easy, and before anything else you would have to find the cave.'

'Sounds impossible,' said Jack.

'Well, it's true that no one, although over the centuries many had tried, had ever been able to locate the entrance to this cave. That was until a local shepherd, and it was only about 60 years ago, was trying to put a tether around an unruly ram, and, when the ram resisted, he dropped the ball of string he was using and saw it fall to the ground, start to unravel, and roll into a mess of briars and nettles where it seemed to get stuck.'

'When he went to untangle it from the thorns, he saw, underneath these clumps and bushes, what looked like a big hole and, when he looked more closely, he could see that it was the entrance to some kind of tunnel.'

'Being an inquisitive kind of chap, he got down on his hands and knees and made his way through the prickles that mysteriously parted to let him through, and there before him, clear as day, was the entrance to a vaulted passage.'

'Without thinking he entered the passageway and soon wished that he hadn't because the floor was covered with warty toads and slithering lizards and above his head flitted the dark wings of bats. Nevertheless, he ventured deeper and began to leave the sunlight behind him. As the tunnel twisted and turned, it became darker and darker, until, at length, his courage was almost gone and he decided that he should turn back.'

'Just at that moment he saw a dim light ahead of him. This made him curious and he wondered if it was a sign that there was another way out so that he wouldn't have go back past the toads and the lizards and the bats. So, he went on a little further. As he did so the light grew brighter until, all at once, the tunnel opened up and he found himself in a vast and vaulted hall. In the centre of the hall there was a hole in the floor and from this hole a fire blazed, a magical fire that burned without fuel and filled the hall with a bright and flickering flame.'

'In the fire's light the shepherd could see the carved walls and fine roof and, on the far side of the hall, was King Arthur, his Queen and his Knights, lying slumped on thrones and chairs, asleep.'

Jack gasped.

'On a table, beyond the fire, lay the spell-dissolving horn, the magical sword Excalibur, and the ribbon. The shepherd went forward and firmly grasped the sword and, as he began to draw it from its scabbard, the eyes of the King, the Queen and all his Knights began to open, and their bodies straighten until they were sitting upright.'

Grandpa paused.

'And then?' said Jack.

'The shepherd was amazed but he continued to draw the sword from its scabbard and when it was completely free, it was so heavy he could hardly lift it, he took hold of the ribbon and cut it with the sword. Then he began to put the sword back into its sheath and as he did so the spell resumed its ancient power and everybody began to slowly sink back into sleep.'

Jack listened intently.

'But before they did,' continued his Grandpa, 'King Arthur lifted up his eyes and hands and exclaimed,

"Oh, woe betide this evil day, on which this witless man was born, who drew the sword, the ribbon cut, but did not blow the bugle horn."

'This frightened the shepherd and he turned and ran from the place, running down the twisting passage as fast as his feet could carry him, not even pausing to worry about the toads, the lizards and the bats but hoping against hope that he could find the exit and once more be in the light of day.'

Jack's Grandpa paused, and then he said,

'And he did find his way out. When he ran around one of the corners he saw a glimpse of sunlight and this made him run even faster, faster than he had ever run before, afraid that the tunnel exit would close before he got there and that the sunlight would disappear. But that didn't happen and he rushed headlong out of the tunnel, through the brambles and nettles and back to where he had left his ram.'

'When he reached the spot, his ram was still there and he grabbed one of its horns and kept running, pulling the ram along behind him, trying to get away from the memory of what he'd done. Ashamed of his mistake.'

'Over that night and the next morning the horror of what he had done, and not done, sunk in and garbled his mind.'

'Though he tried to tell and retell his story to anyone who would listen, he could never tell it in a way that made any sense and so, because people didn't understand what he was talking about, they stopped listening.'

'For the rest of his life he tried to retrace his steps and make good his error, but he could never again find the entrance to that enchanted hall.'

'So now, Jack, the question is this, is King Arthur still there, asleep, waiting for our call, or is he doomed to sleep forever… or did the shepherd just fall asleep and imagine the whole thing?'

There was quiet as Jack thought about it.

'That's not a true story, is it?' he said.

His grandfather shrugged his shoulders,

'Why would you think that?'

'Well,' said Jack, 'if the shepherd couldn't remember anything then who was there who knew what happened and could tell the story?'

His grandfather smiled, pleased at his grandson's logic.

'There is a little bit more to tell,' he said, 'but I don't know if it will change your mind.'

Jack listened.

'This is not a story I made up,' he paused, 'and that's a fact.'

Jack nodded, willing to accept this point.

'I heard it from a man whose brother met a man who was going around collecting stories. He said that the man who was collecting stories was collecting them to make sure they were not forgotten. He said that, because there is so much moving around these days, stories that had been handed down by word of mouth from one generation to the next were in danger of being lost and that he wanted to capture as many as he could before that happened. He wanted to write them down and put them in a book so that they were safe.'

Jack thought about this, and then he nodded. Books were a good thing, and keeping stories safe was a good thing too.

'Well, it was this man, the man who was collecting stories, that met the shepherd. He had been asking around everywhere he went about whether there were any good stories to collect and when he came to this particular place the shepherd was pointed out to him. He was an old man by then and was sitting drinking on his own in the corner of a pub.'

Jack nodded again. That was possible.

'The man went and talked to the shepherd, who was a bit reluctant at first, but after a while, and a few drinks, the shepherd agreed to tell him what he could remember.'

'Over the next few days, the man listened to the shepherd. His memories came in bits and pieces, some blurry, some clear. His story was all over the place, but the man wrote each bit down and then, when he thought he had enough, he pieced them together like a jigsaw. Then he read the story back to the shepherd and the shepherd opened his eyes wide, "That's it," he said, "that's exactly what happened.".'

Grandpa looked away.

'Unfortunately, the shock of remembering what had happened to him, and the terrible mistake that he had made, was too much for the shepherd and tears flowed down his deep-wrinkled cheeks and he got up and left the pub. He died two days later.'

'That's sad,' said Jack.

'Sad for the shepherd but good for the story because it had been rescued, and written down, and the story was now clear enough to be told and retold… and through that line of retelling I heard it. And now I've told it to you.'

'So, I'm part of the story's history?'

'Yes.'

'Did he put it in a book?'

'I don't know, he went back to London and nobody I know ever heard of him again.'

Grandpa tapped his pipe on the arm of his chair.

'Now what do you think, is the story true?'

Jack still wasn't convinced.

'It might be, but if King Arthur is waiting for our moment of greatest need, then even if the shepherd had done it perfectly, it wasn't the right time.'

'That's true,' said Grandpa, 'but then King Arthur would have asked and when told that the time had not yet come, he would have gone back to sleep happily and waited to be woken again at the proper time.'

'How do you know that?'

'It's the legend.'

'Seems to me this is a more complicated story than it first appears.'

'Most stories are,' said Grandpa.

'Hmm,' said Jack.

'Maybe it's more important what the story tells us.'

'And what's that?'

'Maybe it's saying don't meddle with things you don't understand, or maybe it means that if you want to achieve something you have to know the steps you to take, and you have to take the time to take all those steps, and in the right order.'

'Hmm,' said Jack.

'Or maybe it's just a good story,' said Grandpa.

Jack considered.

'I think you can definitely learn things from stories,' he said.

'I think you can too,' said Grandpa.

Chapter 15

The Moore's arable land was divided into four fields of equal acreage and, over the years and generations of Moores, a method of crop rotation had been developed that had become a tradition.

In the first year, winter corn was sown, either wheat or winter oats. In the second year, spring corn, oats and barley. In the third year, half was in clover for hay and the other half in rye, winter barley and vetches to feed the sheep in the Spring, followed by swedes and kale for winter feeding. The halves were alternated every four years as Jim had it from his father that the clover would only grow successfully in this system once every eight years, and he had no reason to doubt it nor to test its voracity. If something was proven and could be seen to work, then why tamper with it? Then in the fourth year, summer roots, usually turnips, were grown.

This rotation was unalterable. The beauty was that you always knew which crop a particular field would be growing two or three years ahead and could work to that end.

Any variation was considered a sin. This was a proven, sustainable, way to farm. It may not maximise profits, but it ensured that Mr Moore could husband his land and fulfil his duty of maintaining the farm both for himself and for future generations.

Such a tried and tested system was the chief reason why there was resistance to, and mistrust of, new things.

If any new method were tried in the area, then a local farmer would not only look to its advantages, he may even ignore them, but would be quick to point out any shortcomings.

Mr Moore could not stop progress however, and he, as well as his neighbouring farmers would move, albeit reluctantly, to new methods and new machinery, that was expensive, unreliable, and needed new skills to use and maintain, only when they felt that there was no other choice. At the end of the day, they had to remain competitive in order to keep their families fed.

After centuries of striving for enough, now was the age of efficiency and profit, the ratcheting aim of achieving more, of doing it faster, of replacing human and horse with metal, steam and electricity. And it took some getting used to.

As a farmer, Jim Moore was and would always be, for better or for worse, a part of his own landscape, his role within it ruled by and buffeted by the weather and the seasons.

With the skills he had learnt from his father and grandfather he knew how to ride the naturally cyclical tides of chance, how not to fight against them, but to take losses and failures with stoic indifference and how not to celebrate too volubly the good years that may happen along.

As far as Jim Moore was concerned, being a farmer needed a thick skin, resilience, perseverance and nerve. The profit he made was a by-product of his application of experience and the tight rein he kept on expenditure.

With all its trials, he still thought it a good life and was sceptical about ideas that challenged his system of crop and livestock rotation in favour of a mechanised future full of new artificial nutrients, pesticides and treatments designed to squeeze ever increasing amounts out of the same soil.

At best it seemed too good to be true, at worst it seemed to him to risk tipping the balance, of denuding the land and storing up greater problems for the future.

His son, Peter, however, was beginning to see the world differently.

When Peter showed enthusiasm for new ways or new machinery his father would shrug his shoulders, take off his tweed cap, and scratch his head. If Canute could not hold back the tide then what chance did he have?

There was one thing Jim Moore was sure of though and that was that as a farmer you had to know your sums and there was no one quicker at reckoning than Jim Moore, he'd been cheated too often as a younger man to let even farthings slip through his fingers now and he ran his farm as if it were his extended family.

The Carters harnessed the horses at 6:45am and Jim Moore would give them instruction so that they could be about their work by 7.

The Dairyman and Shepherd were different; they had charge of their respective areas and were trusted to go about their work undisturbed.

The sheepfold was visited every morning and each sheep given a careful eye. To an outsider it might seem that the farm was run entirely for the sheep they were so carefully looked after; lambed, run out and grazed, marked, dipped, put to the ram, the shepherd always on the lookout for foot rot or other ailments that could be nipped in the bud. They were hungry animals with a large appetite and, if necessary, their diet was supplemented with bought-in feed.

There were so many things that could happen to a sheep, especially as they seemed to take perverse pleasure in getting into trouble. If there was a hedge it was possible to get stuck in, if there was a bog to become mired in, if there was a hole to fall into, a fence to poke a head through, a gap to escape out of... then at some time or other a sheep would find a way to do it. From its birth to the time that it left the farm for sale or for slaughter a sheep needed to be watched and rescued, and it was important that the shepherd was a man who could maintain an even temper and a positive outlook in trying circumstances.

The Dairyman needed a different demeanour.

Producing milk twice daily, seven days a week, and getting the milk hygienically into the churns ready for despatch, was more akin to factory production than farming. Those who worked in the dairy knew that it was their efforts that ensured a daily income to the farm and bridged the uneven and seasonal income from sheep, pigs, crops and beef cattle. It was not unusual for the Dairyman to be a little scornful of the amount of attention the sheep got whilst they managed their cowherd with smoothness and simplicity; giving them food and drink, bringing them in to calf and milk, and allowing them to do most of the rest for themselves, intelligent and docile animals that they were.

The cows were split into two herds. The first was the main milking herd and the second consisted of the dry cows waiting to calve and the cows that were nearly dry.

Jim Moore was a man who looked after his workers, a man who found people he could trust and, in general, would then leave them to their work, knowing that if anything needed his attention they would bring it to him. As a result of Jim and Ella's efforts the farm made money, not a great deal but enough for them, Peter, and their extended family of itinerant and permanent workers to survive on.

The farm was a place of life and death husbanded by humans. The birthing of lambs, calves, foals and piglets, not all of whom survived. The rearing and slaughter of sheep, pigs and cows. The choice of which animals would live and be bred from and which sold on or sent to the slaughterhouse. Over all of these things the farmer and his family of helpers reigned superior and god-like.

Amongst other things, Jim Moore had the right to shoot rabbits and pheasants on the farm and Peter and Jack learnt how to chase rabbits, running them down and falling on them. Then later, when the boys were older and Mr Moore thought they could be trusted with a gun, they went on hunting expeditions, creeping or crawling, going carefully, avoiding any noise, the scrunching of pebbles, or inadvertently snapping a twig, Above all they learnt how to shoot the gun, as their prey darted between trees and undergrowth, and that a bullet goes a very long way.

The first time Jack fired the rifle it put him on his back. Mr Moore stifled a smile, but Peter laughed out loud. As Jack got disconsolately back to his feet and was dusting himself off, the farmer said,

'Take a firm stance and hold it into your shoulder, everybody has to learn.'

'Here, I'll show you,' said Peter, reloading the gun and lifting it to his shoulder, 'see that tree trunk, I'm just going to aim at that.'

Jack watched admiringly, his father had never let him touch a gun, never mind teach him how to fire one.

Practise makes competent, and so it was with Jack, he soon got the hang of it.

Once, when the boys brought their haul of game home to the farmhouse, Jack asked,

'Can I take a rabbit home with me?'

'The problem is, Jack,' said Mr Moore, 'that I have permission to shoot on my farm and I can give permission to you, otherwise it would be poaching, and poaching is a serious offence. If anyone saw you and didn't know where you'd got it from then you could be in serious trouble. You might even be thrown in jail before I heard about it.'

Mrs Moore sighed, 'Sorry, Jack, but Jim's right.'

Jack never asked again but at the end of the next visit he was presented with a pie to take home.

'Thank you,' he said, 'what is it?'

'Let's just say it's a meat pie,' said Mrs Moore, 'now you just hop it home and enjoy.'

He was halfway home before he realised what it was.

The family loved it, even Jenny was impressed.

Chapter 16

Jenny spent a lot of her time feeding the family; getting the food, preparing it, cooking it, serving it, cleaning up after it... it was a never-ending task. She took it as a source of pride that there was always a meal ready, and water heating for a bath, when either Frank or Edward returned from their work underground.

Jenny ran her household by developing, and sticking to, a routine that she knew would keep everything ticking over, and was even able to squeeze in time between chores in late morning, mid-afternoon and late evening, to do something of her own.

God help anyone who tried to meddle with her methods. They would find out very quickly that neither meddling nor the attempt to suggest change or improvement were welcome in her house.

Thursday was breadmaking day as, although the colliery village had a general shop, there was no bakery so, each Thursday, Jenny would be busy using the oven to turn her shop bought flour into loaves and rolls, or the well-loved 'stotty cake'.

She prepared for each weekend by black leading the kitchen range, washing the front step and cleaning her few brasses. On a Friday the family would be dosed with cod-liver oil and hair would be cut. On Saturday afternoons, while the men were out, she would wash herself more thoroughly than the daily rinse, additional privacy being provided by a strategically placed clotheshorse draped with blankets.

It was important to be well prepared for the weekend as this was the men's main time off, with the pit closed down on a Sunday.

Sunday might feel like a holiday for the men and the children but there was never a holiday for the women and it paid to be as well prepared as possible.

Jenny and Frank slept on a bed in the parlour. Grandpa slept on the floor in the kitchen. He wouldn't have it any other way.

He said that his army days had spoiled him for beds and that he needed the solid ground under him to get off to sleep. The kitchen was also the warmest room in the house, a fact that was not lost on Jenny.

As Grandpa curled up in a corner and had the ability to sleep through any kind of night-time or early morning activity without waking, Jenny was content to put up with this rather eccentric sleeping arrangement. The only thing she demanded was that no one, and she meant no one (looking particularly at young George), ever told any of their neighbours that she'd made Grandpa sleep on the kitchen floor.

As far as she knew, no one had ever let slip this family secret. Reputation was important to Jenny.

For the women of the mining village, shopping was an important part of their lives. Some hated it, others loved it. It was both an art and a necessity and spreading their income across all the needs of the household was a skill that each woman aspired to perfect.

Some households had only one income but several mouths to feed, others had more than one worker under their roof and therefore more than one income coming in. These were the lucky ones and, after years of scraping by, Jenny and Frank now had the luxury of two incomes and the prospect of more when Jack and George reached working age, although by that time Edward might have met a girl and moved into a place of his own. Good times were not built to last, and Jenny was determined not to take anything for granted. She lived her life one day at a time, focussing on what needed to be done… and there was plenty of that.

The Cooperative Wholesale Society, CWS, or 'the store' as it was known in colliery villages started way back in 1873.

In a number of mining communities the coal mine owners thought it good business to not only build and have control over the housing but to also build and run the only store in the village. In this way they could recover a large proportion of the wages they'd paid out by charging inflated prices for food and other basic household goods.

Thankfully this was not the situation everywhere, but there was enough unrest to precipitate change.

It was a group of Lancashire weavers who first set up the Cooperative movement. They felt that if customers could be encouraged to pay to join a co-operative organisation, by purchasing shares, then the money raised could be pooled together to buy staple items like tea, butter, sugar, flour, oatmeal and candles. Once these items had been re-sold at reasonable prices then the money could be reinvested to buy more items and extend the product range.

This method was so successful that it was rolled out all over the country with people in towns and villages being responsible for forming committees and setting up their own co-operative stores.

The committees would locate premises and allocate jobs; finding people to collect the joining fees, go to the wholesale warehouses to buy products, work in the stores to sell the food and then reinvest the money in more products.

This was a virtuous circle bringing cheaper basic foodstuffs and household items to their customers and still making enough money to repeat the process and build the business. The fact that this was so easily achieved gives a clear idea of just how much of an advantage had been previously taken.

Purchases made by individual members were made a note of so that, when dividend day came around, they would receive a refund related to the amount of purchases they'd made. This payout of shared profits was known as the dividend or 'divvi'.

One benefit of a large membership was that the Co-op had substantial buying and bargaining power, and a warehouse was opened in Newcastle upon Tyne which supplied all the local stores in the north.

The organisation became so successful that the Co-op launched their own range of goods and operated factories making soap, clothing, biscuits, and textiles throughout the country. They even opened a tea plantation in India and called their own brand 'Indian Prince'.

The additional economies made by manufacturing their own goods were passed on to the customer and the Co-op operated overall as a nonprofit making organisation.

Not only did the store provide basic foodstuffs at realistic prices, it also brought communities together in a common cause and was an opportunity for working people to govern and run something for themselves for the benefit of themselves and their community.

Once established, a Co-op store became a recognised source of employment, and, largely for women, these jobs provided an alternative to seeking work in the colliery or 'in service'.

Being a member of the store became something of a badge of honour for mining families, whilst having your order delivered to your door was a mark of respectability.

In Jack's village the 'order man' visited Jenny on a Monday and took a note of her requirements. The groceries would then be delivered at the end of the week by the store horse and cart, although meat was delivered on a Wednesday and the greengrocer, with his cart, came round on a Thursday.

Families used the store for most things including hardware, drapery, millinery, clothes, shoes, furniture and the tools of the trade that the miners would be responsible for buying for themselves

Some families tried to buy everything through the Co-op as that maximised their divvi. Dividend day was a day to look forward to and children would look on eagerly, in the hope that something good might come their way.

Alice Hudson could not afford this luxury.

It was not that the Co-op prices were unreasonable but as her husband limited what he passed on to her from his pay, she had to go around the small dealers in the hope of saving a few pennies. She would haggle over the prices and, were possible, buy what she could 'on tick'.

When she could, she took Sarah along with her and taught her how to examine the articles and their prices with a critical eye, and how to haggle with an 'I can always go somewhere else' attitude, showing a confidence that she did not really feel.

When payday arrived and she'd received her money from Neville, she would often send Sarah out on her own, secretly and quietly, with a list of things to get. She didn't want the neighbours to know what she was reduced to.

Without feeling the responsibility, Sarah quite enjoyed the challenge. She would buy what was on the list for as little as possible, comparing prices between dealers, and if she saved enough from the money she was given, she would look for a bargain and bring home, for example, half a pound of corned beef as well. She would bring the purchases back in plain, brown paper packages to avoid prying eyes and would sometimes be praised for her initiative and sometimes told off for not bringing the spare money home.

Alice didn't avoid the Co-op altogether though.

It was still a good place to shop, and she used to go with Jenny every other Saturday for a 'special shop'. She would not buy as much, she would not spend as much and, if there was the opportunity to haggle, then she would.

It was important to Alice, for her reputation's sake, to be seen in the Co-op.

The two mothers would drag Jack, George and Sarah along with them to help carry any purchases home.

Top of Alice's mind was the need for a bit more money, and she wondered if she could take matters into her own hands.

'I know you do sewing,' she said to Jenny, 'do you think I could do that?'

Sarah stood listening and interested.

Jack was off looking at the garden tools, George in tow.

'Well yes, I do some sewing,' said Jenny, 'and it does bring in a few extra pennies every now and again. I enjoy doing it.'

'Do you think I could learn?' asked Alice.

'It wouldn't be easy. I picked it up from my own mother, at her knee like. But I suppose you won't know unless you try.'

They wandered over to the fabrics department and were immediately pounced on by Tony Sharpe, one of the assistant managers.

'Careful of this one,' whispered Jenny, 'he could sell a bull to a calf.'

Alice smirked.

'Now ladies,' said Tony, his eyes twinkling, 'what are you looking for today? Perhaps I could help you?'

Tony was a couple of years younger than Alice and had only recently arrived in the store from Newcastle. He was lean and energetic, smartly dressed, clean skinned, bright, friendly and ambitious to eventually own a store of his own.

He had never had any intention of going anywhere near the pit. His was the world of retail, of buying and selling and of being clean. He appreciated where the shopper's money came from, the sight of the winding gear that loomed large on the horizon made that perfectly clear, but for Tony his role was to live by the Co-operative code; negotiate hard with suppliers, miss out as many middle-men as possible, provide quality and value for money and generate the divvi that would hopefully be spent back in the store. It was a beautifully virtuous circle as far as he was concerned, everyone won except the margin grabbing hustlers who tried to control prices and supplies, and he was happy to be a cog in the fair-trade wheel.

And he oozed charm.

'I'm looking for some white cotton to make a blouse or two,' said Jenny, 'it needs to be soft but hard wearing, it's for Elsie Walton.'

In his position in the store, Tony knew most of the women in the three streets and a lot of the men. He knew Elsie and he knew what important work she did, amateur and unpaid, for so many people.

'Funny you should say that Mrs Lawley, we have a special discount on an end of roll. Let me show it to you.'

He darted away to a far corner and started going through a pile of assorted cottons.

'He's a real charmer, isn't he,' said Jenny, 'I like him.'

'Don't let Frank hear you saying that, you'll make him jealous.'

Jenny laughed.

'Frank's got nothing to worry about, this lad's young enough to be my son, he's more your age.'

Alice blushed.

'Jenny!' she said, 'you can be so…'

The sentence was cut short by the returning retailer.

'There you go,' he said, 'feel this, what do you think?'

Jenny rubbed the fabric between her fingers, pulled about a yard from the roll and inspected it for defects. It was good quality, and she enquired about the price. It was very reasonable.

On the way home, Jenny returned to the conversation about sewing.

'I suppose I could show you a bit of dressmaking if you like,' she said, 'maybe even show Sarah.'

Alice accepted the offer willingly. Sarah was overjoyed.

Jack and George weren't listening; they were discussing the essential differences between a spade and a shovel.

Chapter 17

Jack's grandfather was at his allotment, leaning on a spade. In his hand was a letter that he had just finished re-reading,

Dear ex-Corporal A. Lawley,

I am sorry to be the bearer of sad news but as executor of the estate of ex-Private Harold Carpenter I have the duty to inform you of his death.

Mr Carpenter left no family and no realisable assets and died in West Morton Workhouse on the 15th inst. His last days were not pleasant ones I'm afraid, but he has now passed into the 'peace of the Lord.'

He left few instructions other than to request that some handful of people be informed of his passing. You are one of those people and Harold wished you to know that his time in the British Army was amongst his most treasured memories.

Again, we would like to assure you of our condolences. Harold found himself down on his luck but was still able to raise a smile to the last with reminiscences of his escapades in warmer climes.

Yours Sincerely
M. Markham
West Morton Workhouse

P.S. Corporal Carpenter's funeral has already taken place, at the cost of the Parish, and he has been laid to rest in an unmarked grave.

'I didn't know,' Grandpa said to himself, 'you silly bugger, why didn't you write, you know I would have helped if I could.'

He folded up the letter and put it in his pocket.

'It's too late now, so much for looking after us like heroes, so much for the service we gave, the danger we put ourselves in, the lives that we lost… what was it all for, Harold? For a bit of metal and a ribbon to wear on your chest?…'

As Jack approached, he saw his grandfather bent over the spade. He didn't seem to be moving.

'Hello, Grandpa,' he called.

The old man looked up as if awakened from a dream. The news had brought him up short and, as he needed to talk, and Jack was there, he raced through the pleasantries and began to ruminate out loud. He would couch his words to protect the boy and maybe, as a consequence, they would have no meaning, but they were so filling his mind that he could do no other than to let them spill out, and it was Jack's lot to hear them, for better or for worse.

'As I grow older,' he said, 'I realise that I understand less and less. There were times when I thought everything was clear and simple; I was born British, the British Empire was the greatest empire that there had ever been, and we were obliged to revere and protect it. We thought that to be a part of something so great was in everybody's interests in the end. And to be a soldier, to be in the front line and to contribute towards this noble enterprise, to be willing to die for it, seemed to be an adventure, an honour and right.'

He looked down at his hands, soiled from his labours,

'I've got a primus here,' he said, 'I'll boil a kettle, and we can have a cup of tea.'

He left the spade standing, it looked like a kind of headstone with its shadow stretching across the dug ground and walked over to his ramshackle shed.

Jack followed him willingly, he loved to listen to his grandfather's reminiscences, although this time he sensed a more sombre mood, this time it felt different, that what his grandfather was trying to say was more than a story or a humorous anecdote.

With mugs of sugared black tea in their hands, his grandfather continued,

'Life is like a horse cart, Jack. You just keep going merrily along until one of the wheels falls off. Then you fix the wheel and get going again. The cart's a bit more worn and a bit more wobbly but it still does the job. And you just keep going like that, doing your work, looking after the cart as best you can, fixing bits and pieces here and there… and that's the way it is … until the axle breaks,' Grandpa paused, took a drink of tea, 'and then the cart's no good anymore and it's scrapped or burnt and a new, maybe a better, more modern, cart takes its place. That's the way it is, Jack, that's the way it is. Nobody remembers the old cart once it's gone.'

Jack felt like his grandfather had tried to say something profound, pass on some pearl of wisdom, but all he could see in his mind's eye was a cart with a broken axle, and he knew even that could be fixed. Did that mean a cart could go on forever?

'The wealth of a few is built on the effort of the many,' said his grandfather, 'we are at the root of the tree, and just like a root, we can never hope to become a branch, or a leaf, or a flower, but without us the tree would not be fed, it would not grow, there would be no branches, there would be no flowers, there would be no seeds, there would no new trees spawned. Best to be happy that you're in amongst the roots I suppose and know your place, know that you're a part of the tree and that what you do counts.'

Jack sat quietly, sipping at his tea. He didn't know why but he felt that his job was not to understand or question but simply to let his grandfather finish.

'When you start to read a book, you don't know where it's going to take you,' said Grandpa, knowing that a love of books was common ground, 'but the author does. The author has carefully constructed the pathway, the twists and the turns, the ups and the downs. All are already mapped out, unchangeable, yet a mystery to you, the reader, hidden in the pages that you have yet to turn. So, the question I ask is … is life like that? Is everything predetermined yet still a mystery for us to discover as we go on our journey… as we turn the pages from beginning to end? Or are we writing the story as we go along and the next page, before we turn it, is still blank?'

Jack was now on firmer ground. The mention of books gave him the opportunity to respond.

'When I read,' he said, 'when I really read, I start to feel like I'm part of the story,' Jack knew that he couldn't talk like this to anybody else, it sounded so silly, but he thought that his grandfather would understand, 'it's like the story is in my mind, I'm inhabited by it and so I've sailed the seas with Treasure Island, followed clues with Sherlock Holmes, and dared to ask for more with Oliver Twist...'

He looked up at his grandfather.

'Am I being silly?'

The old man smiled.

'Try never to lose that, Jack, don't let reality destroy your imagination.'

Jack looked puzzled.

'Keep enjoying reading your books,' said his grandfather, ruffling his tousled hair with his hand.

Jack laughed.

'I will, Grandpa,' he said, 'I will. I promise.'

Around them the summer day shimmered; just like in a book.

'Now let's get some work done,' said his grandfather, 'you go and check the hens, I'll dig us out some vegetables.'

When Jack walked back towards home, hand in hand with his grandfather, a newly laid egg in his pocket, fresh dug carrots in his other hand, the sun was low on the horizon and spread a deep red glow across the roofs of the colliery rows. In a short while the sun would set and the roofs would turn to black, but for the moment it looked beautiful.

Chapter 18

Jenny was always busy.

She would rise before Frank and Edward, at three in the morning, rake out the cold ashes, reset and relight the range, heat some water for the men to wash in, take the bucket of ashes to the privy, get breakfast ready and see the men off to work with the lunches she had prepared the night before.

To Jenny it was unthinkable for her men to leave for work while she remained in bed. She never said why, but it was an unwritten rule of the colliery women to see their men safely out to their shifts. It was a way of managing the fear that it might be the last time they saw them alive. Unfortunately, at the root of this fear lay a grim reality.

Later, at around 7, she would wake Grandpa, who could sleep through a hurricane, and, after he had put away his bedding, she would scrub the kitchen floor in a never-ending quest for cleanliness, put more coal on the fire and more water on to heat. Then she would wake Jack and George and see them and Grandpa washed, clothed and fed in time for Jack and George to get off to school. Grandpa would help by filling up the coal scuttle from the shed outside and by bringing in two new buckets of water. Then, if he had no work on the Moore's farm that day, he would get out from under his daughter's feet by going off to his allotment and tending to his veg and his chickens.

Jenny would then wash herself using a jug of hot water, an enamel bowl, and soap, and finish by tying up her hair for the day. Then the kitchen table would be given a rub over, the breakfast things cleaned and put away.

Then she would make the beds and air the rooms if the weather was mild enough, and after that she would face up to the job she disliked the most: the chamber pots.

First they were emptied into a slops bucket, then that was taken out and emptied into the privy, that was dug out and into a dust cart, using a hatch in the back wall, 3 times a week. Then she would scrub the chamber pots with washing soda, put them back under the beds, and then wash her hands thoroughly using Lifebuoy soap.

At around 10 am she took a short break and had a cup of tea.

It was only by establishing and sticking to her routines that Jenny had any hope of making 'spare' time for herself.

Monday she would do the laundry using a metal dolly tub, working with a posser, warm water and soap, removing the dirt and then squeezing out the water through the mangle, tipping the dirty water into the gutter that ran along the middle of the back street.

Tuesday was for drying.

Wednesday was for ironing.

Thursday was for baking.

Friday was for cleaning.

Saturday was for finishing up whatever was not already done.

Sunday, the men's day off, was for church and the 'big cook', preparing food not just for the day but food that could be used, with careful shepherding, over the next few days.

By doing all of this and cooking dinner, preparing supper and hot water for her men's return, shopping, cleaning and dusting, and the myriad of other things I've forgotten, Jenny managed to still find a few hours in her day, perhaps not every day, that she could devote to the thing that she loved doing… and that was her sewing.

Over the weeks that followed Jenny tried to fulfil her promise to teach Alice and Sarah to sew. They met up when they could, sitting around Jenny's kitchen table drinking tea, talking, listening and trying to learn from her by doing and then through repetition.

Jenny took them through each of the stages. She demonstrated how to cut out a pattern, leaving a good margin at the seams to allow for alterations. They practiced on a simple skirt, and she showed Alice and Sarah how she'd learnt to tack and fit, using each other as models.

Then they moved on to linings; how to cut identical pieces of lining and main material, how to firmly tack them together and join the various pieces together, starting at the waist and working downwards.

'If you do it like this,' said Jenny, 'any alteration you might need to do later to the length can be done at the bottom.'

'This is more difficult than I thought,' said Alice.

And indeed it was evident that Alice was finding it difficult to concentrate, to deal with the detail. She was always trying to do everything in a rush and pricking her fingers regularly.

'Slow down, Ma,' said her daughter, 'look, Jenny, what do you think of mine?'

'That's good, Sarah,' said Jenny, 'and don't worry, Alice, it took me a while to get the hang of it.'

They kept the emerging garments in a clothes chest in Jenny's parlour and took them out at intervals, getting on with them step by step, as time allowed.

When the seams had been firmly pressed, a band was added, the skirt regularly tried on for length and carefully adjusted by helping each other make measurements and pinning the material up to the required length.

'Remember we're cutting this a few inches longer than the length we want in the end,' said Jenny, 'so we can turn it back on itself and make a hem. If you think it's a bit too full, don't worry, we can add a few pleats. If the material were heavier then I would put in box pleats and keep the pleats in position by adding a bit of broad elastic a few inches below the waist and then sewing it in from either side of a back seam, and attaching it here and there between the pleats. That would make it look better, but we're using a lighter fabric so that shouldn't be a problem.'

Alice had cut her skirt too short and sighed.

'All that work,' she said, 'and I've ruined it! I'm so stupid!'

Jenny saw that Alice was on the verge of tears and how stiffly she was sitting, how painful it was for her to move her left arm. With Sarah in the room, Jenny couldn't ask all the questions she wanted to ask, but she could guess the answers.

'Don't worry,' she said, 'we can add some length back by adding a false hem. I'll show you how to do that next time, we have to be careful not to carry through the stitches to the material or it won't hang right. It might all sound confusing, but once I show you, you'll see what I mean,' she paused, 'but right now I think we've earned a cup of tea, don't you? And I might even have a slice of fruit cake,'

Jenny did her best to teach them.

Sarah was a natural, her attention to detail, the evenness and straightness of her lines. Alice, on the other hand, just couldn't get it, her stitches were all over the place, the more she tried the worse it got.

After another few weeks of unavailing effort she said, looking down at her work,

'It's just not for me, I'm all thumbs.'

She had tried her best, Jenny knew that.

'It's not for everybody,' admitted Jenny, 'maybe it's the way I'm showing you. I take so much for granted you know. I've been doing it for so long and I enjoy it, I find it relaxing. We can keep trying if you like.'

'No, I don't think so Jenny, I'm wasting your time and there's so much else to be doing.'

That was always true.

'I'm going to stick with what you've shown me so far, and I thank you for that' she paused, 'I had hoped to follow in your footsteps and do a bit of work here and there, for other people you know, to bring in a few extra shillings, we could do with that. But this isn't going to work, I'm going to have to think of something else.'

Sarah looked downcast. Jenny noticed and nodded at her.

'Sarah's work is very good,' she said, 'I'm not sure I was as neat at her age.'

Sarah beamed.

'I've got a bit of work on at the moment,' said Jenny, 'maybe you could loan me Sarah for a few hours every now and again, I couldn't pay her very much, but I could give her a bit when I get paid myself.'

Alice turned to Sarah,

'What do you think, pet, do you enjoy doing this?'

'I love it, Ma,' said Sarah, 'I'd love to help Mrs Lawley, if she'd like me to.'

'Alright,' said Alice, 'as long as it doesn't get in the way of your schooling or your chores.'

'It won't, Ma, and you'll know where I am if you need me.'

Such small moments change lives.

From then on Sarah was a regular visitor to Jenny's back kitchen and proved herself both a willing pupil and a hard worker. Jenny soon found that, because of Sarah's help, she could take on more work and, over time, that her work and Sarah's became almost indistinguishable.

Chapter 19

Frank's local pub, 'The Stackyard', was named after a time when all around was farmland. It was always busy, particularly after payday, and the atmosphere was lively and fogged with cigarette and pipe smoke that became denser as the evening wore on.

The pub had a flagstone floor, small round tables, wooden chairs and benches, a fireplace, a piano, and a simple bar with a line of pewter and glass tankards hanging on the wall behind. The regulars gathered there to sip their tipple, drop by drop, to make it last, to discuss local events, wrangle over politics, football or women or to sing a few songs with gusto.

The general hubbub rose and fell like waves breaking on a shingle beach, the pulsating chatter punctuated by bursts of laughter and raucous singing that issued from an impromptu choir of miners clustered around the old, beaten, piano.

This was a place predominately for men, a men's haven in a man's world. If now and again it was impossible to prevent a person of the female persuasion from crossing the threshold then it was an unwritten but golden rule that she would take her place solely in the small snug that nestled at the back of the establishment.

Here she and her male escort would sit at a table and take a small drink in a civilised manner, maintaining a pretence of deafness to the blasphemous swearing that issued forth from the men at the bar.

But most of the time the snug was empty or, in extremis, acted as an overflow to the bar-room.

A number of the men were not allowed to swear when in their god-fearing homes and made up for this lack of linguistic freedom by relaxing their vocabulary within the walls of the pub.

The pub satisfied the rasping thirst that was a natural consequence of the long and sweaty shifts underground and also gave the men an excuse for a break from their womenfolk and, if the truth be known, the womenfolk a further break from their men, who, when at home, would be forever demanding food or cups of tea or getting in the way of the endless chores that their wives had to contend with.

That the women worked harder than the men would never have been admitted. It was the men who brought in most of the money and kept the roof over the family's head. The women's tireless work was not paid and was therefore not socially valued as highly. Their worth was however starkly evident when they weren't there, through illness or childbirth, and the chores were left undone.

Now and again children would trail a stoneware jug over the flagstone floor, pushing their way through the crush. Finding their way through the smoke to the bar they would climb the couple of wooden steps provided for the purpose, peer over the counter and ask for the jug to be filled with the warm, dark brown, strong bitter beer that they had been sent to bring home.

The publican, his white apron tenting over an extended belly, would fill the foamy jug and offer the young beer carrier a stick of rock from a candy jar kept under the bar. The sweet, to be consumed on the way home, was supposed to act as a diversion, making it less likely that an inquisitive child would be tempted to sample the contents of the jug. Jack had completed this errand many times and had not always avoided the temptation.

The pub was also a meeting place, a place where the world was put to rights, or wrongs amplified, a place where events were instigated, agreed or organised.

The 'Stackyard' welcomed and survived on its regular clientele, some of whom had their own personal glass or tankard hanging over the bar or held first rights to a particular seat at the bar, in a corner or by the fire.

Such a man was Earnest Weightman, who was perfectly named. Just like a Taylor who was a tailor, or a Carpenter who worked with wood, Earnest Weightman was a Check Weigh-Man, a position that came with both respect and responsibility.

Voted into the position by the hewers because of his attention to detail and acumen with numbers, and paid through their contributions, he acted as their legal representative on the surface. It was Earnest who checked the amounts of coal that each hewer had sent to the surface, which in turn determined their pay and that of the piece-workers.

He had to not just be above reproach, fair and unbiased, but he had to be strong enough to withstand the barrage of questions and abuse that would come his way from each of the hewers, who would be eager to fight their own corner.

Although the underground workers could resent the cushy jobs of the surface office personnel and were suspicious of their closeness to management, it was not in anybody's interests to fall out with Earnest. He had his hands too close to their purse strings.

Earnest knew which hewers were down the pit, when, and for how long. He was a man that it would be best to cultivate as a friend. It amused Earnest that people were sometimes so particularly nice to him and how some of the hewers could conjure up such creative reasons as to why their weight tally was somehow mysteriously and unaccountably undercounted.

Although balding, pale skinned and pallid, he was always clean and neatly dressed in a waistcoat with a prominent watch chain, but no watch. In his youth he had been a good boxer but now, and there's no getting away from the truth of this, Earnest Weightman was rotund.

His voice was loud, his stories long and his tales could be tall.

'If it were not for my lungs,' he would often boom, 'I would be down there with you all my boys, hefting the black stuff, doing a real man's job. But alas I have not the capacity,' here he would normally produce a single dry cough, 'an infirmity has put an early end to those dreams and now here I am, stuck above ground, oh such a fickle mistress is fate.'

He meant no harm and would generally raise a smile in those who chose to listen. If any of his audience did pause to think about it then they would probably conclude that having someone of Earnest's girth down the mine with them, sharing the dark with its low ceilings, tight corners and narrow passages would not have been to their advantage, although his voice would have carried.

Earnest always occupied the same spot at the bar, at the farthest end from the door, and the stool he sat on may as well have had his name carved into it.

He was more than tolerated, he was liked, and there would always be a willing enough audience for his stories that ranged from the hunting habits of tigers in India, to the reason why some of them learned a taste for man and what could be done about it without simply killing these noble beasts, which in Earnest's opinion would be a crime against Nature herself, to how he almost got a tattoo that he would surely have been ashamed of for the rest of his life.

His disciples encouraged him, making ribald remarks, raising eyebrows, exchanging winks, pressing their own anecdotes into the narrow gaps that occurred in his flow. And there were gaps, gaps when he paused for a drink, gaps when he called for his personalised tankard to be refilled, loud but polite, 'Please, my good man, if you would be so kind,' he would say, holding his empty tankard high above his head.

And he was good for an argument on any subject. Never heated, mind, just an intellectual fencing of diverse opinions, interspersed with light remarks. It was a sharp mind that would come out on top of any argument with Earnest Weightman.

And there was no subject that he was afraid to tackle, no opponent, however brusk or of muscular build, that he would shy away from. Once he got into his stride his back would straighten and his stomach would protrude, his watch chain sparkling in the lamplight.

Because he was generally inoffensive and would give help and advice to anyone who asked him, he was almost universally liked. There would be those who thought him pompous, others that sniggered at his bow tie and shiny brown leather shoes, but they tended to do it good naturedly and, of course, behind his back.

As a matter of fact, there was only one thing that Earnest Weightman was scared of, only one thing that would instantly silence his bluster and have him timorous as a schoolboy... and that was his wife.

Elizabeth Weightman was a good foot and a half shorter than her husband, but she had the heart of a lion. If Earnest got carried away with his own rhetoric, which was not unusual, he would miss his agreed time of departure, the time held sacred in Elizabeth's household for sitting down to dine. When this happened the door of the pub would open with a crash and there, silhouetted, would stand Elizabeth, her arms folded.

'Earnest!' she would call out. Only once, but once was enough.

A spasm, like an electric shock, would pass down Earnest Weightman's spine. The pub would fall silent.

'Yes, my dear,' would come the already apologetic reply.

'Now.'

'Yes, my dear.'

And the great man would slide his bulk from his stool, the men in the pub would part before him like the Red Sea, and Earnest Weightman would hurry out, tail between his legs, unable or unwilling to respond to any of his compatriots' parting remarks, 'Hope, for your sake, it's still hot...', 'See you again tomorrow night, Earnest...', 'Still think you should just shoot those bloody tigers...'

On this particular evening, Edward had elbowed his way to the bar and ordered two pints of the local brew, Burtons bitter, in moulded glass tankards. When he returned, his father was already in conversation with Joshua Tindale, father of the recently deceased twins.

Joshua had his hand on Frank's shoulder, unsteady on his feet from the number of liquid condolences he had consumed.

'They were good lads really,' he slurred, 'Had to take the belt to them now and then, but that's how it is with lads isn't it? I used to get a good leathering from me own dad and hasn't done me no harm. Maybe I was too soft on them, let them run around like wild things, too free for their own good.'

'It was a terrible accident,' said Frank, 'nothing that anybody could have done about it. Our youngest, George, got on well with your lads and I'm sure he misses them.'

'You know the worst of it is that in a few years they'd have been earning. A bit more money coming into the house would have done us no harm, and that's for sure.'

He paused, looking into the far distance,

'Dammit you do so much work, you have plans you know, you get so close to something better and then it's bloody snatched away and there's nowt you can do about it. Damn, damn, damn.'

'Would you like another drink, Joshua?' asked Edward, 'Get you a whisky perhaps?'

'No Edward, I can feel meself going. I know I've had too much already. Thanks all the same, I'd better be getting home.'

Joshua turned and headed for the street but before he could get to the door he was waylaid by two more of his workmates who put their arms around his shoulders and lead him, with little complaint, back to the bar.

Frank and Edward shook their heads.

Neville Hudson, Sarah's father, was also at the bar. Large and sour he was one of the few miners who was still dirty, having come straight from the pithead to the pub. Neville did not pass on his pay to his wife, Alice, but gave her an allowance to eke out on food, clothing, and all the other household essentials.

Alice was well known to her neighbours for needing to scrounge a little bit of this and a little bit of that to make ends meet and explaining away the cuts and bruises that were sometimes evident on the little flesh she exposed, as marks of her own clumsiness. According to her she was always bumping into something or tripping over something else. However, the walls of the houses were thin enough for neighbours to hear other causes. But a man's home was his castle, and no one had yet felt that it was their place to intervene.

Neville kept the rest of the money for himself, feeling that he'd earned it and with only one child at home he may as well spend it.

There was the odd coarse remark about Neville's lack of fertility, particularly as his one success had turned out to be a girl, but as he was known to have a temper awakened by drink, it was a brave man who would say anything to his face.

He was, amongst other things, a gambler. If he thought there was a good bet to be had, good odds and the prospect of sizeable winnings then he was up for it.

Although he was loud when he had a drink in him, underground he was hard working and formed part of a close-knit team, a team that Frank was also a member of. It was Neville's above ground behaviour that got him into trouble, most of it of his own making.

It was clear that he was unhappy as he pushed and shoved his way to where Adam Thompson, a more recently arrived miner, was talking football. He was one of a small group of men trying to decide who the best Newcastle players were, past and present.

Neville barged in. With his face only inches away from Adam's he glared at him accusingly.

'You bastard,' he hissed, 'that bloody bird of yours was a dead cert. You did a deal didn't you? Held her back from the clock, bet against your own. Made yourself some good money I'll be bound and took bastards like me for fools.'

Adam's prize pigeon, Nero, a red-hot favourite in the previous weekend's race to home, had unaccountably failed to show.

Adam stood his ground.

'It happens,' he said, and turned away.

Neville was having none of it. With a couple of men egging him on and fuelled by the amount of beer that he'd already supped, he was up for a fight. He reached out a coal-blackened hand, grabbed Adam by the shoulder and gruffly swung him around.

'You're not getting away with it that easy,' he growled.

As the exchange grew more and more heated it attracted more and more attention. The piano music faded, and an increasing number of eyes turned to see what all the fuss was about. Neville was known to be good entertainment when he was riled, as long as it wasn't you who were in his firing line.

'Get your hands off me,' said Adam, keeping his voice calm and even, although there was no mistaking the underlying grit.

Frank tried to intervene, but Adam signalled him back with a wave of his free arm.

'I can handle this,' he said, 'Now Mr Hudson, what exactly is your problem?'

'I want everybody to hear. I'm calling you a cheat, Adam Thomson. A cheat and a liar. You know as well as I do that that bird of yours is a champion and should have won easy. You held it back. I know you did.'

'You must be mad,' Adam was clearly losing his own temper now, 'I've never cheated in a race, and I never will. Why would I?'

'You knew I was betting on your bird. You did it to spite me. To make me look daft.'

'You can do a grand job of that yourself, without any of my help. Look at you man, you've had too much to drink. Get yourself home before you start to regret it.'

'I'm not going to regret this...'

Neville Hudson swung a clenched fist in a haymaker of a blow.

But the blow never landed, it was deflected aside by a smaller, cleaner man, deceptively strong, who now stood between the two combatants.

Earnest Weightman had been watching from his customary seat at the bar, he had seen the situation escalating and had wandered over in time to grab the swinging arm.

'I think that's enough now,' he said, keeping hold of Neville, 'I think you've given enough entertainment for one evening,' and then to everybody, but nobody in particular, 'alright, the show's over.'

Neville stayed silent, but continued to glare at Adam, who held his gaze.

Slowly but surely the attention of the onlookers drifted, the piano started playing again, the sound of singing, led by Edward's rich baritone, again filled the room. Earnest took Neville by the arm, more gently this time.

'I'm just off home now, Neville,' he said, 'why don't you walk with me. You know how scared we surface workers are of the dark.'

'I'm up for a bit of fresh air,' said Frank, 'mind if I come a long?'

Once outside in the cool night air Neville Hudson sagged morosely, glaring at the ground. He swayed as he walked, supported on either side by Earnest and Frank.

'You'll never bloody learn, will you Neville,' said Frank.

'He's cheated me out of money,' said Neville, 'you know how hard I had to work for it, but there's still time yet for me to get me own back.'

It was a clear night and the moon was high, lighting their way. Behind them the glow from the pub windows gave the impression of a sunset or a dawn that never rose nor set.

On reaching Neville's house, Earnest lent in close and whispered into his ear.

'Just one more thing, Neville. I'm a family man myself and I know it isn't sensible for a man to take out any frustrations he might still have in his mind, no matter how just or unjust he thinks his cause, on those weaker than himself. No Neville, such a man might just be getting himself into more trouble. Wouldn't be sensible at all. You do understand me, don't you Neville?'

With glassy eyes Neville looked at Frank, who nodded his agreement.

With a new energy, Neville Hudson shook himself loose and walked towards the door of his house. The back lit silhouettes of his wife and daughter could be clearly seen peeping through the front room curtains.

Sarah saw Frank and Earnest. She hung her head and turned away. She knew that her mother would need help to get her father washed and into bed. She was just hoping he wouldn't be too difficult.

When Frank got back to 'The Stackyard', Adam had already left. Their conversation on the best Newcastle team would have to wait for another day. Edward subtly mentioned that the singing was making his throat dry and Frank brought the appropriate remedy in two pint glasses. They left the pub at the same time as Joshua Tindale was staggering to the exit for the umpteenth time and helped him to finally make his escape.

For the second time that night Frank found himself walking somebody home, this time with his son helping. They walked together through the streets, their hobnailed boots scraping and scrunching on the gravel surface. Joshua leaned heavily on Edward, and when they pushed open his front door and shouted in Mrs Tindale asked if Edward and Frank could help to get Joshua to bed as, in her condition, she felt it was currently beyond her. They happily obliged.

A few days later Frank looked up from his breakfast plate.

'I hear there were goings on again in the pub last night,' he said to Edward who, along with Jenny, Jack, George and Grandpa, was sitting at the kitchen table, eating.

'Storm in a teacup, Da,' said Edward, 'You know how Neville Hudson gets when he's got a bevy or two inside him.'

'Aye well, like as not he's got a few things to worry about,' said Frank, 'There's always rumours of shifts and maybe jobs being cut back. Stocks of coal are too high apparently, prices too low, the normal rubbish you hear before the axe begins to fall. And Neville's a worrier.'

'That's no excuse,' said Jenny.

Chapter 20

Jack was running.

He splashed his way down a farm track on his way to the Moore's farmhouse. He skipped over the ankle-breaking potholes and scuffed his boots on the grit and gravel and raised up a small cloud of dust that smoked in his wake. He was a boy in a hurry.

When he approached one of the wide wooden, barred gates that controlled access to a hedge-rowed field he saw the farmer leaning on it, his sleeves rolled up, his weather worn arms bare to the elbow, pipe in his mouth, his fraying flat cap on his head. He'd heard Jack coming, it was hard not to, and turned to greet him,

'Now, Jack, what's all the rush?'

Jack came over, panting, and tried to mirror the farmer's relaxed stance by leaning on the gate.

'Taking a break, Mr Moore?' he said.

The farmer smiled.

'No, young man,' he said, 'I'm working hard just like I always do.'

Jack put his face up to the sun and allowed the ultraviolet rays to wash over his young features.

He could feel the warmth and regained his breath.

Following the farmer's gaze he looked out across the fields to the land that rose up and into the distance. He couldn't see what hard work it was to lean on a gate and enjoy the view.

The farmer read Jack's disbelief in his face. He took the pipe from his mouth and used it as a pointer, almost adopting the role of a teacher with a stick, pointing at a blackboard.

'Look there,' he said, 'you see that bare bit of land in the middle of this field?'

Jack looked and nodded.

'Well, there's something not right there and I'm going to get one of the lads to take a look. Could be it's been trodden down in those wet days we had, been compacted by horse or cows we've had in here, so it might need a bit of turning or maybe a bit of muck spreading or a bit of potash or lime. And over there in the corner, see that?'

Jack looked but couldn't see anything. He said so.

'If you look closely, you'll see there's a break in the fence, won't do to have the animals wandering in amongst the crops, so that'll need fixing. And that horse over there, what do you notice?'

Jack looked closely.

'It's limping,' he said.

'That's right, maybe shed a shoe, maybe worse, needs looking at, best catch it early so it doesn't get serious.'

Jack was beginning to realise that the farmer was working. They were seeing the same things, but the farmer was understanding a lot more.

'And if you look at the sky, Jack, and the ground, you can see it's a good day for ploughing and maybe a bit more muck spreading. You've got to grab these chances when you can, you never know what it's going to be like tomorrow. I've given the lads instructions for the work already and I don't see any need to change them.'

Jack could see teams of horses in the distant fields, some pulling carts, others pulling at the plough. Voices of encouragement carried faintly to their ears.

'Let me tell you, Jack, it's the soil you need to look after, that's a lesson my father taught me. Nothing grows if the soil's no good. There's no feed for the animals and no money for the farmer. Look after the soil, he used to say, and not just for now but for tomorrow too… look after the soil and the soil will look after you. And that's what I try to do…'

He paused and after a moment's consideration said,

'Like all farmers I'm always just one bad year away from the Workhouse, constantly living on a knife's edge without any large savings to fall back on. Bad weather at the wrong time, injuries, diseases and other disasters. We're in God's hands is what it boils down to, so's best we try to keep in his good graces.'

'My dad works at the face,' said Jack, 'comes back covered in it. He and Edward have it tough.'

'To townsfolk maybe, or to the uninitiated you'd think the miners had the harder work,' said the farmer, sucking on his pipe, 'You'd look and you'd see the dirt, the black faces and hands, the coal-dusted bodies, the grime and the dried sweat. But that's all on the surface, not even skin deep, it'll scrub off! I'm not saying they don't work hard mind, no, I mean, who would want to work at the bottom of a hole without the sun for company? Not me, that's for sure. No, what I'm saying is that farming is hard labour too, we just don't get the credit for it.'

'There's no end to the work and no end to the working day. You're always thinking about the problems, and there's always enough of those, and trying to guess what might come at you next so you can head it off.'

'There's always something could have been done better, there's equipment and supplies to buy,' the farmer took a breath, 'aye, it's hard work on the land as well as under it, you just remember that, Jack, and don't be thinking we've got it easy compared to your family.'

Jack wasn't going to argue. As far as he was concerned, everybody worked hard, his mother included, whether they'd chosen their work or had it thrust upon them. He wondered for a moment about his own future.

He would be following his father and brother into the mine… whether he liked it or not.

The farmer put the empty pipe back in his mouth and sucked on it. Jack felt that this signalled the end of the impromptu lesson. The farmer had work to do and Jack didn't want to get in his way. He stood away from the gate.

'You off to see Peter?'

'Yes, sir.'

The farmer smiled at the politeness.

'Expect you'll find him in the barn or collecting the eggs.'

'We were hoping to go fishing,' said Jack.

'Good day for it,' said the farmer, 'and if anyone asks you, give 'em my name, I don't want you boys being accused of poaching.'

Peter and Jack set off fishing. They were after wild brown trout.

Peter had his own and his father's split cane rods and the tackle to go with them. Most important of all he had a small collection of artificial flies.

'We need to find a good spot, a spot where we can see the fish rising,' said Peter.

His mother had provided them a flask of cold tea and a lunch box with sandwiches and apples before they set off.

Peter led the way and after about a half hour walk they approached the river. Walking through a small woodland they heard it first and then glimpsed the silver waters through the last of the trees, chattering across broken stones.

'This is a good place,' said Peter, whispering, 'keep your voice down now, and crouch down as we approach the bank.'

Jack obeyed and when they were a few steps away from the riverbank, Peter pointed,

'There's a series of pools here,' he said quietly, 'and there's space behind you, so you can cast without getting the line caught in the trees all the time.'

Jack nodded, he'd lost count of the number of trees he'd caught, more than the number of fish, that was for sure!

As they approached, they heard a plop, as if someone had dropped a stone into the river.

'We're not alone,' said Jack.

'It's OK,' said Peter, 'it's just a water rat. I've seen them round here quite a lot. If you spot them, you'll see most of their body is under water. They're hairy, long deep brown hair, don't do any harm, so I leave them alone.'

They looked up and down the river, searching for signs of fish. The water flowed fast and full in the centre, slower and circling under the shadowing greenery that hung out over the glass-clear water.

'There's a lot more flies by the river,' said Jack, watching the latest hatch spiral and skate over the flashing water surface.

'That's 'cos there's everything they need right here,' said Peter, 'water to lay their eggs in, and hatch, water to grow and hunt in as nymphs, and then water to emerge out of and feast on the odd angler!'

'I'm not odd,' said Jack.

Peter laughed.

'The occasional fisherman then.'

'They are doing a good job of feasting on me!' said Jack.

'Stop complaining, it's a nice day and … look… over there … a fish rising.'

Jack followed Peter's pointing finger to where a concentric series of circular ripples were spreading out and merging back into the surface.

'That's a good sign,' he said, insect irritation forgotten, 'let's get the dry white daddy-long-legs on and see what happens.'

'You try that,' said Peter, 'I'm going to try a black buzzer.'

They tackled up and Peter went a little further downstream so they each had a comfortable stretch of water to cast into.

Jack tried to cast to the far side of the river, to a likely spot under an overhanging tree. He immediately got his line stuck in the foliage.

'Shit!' he muttered.

'First blood to you,' said Peter, 'though if I were you I'd try to catch a fish next time, trees are hard to land.'

'Ho, bloody, ho,' said Jack as he hauled on his line, eventually breaking it, and needing to tie on a new fly from his small supply. He hadn't touched the water yet!

'Whoa!' said Peter, snatching up his line, 'got a bite then… missed it.'

'What a shame,' said Jack, casting out his line and watching as it flew under the overhanging tree and plopped into the water.

'The fish seem to like a bit of shade,' he said, and started to steadily wind in his line, trying to tempt a hungry trout.

Further down the river a fish rose.

'Damn!' said Jack and Peter together.

'Patience,' said Peter, 'that's what we need.'

The boys settled down to the task in hand; casting, retrieving, casting again, looking for signs that there were fish, and they were feeding.

30, 40 minutes passed.

Then Jack felt a pull on his line.

He struck.

The line went tight, water droplets sprang off it, filling the air with sparkles.

'Get the net!' shouted Jack.

Peter dropped his rod and ran to help.

'Play it, Jack, not too tight, don't break the line, give a little when you have to, let it tire itself out.'

Jack wasn't listening.

He didn't need the instruction. He knew what he was doing. He played the fish, gave it respect for its strength and speed, kept the line tight, let the fish pull line back through his fingers, wound back as the pull slackened, and all the while Peter waited with the net and the sun glittered on the surface of the sparkling water.

'Here it comes,' said Jack eventually, guiding the fish towards the bank, towards the net that Peter had lowered into the transparent shallows.

'Just a little bit more… just… a … little… Got it!'

Peter raised the net. The fish twisted and turned but was caught.

'Here, I'll take the fly out its mouth and we'll have a good look at it.'

Peter tipped the fish onto the green riverbank and held it in his hands to prevent it twisting itself back into the water.

It was a brown trout, golden-brown body, darker back, cream-yellow belly, it's back and sides displaying clear, reddish spots with pale borders, in all its wild splendour it flapped and gasped.

Peter took his lead-weighted antler 'priest' and smacked the fish once on the head. It shuddered and then lay still.

'First fish of the day,' said Jack, 'and what a beauty, must be over a pound.'

'Maybe,' said Peter, 'you were just lucky.'

Jack smiled in triumph.

'First fish of the day,' he said.

They fished on for a few more hours, stopping to eat their bait, moving up and down the riverbank looking for the telltale signs of fish feeding. Along the way they had time to talk.

'So, you're going down the pit,' said Peter.

'Soon as I leave school,' said Jack, 'I think I'll be starting with the ponies.'

'Do you want to go down the pit?'

'Why not? Me Dad's down there and Edward, they'll show me the ropes. It'll be good to be making a bit of money, to help out at home, like.'

Jack paused.

'Why do you ask? It's what we do isn't it? We follow our fathers, me down the pit, you on the farm. We live what we're born into don't we? There's not much choice.'

'No, there isn't, is there,' said Peter.

'Don't you want to be a farmer then? You seem to enjoy it.'

'It's not that I don't want to, it's that I don't have a choice. What I'd like to do is to see a bit more of the world before I settle down, although there's not much hope of that around here is there?'

Jack shrugged.

'Being a farmer, in the open air, its better'n being in the dark underground. You'll make a good farmer if you ask me. Its best to be careful what you wish for, I think,' he said.

The two boys were fishing upstream of the colliery, in waters unpolluted from the outflows. The waters were crystal clear, not black like they were further down.

They could hear the mixture of bird song, calling out in languages that were completely indecipherable to them.

A small bird was crawling up a tree trunk, its long claws giving it a secure hold, its white breast feathers closest to the bark. Its brown back was speckled, and it had a white stripe above the eye, an evolutionary form of camouflage that was designed to protect it from the attention of predators. It scurried over the tree trunks. It was poking its long, slender, down-curved bill into the narrow crevices, seeking out invertebrates, plucking insects from under the bark.

When it reached the top of its climb it flew down, to the bottom of the trunk of the next tree, and began to climb again, bracing its tail against the ribbed surface to increase the security of its hold.

'Look at that,' said Jack, pointing it out, 'what a strange bird; climbs up, flies down, climbs up again. I haven't seen one like that before.'

'You've probably seen one but not noticed it,' said Peter, 'they're quite common. It's a Treecreeper.'

'I can see it's creeping up trees,' said Jack, 'that's not big news!'

Peter laughed. Which annoyed Jack a tad.

'No, what I mean is it's called a Treecreeper, like a bird with a red breast is called a Robin. It's got long claws for a tight hold, but it can only climb in one direction. It can only climb up, so that's why it behaves like it does; climbs up, flies down, climbs up… it's one of the ways you can identify it.'

'Very appropriate,' said Jack, quite impressed but not willing to admit it.

'They make their nests out of spiders' webs,' said Peter.

'Really?'

'Spiders' webs, moss and feathers. I found one once, wedged into a crevice. I thought it was amazing that such little birds could do something so complicated. Imagine how many spiders' webs it had to collect, and they're quite sticky aren't they? So, it had to collect them and then put them in place, using the sticky strands to slowly build a nest.'

'I guess there were two of them doing it,' said Jack.

'That's true,' said Peter. He paused, and then he said, 'Brought one back to life once.'

'No, you didn't, now you're really pushing it!'

'Yes, honestly, it flew into a window, mustn't have seen it, we heard the thud, and I went to see.'

'That bit's possible,' said Jack.

'So I went outside and there it was, lying on the ground, looking dead.'

'So far, so believable.'

'Well, I wanted a closer look, so I picked it up, didn't know what it was, so I took it inside. Dad was there so I showed it to him, and he told me what it was. Then, as it was lying in my hand, it opened its beak, although its eyes were still glazed over. I looked more closely and although its neck was in a peculiar position I could see its chest rising up and down. Dad said that if I cupped it in my hands and kept it warm and still for a while it might have a chance.'

'And what did you do? Didn't you think its neck was broken?'

'I did, but still, I took it back outside and stood with it cupped in my hands. After a few minutes I had a look, its chest was still moving, and it was still warm. Very gently I moved its neck, it was floppy, so I didn't hold out much hope. I had a close look at it, its claws were clenched as if it was grabbing on to an invisible branch, its beak was amazing, delicate, needle-sharp, curved, and slightly open, showing a pink tongue that fluttered as I looked at it.'

Peter paused, held out his hands, cupped them as if the bird was still there.

'I put my other hand back over the top so that the bird was in the dark and in the warm. In farming you sometimes see that animals lose hope through fear or pain, give up the fight, but if you can keep them quiet and calm, take away the fear, then they have a chance. And sometimes a miracle happens, and they recover. I've seen it with sheep, and horses and cows.'

'And with birds?'

'I sat down and waited. It seemed like forever and I thought I'd lost it, but at least I'd done my best. Then I felt a movement.'

Peter looked at his hands.

'I opened my hands, and the Treecreeper was twitching its legs, its claws were opening and closing… and then it righted itself, its eyes brightened, it wrapped its feet around my finger and dug its claws into it, drawing a pinprick of blood. It hurt but I held steady and slowly the bird regained its consciousness and looked more and more alert, ruffling its feathers and beginning to look around.'

Jack held his breath as if this was something that was happening now. Peter spoke in a hushed, reverential, tone.

'As it looked around, I raised my hand. The bird held on tightly. I lowered it. I waited a little and then I raised it again… and the bird took to the air and flew away.'

'That's amazing,' said Jack, 'is that true?'

'As true as the present it left me,' said Peter.

'It left you a present?'

'After it had gone, I looked down at my hand and there in my palm was the present.'

'What was it?'

'Bird shit,' said Peter.

Jack was surprised and then he laughed.

'As it was recovering it must have shit, maybe because it was scared,' said Peter.

'Was it still warm?'

'Oh yes, and slimy and wet.'

'Yeugh, what did you do?'

'It's supposed to bring you luck, bird shit, but I washed it off.'

'That's an amazing story,' said Jack.

'And every word is true,' said Peter, 'But that's nothing, I can tickle trout.'

'Tickle a trout! That's ridiculous, I don't believe you,' said Jack.

Behind them a small bird let out a high-pitched trill, I'm not sure whether it believed it either.

'Look,' said Peter, 'I'll show you. I'm going to catch a fish with my bare hands,'

'Don't be daft,' said Jack, 'it's difficult enough with rod and line.'

'Ssh,' said Peter, 'watch and learn.'

So saying he scouted out the lie of the stream, looking for a place where the water had slowed and pooled under a rock overhang. Once he found the place he was looking for, he got down on his belly and started snaking his way towards the edge.

'What are you...'

'Sssh,' said Peter, 'if there is a fish there I don't want to scare it off with my shadow.'

He continued his crawl

'Fish always face upstream,' he whispered, 'If their heads don't face the current, the water enters their gills the wrong way.'

Peter slowly reached out, over the overhang, and slipped his hand into the water.

'Wow, that's cold,' he muttered, 'now I'm going to see...'

He stopped in mid-sentence.

'There's a fish here,' he said.

Jack held his breath.

'Now,' said Peter, talking to himself, 'take it slow, Peter, work your fingers from the fish's tail towards its head, that's it, just like that, that's good. Now gently does it, just the tips of your fingers, rub its belly, and keep going, slowly now, don't scare it off, that's it, towards its head and…'

Peter gripped the fish hard and in one movement lifted it out of the water. It was flapping. Peter held on tightly.

'Quick, Jack, bring me the priest.'

Jack closed his mouth and did what he was told.

A few seconds later, the fish lay still on the bank, a beautiful brown trout.

'That's one of the most amazing things I've ever seen,' said Jack.

Peter smiled.

'And it's bigger than yours,' he said.

'It might be bigger,' said Jack, 'but it's not the first, it's the first that really counts, it sets you up for the rest of the day.'

'The rest of a day where you don't catch any more and I get a bigger one,' said Peter.

'You should thank me,' said Jack.

Back at the farmhouse they turned their catch over to Mrs Moore and by the time they'd cleaned off their tackle and put it safely away, as good workmen always look after their tools, the fish had been gutted, cleaned and were sizzling in the pan.

'I was going to do that, Ma,' said Peter, 'you needn't have bothered.'

'If you think I'm going to let you anywhere near my pans you've got another think coming,' said his mother, 'it would be more bother cleaning up after you than doing it me'self,' she smiled, 'besides they're nice fish and I thought you might be hungry.'

'The biggest one's mine,' said Peter as they sat at the kitchen table, empty plates in front of them.

Ella Moore slid the fish onto their plates and silence fell as they began to eat, cutting themselves thick slices of bread from a farmhouse loaf and covering them in fresh butter, occasionally slurping gulps of milky tea.

Mr Moore arrived halfway through their meal.

'So, you were successful then,' he said.

The boys nodded, but did not speak.

'You'll never get fresher fish than that,' he said as the boys navigated around the bones and tucked into the succulent flesh.

'They've not left us any,' said Mrs Moore, 'just caught the two.'

'Sorry, Mr Moore,' mumbled Jack, his mouth full.

'Oh, don't you worry,' said the farmer, 'I'm sure Ma'll have something to fill my stomach, don't you Ma.'

'I do that,' said his wife, 'get yourself cleaned up and I'll get it on a plate.'

Her husband duly went off to obey.

'I got the biggest one,' said Peter, to his father's retreating back. 'tickled it out of the water, like you taught me.'

Jack gave him a dig in the ribs for his troubles.

When they were finished there was only the head, the bones, the fins and pieces of skin left. They mopped the juices up with the bread.

Chapter 21

Sarah continued with her sewing and became particularly good at the choice and the application of trimmings, pinning them in place before asking for Jenny's opinion. She had a good eye and a neatness in application, always ensuring that the braid or ribbon looked exactly the same on both sides.

She learnt how to press pleats with a warm iron and to ensure that the iron was not hot enough to damage or permanently mark the material.

Jenny used good quality pins, cottons, hooks and eyes and said that it was always worth that bit extra, using cheap ones could easily prove a false economy if they snapped or punctured the skin, and Jenny was sure that building a reputation for care and quality was what made people come back for more.

It wasn't all new clothes though, they also did a fair amount of patching, mending and altering. Making clothes last was an essential skill in managing a household budget, especially if you had a house full of men as Jenny had, and hard-wearing clothes could be usefully passed on to younger siblings if they were still in one piece and presentable.

Jenny enjoyed the help and the chat and had no reticence in sharing some of the income she made from her sewing with Sarah.

Alice was delighted.

She told Neville that Sarah was learning how to sew, but she didn't tell him that she was making a little bit of money and instructed Sarah not to mention it either.

It wasn't long before Sarah could be relied upon to make or reshape clothing for other people and she started to visit farms in the area on her own, in order to carry out needlework tasks.

Alice however was still searching for something that she could do.

For the men, living in such close proximity and working together on their shifts underground, relying on each other for the extraction of the black rock that brought them their pay, and drinking together afterwards in 'The Stackyard', built a bond and, over time, a shared loyalty.

There wasn't much they didn't know about each other; both their strengths and their weaknesses.

That is not to say that such bonds could not be broken, men moved on from one colliery to the next or left the pit through illness or injury, but nevertheless there was a kind of shifting stability within their relationships.

Outside of the mine, out in the fresh air, men who worked together underground would generally help each other out above it.

So it was with Frank.

He was known as someone that was easy to get on with, did not hold grudges and was generally quiet and solid.

The one relationship that he did battle with however, was the one with his neighbour Neville Hudson. When he was down in the darkness of the pit, Neville was strong, a good worker and a solid team player. But Jenny knew what she knew and wouldn't let it go. She'd heard the noises through the adjoining wall as well as Frank had. She'd also seen Alice flinch in pain, and she'd heard her excuses.

It simply was not good enough.

Something had to be done but she, as a woman, could not talk to a man, it would just make things worse.

So she badgered Frank.

He knew Neville well, didn't he?

Worked with him most every day, didn't he?

He had to talk to him.

It was his duty as a man, a father and a husband.

Frank knew that what Jenny was saying, seeing and hearing was all true. What was going on wasn't right and it was wrong just to ignore it and hope it would sort itself out, although this would have been his preferred option.

But it had been going on for too long.

The problem was that, when working underground, Neville did his job as a Putter at the face, loaded the trucks without complaint, always kept the coal moving away. It was getting the coal out of the mine that got them their pay, and it was their pay that kept their family engines running, including the money Jenny spent on behalf of the household. Underground they were all links in a chain and the chain was only as strong as each link… and Neville was not a weak link.

Frank knew that if he were to try and talk to Neville, with the hope of it having any effect, then he couldn't do it underground. The risk of starting an argument was too great and too dangerous, there'd been other instances of fights breaking out underground and none of them ended well. On top of that he couldn't talk to Neville in front of others, he knew that would make Neville feel humiliated, and whatever value there might be in Frank's words, it would all be lost in the defence of his character that Neville would inevitably have to mount. Like Jenny, he knew that this was a delicate matter and that trying to help in the wrong way could easily make things worse, much worse.

So, he'd have to find a way to have a proper conversation above ground.

Frank thought about this.

The opportunities were limited. He couldn't talk to Neville when there were others around and he definitely couldn't talk to him when he'd had a drink. Drink changed his personality. If he talked to him in that state, he may unintentionally fuel whatever was in him, whatever was driving his bouts of aggression. And anyway, if by any chance he did get through to him, he would have probably forgotten the conversation by the morning.

He talked to Jenny about the only sensible idea he'd come up with.

'We're both Newcastle fans,' he said, 'I could take him to a match, just him and me. We'd be surrounded by strangers then, so whatever happened won't matter so much. I'll have to offer to pay for the trip though, say it's for some reason or other that I'll have to think up. Would you be happy with that?'

'How much?' asked Jenny.

She knew that Frank would have thought it through as best he could, but still money was money and things were tight.

'Probably get away with six or eight bob all in,' said Frank.

'I'll give you ten come the day,' said Jenny, 'bring me back as much change as you can, and Frank,' she paused, drew closer and looked him straight in the eye, 'the sooner the better,' she said.

Sport was a subject that frequently featured in the men's talk.

There was only one team... no, hold on... there were three teams; Newcastle United, Sunderland and Middlesbrough, and the greatest rivalry was between the Geordies of Newcastle and the Mackems of Sunderland.

You couldn't support both!

You had to choose.

Newcastle United's shirt was black and white vertical stripes, almost an echo of the colours of the pit, the above and below ground. Sunderland played in red and white vertical stripes, and their fans supported them with equal passion.

But, as I say, you had to choose, and once you'd chosen that was it for life, there was no changing sides later.

It was tribal.

You could no more change your team than change your family. Each game was a battle, each stadium a Colosseum, with two teams of gladiators fighting it out, striving to achieve victory over the other. The only difference was that, although there was often blood shed in the cause, there were no lions, and no death sentences passed by the raising or lowering of a thumb.

Both Neville Hudson and Frank Lawley supported Newcastle United and, luckily for them, Newcastle were doing well.

Formed in 1892 from a uniting of the East End and West End teams they fought for promotion to the First Division and achieved it in 1898. Even this was controversial! Promotion was decided by a series of playoffs between the top three teams Newcastle United, Blackburn Rovers and Stoke, with two out of the three gaining promotion. Newcastle finished third.

However, there was suspicion of collusion between the other two clubs, something that was not strongly denied, in that they had agreed to draw a game that would see both teams go through ahead of Newcastle.

Newcastle complained loud and strong until finally the Football League agreed that Newcastle would be promoted as well, claiming that it had always been their intention to increase the number of teams in the First Division.

As well as the justifiably loud protests it was believed by some that Newcastle's calls for promotion were significantly strengthened by the large crowds of over 15,000 that the team regularly attracted.

From then on there was no holding them back and they consolidated their First Division position, on one particular occasion, in front of a cheering crowd of 26,500 at St James's Park, they achieved the rather perverted pleasure of beating Sunderland 1-0 and thus depriving them of the league championship.

It was little consolation however as all Newcastle United fans were acutely aware that, so far, they had not won either the League or the FA Cup whilst their rivals, Sunderland, had already been league champions four times! That hurt.

The current manager was a man called Frank Watt, a quiet Scotsman from Edinburgh who, although appearing almost shy and unassuming, had an iron will and a single purpose; Newcastle United must win a major trophy.

He had played a great deal of football and cricket in his time and had even been a referee before he was appointed secretary of Newcastle United. This strangely titled role encompassed almost anything and everything. Technically he did not hire or fire players or pick the team, that was the job of a selection committee of directors, but in practice he did, and he had, over time, built the best team that the North of England had yet seen.

In appearance he was stocky, customarily wore a three-piece suit, watch chain prominent across his waistcoat, white shirt, dark tie and a bowler hat. Most notable amongst his features was a huge handlebar moustache that he groomed and nurtured. Although he appeared dutifully in team photographs, he was not one to push himself forward, preferring to stay in the background and let others take the credit whilst he went about his work methodically and efficiently

As a man he was a father figure to a lot of the young players, sitting, smoking a cigar, and listening patiently to what they might have to say, although he didn't shy away from the difficult decisions when a player had to be told that his time with the club was over, or that unfortunately a bad injury had brought an early end to his playing career, or even that he had not been picked to play the next game.

Frank Watt had realised that Tyneside could produce its own local players, drawing on the popularity of playing the game in men from the coal mines and the shipyards and, being a Scot, he saw nearby Scotland as a source of more good players. The fact that Sunderland had done so well recently was deeply unpopular in Newcastle, but it was also a stimulus, and Frank Watt did little to discourage any feelings of jealousy.

Jealousy could be a good thing, as long as it was used constructively.

Before embarking on the trip, Frank tried to explain the state of play to Jenny.

'It's a close finish this season,' he said, 'there's three teams can win the Championship: Newcastle, Everton and Manchester City. Everton are favourites but have just lost so now the best they can do is 49 points. Manchester City have two matches left and they could get 48 points, they had a winning streak of 8 games in a row earlier in the season and have just beaten Everton, so I don't think they'll drop any points in their last two games. Newcastle now have 3 games left and so, with Everton losing to City, if they won them all they'd be certain to be champions because that would net them 50 points. So, it's a big game against Sunderland, win that and we're almost there.'

Jenny had only been half listening and half making sure that Frank had a set of clean clothes to go in.

'Oh, very nice,' she said encouragingly, 'but don't forget your real purpose.'

Frank fell silent.

'Make sure you talk to him, make sure you talk to him like you promised.'

Frank realised his suggestion, his idea, had now become a firm promise, and Jenny didn't want him to let her down. The excitement of attending this critical game had suddenly lost its edge.

Chapter 22

The railway system was by now well developed and Frank and Neville set off on what was an overcast day, prone to torrential, but passing, outbursts of rain.

Newcastle United played in what was known as the pyramid formation; two backs, the right back and the left back in front of the goalkeeper, then three half-backs, left, right and centre and ahead of them the five forward positions, outside right, inside right, centre forward, inside left and outside left. Although they would cover for each other, roughly speaking five outfield players were there to support the goalkeeper and stop their opponents scoring and five outfield players were there to try and score in their opponent's goal.

'It's a good system,' said Frank, 'and in Bill Appleyard we've got one of the best forwards in the league.'

'He certainly knows how to barge a goalkeeper into the net,' said Neville.

'All fair and within the rules of the game,' said Frank.

'And Howie, Veitch and Rutherford can score as well, yes, we've got a good attack,'

'Don't forget Gosnell, he's a talented winger, got a good left foot.'

'He's not a patch on Bobby Templeton, now there was a player, shame he didn't settle, and besides Gosnell's a Southerner!'

'You can't hold that against him.'

'I can if I like,' said Neville.

They both laughed.

'Our half-backs are all Scotsmen,' said Frank, 'best three in the country if you ask me; Gardner, Aitken and McWilliam, all good players in their own right but together, unstoppable.'

'Aye, true, and with Lawrence in goal and Carr and McCombie as full backs we should be too strong for Sunderland. After all we had an easy win against Stoke on Friday, 4-1.'

'That's just the thing; we should win but…'

'But what?'

'But we're Newcastle, we should have won the cup, getting to the final is something, but we should have won, but we didn't, we hit the post, the fates were against us.'

'Don't be daft, the fates, that's just crazy.'

'Well, we've only had a day between games, the players'll be worn out, Sunderland've had much longer to prepare.'

'But we're the better side.'

'Better if we're fit and all on the pitch. Sunderland will play hard from the whistle; you mark my words. They beat us earlier in the season and they'll want revenge for what we did to them a year or so ago.'

'You mean when we beat 'em and stopped 'em winning the league?'

'They weren't impressed and now they'll do their best to return the favour.'

As they talked their train made its way towards Newcastle upon Tyne, a busy city with a population of some 280,000.

Lying on the north bank of the River Tyne, 9 miles from its exit into the North Sea, it was located amidst the coalfields and was an important coal shipping port and the source of the saying "…like taking coals to Newcastle" meaning something that would make no sense.

It also had large ship building yards and factories for the manufacture of locomotives and iron goods.

In Roman times it had been called Pons Aelius, a significant river crossing point, and was a garrison fort on the Roman Wall.

In the Saxon period it was called Monkchester a name derived from the number of monastic institutions that were then in the area.

The name on the sign that greeted Frank and Neville as their train pulled into the station dated from the castle, founded by Robert Curthose in the 11th century, though the Keep (85 feet tall with walls 12-18 feet thick) was the only part that remained and dated from 1172-7.

On platform 9, near to where they alighted, was preserved 'Stephenson's No.1 engine' the first steam locomotive to carry passengers and the brainchild of George Stephenson who died in 1848, at the grand old age of 67, and who was commonly acknowledged to be one of the Northeast's greatest engineers and the 'Father of Railways'.

Frank and Neville exited Newcastle Central Station and joined the hubbub of people and horses, cars and trams that flowed busily around the city.

To the right was a statue of George Stephenson, Frank pointed towards it,

'There is a theory,' he said, 'that it was from Stephenson, 40 years or so ago, that we got called "Geordies" because of his Geordie Miner's Safety Lamp that we used to use.'

'Then he's got a lot to answer for,' said Neville, 'it gave out only about half the light you could get from a candle!'

'He was apparently too rough a talker for the Parliamentarians down in London, he said what he thought, so they thought him too uncouth and uncivilised.'

'He was one of us then, good on him.'

As if in reply the heavens opened, and the two men pulled their coats and scarves tighter and made sure their caps were secure.

With the imposing sight of St Mary's Roman Catholic Cathedral on their left, they hurried across Neville Street and up Grainger Street where, after a few hundred yards, they turned left onto Newgate Street where a steady stream of people, some wearing the black and white colours of their team, shouldered their way onwards.

'This rain's not a good sign,' said Neville, 'Newcastle are going to find it difficult to play their style of football on a muddy pitch.'

'And it'll drain more energy from already tired legs,' said Frank.

Fortunately, the downpour was soon over, but it was still blowy and overcast. They continued towards Percy Street, pausing to buy a couple of meat pies from a street vendor, to keep themselves going.'

'We need to get into the ground early,' said Frank, 'I think it's going to be full.'

'They might even shut the gates,' said Neville, 'especially as at the last game the papers said that the crowd was too big and one of the barriers collapsed with the pressure. They won't want that to happen again today.'

They hurried through the bustle and turned off at St Andrew's Church. The streets were alive with horse drawn vehicles, city trams and the ever-increasing number of internal combustion engines.

The closer they got to the ground the more intense the crowd. The pubs were heaving and the drinkers overflowed onto the pavements. The talk was all about the game. The general opinion seemed to be that Newcastle were the much better side and simply couldn't lose. The betting shops were doing a roaring trade.

The crowd was even more thickly bunched as they made their way up Leazes Lane.

'By the way,' said Neville, 'I'm pleased you invited me to the game but where did the extra money come from?'

Frank had been rehearsing an answer.

'Got lucky on a horse,' he said, 'thought that if I didn't spend it quickly then Jenny would have it off me and it'd disappear into the housekeeping.'

'But you don't normally bet,' said Neville, 'strange you should do it just as these critical games are coming up.'

'Not strange, calculated,' said Frank, 'I did it to try and get enough to go to the match and I ended up getting more, so I thought I'd invite you along. I know what an ardent fan you are.'

'Well, I know I shouldn't look a gift horse and all that... which horse did you put it on?'

The hallowed ground of St James' Park, the home of Newcastle United, now rose before them and they joined a disorderly queue that was bustling towards the turnstiles. Frank took a shilling out of his pocket.

'If we get separated,' he said, 'here's your entrance money, I'll see you on the inside. I'll wait by the "Gents". Now it's time to do a bit of pushing of our own.'

It was a shuffling mob that made its swaying way to the gates, and although the pushing and shoving was generally good humoured it was still every man for himself.

Finally, they made it through and, after emptying their bladders, they got themselves into the East Stand and found a vantage point sandwiched together in an already large and boisterous crowd. Looking around there was a sea of black and white, but plenty of red and white too.

'There's a lot come over from Wearside for this one,' said Frank.

Soon word spread that the gates had been shut, the ground deemed to be full to its capacity of around 30,000.

The playing surface was affected by the rain and Sunderland won the toss and elected to play with the wind and the slope in their favour in the first half.

The sound of the referee's whistle to start the match was met with a huge roar from the crowd and the onset of chanting; "New-cas-el", "Sun-der-land", that continued almost none stop.

From the start Newcastle went on the attack and Frank and Neville joined in the cheering and shouting. A shot was deflected but the ensuing corner was not a good one and Sunderland broke away with pace, a warning of things to come, and, playing with power rather than finesse on the greasy ground, they gave the Newcastle defence something to worry about, McCombie breaking up the Sunderland move at the last moment.

The Wearsiders played with strength and cleverness so that Lawrence, the Newcastle keeper, was called into action to clear an effort from Bridgett, one of the Sunderland forwards.

The game went back and forth and a combination between Veitch and Gosnell found a way through the Sunderland defence, but Gosnell was blown for offside.

At a time when completely impartial officials were not universal this decision was met with derision by the Newcastle supporters and applause by the Sunderland fans.

To be on-side there needed to be three players; two outfield players and the goalkeeper, between the player and the opponent's goal and many a method was devised to set an 'offside trap'. This was a dangerous game however as not every offside was given and no matter how loud the protestations the official's decision was final.

So far Carr, in a Newcastle defensive role, had tackled the Sunderland forwards strongly but then he handled the ball and from the free kick Lawrence had to make a great save from Bridgett.

One of Newcastle's moves ended with Rutherford making a pass to Gosnell, but the forward was not well placed and shot wide. Newcastle took a lot of pressure, although it was obvious that they were playing much below their normal form.

When Sunderland made another fast-paced attack, Carr tried to stop the advance but unfortunately only managed to kick the ball off a Sunderland player who chased it down and took a shot at goal, Lawrence again saving.

Neville Hudson was shouting his support, the two men were swaying uncontrollably with the crowd-mob as the game flowed from end to end and people stretched to get the best view of each attack, each tackle, each incident.

Newcastle's best effort was worthy of a goal. Veitch took the ball and worked it forwards, moving down the wing and lifting it into the centre. Appleyard pounced on the opportunity, but his effort went agonisingly wide, and he put his head in his hands.

Excitement was high and again Newcastle advanced, this time Rutherford almost scoring.

But then Sunderland came into their own and took control. Lawrence was called into action again and again and Carr did some stalwart defending, darting in just in time with a smart interception and clearing the danger.

The game was being played at pace, with Newcastle showing the cleverer moves, and the smarter passes, despite the conditions, but Sunderland playing the more straightforward, the more resolute game, and this began to tell.

In one burst forward by the Wearsiders Aitken, fouled, and Carr made a mistake, thinking the ball was out of play. But it stuck on the muddy surface and Holley, seeing the opportunity, gained possession, ran forward, and hooked the ball into the net.

A loud groan went up from the Tynesiders and a tremendous cheer went up from the Wearsiders.

Frank groaned.

'Damn it,' he said, 'we needed the first goal.'

'Stupid mistake,' said Neville, 'got a mountain to climb now.'

The game was now about 30 minutes old and, flushed with their success, the Sunderland team played with more confidence and were in danger of over-running the Newcastle team, who were struggling to contain them.

The second goal, when it came, was deserved and not unexpected.

Buckle carried the ball from midfield, beat three men and scored with an unstoppable rifle-bullet of a shot.

Things went from bad to worse for Newcastle as Gardner, one of their best players, got so badly injured that he could not continue and, as there were no substitutions for injured players, Newcastle had to play the rest of the game with only 10 men.

They put up a spirited fight however and got their reward when Gosnell put over a centre and Appleyard got on the end of it and beat the Sunderland goalkeeper to put the ball in the net.

But the goal was disallowed for offside!

'Never!' shouted Neville, who was far too far away to see if it was or if it wasn't.

The crowd roared their disappointment and this support spurred on the Newcastle players who kept up the pressure. Howie worked his way through and gave the ball to Appleyard who was fouled as he was about to shoot, and the referee awarded a penalty.

There was a huge cheer and then a hush as Veitch stepped up to take the kick.

He steadied himself and then ran to the ball, kicking it with tremendous power. The ball sped from his foot past a helpless goalkeeper and into the net.

The crowd went wild, the swaying masses putting tremendous pressure on the crowd barriers which, this time, held firm.

'We're back in the game,' yelled Frank.

'Damn right,' shouted Neville.

From then on, and up to the half time whistle, the play was evenly balanced.

The crowd were restless all through the halftime period. Things were not going Newcastle's way. The Sunderland fans wanted the game to be over now, the Newcastle fans wanted the second half to start and their team to get an early equalising goal.

Any result was still possible.

'We've still got a chance,' said Frank.

'10 men,' said Neville, 'it's going to be tough, we're losing energy, what we don't need is any more rain or any more injuries.'

'But we are Newcastle…' said Frank.

'So there's still a chance,' said Neville.

After the change of ends, Newcastle had the incline and the wind in their favour, but being a man down meant that the task before them looked like a big one.

Whatever the moustachioed Frank Watt had said to his team at halftime certainly provoked a response and Newcastle started the second half playing with the style that had won them so many games. They swarmed around the Sunderland goal, Webb, the Sunderland keeper, needing to save and clear several times.

Even though they won numerous corners Newcastle could not get the ball into the net, and Sunderland were lucky to keep their lead. Appleyard, Gosnell and Rutherford all came close, one of Gosnell's efforts only just being kept out.

The game was exciting, the crowd roaring Newcastle on, conscious of how well they were doing with only four forwards.

Then Aitken was hurt.

'Oh no,' said Newville, 'we can't go another man down, and not Aitken, he's holding the team together.'

'Playing with 9 against 11 would be impossible, we're doing well to out-play them with 10,' shouted Frank.

Andy Aitken struggled back to his feet; he was obviously hampered but he recovered sufficiently to carry on. The crowd roared their approval.

Then there was another heavy shower of rain.

'What is going on,' moaned Neville, putting his collar up and pulling his already damp scarf tighter around his neck.

The vertical rain thudded onto his cap and cascaded down his shoulders. Frank and 30,000 others were in the same predicament,

'This is exactly what we don't need, its playing right into Sunderland's hands, even the heavens are against us.'

Certainly, the downpour left the pitch in a bad state, and the surface was very slippery, causing mistakes. Newcastle battled on however and Rutherford almost scored the equaliser.

But in these conditions, a man down and a key player injured, Newcastle's supremacy couldn't last and Sunderland, continuing to play their straightforward game on a slippery surface, began to dictate the play. The crowd sensed this, and after so many years of hoping, there was a growing feeling that the game was slipping away from the home team.

From a free kick, Sunderland almost got another goal, but Newcastle held on, and, as long as the difference remained at only one goal, there was always the chance that they could grab an equaliser, the least that was expected and the least that, on balance, they probably deserved.

It was not to be.

George Holley, one of Sunderland's forwards and the man who would hold the record for goals scored in Tyne-Wear derby games, took a pass from Jimmy Gemmell and, ignoring the shouts of the Newcastle defenders and the home supporters for offside, ran through on goal and slotted the ball past Lawrence and into the net.

Some of the Newcastle players had actually stopped, so sure were they that Holley was offside, and to any objective observer in the crowd, and there weren't many of them, he certainly looked offside.

Newcastle's players protested loudly, the Newcastle crowd booed, but all to no avail, the linesman and the referee stuck to their guns and the goal was given.

The Sunderland supporters cheered themselves hoarse, jumping up and down, swaying from side to side in a frenzied wave of joy. For a moment there was a fear that the barriers would give way under the pressure, but they held, only just.

Having had an earlier goal ruled out for offside and now this, the Newcastle fans felt doubly hard done by.

A two-goal lead was too high a mountain to climb and it knocked the stuffing out of the team and the crowd.

Although they continued to push forward when they could, the rest of the game was played to the victorious chanting of the Mackems and the jeering of the Geordies.

When the final whistle blew, Sunderland had beaten Newcastle for the second time that season and the Geordie's hopes of finally winning the title, only two weeks after losing the cup final, were in tatters.

Neville and Frank hung back and waited for the crush of the departing crowd to lessen.

'Newcastle weren't at their best,' said Neville, 'but I still think they deserved something out of the game.'

As they filed out of the ground, carried along in the tail of the streaming crowd, Frank said,

'Well, the weather was against us, the injuries on and off the pitch… having to play so many games in so few days had an effect I think, our individual fitness suffered and the overall quality of our play. Sunderland didn't have the same problems, and their greater fitness told in the end.'

'10 against 11 for the whole of the second half,' said Neville, 'Gardner's injury was a real blow.'

'And the offsides… that was the last nail in the coffin. I wonder about the impartiality of that linesman.'

'Yes, he seemed to be favouring the Mackems the whole game.'

'But even with all that, we were still in the game until that third goal.'

'I think we've got to say the lads did their best.'

'Typical Newcastle, so close…'

'Sometimes it doesn't matter how hard you try, you still lose.'

Wandering on down Grainger Street they stopped to join the queue for fish and chips.

'There's nowt like a fresh paper of fish and chips, showered in vinegar, and sprinkled with salt,' said Neville.

Frank laughed.

'That sounded almost poetic,' he said, 'but you're right, there's nowt like good fish and chips; fresh fish, crispy batter, thick cut chips, soft inside, browned and crispy on the outside.'

'Now who's the poet,' said Neville.

They walked on to Newcastle Central Station, eating with their fingers. The rain had stopped but it was still dull and a bit blustery. The two men sought shelter inside the station to dry out, finish their meal, and wait for their train.

Once inside they found a vacant bench by one of the platforms.

Frank knew he had to complete his mission, he couldn't go home to Jenny and admit he'd not talked to Neville about their concerns.

The station smelt of smoke and steam, the trains constantly arriving and departing or, with many trucks fully laden with coal, simply rumbling through.

With its vaulted roof of metal and glass the place was like a modern cathedral, a monument to the success of industrialisation and the power of progress. From where they were seated the two men could see the be-suited business types with bowler hats atop, the well-dressed matrons with fancy hats and luggage, the porters trolleying suitcases hither and thither and the chaos of children running in between, under or dodging around the whole scene, distraught parents trying to be heard above the din, the clanking, chugging, squealing of metal on metal, the hissing of steam.

Frank leant in close.

'We can hear you through the wall you know.'

Neville froze, chips halfway to his mouth.

Frank could tell what he was thinking; should he ignore it and change the subject, should he deny it, should he… he put some chips in his mouth, kept looking down at his shoes, chewed slowly,

'No point denying it is there? What do you think you're hearing?'

'You, with drink inside you, lashing out, breaking things… and Alice…'

'Stop,' said Neville, 'that's enough.'

They sat in silence for a while, finishing their food.

'Here,' said Frank, 'give me your paper, I'll put it in the bin.'

When he came back Neville was no longer on the bench, he'd walked off towards the end of the platform and stood gazing out along the tracks as they ran out of the station, turned away under a road bridge and were lost to sight.

Frank walked slowly up to him.

'Train's about due,' he said, 'bound to be a busy one so we better get ready.'

'Is today all about this?' said Neville.

Frank tried to smile.

'Don't need an excuse to come to St James's,' he said, 'even if we did lose!'

'Aye, and to the Mackems!'

'Still got a chance at the title though.'

'True, not as good a chance now, but still a chance.'

'Not impossible.'

'No, not impossible, just very difficult.'

'Nothing's impossible,' said Frank.

They fell silent again, made their way to the right platform, boarded the train, which was on time, and didn't speak during the journey, jostled as they were by fellow passengers, some the worse for drink, others singing tunelessly, the atmosphere increasingly fogged by cigarette smoke.

On the walk home Frank allowed the silence to hang. He would have preferred to talk about the game, the team, the poor decisions by referee and linesmen who seemed to be playing for Sunderland, but, having broached a bigger subject, he knew it was best to keep quiet.

'I don't mean to, you know,' said Neville, looking at Frank for reassurance.

Frank said nothing.

'It's just, I don't know, I've got this anger inside me and the drink...'

'I give my money to Jenny, you know,' said Frank, 'she sees to everything in the home, gives me a bit for meself like, not enough to get drunk on though.'

'Alice's younger than me, thought she might not be able to manage money.'

'Seems very capable to me,' said Frank, 'your Sarah looks well looked after and Jenny's always telling me that Alice is the best at haggling when they go to the Co-op together. Jenny lets your Alice do the work and then asks for the same price. They can't say no.'

Neville smiled, 'I didn't know that,' he said.

They were close to home now.

'Alright,' said Neville, 'I'll give it a go.'

'You can't do a thing if you haven't got the money for it,' said Frank.

'Aye, that's right I suppose, and that reminds me, how much do I owe you for today?'

'My treat, I told you it was, I don't want any money…'

Frank left it hanging, he didn't want Neville's money, he wanted something else.

As Neville was opening his front gate, he turned to Frank.

'Thanks,' he said.

'No problem, here's to winning the League.'

Jenny was waiting.

Frank shrugged off his damp coat, took off his scarf and cap.

Jenny put them near the fire to dry. Frank sat down in his chair.

'Where is everyone?' he said.

'They're out.'

'It'll be dark soon.'

'Then they'll be back soon… did you talk to him?'

Frank sighed.

'Yes, I talked to him.'

'And?'

'And he listened, and he didn't get upset.'

'Is that it?'

'What do you expect?'

'Some kind of promise!'

'That was never going to happen, Jenny, and even if it had I'm not sure how much it would be worth.'

Jenny paused for a moment, thinking.

'Well, at least you talked to him.'

'Yes, I talked to him.'

Her tone changed.

'Would you like a cup of tea?'

'I definitely would,' said Frank.

'Oh, and by the way, how did the match go?'

'Don't ask,' said Frank, reaching for his pipe and newspaper.

Chapter 23

The conversation underground, when there was any, was mainly about the football and 'The Toon's' chances of winning the league. One of Frank's crew, called Pat, was a Sunderland supporter, but they tried not to hold that against him.

'I don't know what all the fuss is about' said Pat, as they were sitting down to their bait, the only light coming from their combined lamps, 'we've already won it four times, it can't be that difficult.'

Neville huffed.

'You won it when it was easier,' he said, 'to win it now you've got to be better than top teams like Villa, Everton and Manchester City.'

'And Sunderland,' said Pat, 'Just look at the record books Neville, it's all there, for all time. Would have won it a fifth if you Geordies hadn't got in the way.'

'Yea, sorry about that,' said Frank, smiling.

'So, it was nice to return the favour,' said Pat, 'beat you twice this season, home and away, haven't we?'

That hushed the conversation; it was true and it had put a dampener on Newcastle's chances… but it was still possible. There was still hope.

Neville glanced into Frank's bait box,

'Looks like Jenny and Alice have been shopping together again.'

Frank laughed, they both had the same; a pork pie and a stotty sandwich of ham and pease pudding. All to be washed down with their flask of cold, milky, sweet tea.

'There's nothing like a fresh stotty to make a good sandwich,' said Frank, even though everything they ate was flavoured 'coal dust'.

'Well, we can agree on that,' said Pat, 'I've only got the wholemeal today, want to swap?'

There were no takers.

Back on the surface, cleaned up and sitting in front of the range, Frank was looking at the small print of his newspaper intently, his brow furrowed. He seemed to be trying to pierce the page with his gaze. Jenny wondered if he was having problems with his eyesight.

'What's wrong?' she asked.

'Just trying to work this out,' he said, 'Newcastle lost to Sunderland. so now we can only get 48 points if we win both the remaining games. They're both away so it won't be easy. One at Sheffield Wednesday and then the last one down the road at Middlesbrough.'

'Middlesbrough,' said Edward, 'so Newcastle end the season with another local derby… and away at that, that's a tough one.'

'They're all tough at the end of the season,' said Frank, 'look at Everton, they lost again to Woolwich Arsenal, so with one match left for them, the best they can do is 47 points. Manchester City, on the other hand, could get 48 points if they win their final game, which they probably will, even though it's away at the Cup Winners, Aston Villa.'

'You mean the team that beat us in the final?'

'I was trying to forget that, but yes, it just seemed to be their day, we hit the post, so close…'

'And now we're close again?' said Edward.

'Yes.'

'And when it's close we normally lose?'

'Has to change sometime,' said Frank.

'And what about if we finish equal on points?' asked Jack, who'd also been listening.

'If it's equal on points the team with the best goal average, the number of goals scored divided by the number of goals conceded across all 34 games, takes the title. And here's the good news; Newcastle's goal average is much better than Manchester City's. They'd have to score more than 12 goals against Villa, at Villa, to catch us up, and not even they are going to do that.'

'So, if Newcastle win both their games, they're Champions?' said Jack.

'That's right, they'd be Champions for the first time in their history, crowned the best team in the country.'

'So, why didn't you just say that,' said Jenny, 'without all that if-ing and but-ing and fancy maths. Newcastle have just got to win, that's all.'

Frank, Jack and Edward looked at each other. As a wife and mother Jenny was one of the best, but even though her conclusion was correct, she didn't understand the emotional rollercoaster of being a Newcastle United supporter.

It would all be settled in a week.

Progress in away games was telegraphed to Newcastle and the news spread out, by word of mouth, by train and in speedily compiled print.

The day after the game Frank read out the report,

'Sheffield Wednesday versus Newcastle United
An Exciting Encounter
United one goal down with 13 minutes to go

This important league match, on the result of which so much depended for Newcastle, was played at the Owlerton ground in Sheffield. The weather was inclement with rain threatening.'

'Nothing new there,' said Edward.

'At the start there were about 12,000 spectators. United won the toss and played with the light breeze at their backs in the first half.'

'The first incident of note came from a strong run by Gosnell who worked his way into a central position before sending in a shot that was saved well. A few minutes later Gosnell again broke away on the Newcastle left before cutting into the centre.

He engineered a great chance to shoot but his hard shot flew past the post.'

'Newcastle were playing well and from a corner the clearance came to Gosnell and he put in a great cross to Appleyard, who was unfortunately ruled offside.'

'But Wednesday were never to be discounted and, after Appleyard was pulled up for a foul, they streamed forward, the ball flying up the right wing before being centred and cut out by the Newcastle defence.'

'Encouraged by this success, Wednesday pressed forward, putting in a long shot before their forwards combined together to create an opening, which was saved before being collected by another of Wednesday's forwards, who wheeled round and shot just wide. Wednesday had other chances, and a fast breakaway saw an accurate pass slipped through to the centre forward who's hard shot went just wide.'

'Sounds like Wednesday were on top,' said Edward.

'Happens in a game, son,' said Frank, 'one team has a good period and then the other, you've just got to ride it out and wait for your chance, its goals that count, not time on the ball.'

'After this Gosnell and the other Newcastle forwards began to press the Wednesday defence but could not score. One shot was saved by a diving goalkeeper who then sent a long clearance direct to the home forwards who combined to break away through the Newcastle half backs and take a shot that the goalkeeper punched clear, only to see one of Wednesday's forwards take an overhead kick that flew back past him and into the net.'

'Wednesday were ahead and there were 25 minutes gone.'

'Knew we went one nil down,' said Frank, 'sounds like Wednesday just about deserved it, unlucky for a clearance to go straight to the opposition.'

'What do they mean by an overhead kick?' asked Jack.

'Probably means he kicked it without looking where it was going. Bit lucky if you ask me,' said Edward.

'Newcastle responded by pressing hard with shots going in from Gosnell and Appleyard, the Wednesday goalkeeper having a great game. Wednesday's defence was also strong and though the Newcastle forwards played well they could not breakthrough to score a goal.'

'Towards the end of the half Rutherford and Howie combined to create a clear chance but when the ball was centred, resulting in a terrific shot, the goalkeeper again made a fine save. Wednesday then attacked with pace and almost scored another goal themselves.'

'That's the problem,' said Frank, 'when you're pushed to attack you're always open for a fast breakaway. Thank goodness the lads didn't go two down.'

'Newcastle didn't deserve to be behind and two goals down would have been particularly unfair, they had played well and as the half-time whistle blew, the Newcastle supporters, who'd travelled a long way, were growing more restless, knowing how critical a win was for their team.'

'The second half brought more of the same, Newcastle pressing, Wednesday defending stoutly and breaking away with pace and threatening to score a second when they got the chance.'

'As the game approached the final 15 minutes Newcastle got another corner and from this the ball found its way to Howie who bent the ball into the corner of the net.'

'The equalising goal was met with euphoria from the Newcastle fans.'

'Thank goodness for that,' said Edward, 'that must have settled a few nerves.'

Frank smiled and then turned back to the paper and continued reading.

'This breakthrough seemed to spur on the Geordies and deflate the opposition who had held on so bravely and for so long. To the roar of the crowd, Newcastle continued to press forward and, within a few minutes, were rewarded with a second goal from Howie. Newcastle had taken the lead and from their play they were determined not to lose it. With time running out, Wednesday gave away a penalty and Orr scored from the spot to give Newcastle some breathing space.'

'Newcastle saw out the remaining minutes and when the final whistle blew, they were winners by three goals to one.'

'I knew we'd won,' said Frank, 'but I didn't realise how close it was, or how nervy.'

Now all depended on Newcastle's last game of the season which would be against their Teesside rivals, Middlesbrough, in barely three days' time.

The success, or otherwise, of Newcastle's whole season came down to this last game.

The intensity of hope tempered with pessimism brought Frank and Neville closer together.

They talked about football on the way to the pit, in the cage going down, on their increasingly stooped walk to their part of the face, during any break in the job of cleaving coal, shovelling it, piling it, transporting it, they talked about football on their way home, they wished each other a 'Good evening and come on the Toon' at their front gates, and they did it all again the next day.

And then the final game arrived.

Jenny was concerned that Frank was becoming too friendly with Neville. She knew that her husband was intrinsically a kind man, and with kindness could come a level of forgiveness, a forgiveness that Jenny did not share.

A number of men were known to have a temper, some of them fiery, and even Frank was known to fly off the handle on occasion, but it was the marks that Jenny had seen on Alice's face and arms that grieved her, that and Alice's explanations of her "clumsiness", her knack of falling over or bumping into things.

Granted there had been no new outbursts since Frank's chat with Neville, no worrying sounds coming through the wall, but Jenny did not believe in miracles, and she knew that Frank would find it more difficult to talk to Neville again the deeper their friendship grew.

Frank and Neville went to the nearest railway station to keep as close to the news as possible.

When the Newcastle team left for Teesside at noon, the weather conditions were not encouraging, rain was falling as if it intended to continue all day. Before they reached Darlington however, the rain stopped and was replaced by a blanket of fog that hung over Middlesbrough, the sun struggling to break through.

The Stockton races were on, on the same day, and affected the number of home fans that attended the game at Ayresome Park, that and Middlesbrough's poor recent form. Ardent Boro fans had no wish to go and witness one of their local rivals lifting the league championship by winning at their home ground.

At kick off the crowd was about 12,000.

Newcastle lost the toss and would play the first half from the east end.

From the kick off Middlesbrough mounted an attack but fortunately for Newcastle the centre forward was given offside when he was otherwise through on goal. Carr defended well and Newcastle began to show their style, Orr testing Middlesbrough's goalkeeper. Appleyard led the forwards in good style and Howie started well, sprinting into the home penalty area and putting the ball across for Orr to shoot and beat Williamson.

A goal!

Newcastle were one nil up with only five minutes played.

If there was nervousness in the team or in the crowd, then this early goal partially dispelled it.

The same was true when news of the goal arrived in Newcastle and then into the ears of Neville and Frank. Their faces lit up with joy, their hearts beat faster, could this be the day?

'It's early in the game,' said Frank.

'A lot could change,' said Neville.

'It is Newcastle.'

'But it's a good start.'

From the kick-off Newcastle regained possession, Appleyard shooting just wide after connecting with a centre from Gosnell who had taken the ball up the wing. Carr and Veitch worked well but then, clearing strongly, McCracken sustained an injury. The Newcastle crowd fell silent, was this going to be a repeat of the Sunderland match, a key player off injured and down to ten men?

They waited in trepidation but when, after a few moments, McCracken recovered sufficiently to carry on there was a huge roar of relief.

Newcastle had been rocked though, and Middlesbrough went close.

The game was being played at a fast pace and Newcastle were playing well and with purpose, Middlesbrough were energetic, but without the same intuitive teamwork.

After a strong clearance, Rutherford got the ball and his shot rattled the crossbar. The Newcastle fans roared their team on, the noise consistently loud, and Williamson, the Middlesbrough goalkeeper, had to make a sharp save from Appleyard.

The game flowed for end to end, and Middlesbrough were presented with a couple of chances, but they did not make the most of them. At the other end, fierce shots from Gosnell and Rutherford went close.

At the railway station, no news was good news as the minutes ticked slowly by, like an ant treading through treacle.

Frank and Neville did not talk; they just waited and listened.

Newcastle began to pass the ball about and there was always danger to the Middlesbrough goal, Williamson making a diving save from Appleyard. He failed to hold the ball however, but was on his feet again as Rutherford crossed the ball to Gosnell who had expected Rutherford to shoot so was unprepared and his shot went wide.

The game was far from one-sided, but there were no weaknesses in the Newcastle team, and their level of play did not slacken even when it began to rain and the ball and the ground became greasy.

When the whistle blew for half-time Newcastle had a well-deserved one goal advantage.

Frank and Neville retired for a cup of tea and a scone at half time in the station's tearoom.

'What do you think?'

'Anything could happen.'

The second half began with Middlesbrough on the attack, but they soon gave way to Newcastle's determined teamwork, their precise passing from front to back produced new openings and Howie took off on one of his dribbles and fired off a drive that scraped the bar.

It was evident that Middlesbrough were tiring and less than 10 minutes into the second half Newcastle had their second, Rutherford taking the ball into the centre, beating the halfbacks and scoring with a magnificent shot that flew past Williamson and into the Middlesbrough goal.

When news reached the two men their relief was palpable. Others around them shouted and cheered.

Could this really be the day?

But they were Newcastle United supporters, they knew what could happen, tantalising hopes of victory had turned to disappointment too many times before.

They held their breaths.

After the second goal the cheering was deafening, and the hubbub was intensified when Newcastle immediately got away again and the flying Gosnell sped up the left wing like a hurricane. Arriving at the by-line he centred the ball and Appleyard scored a third with a powerful volley that gave the Middlesbrough goalkeeper no chance at all.

Newcastle were now three goals up with 54 minutes played.

This third goal removed any chance that Middlesborough might have thought they had of getting back into the game.

When the news spread there was disbelief followed by euphoria. There was dancing and singing. Ladies in fashionable hats were grabbed and swung round by miners in their flat caps and scarves. A tsunami of chaotic exultation swept through men of all ages and even infected the top-hatted gentlemen and some members of the fairer sex. It was as if a war had been won, and victory declared.

Meanwhile in Middlesborough the game continued.

Every Newcastle man played up to his best and the rest of the game was uneventful, even though Middlesbrough got some shots on the Newcastle goal the goalkeeper was never seriously challenged, and yet there was always the chance of another goal from Newcastle, Gosnell and Aitken sending in shots that tested Williamson in the Middlesbrough goal.

When the whistle blew for the end of the game, the cheering from the visiting supporters was full of unadulterated joy. Newcastle had shown themselves to be the better team on the day, had won three goals to nil and had secured the League Championship!

After the match the Newcastle United players, officials and friends sat down to tea at the Grand Hotel in Middlesbrough.

The Newcastle United chairman, Mr John Cameron, expressed his gratification, that he was sure they all felt, at the team's performance and the proud consummation of their season's work. In London, after they had been defeated in the final for the English cup, he had been proud to call this team the best in England, and he thought that that remark had since been amply justified. Of the two trophies, winning the league undoubtedly possessed the greatest merit, for it could only be won after eight months of consistently good play. The players had had their ups and downs, but this was to be expected as they were not machines but men who must keep themselves fit, deal with injuries and who had thoughts and feelings of their own. He wanted to end by expressing, on behalf of all the directors, his satisfaction and pride at the team's achievement that day.

Andy Aitken, the Newcastle United captain, was then called upon to say a few words and he said that he was very pleased to have won the league as it was as much for the sake of all the Newcastle supporters as that of the directors. The people of Newcastle deserved this win as some compensation for the cup disappointment, even though they gave such a fine reception to the team when they returned from London as beaten finalists.

They left Middlesbrough by special train a few minutes after 7 o'clock and a large crowd, assembled around the station and for some distance along the line, cheered them on their way.

Newcastle United were winners!

For the first time in their history, they had won a major trophy.

The record books would show it, it was unalterable, it had really happened, and it could never be taken away.

Such an achievement was met with a mixture of euphoria and disbelief. The most northerly first division team, a team that represented industrial communities, a team that represented miners, manual workers, a team that somehow encapsulated an impossible dream, a dream that had just been realised.

Somehow it mattered more that Newcastle had won their first championship than that Sunderland had already won four. It made no sense, but it was so.

Newcastle had flattered to deceive, they had fallen at the last fence, they seemed fated to be no better than second. Such fanatical support deserved more. They were a big club, but they had failed to win a major trophy… until now.

And now that it had happened there was a huge communal sigh of relief, a weight had been removed from the collective shoulders, heads could now be held high. Never again did they have to look away when trophies were mentioned. A hundred years or more from now it would still be remembered, still celebrated, as a proud memory.

Newcastle had won their first league championship and now there was only one thing to do, to win more and, in particular, to win the FA Cup.

Neville and Frank were in 'The Stackyard', it was full to overflowing. The atmosphere of communal joy was thicker than even the fog of cigarette smoke.

Neville had drunk enough to be 'happy' and Frank steered him away from the bar and towards the piano where they joined a the chorus of 'Cushy Butterfield'

"She's a big lass an' a bonny lass,
An' she likes her beer
An, they call her Cushy Butterfield,
An' aw wish she was here."

Later, they walked home together, leaning on each other for support,

'I don't think I've ever felt this happy,' said Neville.

'I think I must still be dreaming,' said Frank.

'There'll be no stopping us now,' said Neville, 'it's upwards all the way from here, things have just got better and they're going to stay better, maybe get even better, you mark my words.'

'I hope so,' said Frank as he helped Neville through his back door, Alice and Sarah were waiting for him in the kitchen.

Unsteadily Frank made his way through his own backyard and into his own kitchen, still humming his own variation of 'Cushy Butterfield'. It was unlikely to catch on.

Inside, Jenny was sitting at the table.

'We won,' said Frank, moving towards her, his arms open, 'Newcastle are champions. Yahoo!'

Jenny looked at him severely and pushed him away.

Frank was surprised.

'Ah know I might be a bit tipsy luv,' he said, 'but fair's fair, this is a big day.'

'It's not that, and I'm pleased for Newcastle but…'

'But what pet? What have I done to upset you?'

'You let him drink,' she said, 'worse than that, you led him to drink, you drank with him!'

Her words brought him down to earth with a bump.

'It was only a couple of pints Jenny and it's a big day…'

Frank sat down, he looked like a small child that had just been told off by his mother, one that was still not completely sure of the fairness of it.

They sat quiet for a while and then Frank said,

'I'm sorry.'

Jenny softened, put her arm around his wide shoulders, he was still wearing his coat.

'Why did you let him drink?' she said.

'But Jenny…'

'But Jenny what, you know the problem, you've talked to him and what's the next thing you do? You go drinking with him!'

'But Jenny… Newcastle…'

'It's just a game, Frank, this is real life.'

Although Frank thought it was more than just a game, what Jenny was saying penetrated his befuddled brain. His shoulders slunk and he sighed heavily.

'Just get yourself off to bed,' said Jenny, gently.

After she'd helped Frank undress and fall into bed, she began to get herself ready and continued to worry about next door, the last thing she wanted to think was that her Frank had been the cause of more problems.

She stepped closer to the wall they shared with the Hudson's and listened carefully. All she could hear, and that faintly, was a tuneless version of 'The Blaydon Races' and what sounded like Sarah laughing.

Frank, who had fallen asleep as soon as his head hit the pillow, was snoring softly as she slipped under the sheets beside him.

Chapter 24

Sunday was a special day.

The pit and just about everything else was closed. It was a day for recuperation, for rest and recreation and, of course, for Church. Most families went to church at least once on Sunday, a lot went twice, attending both the morning and evening services. And then there was the Sunday school for the children, a time when parents might have a little adult time if they were lucky.

There might even be time for the allotments, or the pigeon lofts, or reading the newspaper or even a book. For the women chores didn't stop just because it was a Sunday, but if you had a good weekly routine then there was a chance of a lighter burden for at least a part of the day and church was a good reason for everyone to be cleaned up and in their 'Sunday best', the women in their hats.

At church and after there was the chance to meet a wider group of people, to chat, to exchange news, perhaps even for the younger members to eye each other up and begin to get acquainted.

Jenny made sure her whole household, including Grandpa who wasn't too keen, attended the morning service. It was like a military manoeuvre to get everybody up, washed, fed and ready, but Jenny would not take "no" for an answer.

The church bell rang to call in the congregation and they were in reasonably good time when they reached the arched stone entrance, pausing to meet and greet people they knew before making their way to their customary pew.

People somehow knew to file in quietly, even the children were mostly well behaved, or brought into line if they erred. Regulars would have places where they would normally sit and, by some kind of unwritten rule, these arrangements were acknowledged and adhered to.

There would be almost no talking after walking into the church, or if there was then it was in hushed tones and subject to severe glares if it overstepped the mark. The preaching was generally stern, instructional and full of warnings.

Once the welcome had been delivered, resonating from the high ceiling, and the first hymns had been sung, the visiting preacher, a short wiry man who made his cassock look oversized, climbed the few stairs to the pulpit and began to speak,

'Unto a Christian man there can be nothing either more necessary nor profitable than the knowledge of Holy Scripture; forasmuch as in it is contained God's true word, setting forth his glory and also man's duty. And there is no truth nor doctrine necessary for our justification and everlasting salvation, but that is, or may be, drawn out of that fountain and well of truth.'

'So, with that in mind, let me read to you from the Gospel of Saint Luke, Chapter 2, Verse 7, "and she brought forth her firstborn son, wrapped him in swaddling clothes, and laid him in the manger, as there was no room for them at the Inn".'

'Although we normally read such verses at Christmas, they have a message for every day of the year for today, my friends, there is no room for Jesus at the Inn,' he raised his head and cast his eyes around his congregation, 'or at the pub,' he said, 'the pub that is full of sinful passions, of evil desires and wanton wickedness, and all of this fuelled by that devil's brew, alcoholic beverages,' Neville, along with a number of others, shifted uncomfortably in his seat, 'A brew that's only purpose is to dull the mind, dissipate the heart, and destroy the conscience. So, I ask you all, where will you be these coming hours? Will you be at the pub where there is no room for Jesus or will you be at home, in the bosom of your family, eating God's food, seeking his forgiveness for your sins and conversing in a wholesome manner on all that is worthy?'

'Or,' he added, his eyes seeking advice from on high, 'should total abstinence prove impossible, as we are, after all, only imperfectly human, will your sustenance be taken only in a healthy moderation. A man who knows his limits is a wise man indeed. Yes, moderation, my friends, let that be your watchword.'

There was an uncomfortable rustling from the ladies present and many a quiet smirk on the faces of the men. They knew from experience that the visiting preacher was quite partial to a drink himself and, rather than prove himself a hypocrite, had provided a platform for a little flexibility, for which they were grateful, although a number of the wives weren't.

To give him his due, the preacher rarely, if ever, exceeded his limits, helped by the fact that his capacity was much higher than other men's.

'And now, my friends, please stand and let us sing one of my favourite hymns, "All things bright and beautiful, the Lord God made them all".'

The service continued with hymns, prayers and the Blessing and, as they filed out of the church, they put their donations into the collection bowls and shook the preacher's hand and some people indulged in a few pleasantries.

The preacher was popular in the village, not just as a man of God, but as a man of good sense too.

The sermon had worked on Jenny's fears however and, when they were next alone, she said to Frank,

'If he does it again, you'll have to do something.'

'Do what?'

In mining communities, as well as there being a limited police force accountable for upholding the Law, uniformed and authoritative, there were also other ways of dispensing a form of 'natural justice'.

It was not uncommon for problems to be mysteriously solved. There might be cuts and bruises that appeared by themselves, or families who decided to leave the area one night, without a forwarding address, or some miraculous, and generally permanent, change in behaviour.

There was no leader or organisation to this self-policing, it just seemed to be something that sometimes happened and was met with a general level of acceptance and approval.

The police knew that it happened but also understood that it was better not to investigate these incidents too deeply. As long as the community was peaceable and generally well behaved then their job was done.

'I don't know what,' said Jenny, 'but mark my words.'

'Let's hope it never comes to that,' said Frank.

Over the next few weeks Jenny could see a difference in Alice. She no longer wore long sleeves all the time, had a gleam in her eye, and a new lightness in her bearing. It was like a miracle.

'You wouldn't believe it,' she said, 'but Neville's handing me his pay these days. I mean, all of it! And then he takes back a bit for himself but always asks if it's too much and should he do with less. Jenny, it's amazing, it's like the man I thought I'd married has come back!'

Jenny was old enough and wise enough to temper her joy at this apparent change of fortune. She was pleased at the positive difference in her friend and was happy to ride the wave for as long as it might last.

She told Frank about the change. He was similarly reticent.

'Nothing's changed underground,' he said, 'he's just the same old Neville; strong, solid and dependable.'

Taking up his paper he pointed to an article,

'Maybe it's not of interest now but I thought I'd show you this.'

Jenny read the article quietly.

Wife Takes Husband to Court

Phoebe Cartwright has taken her husband to court on a charge of cruelty. Those in her village were said to be surprised as the couple have one child, a boy, aged eight. The events leading up to the charge began when neighbours complained to the police about hearing what they took to be fighting in the

Cartwright's house. PC Walker responded to the call on behalf of the police and when he entered the house immediately saw signs of a disturbance. His first reaction was to calm the parties and suggest that there were probably faults on both sides. On witnessing the extent of Mrs Cartwright's cuts and bruises however he believed that, on this occasion, her husband had gone too far. In addition, Mr Cartwright was freely issuing threats of more violence to come.

'Why is this article here?' asked Jenny, 'it's not normal to write about this.'

'It's an unusual case,' said Frank, 'so worthy of publishing. With so much going on about women fighting for the vote and other rights, I guess its topical.'

Jenny nodded, she saw no problem with women fighting for their rights, she just wasn't sure how they found the time.

The Victim's Dilemma

Although there must be an awareness that, unfortunately, instances of domestic violence do occur in the privacy of people's homes it is also self-evident, from the extremely small number of cases that revert to the law, that it is notoriously difficult to prove. The wife often changes her mind about bringing charges once the official police force becomes involved, or has her mind changed by her husband once they have reconciled their differences. It is therefore understandable that the police, in their turn, prefer not to be involved in cases of violence between a man and his wife as it often results in a waste of their time and resources.

The reason for dropping charges can easily be understood. If a wife goes ahead and takes her husband to court, she stands to end up homeless as, more often than not, the house is in the husband's name and he is the one entitled to stay in it. Under such unhappy circumstances a wife, no matter the strength of her case, could find that there are no family or friends willing to take her in as the old saying 'once you've made your bed you must lie in it' holds some sway among those who live cheek by jowl in these communities. A wife's only option would then be the workhouse, and no woman wants that either for herself or for her children. Therefore, a wife will often put up with ill treatment from her husband in order to keep a roof over her and her children's heads.

'No marriage is perfect,' said Frank, 'everybody has arguments.'

'Even us,' said Jenny.

'Problem is knowing the line between an argument and abuse.'

'And whether it's a one off or not.'

'Exactly, so if we have difficulty knowing, what chance have the police got.'

'Or a judge.'

'It's true what it says here,' said Jenny, 'I wouldn't want the police involved in anything that might happen next door.'

'Read on,' said Frank, 'see if you're still sure of that.'

Phoebe Cartwright's Case

Phoebe Cartwright knew of the risks but after that night she said that she had had enough, and she removed herself and her son to her mother's and told the police that she was determined to see it through. At first there was justifiable scepticism but true to her word Phoebe Cartwright held steady and her case finally came to court.

Following the case hearing, the ruling was in Mrs Cartwright's favour, and she was granted a separation order on the grounds of her husband's cruelty. The court also ordered him to pay her eight shillings a week to support her and their son. This was deemed enough money for Mrs Cartwright to find a place to rent and feed and clothe herself and her son.

From a legal perspective this was believed to represent a fair and welcome resolution to a difficult marriage.

Judge's Closing Remarks

In his closing remarks the judge said, to general applause from those ladies present, that he hoped that this case showed that the law could be relied upon in these difficult cases and that it may give other women the hope that, if they were brave enough to go through the court process and gain the order, that they might still be able to survive on their own and with their children. Such a judgement strengthens the case law that could be used in future cases against abusive husbands and should give husbands pause for thought at the prospect of losing 8s a week and having no one to cook their meals, mend their clothes, prepare their baths and the myriad of other tasks that they might take for granted.

'Just because one case ends well doesn't mean others will,' said Jenny.

'True,' said Frank, 'but maybe if someone were to read this it might give them hope on the one hand or pause for thought on the other.'

'Hmm,' said Jenny, 'You don't even know if the husband will keep paying his 8s a week. Most likely he won't.'

'He'd risk a fine or maybe even jail,'

'Which just makes things worse for everybody.'

Frank didn't answer.

Jenny considered for a moment.

'The result is a broken family, whichever way you look at it.'

'It was the neighbours who first drew attention to it,' said Frank, 'they did something and look where it led.'

'As I said, I wouldn't want the police involved,'

'Be careful Jenny, that's all I'm saying.'

'I'll keep this article,' she said, 'I'm not thinking of showing it to anyone,' she paused, 'but if things get worse…'

Frank never spoke to Neville again about matters at home.

They continued to work together underground, through the hard shifts and the comparatively easier ones, and they continued to both support Newcastle United, following their fortunes with a mixture of hope and trepidation.

'We've got to win the Cup,' said Frank, 'we've won the League now we've got to show we can win the Cup.'

'We keep bottling it in the final,' said Neville, 'that Palace ground is like the stadium of doom as far as Newcastle are concerned.'

'We've come so close; we must be able to win it eventually.'

'Maybe,' said Neville, 'but I'm not expecting it to be in my lifetime.'

Chapter 25

Each time Alice visited the Co-op it seemed that Tony Sharpe was right there to help her. In the past he'd noticed the marks she'd occasionally had, the awkwardness with which she'd sometimes moved around and the way she'd winced when she bent down to look at something. He didn't say anything, it wasn't his place, but it raised a feeling of sympathy in him, a latent desire to help if he could.

Alice would talk to him as she shopped and when he asked if she wanted any more material, she told him that she'd decided that dressmaking wasn't for her and that she was trying to think of something else that might bring in some extra money.

'Do you know,' he said, 'there's one thing I've always thought the village needs.'

'What's that?' asked Alice, more out of politeness than anything else.

'A fish and chip shop,' said Tony, 'they've got plenty in Newcastle and they're very popular.'

'A fish and chip shop?'

'Yes,' he said, 'all you need is a ready supply of fresh fish and good potatoes,' he paused, 'and some premises of course.'

'Oh, is that all. Sounds like a piece of cake.'

'Not cake, but a good crisp batter on fresh fish, fried in lard.'

Tony's idea was not a bad one. It was the growth of the railways that enabled the speedy distribution of fresh fish and farm produce. Cod and haddock caught in the North Sea and landed on the East Coast were rapidly transported to the markets of the industrial towns and cities. People would then set themselves up as friers and a boom in 'Fish and Chips' shops was the result, served in newspaper, sprinkled with salt and splashed with vinegar, and eaten with your fingers while still hot.

Although at first it struck Alice as a stupid suggestion, over the next couple of days it stayed in her mind.

The next time Brian Goodson, the fishmonger, came around the streets with his cart, she decided to have a word with him. He sold good fresh fish, mainly cod and haddock. Because of the lack of refrigeration, they had to be sold fresh and consumed quickly.

Alice hung around at the back of the queue and when it was finally her turn, she bought a couple of tail-end pieces of cod and, as the fishmonger was wrapping them, she said,

'How's it going in the fish business?'

This was an unexpected question and Mr Goodson's surprise at such a sudden interest was obvious.

'It's alright, I suppose, keeps the wolf from the door.'

'Plenty of cod about?'

Brain Goodson handed over her purchase, wiped his hands on his apron and then stood looking at her.

'Now then Mrs Hudson, what's all this?'

Alice coloured slightly.

'I was just thinking, that's all.'

'Thinking what?'

'Well, you know we all appreciate the quality of the fish you bring us.'

'Hmm…'

Mr Goodson, a fishmonger for some twenty years, was unused to compliments.

'Well, I was just wondering… if someone was to open a fish and chip shop, say here in the village…'

'Someone?'

'Er, well, me for example… if that were to happen… could you supply the fish?'

'Every day?'

'Not at the start, maybe Wednesdays, Fridays and Saturdays?'

'You've thought about this then?'

'A little bit.'

Mr Goodson smiled.

'What does your husband think?'

'Oh, he's very keen,' lied Alice, who had yet to broach the subject with Neville, 'he loves his fish and chips.' That much was true.

'The fish I buy is landed at North Shields, gutted and packed in ice, I inspect each box before I buy, then a put it on the cart and sell it on my round.'

'You don't have a shop?'

'Thought about it, but I can't be everywhere, I've got the set up I need, somewhere for the horse…'

Mr Goodson's horse was a placid animal, chestnut flanks with a white flash on her head, friendly even with noisy children and happy to munch on her nose bag. Any deposit she left behind was gratefully scooped up whilst still steaming by the first to fetch a bucket and applied to an allotment or front garden. It was good stuff.

'Anyway, how much fish would you be needing?'

'I don't know, I wouldn't want to have any left over.'

'Hmm… well if you started with, say, twenty fillets and see how it goes?'

'That sounds about right… what do you think?'

'I'm thinking that if it becomes a real thing then you can talk to me. I could put the fish on the train in Newcastle, but you'd have to collect it.'

'Obviously the price would have to be right.'

Mr Goodson laughed.

'You're talking like a business owner already. I'd have to see what I could do. I have to make a living you know, and if there were a fish and chip shop here maybe I'd sell less fish off the cart.'

Alice left it there, wondering if this idea was becoming just too complicated.

The next time she was in the Co-op she gave Tony Sharpe a whispered update. She was increasingly determined to somehow have a source of income of her own. Tony was impressed by her strength of character and put her in touch with a greengrocer friend of his who Alice talked to about a suitable supply of local potatoes,

'It's seasonal you know,' he said, 'not like your fish were you can probably get your haddock all year and cod most of it.'

'I've talked to someone about that,' said Alice, 'but you can't have fish without chips.'

'Well, if you trust me to know what I'm doing then I could supply you a sack or two at a time.'

'I will trust you,' said Alice, 'a single sack would do at the start.'

'I'd have to shake hands with your husband of course, he'll be the wage earner in the family.'

'Yes, of course,' said Alice.

Having got this far what Alice needed was a place to set up and the money to get it started. When she mentioned it to Tony, he said that she would have to find the premises and run the business but that he had savings and, as it had been his idea in the first place, he would loan her some money if, and only if, her plans were viable.

If he did this he wanted, in fact he insisted, that no one should know about his investment. He would be a 'sleeping partner', would want his money back within a year and a percentage of the profits from then on.

Alice couldn't take it in, she needed to think things through carefully and most importantly… she needed to find the right way to introduce the idea to Neville.

Before talking to Neville, she talked to Jenny about it. They were sitting at the kitchen table, teacups in their hands. After Alice had explained how far she'd got she said,

'What do you think Jenny, is it a stupid idea?'

Jenny could see that Alice desperately wanted some positive support. Her idea of becoming a dressmaker, or at least making a little money with her sewing, had come to nothing, she did not have the patience for it. Now here was an alternative idea, and it couldn't be more different; running a shop, dealing with suppliers, frying… Jenny paused in her thinking,

'Do you know what equipment you need? Do you know how to operate a deep fat frier? It can be a dangerous business.'

Alice looked downhearted.

'No, I don't,' she said, 'it probably was a stupid idea. I could never do anything like that.'

Jenny smiled sympathetically and sipped her tea.

'You're capable enough Alice,' she said, 'I'm sure about that, but it's like anything, you have to learn how to do it, you can't just jump straight in.'

'Like sewing you mean?'

'No, I didn't mean that and anyway, nobody's good at everything, but you'll need to learn more about it before you can say whether it'll work for you or not. It's a good idea mind; we could do with a chippy.'

Alice was almost in tears.

'And how can I do that?' she said.

'Well, you could go to the nearest chippy and ask if you could lend them a hand, to learn the ropes, do it cheap and they might welcome the help.'

'Do you think it's possible?'

'Oh yes, it's possible, you'll need Neville's support of course, you can't do this without him knowing and because of the time involved he's going to have to go along with the consequences.'

'Consequences?'

'Cold suppers, Sarah looking after herself, although we can help there if you want, she's welcome round here.'

Alice started to brighten and then an anxious look came onto her face.

'I am going to have to talk to Neville. Things are so much better at the moment. I don't really want to upset him. I don't know what he'll say.'

'You won't know if you don't ask him,' said Jenny.

Alice didn't know it, but she'd picked a good time to talk to Neville. He wasn't drinking as much; he didn't have the money and 'The Stackyard' refused to serve him 'on tick'. He had begun to feel a longing for a drink that he couldn't explain and at the same time he felt depressed and guilty.

The guilt was a new one. He'd never felt that before. He'd just ridden the wave of his existence and couldn't believe that drink, his friend and crutch through life, could ever be a problem. He knew he was physically stronger than Alice, he knew that sometimes he hurt her. He knew that sometimes something inside him snapped, and that alcohol fuelled a blessed release of pent-up anger. Anger that he wasn't a better man. Anger that nobody understood him. Anger that people, and he knew he meant Alice and Sarah, depended on him. There was no escape.

He increasingly hated going underground, the darkness, the humidity, the unforgiving manual labour, the unrelenting fog of coal dust, the sharp particles, like annoying little midges, prickling your skin, sticking to your clothes and body, breathing them in and coughing them back out again, well most of them, other than those that settled in your lungs or found their way into your stomach. When he looked in the mirror, he did not see himself, he saw someone that he had become, through no fault of his own.

With no parents living, no siblings, no relatives within reach, no friends close enough to open up to, he felt alone, permanently down in his own pit, the darkness closing in. The only person close enough to care, the only person he could perhaps open up to was Alice.

But he couldn't.

He saw how hard she worked. He saw how little they had, and he resented it. He wanted to say sorry, but he was a man, and men didn't behave like that.

Sometimes he wanted to get out, to go somewhere else, to do something else, to have a different life, to have a better life. But being a miner was all he knew. If he moved collieries, he would just be swapping one frying pan for a different fire. When he thought of the future, which he tried not to do, it looked even bleaker.

So far he was still healthy, but around him he saw men with bent backs, with raking coughs, coughing up blood, staring with increasingly hollow eyes, and he knew that in all likelihood it was only a matter of time before his own physical decline took root and he followed them down the same road.

The most frightening thought was that this, this time now, was the best it was ever going to be. He wasn't working for a better future, he was holding on, and alcohol had been his crutch, and once its hold was loosened, he was left feeling even more adrift.

In some perverse way he felt that his predicament was Alice's fault. If they'd never met, if Sarah had never been born, if he had no responsibilities other than for himself, then he could have bettered himself, could have gone where he wanted, when he wanted, done what he wanted, with only himself for company.

In reality his thoughts would wander, he would never analyse things with any kind of clarity or conclusion, he did not have the ability, but in some self-fulfilling form of self-deception he felt that his aggression, when it burst out, was Alice's fault, somehow, she deserved it.

But now he was beginning to feel guilty; to feel that maybe everything was his fault, and that he was alone. He was a worthless man, a worthless husband, a worse father and unable to give the only two people who cared about him the life they deserved. He wanted to say sorry, but he couldn't. Instead, he sat in the corner of the kitchen reading his newspaper, smoking his cigarettes. The least he could do was to be as little of a burden to them as possible.

When Alice broached the idea of a fish and chips shop, he didn't really listen to the words, just saw the excitement in her eyes. He didn't really listen to her garbled explanation of a loan and a property and working in the next village, in their fish and chip shop, to learn what to do and how to do it.

'I have talked to Mrs Lewins,' said Alice, talking fast, her fingers twisting and untwisting in her lap, 'and she says I can help if I like though she won't pay me very much.'

She paused, her eyes on the floor.

'I will be out more,' she said, 'but if I arrange meals and leave things for you, I think I can make it work.'

The idea that Neville was being asked to make some kind of sacrifice felt to him completely appropriate, a kind of penance he could pay to partly make up for his misdemeanours, both past and present.

'Do you really want to try this?' he said, 'it sounds like hard work.'

Alice let her guard drop, lifted her head.

'Oh, I'd love to Neville, I'd love to give it a go.'

When he looked into her face he felt a pang of jealousy. His wife wanted to make her life better, to do what he couldn't do, and she still had the energy to do it. His first reaction was to take the opportunity away, why should she have the freedom he craved when he could not? But his better self, or his guilty self, won out,

'Go on then,' he said, 'why don't you give it a go and if it doesn't work then…'

He didn't finish the sentence because Alice had jumped to her feet, run over to him and kissed him on the cheek.

'Thank you,' she said, 'thank you, I won't let you down.'

Neville was stunned, he couldn't decide whether he needed a drink or not.

Mrs Jane Lewins was a friendly woman.

Described as 'well covered', she was tall and a chain smoker. Her husband, Joseph, was a miner, a hewer in fact, and worked in the business with his wife when he wasn't down the pit. Alice envied the closeness of their partnership.

'Joe can't work down the pit forever,' said his wife, 'this business is a way out if we can keep it going, saving what we can. He wants to go into transport but it's the cost of the vehicles that's getting in the way. He's looking at those steam driven lorries, don't understand them meself, but Joe's got a mechanical head on his shoulders, so he'll understand them alright.'

Alice was amazed at the clarity of Jane Lewins' vision for the future. It almost frightened her.

'If all goes to plan,' said Jane, 'we can bring our sons into the business, so they don't have to go down the pit, that's Joe's ambition anyway.'

She was happy to teach Alice the ropes, another, cheap, pair of hands would be useful, and she wouldn't be shy to let Alice work as hard as she wanted.

'But what's your idea?' she asked.

'Need some extra money,' said Alice, getting directly to the heart of the matter, 'can't sew, but I can work hard.'

Jane Lewins was as good as her word; she took Alice to the fish market, her greengrocer's, the butchers for the right quality lard, got her on the fryer and laughed when she splashed herself or undercooked the fish,

'We all do it,' she said, 'it's the battle scars of learning the trade. Just slide the fish through the batter, make sure you haven't missed a bit, see like this, then lift the fish by the tail end and lay it into the fryer, see how it sizzles, and then let it go, don't throw it in, that's how you get splashed, and then keep an eye on it until you can see it floating on the top, all nice and crispy yellow, don't leave it in too long, overcooked fish is dry and the batter's too dark and hard, collect the floating bits of batter and give them away as 'scraps' to those who like them, there's a lot that do.'

Alice listened, a bit of a slow learner she was enthusiastic and kept trying until she eventually picked things up and made them work. One of her characteristics was that she was not shy to ask the same questions over again.

'Alice,' laughed Mrs Lewins, 'you've got a head like a sieve, but don't you worry, you ask as many times as you want, you'll get it in the end.'

It soon became apparent to Alice that the Lewins' fish and chip shop was a bigger operation than she could hope to cope with. Mrs Lewins employed 4 part-time helpers, all women, who she managed so that all the necessary jobs were covered.

'Women are the best for this job,' she said, 'more organised and more pleasant to the customers. My ladies can't do full time jobs, there's too much to do at home, but a few hours out the house every week and a few extra pennies in the purse is no bad thing.'

Alice watched the way Mrs Lewins handled 'her ladies', she was pleasant but firm, and there was no doubting who the boss was.

Alice was not sure she could do that, what she wanted was something she could do herself, perhaps with a bit of help from Sarah now and again, even if that limited the size of the business.

She talked to Mrs Lewins about this.

'It'll be hard work doing it all yourself with nobody to do a bit of fetching and carrying and helping out,' she said, 'but it's possible, look at those who sell out of a fish and chip cart.'

It was true, Alice had seen one, pulled by a horse, unhitched and set up by the side of the road. It was a dangerous arrangement; a coal fire heated two deep-dished pans full of lard, the fish and chips were cooked in small lots, wrapped in greaseproof and newspaper while piping hot, salted, and served to the patiently waiting queue.

That was not what Alice wanted either, it was too cramped, and too dangerous.

She told Mrs Lewins what she thought.

'Well then,' she said, 'you're going to have to find yourself a small premises, your front parlour for example.'

Alice crinkled up her face. She could not even imagine suggesting this alternative to Neville. Having his passive support was all she'd asked for and, although she envied the collaboration between Joe and Jane Lewins, was all she wanted. Their journey was not the same as her's.

'Others have done it,' said Jane, seeing Alice's reaction, 'small premises, in the home, or close to it, a couple of small coal-fired fryers, one for your fish and one for your chips, a serving counter, then you could open up and, starting small to judge your trade, keep serving until you run out of fish.'

Alice thought this through, asked Jane to repeat the idea just so she understood it properly.

'That's what I want!' she said excitedly, 'you've hit the nail on the head, Mrs Lewins, yep, right on the head.'

Jane Lewins smiled and raised a hand,

'Whoa, Alice, there's a way to go before you get there.'

'Yes,' said Alice, not to be deterred, 'but now I know where I'm going to get to.'

'Trying to get to,' corrected Jane Lewins.

'No, Mrs Lewins, no, I'm going to get there, I'm going to do it.'

If determination, enthusiasm, and perseverance provided a road to success then Alice was on that road, had already taken some steps along it and now she could lift her head from her shoes and look forward and see, on the far horizon, the shadowy shape of her destination.

Chapter 26

Jack had been in the fields, helping Peter and working with the herdsman to move cows from one field to another.

'There's a few things to know,' said the herdsman, 'don't get between a cow and her calf, some mothers can be very protective, don't get hemmed in a corner because you don't want to great leant on by a cow, they can weigh over a ton… and if there were a bull in the field, then pay him respect and don't upset him.'

Under the herdsman's guidance they'd moved the beasts out onto the track, along and safely into another field where the grazing was better. The cows were placid the whole time and responded with familiarity to the herdsman's calls and cajoling.

Now they were back in the farmhouse and were chatting about their experiences over cups of tea and slices of cake.

Jim Moore had been listening to their chatter and reached over and took his pipe down from the mantle shelf, filled it, and tamped it down. Then he lit a taper from the live coal fire and sucked his pipe into life.

Settling into his customary chair he waved the boys over and started to talk about the way that farming was changing,

'I never thought I'd see the day,' he said, 'but it's not just industry that's having a revolution, it's farming too. Every day, almost, I read of some new, clever, contraption that somebody's invented or one of my neighbours is showing off this or that new thing. I'll tell you what,' he said, tapping the end of his pipe against the arm of his chair, 'I wouldn't be surprised if engines started to take over from horses,' he paused, 'it would be a shame that, but you can't stop progress, can you?'

Jack knew that the farmer, like his son, had an affinity for horses and even took some of the pit ponies onto his fields, either for recuperation or retirement, rather than see them shot.

'It'll not be in my lifetime mind you, but I can see it coming.'

The farmer reminded Jack, in some ways, of his grandfather. They both liked to tell a good tale although the worlds they'd lived through, and from which they drew their inspiration, were very different. The farmer was proud to be a product of the land, this land, just like his father and his grandfather before that. He took an interest in anything or anybody that increased the standing of the North East.

'It's good to know that people from this part of the world can make a difference,' he said, 'like Captain Cook, from Middlesbrough, and Thomas Bewick, a man of the North East, a man who was lauded, even in his own lifetime, for his groundbreaking method of making woodcuts, and illustrating books.'

Jack's ears pricked up at the mention of books, but he'd not heard of Thomas Bewick, and he said so.

'Bewick came from farming stock,' said Jim, 'stood at nearly 6 feet tall and was sturdily built. He had, to all accounts, a prickly side, and was not slow to repay an insult,' he settled back, eased into the tale, happy to have a ready audience. His wife kept a comfortable distance, working over by the sink, 'There was one occasion that has been recorded, when two pitmen decided to chastise him for some reason, but it was Bewick that turned on them and set them on their heels with bruises to remember him by. His ability to provide detail in his illustrations was unparalleled and he added small pictures, called vignettes or some such, and used them to fill otherwise empty spaces,' he sucked on his pipe, 'and these little pictures told tales of their own. Very clever really. So detailed was his work that you would need to look at them with a magnifying glass to fully appreciate the artistry.'

The farmer went over to a cupboard and returned with a book in his hand,

'Here, this is one of his, take a look.'

Jack took the book from the farmer's large and work-worn hand, its title was "A General History of Quadrupeds". Peter looked on.

'I'm not the best reader,' said the farmer, 'but I made my way through this one, and Ma has sometimes read bits out as well.' Peter nodded, 'Take a look, Jack, there's animals in there that I'd never have imagined.'

Jack opened the book.

'There's a lot about horses at the start,' he said.

'Yes, Thomas and me are of like mind when it comes to the beauty and importance of horses, even though he's been dead these eighty year or more I feel like me and him could have had a right good talk about horses.'

Jack didn't doubt it.

He skimmed through the book, glancing at some of the illustrations and then turned back to the beginning and browsed through the Index, the animals were not presented in any order that he could fathom.

At the end of the Index was one of the vignettes that Mr Moore had spoken about. It was undoubtedly a scene from the banks of the Tyne in Newcastle; an elevated wooden gantry had tubs full of coal which were being pulled into position by ponies and then tipped down slides into the bowels of the waiting boats below. In the background, industrial chimneys belched out smoke and warehouses lined the riverbank.

The farmer saw where Jack was looking.

'Aye, that's a good one. It takes a proud and a confident man to begin a book all about nature and animals with a picture of industry. It's hard to say whether the contrast is purposeful or not. But I think it is.'

'Why would it be?'

The farmer chewed on his pipe stem.

'Here is man with all his cleverness; the coal, the ships, the factories, the warehouses, taking over and controlling nature to his own ends, the ponies to pull the tubs, the river to float the ships, the wind to fill their sails, but we must not become so self-obsessed as to think that only we matter, rather we should wonder at the other animals that share this world with us, though some of them we'll never see in life.'

Ella Moore had been listening to her husband's explanation and tutted.

Her husband looked at her.

'He gets like this sometimes,' she said, 'maudlin is what I call it. That picture might have just been the one closest to hand. Best we concentrate on our own selves, I think. There's plenty work needs doing and not much time to do it in.'

Her husband smiled.

'You bring my feet back to the floor,' he said smiling.

'I must be going,' said Jack, 'Ma'll be waiting.'

As he was about to leave, the farmer said,

'Take the book if you like, Jack. As long as you bring it back mind.'

'Thanks, Mr Moore,' said Jack, 'but I'd rather leave it here. I know you like it and there's no saying what might happen if I take it home, specially if George gets his hands on it. Maybe we could look at it again sometime when I'm here.'

'You're a smart lad,' said the farmer's wife.

'You've got a good head on your shoulders,' said the farmer, 'but I've got another idea.'

'What's that, Mr Moore?' said Jack.

Jim Moore looked at his wife and she nodded, seeming to understand what her husband was about to say.

'It's them small pictures of Bewick's that intrigues me,' he said, 'He didn't have to do them, no publisher would've even thought of asking for them. It was for the love of the work, the love of the look of the book, that he did them. They made his works different, attracted interest and went on to make his fortune and name. It could have gone the other way, or simply be passed off as irrelevant or worse, unnoticed. He might have hoped but he didn't know. Aye, that's what I like, that he did what he wanted to do, and was ready to accept the consequences. And now, Jack, I want you to take this book and keep it, its yours.'

Jack's mouth fell open, even Peter was surprised by his father's generosity.

'I don't have many books of my own,' said Jack, 'though I get a lend of some good ones from the school library, Mr Hughes sees to that.'

'He's a good man, Mr Hughes,' said the farmer, 'I knew him before his accident, knocked him back that did, but he's made a good go of it since.'

'It'll be nice to a have book like this of your own,' said Ella Moore, 'build your library, one book at a time.'

'And this would be one of the first,' said Jack musing.

'And what a good one,' said Mr Moore.

'But I can't...'

'It's alright, Jack,' said Peter, 'Dad wouldn't offer it if he didn't mean it.'

Jack hurried home, the book inside his coat, held close to his chest. His mind was full of the strange creatures he'd glanced as he'd flipped through the pages; a tiger, a camel, a reindeer. It was a glimpse into a different world, an exotic world, a strange world, a world that he doubted he would ever experience for himself.

When he got home, he showed the book off proudly. Frank, Edward and Grandpa thought it a nice and extremely generous gesture. George was only jealous he didn't have one too.

Jenny stayed quiet, her mind turning over different ways she could pay back the favour.

Chapter 27

Alice updated Jenny on her progress and ambitions. Edward was listening.

'There's an old shed at the end of Third Street,' he said, 'it's an old works shed for the railway trucks. They used it when they were starting things up, I think, but we've got a bigger one down by the pithead now, so it's not used and in a pretty poor state.'

Alice was immediately interested.

'Can you show me?'

'I don't see why not; it's on common ground.'

'Can you show me now?'

'Now?'

'Why not? Before it gets dark.'

Edward looked at his mother.

'Why not?' she said, 'your dad's not in yet, Grandpa's on his allotment, goodness knows where your brothers are, you've got time.'

'Alright,' said Edward, reaching for his coat, 'let's go.'

Edward led the way.

Beyond the end of Third Street the ground gave way to gravel and cinders interspersed with clumps of grass and weeds. The shed was about 50 yards back. The timber frame that had once been painted white but was now peeling, there was a single door in the facing wall and broken windows, in rotting frames, front and back. The roof was of corrugated iron, rusted and unloved.

'Can we go in?' asked Alice.

Edward went up to the door. It was padlocked.

'Doesn't look like it,' said Edward, 'but we can look through the windows.'

Through the splintered glass and cobwebs they could see that the inside was a mess. It looked like the shed had been ransacked and then left to rot. That probably wasn't too far from the truth.

'I guess they just took out everything they thought was useful,' said Edward, 'looks like nobody's been here for years. I only know of it because I used to play around here when I was a kid.'

'Did you break the windows?'

'Of course not,' said Edward, far too quickly for comfort.

'Who owns it now?'

'I guess it's company property.'

'Hmm,' said Alice, 'do you know anyone I can talk to?'

Edward thought for a moment.

'You could ask Earnest Weightman,' he said, 'he's closest to management that I know of.'

'Thank you, Edward,' said Alice, 'now I suppose we better be getting back, you've got supper to eat, and I've got a meal to prepare for my two.'

Earnest Weightman bore the weight of his responsibilities with calmness and aplomb. Unflappable in the most vexatious of circumstances, he would watch over everything that affected the wages and conditions of the hewers, and was also a trusted advisor on domestic questions, the law, and matters of dispute. He was used to speaking to both management and owners as well as all those who worked in the colliery, both above and below ground.

'The problem with my job,' he had once confided to Frank at the bar of 'The Stackyard', 'is that I have to be a jack of all trades, resolving all kinds of disputes, able to be a spokesman, representing you all in management meetings, being available all of the time, and, without any sign of embarrassment or lack of self-confidence, give advice, sometimes on the most intimate of matters, to older miners, who are actually wiser and more experienced than me yet fail to realise it. And worst of all, I have on so many occasions to weigh my words, conscious that people may assign them a value, even if they don't deserve it. That's why I so enjoy my time at the bar. I feel it is a place where I can relax a little, tell some tales, be me and get away with it, for a few moments anyway.'

Frank had listened. He liked Earnest and partly sympathised with him, but then he thought of the conditions underground and concluded that a desk job couldn't be that bad no matter what the stresses and strains were.

Earnest Weightman was not used to miner's wives coming into his office.

Alice was told to wait outside while he finished what he was doing. When he went and opened his office door she was still there. He only knew her vaguely, he knew her husband better, but the reason he knew of him was not a good reason.

Fortunately for Alice, Earnest Weightman was not a man to hold the sins of the husband against the wife.

'Alright, Mrs Hudson, I can give you two minutes, I'm very busy with payday so close.'

'Of course,' said Alice, sitting, facing him across his polished mahogany desk, piles of paper right and left.

She explained about the shed and about what she wanted to do with it.

'I see,' said Earnest, 'and you would pay for every and all repairs?'

'And the refurbishment,' said Alice, 'and the upkeep.'

'I see,' he said, and picked up a pen and scratched behind his ear with it, 'and rent?'

Alice laced her fingers together in her lap, white knuckles showing,

'As I would be making an investment in an otherwise worthless property,' she said, just as firmly as she'd rehearsed it to herself in the mirror, 'I would expect it to be rent free for a year and then to agree a fair quarterly rental after that.'

This was not what Earnest Weightman expected this day would bring him. He was used to arguing with disgruntled miners, not talking about an abandoned shed with one of their wives.

His calculations of individual shifts and weights for each miner and conversion of those into pounds shillings and pence for their pay-packets were complicated, but also tedious, so that in a way Alice's intrusion was a breath of fresh air, but it was also a new complication. He finished scratching and put his pen back on the desk.

'Please write all this down, Mrs Hudson, and send it to me. I'll then give your idea some consideration.'

'Thank you,' said Alice jumping up and reaching over to shake his hand.

'I can't promise you anything, mind,' he said, a little flustered by Alice's enthusiasm, 'I'm only a small cog in a big machine.'

'I'll write you the letter,' said Alice, 'and deliver it personally tomorrow.'

After the door had closed behind her, Earnest said to himself,

'I'm sure you will, Mrs Hudson, I'm sure you will.'

Then he shook his head, smiled, and returned to his sums.

Alice was as good as her word, as was Earnest Weightman, and by some minor miracle, or perhaps Earnest's advocacy, the use of the hut was granted to Alice for the purposes of the frying and sale of fish and chips, and for that purpose only.

The formal application, made on behalf of Alice Hudson by Earnest Weightman, was signed off by the Secretary of the Company on behalf of the Board.

Once the way was cleared, Alice was given the keys to the hut. She was pleased and nervous in equal measure, aware of the daunting task ahead.

The first thing she did was clean out all the miscellaneous junk and debris that had been left behind. Edward and Jack volunteered to help with the lifting and carrying and George did his best to help his brothers.

Once the place was cleared a tile-covered concrete floor was exposed, the shed had obviously been built for the handling of heavy bits of metal equipment and, although some of the terracotta tiles were cracked, Alice decided that scrubbing it clean of the dirt and oil and grease that had been left behind was going to be enough.

'Defects add character to a place,' she said to Sarah as they knelt, scrubbing brushes in hand, pails of soapy hot water alongside them, working their way across the floor and into each nook and cranny. It would need doing more than once, but this labour of love would yield a clean floor eventually, one that you could almost eat your meal off; almost.

The windows were replaced. Edward contributed 2 shillings 'on behalf of a friend' who might have been responsible for a couple of the breakages. Alice didn't want to take the money, but Edward insisted. It was worth it for a clear conscience.

Earnest Weightman discovered some 'left over paint' somewhere and sent it up with paint brushes and a ladder and a request to have the brushes and the ladder back 'whenever possible'.

The corrugated metal roof was sound and not leaking so Edward scraped it off and painted it black. Grandpa and Jack, aided by George, scraped off the timber walls and painted them white, inside and out.

The gods were kind and provided some dry days for the work, though it took some time.

Alice had the door replaced and a new lock fitted, keeping the key safe.

Jane Lewins suggested somebody that could perhaps fit out the inside with the fryers, the counter and other fixings. She even talked to them on Alice's behalf to ensure she got a 'good and fair price for the work'.

In the end Alice got two coal-fired fryers and a hot plate for boiling water, a metal covered counter, a sink, a cupboard and some shelves, all within the limit of expenditure that Tony Sharpe had given her.

Tony paid any big invoices direct to the supplier and handed Alice the balance to spend as she wished. He trusted her and he trusted her judgment and was pleased with his investment. He was taking the first steps to becoming the businessman he'd always wanted to be, and somebody else was doing most of the work.

The range was a combination of black and silver, the black of the cast iron fire boxes below and the silver of the gleaming steel surfaces above. As she looked at it, Jane Lewins' words echoed in her ears.

'Some of the buying is done with the eyes,' she used to tell Alice, 'if somebody sees a clean and shiny range then they know it's hygienic and the food will be cooked well by somebody who cares about what they're doing. You imagine going into a chippy and seeing lots of grease everywhere or charred bits of black, you're not likely to make that your local, are you?'

Well, this range was going to shine. It was her's and she was going to treat it like it was a member of her family. After all, she'd be spending a lot of time with it.

They'd had to break through the wall to put in the flues, but that had seemed to go well, although they had had to construct a brick section to both support the pipes and also separate the hot metal from the wooden construction.

The deep-frying troughs were lidded to keep in the heat and vapours as well as minimise splashing and reduce the amount of oxygen getting to the hot fat and causing degradation. Alice had learnt that if you looked after your fat then you would only have to keep replenishing the losses, about a fifth every night, rather than cleaning it all out and starting from scratch again, a much dirtier, time consuming and expensive job.

Between the frying sections was a chip box into which the scooped up chips would be dumped, allowed to drain, and kept warm, ready for serving. The fish, when ready, would be scooped out of the hot fat with a metal-mesh scoop and lifted into a bureau-type cabinet above the fryers. This had a quarter-circle configuration and a lid that slid back and forth along the arc. Here the fish would lie, keeping warm, draining and ready to serve.

The last big thing to be added was the sign.

Grandpa joined together two planks of wood and painted them white. When they were well and truly dry, Alice, in her best writing, painted **"FISH AND CHIPS"** in 12-inch black letters on it and then supervised the precise placement on the front of the building.

The derelict shed had completed its resurrection and was ready to start on its new journey.

Alice was proud of the result and content that Neville had left her to it and not complained at the cold meals he'd had, the less clean house and the long hours that Alice had been missing.

Neville on his part was pleased to see his wife's enthusiasm and amazed at the new capabilities she had demonstrated. He never thought her capable of anything like this. He stayed away because she didn't ask him to help and felt that if he stuck his nose in it would be unlikely to be appreciated.

He was particularly impressed that Alice had secured a bank loan, or so he assumed. Banks filled him with dread, and he was sure that if he were to approach them, then they would either lose all his money and not be able to find it again or loan him money at a rate that would quickly see him into the workhouse. He was happy to leave that interaction to Alice and hope and trust that all would be well.

When he saw the finished hut, and had looked inside it, Alice nestled close and took his hand,

'What do you think?' she said.

In his mind he was conflicted; she had done this without his help, without the need of his help, so he was useless, that was bad, on the other hand, she had done this, and that was good.

He squeezed her hand.

'It looks like a proper chippy,' he said.

That night, to the amazement of both of them, they made love for the first time in a very long time. The unaccustomed tenderness brought back memories of the early days of their marriage, before Sarah was born, when Neville harboured hopes of building a new and a better life, when hope and energy had yet to be ground out of him by the hard labour down the pit.

Maybe this venture was healing some wounds, bringing them closer together as man and wife, beyond the purely transactional relationship of wage-earner and housekeeper that it had become.

Chapter 28

Wilkinson and Enid Hughes had been going over the school accounts on Sunday. Enid was the patient one. Wilkinson wasn't.

On the Monday Wilkinson's mind was still full of it, and when Wilkinson's mind was full of something it normally found an outlet.

The afternoon lesson was Maths, or more accurately £'s s's and d's. As a teacher he was a big believer that his job was to equip his students to cope with the world outside and that that world had two languages; English and Money, and it was best to be fluent in both.

'You will remember,' he said using his stick to point to the blackboard, 'that there are 20 shillings in a pound and, what's more, there are 12 pence in every shilling, therefore,' and here he looked seriously at the upturned faces, 'how many pence are there in a pound?'

There was silence.

'Work it out' he said, 'and then put up your hand when you have the answer.'

The children knew the risks; if you didn't eventually put up your hand you were in trouble, if you put up your hand and didn't know the answer, or got it wrong, and were picked on to answer, you were in bigger trouble. Heads dropped to their slates, chalk squealed.

'Why does it have to be so complicated?' said Sarah in a whisper to Jack.

'Yes,' shouted the teacher, whose hearing was remarkably good, 'is there a question?'

Sarah tentatively put up her hand.

'Yes, Miss Hudson.'

'Sir, why does it have to be so complicated?' she said.

'Complicated?'

'Sir, I mean why 12 pence in a shilling, why not ten, why 20 shillings in a pound, why not 100?'

'Because, young lady, that's the way it is…,' and here was the chance for Wilkinson's inner thoughts to gain expression, 'We are the only animal that has invented money. I wonder how far we need to go back in our own history to discover the point at which we considered that bartering was no longer good enough. Trying to ascertain what proportion of a live hen would be fair compensation for a loaf of bread would have been a problem and the invention of an intermediary device that would overcome these problems must have been very welcome.'

'Certainly, the Greeks were well versed in coinage as were the Romans, so that the human race's dependence on money goes back several thousands of years. Even in those times an individual's or a family's status was dependent, not only on its land holdings but also on its monetary wealth.'

'Indeed, there came a point when it was the possession of money, and not property, that maintained solvency and kept the wheels of life turning. No longer could you walk into a shop and offer an armful of leeks for a pound of butter, you would have been considered deranged.'

'No, it is money that has become pre-eminent in the developed world, without it you cannot eat, house or clothe yourself. So, it is not extraordinary that the colliery owners look first to their accounts and second, if at all, to their employees. They have been educated on how their world ticks, and they do nothing but follow those rules.'

'So however complicated this may seem, Miss Hudson, we must accept it as a fact no less sure than the rising of the Sun in the East and learn how to deal with the consequences. Money impacts each and every one of us, you could say that it controls our daily lives.'

Sarah wished she'd never asked.

'Now,' said the teacher, 'how many pennies in a pound?'

Sarah asked her mother about this when she got home. Alice saw the sense in what the teacher had said and told her daughter so. She herself was good at the mental gymnastics of monetary arithmetic and put that down to the fact that their money was tight and she'd had to learn the art of hunting for bargains and haggling over prices, as well as the science of counting the coins and working out and checking the change. Such forced learning was likely to stand her in good stead when the fish and chip shop opened, she thought, and encouraged her daughter to pay attention to the Maths lessons.

Alice was the daughter of a miner and married to a miner for more than 10 years. The fish and chip shop would be the first thing that she had owned and run by herself, and she was almost overawed with how close she was to earning her own money, money that would be directly under her own control.

To be able to run it herself, she had had to streamline the business compared to the end-to-end attention that Jane Lewins gave to hers.

The first major difference was with the suppliers. Here Alice relied on Brian Goodson to deliver her fish which had been landed at Cullercoats, entrained to Newcastle, chosen by him and then shipped onwards for Alice to collect. A similar arrangement was made for the supply of potatoes and lard.

The second simplification was the menu. It was a simple one, fish of the day, mainly cod but sometimes haddock, and chips. The only possible alternatives to the standard fish and chip supper were just a piece of fish, or just a portion of chips. Alice intended to collect the batter bits from the fryer and, if asked, would sprinkle a small scoopful on top of a meal. Salt and vinegar were available, of course, and she would add this to each order as directed by the customer, before wrapping the food in a combination of greaseproof paper and yesterday's news.

A piece of paper was pinned to the church notice board and another one in the window of 'The Stackyard', announcing the opening. There weren't that many new ventures in the village to compete, and the news got around.

'What you need to remember,' Mrs Lewins had told Alice, 'is that most of the work in this business is done before the shop opens and after it's shut; doing the serving is the easy bit.'

Long before opening time, Alice sorted out the fish fillets, peeled the potatoes and chipped them through a long- handled chip stamper, the chips dropping into a bucket underneath. She then lit a new fire under the fryer starting it off with kindling and nursing it into flame, adding coal as the fire took hold.

With the lids of the two fryers lifted she kept a careful eye on the melting fat, scooping away any unwelcome bits that may have somehow found their way into the new pans.

'The problem with the fat,' Mrs Lewins had said, 'is that it can ignite, and then you have a real problem on your hands, so it's best to keep a close eye on it, throw in a chip or two when you think it's up to temperature and control the air to the fire to stop everything getting too hot.'

In fact, the temperature of fat needed for frying was about 360°F, and it was heated by a coal fire burning at over 600°F. At this higher temperature the fat could ignite and although it would start to smoke first, the time between it starting to smoke and it bursting into flames could be short. Therefore Mrs Lewins was right, it always paid to keep a careful eye on the fryers. In fact, only the previous September there had been a newspaper report of "a fried fish shop" in a wooden building near a United Methodist Free Church that had gone up in flames and burnt to the ground in less than an hour. Fortunately, the church was unscathed.

Faced with these challenges, Alice sometimes thought that sewing would have been a much safer alternative, if she'd had any aptitude for it that is, as with sewing the worst you could do was prick a finger, here she could burn the whole place down. However, she, like all the women of the village, was used to managing a coal fire. Their whole house was run on coal and managing the coal-fired range in the kitchen was an all day and everyday activity, so Alice knew what to do and how to do it.

'One of the most important things,' Jane Lewins had told her, 'though it may not seem like it, is learning how to wrap the fish suppers properly. Wrapping them properly does not just mean keeping them warm and secure it means doing it so they can be opened outside and eaten with the fingers; the best way to eat fish and chips in my opinion.'

It had taken some time for Alice to perfect this ability but perfect it she had and, now she had the knack, she could do it without thinking.

Alice wore a white apron over her clothes, it was her uniform of duty, and her ambition was to always look clean and tidy, although wiping her hands on her apron, or wiping up a spill with it, was already a big temptation and sometimes a necessity, as, although there were cloths around, they weren't always within easy reach when an urgent need arose.

Alice had bought 50 pieces of cod for the first evening. She'd prepared the batter by mixing flour and water and adding a little baking soda and vinegar, as Mrs Lewins had taught her, to create bubbles in the batter and therefore a light and crispy end product. Such was her hope anyway.

Having got everything fired up and hot she fried some chips and four or five pieces of fish, so she had something ready at opening time. Even if nobody came, she was sure somebody could be found to eat those.

Before the designated opening time she could hear noises outside and saw silhouettes through the window. When she opened the door, she couldn't believe it; there was a queue!

Overwhelmed by the response she became lost in her tasks; battering, frying, cutting more chips, serving, taking the money, giving out the right change.

A split-level counter separated her from her customers, on the lower level she could assemble the fish suppers and wrap them, on the upper level the customers could lean without getting in the way or interfering with the operation. Before wrapping she asked each customer if they wanted salt or vinegar and quickly became used to being closely scrutinised at this stage of the proceedings,

'A little bit more salt, if you please…', 'splash the vinegar on the fish, pet…', 'just salt the chips now Alice…'

The money was kept in a cash box. Alice would go through it at the end of the evening to establish the takings.

She talked to people, shared a joke now and then, but she wouldn't have been able to tell you who she spoke to or what she said, it was all part of the same whirlwind of activity. All the fish was gone in less than an hour and she had to apologise to those who could only have chips.

She closed the shop an hour and a half after it had opened.

It had all happened so quickly; the only blemish was that at some time or other an ember of coal had fallen out of the grill and started to smoulder on a pile of newspapers. Fortunately, someone had pointed it out quickly and Alice had stamped it out.

'Seems you've got to have eyes everywhere in this business,' she'd said, trying to laugh off what could have been a first night disaster.

After she'd closed the doors to customers the first thing she did was move things around, moving anything flammable as far away from the fryers as possible.

'You've got to learn by your mistakes,' she muttered to herself, 'don't want that to happen again.'

Then she wiped and scraped down the surfaces, easier done when still hot, dampened down the fire, scooped out any bits from the surface and bottom of the fryers, took out any remaining food, including the 'scraps'.

'It's a strange fact,' Mrs Lewins had told her, 'that a pile of scraps left in a too hot place for too long can self-ignite.'

Although she had never seen this happen, she had no interest in testing the validity of the theory, so she removed all the leftovers before locking up the shop and going home, the cash box under her arm.

'Clean means customers,' she said to herself, 'if only they knew how much there is to do before and after they come in for their suppers! It can't be that much harder working down the pit.'

She bit her lip, the idea of working in the dark with only your mates and your pit lamp for company actually did seem much harder when she thought about it, so she decided that, in comparison, she had little to complain about.

On his wife's opening night, Neville was down the pub,

'Thought you'd be up at the chippy with your missus,' said Pat, his underground colleague and Sunderland supporter.

'No.' said Neville, 'I'm leaving all that to Alice.'

'Well, I think it's a fine thing,' said Pat, 'I wish my wife showed that kind of initiative, we'd be quids in.'

Neville was pleased,

'Yes, she's really taken to it.'

'Then let me buy you a drink,' said Pat, 'to celebrater her first night of opening, maybe if I get in your good books she'll let me have a free bag of chips every now and again, eh?'

Neville laughed.

'I don't think that would be good business, buy the husband a drink, get free food from the wife. I don't think that works even if you supported the right team, nice idea, but no go.'

It didn't stop Neville from accepting the drink though nor from accepting other offers from men happy to celebrate Alice's success. It was good to have a chippy on the doorstep, just what was needed.

It was a good hour later that Frank saw what was happening, Edward drew his attention to it,

'Dad, I think you better take a look at Neville, seems like he might have reached his limit.'

When Frank found him through the cigarette fog, it was too late.

'Damn!' he muttered to himself.

'Come on Edward, let's get him home.'

It wasn't easy to prise Neville away, he was enjoying himself too much, but finally with Frank on one arm, Edward on the other, they managed to get him outside.

When the cool air hit him, he slouched and said,

'Is it good that my wife isn't at home? Is it really? Hmm, you tell me.'

'You should be proud of Alice,' said Frank, 'she's had to work really hard to get a chippy up and running.'

'Really hard, yea, and what about me, what have I…'

He trailed off.

Frank and Edward held him up.

'Listen Neville,' said Frank, 'I think you should come round to ours. I've got a Newcastle programme I want to show you.'

'Hmm?' said Neville.

'Edward, go and warn your mum, tell her Neville's coming for a visit.'

'Can you manage on your own?' said Edward.

'Yes, off you go.'

Edward unhooked Neville's arm from around his shoulders. Neville slumped, and Frank took the extra weight and steadied himself.

When Jenny saw Alice on the way back from the shed, she went outside and intercepted her.

'Neville's round ours,' she said.

Alice gasped, 'Is he…'

'He's alright,' said Jenny, 'talking football with the boys. Why don't I come round yours for a cup of tea, you can tell me and Sarah all about your first night's opening and then I'll get Frank to put Neville to bed for you.'

'Oh, Jenny…'

'Don't worry, everything's alright, now come on, let's get the kettle on and you can tell me all about it.'

'I've got some leftover chips,' said Alice.

Chapter 29

After the strong start the business settled into a routine, opening on a Tuesday, a Thursday and a Saturday, either until 10:30pm or until the fish ran out. Re-cleaning, maintenance and preparations were jobs for a Monday, a Wednesday and a Friday.

The fish was fresh and the potatoes local. Fish cost a penny, chips cost half a penny if ordered separately, and a fish and chip supper cost one and a half pennies. There was normally a queue at opening time and Alice worked hard and did good business.

The money she made was an essential supplement to her household income and she guarded it jealously and spent it sparingly, never telling Neville either how the business was doing or how much money it made.

Alice built the business to suit the volume of her sales. She preferred to run out of fish and apologise rather than having food left over and having to throw it away.

Tony Sharpe was content to take back only what money Alice could afford so as not to overstretch her finances. However, Alice's pride was such that she wanted to pay the loan back as quickly as possible and, by careful management, was able to start making repayments within 3 months and aimed to have it paid off in less than a year.

Beyond the occasional burns from splashing fat and scalding metal, the most catastrophic risk was that of fire. She was therefore very fastidious, especially at the close of business, making sure that all the fires were made safe, the oil lamps were out, and any hot surfaces were separated from clothes, newspapers or any other form of flammable material. This meant that it was usually late when Alice got home, not always to a warm welcome from Neville, assuming he was home and not still at the pub.

After 6 months it was as if the fish and chip shop had always been there. Everybody knew the opening times, and it was common knowledge that if you wanted to be sure of a bit of fish, then it was advisable to get there early.

On the way home she would occasionally pop a bag of chips into Jenny and have one to offer Sarah and Neville, who were always keen to finish them off, especially wrapped in fresh bread and butter.

It was hard work though, and by this time she was thinking of taking on a bit of help. A big chunk of the money Tony had invested had been returned to him, she'd prioritised that even over taking payment for herself, 'You don't have to pay me back this quickly,' he'd said, 'I wasn't expecting to be paid back for at least two years.'

But for Alice it was important to repay his trust and after a few more months his debt was repaid, and she felt confident enough to take the next step of paying for a bit of regular help.

She wouldn't do it without talking to Tony though.

The next time she went to the Co-op on her own, Alice took the opportunity to give him an update. It was the only place they met, and it seemed to work. She hoped that he felt he'd made a wise investment.

Tony smiled, 'I think I have Alice, from what I hear your place is popular.'

'Don't do plaice,' said Alice, 'just cod and haddock.'

They both laughed.

She asked him what he thought about employing part time help. Tony said that she should use her own judgement but that managing other people wasn't always easy.

Alice decided to wait a bit, she would ask Sarah to give her a hand and see if that made a difference.

A lady from the mining village, we won't give her name, saw them and wondered what all the fun was about. She didn't think much of it, but it set her on a track.

It's easy to draw the wrong conclusions, and when she saw them together for a second time, whispering, the wrong conclusion started to form.

The third time she saw them, she had convinced herself that she was right and surreptitiously drew close enough to eavesdrop on broken parts of their conversation,

'No,' said Alice, 'Neville doesn't know…'

'…you should come round…'

'Perhaps I will…'

That's all she heard before they noticed her and the conversation switched to the price of potatoes.

She wasn't a gossip, if she had been it would have been all round the streets by the end of the day, but she couldn't keep it to herself either, so she told her husband.

'No smoke without fire,' he said.

Later that evening this same man was in 'The Stackyard', he was with his mates but keeping an eye out for Neville.

Unfortunately, this was one of the evenings Neville popped in, just for a single pint, to slake his thirst.

The man found an excuse to talk to him, talked about the football first and then, when he thought they weren't being overheard he dropped the bombshell.

'See your wife is friendly with that chap in the Co-op,' he said.

Neville was startled. The man continued, best to get it off his chest as quickly as possible, he thought.

'Yes, my wife has seen them a couple of times, probably just chatting, eh?'

'What chap?' said Neville, trying to get his head round what he was hearing.

'Tony Sharpe,' the man said, 'Sharpe by name, sharp by nature, eh?'

He laughed; Neville laughed along with him. The laugh was hollow.

'Probably nothing to it,' the man said, 'just thought I'd mention it.'

His job done, he slapped Neville on the back, wished him well, and went back to his mates.

It was like throwing a rock into a pond and walking away, unaware of the ripples that had been created.

Neville festered, scraped the money together for another pint.

He didn't believe it of course. He'd simply talk to Alice about it. But he couldn't do that could he? To do that would mean that he took it seriously. And he didn't... did he?

Back in the house he was morose. Sarah was already in bed. Alice asked him what was wrong. For some reason he lashed out, hit the teapot, sending it crashing onto the kitchen floor, sending hot tea everywhere.

Next door they heard the crash.

'Oh no,' said Jenny.

'You don't know,' said Frank, 'might just be an accident.'

On the other side of the wall, Alice was on her knees picking up the pieces, her silent tears falling into the spilt tea.

It was only a teapot; she'd get a new one tomorrow. The Co-op had some.

Alice was in the Co-op buying a new teapot.

Tony Sharpe came over. He saw immediately that Alice was not herself.

'What's wrong?' he asked.

Alice bent her head, closed her eyes trying to hold back tears.

'I thought everything was going so much better,' she said, and then she told Tony of Neville's outburst.

'For no reason?'

'None that I can think of.'

'Here, take my handkerchief, dry your eyes.'

She handed it back.

'Keep it,' he said, 'listen Alice, you're doing very well. The business is doing much better than I thought. Don't let things get on top of you, not now.'

He put his hand on her shoulder. Instinctively Alice reached out her hand, they touched. It was a moment of empathy between two human beings, nothing more.

But eyes were upon them.

'Tell you what, I'll come up to your shop on Saturday, I'd love some fish and chips and we can talk then, about the business I mean.'

'Yes, please,' said Alice straightening up.

And that was how the fuse was lit, so simply, so unintentionally, not knowing how long it had to burn.

Chapter 30

Alice was out of the house, up at the fish and chip shop.

Neville was hunting around for a new handkerchief. He wanted one before he set out for 'The Stackyard'. Unfamiliar with where they were kept, and without Alice to ask, he hunted around the drawers until he found one. It was a good one, better than he normally had.

It was because it was different that he looked at it more closely, and in looking at it more closely he found the embroidered initials "A.S" in one corner. Puzzled, he put the handkerchief in his pocket, went to the jar on the mantlepiece, took some money out, and left for the pub.

While having a drink, Neville kept putting his hand in his pocket and letting his fingers run over the raised initials. It was a man's handkerchief, there was no doubt about that, but A.S?

Frank and Edward joined him, and the talk turned to football. Newcastle were continuing to prove that they were one of the best teams in the country, so there was lots of good news to chew on. Frank noticed that Neville did not stop drinking after his customary one or two pints.

'Everything alright?' he asked.

'Oh yes,' said Neville, 'everything's just fine, got a bit more money coming in now that Alice's fish and chip shop is doing so well.'

'Must be hard work,' said Edward.

'She's busy all the time,' said Neville.

Another man came over, slapped Edward on the shoulder.

'Hello Ed,' he said, 'you going to the match on Saturday?'

'Might be, not sure,' said Edward.

'Let me know,' he said, 'we can go together if you're going, I'll even buy you a beer.'

'I'll let you know,' said Edward.

After the man had drifted away out of earshot, Edward turned back to Frank and Neville,

'One of my crew underground,' he explained, 'just arrived from the South and keen to make friends. Bit of a loudmouth, but he seems alright, though I don't like him calling me Ed.'

'That's the thing about names,' said Frank, 'better to have one that can't be tampered with, like Frank, for example.'

He laughed.

'Well, it's your fault,' said Edward, 'you gave me this name.'

'You're right,' said Frank, 'sorry about that.'

They laughed again. Neville laughed with them and then he stopped.

'Neville, you alright,' said Frank.

'I'm going to leave you guys now,' said Neville, 'just seen someone I need to talk to.'

Neville shuffled his way through the crowd and cigarette fug, found a spot at the bar and got himself another pint.

'A.S,' he thought, 'A for Alan, Arthur or Anthony… Anthony, and Anthony is the same as Tony, T.S. … Tony Sharpe! What the fucking hell is my wife doing with Tony Sharpe's handkerchief!'

His anger started to burn, the more he thought about it the worse it seemed, he was being humiliated, he was a fool…

He gulped down his drink, ordered another, waved away the bartender's protestations, paid for it, told him he had something to celebrate, that he'd had a revelation and that his life was about to change.

When he left the bar, he did so alone. He was drunk but not drunk enough to forget his mission. He staggered home. He needed to talk to Alice. He needed to know. He needed to talk to his wife. He just wanted to talk. He could control his anger. Of course he could.

When he got home Alice wasn't there. She never seemed to be there. Sarah wasn't there either. He didn't know it, but she was next door sewing with Jenny. All he knew was that the house was empty. All he knew was that he was alone. Alone.

'She must be at the shed,' he thought swaying unsteadily.

And so, he made his way up the hill, towards the white hut, towards the black lettering on the white board "FISH AND CHIPS".

It was the end of the evening's business and Alice was inside cleaning up. Tony was there as arranged, eating his fish and chips and talking to Alice about the business. She'd put a couple of pieces of fish aside, one for Neville and one for Sarah. The door was closed but not locked.

When Neville arrived, he paused to catch his breath and look through the window. Maybe this was a bad idea, maybe he should turn round and go home, he could talk to Alice later, when she was back.

Through the window he sees two people, not one: a man and a woman. The man says something, and the woman laughs. The woman is his wife, the man is Tony Sharpe.

All thoughts of turning back disappear and he barges into the chippy.

Neville has had too many beers and heard and seen more than he can comprehend. He enters the hut ready for a fight and immediately starts shouting, accusing Alice of this and that and threatening Tony. Alice looks at Tony who starts to make his way to the door and tries to leave. He's completely wrongfooted by this turn of events, knows he's at least partly the cause and thinks that if he gets out of the way then Neville might calm down, he doesn't know what else to do.

But Neville blocks his way and sneers into his face

'Coward!' he shouts, spittle accompanying his words and wetting Tony's face.

Alice whispers 'Just go, it'll be alright.'

But seeing his wife talk to Tony Sharpe, in front of him, right in front of him, and so calmly, tips Neville's anger into violence.

'Going to be alright is it, I'll show you what alright is.'

Neville pushes past Tony and without further warning punches Alice in the stomach. She doubles up and Tony automatically steps in between them. Neville turns on him.

'Come on then,' he says, 'get between a man and his wife will you.'

Tony, in confusion, raises his hands,

'I'm not a violent man,' he says, and stands frozen to the spot.

Neville's temper has snapped, the dam holding back his pent up frustrations has burst, and he snarls drunkenly and goes for Tony...

...but he is unsteady on his feet and Tony dodges aside and shoves him away, using both hands, in his own defence.

Neville falls and bangs the back of his head on the corner of the counter; he twists around as he crashes onto the terracotta tiled floor.

He lies there, face down, and blood starts to trickle from his head.

'I didn't mean...' says Tony.

'I know,' says Alice.

They both kneel down beside Neville's prone body. His chest is rising and falling, he is still breathing,

'Thank God!' says Tony.

'Turn him over,' says Alice, more in control of the situation.

Tony lifts Neville onto his side. Neville groans.

'What shall we do?' says Tony.

'You just go,' says Alice, 'leave Neville to me. I don't know what's got into him, other than the drink that is.'

Tony is in shock. He is not a violent man.

'Go!' says Alice.

Tony obeys.

'And say nothing,' says Alice to his retreating back, 'Neville might not even remember this in the morning.'

After Tony has gone Alice decides to try and get Neville home but he's unconscious and too heavy for Alice to move.

She is not sure what else to do or what the consequences might be.

'When he's sober, he might have forgotten all about this,' she says to herself, more in hope than anything else, 'he's going to have a sore head, but I think I'll be able to talk to him. I don't know what's got into him, but I'll find out and then…'

She trailed off, she didn't know 'what then'.

'He might even be sorry,' she thinks, clutching at straws, and tries to avoid thinking that Neville might decide to take the whole thing out on her.

Frustrated and anxious she decides the only thing she can do is to leave him there, let him sort himself out, and let the future look after itself.

Alice leaves a key on the counter so that Neville can let himself out when he comes round, then she turns off the oil lamps, locks up and leaves.

However, in her haste and the pain from the blow to her stomach, Alice does not complete her nightly clean up with her usual thoroughness.

The coal fire beneath the fat fryers is not out and the guard has not been completely moved into place. Worse still a stack of newspapers and empty potato sacks is still on the floor and has not been removed either into the refuse bin or into the cupboard for future use.

After she's gone the fire spits out one hot and glowing ember. Just like it did on the opening night, but this time there is no one on hand to stamp it out.

The ember sparks and skitters across the hard floor, a small piece breaking off and settling under a corner of dry sacking. Nothing happens for some minutes, and then a single tendril of smoke winds its way invisibly into the grey gloom. Steadily the tendril becomes a stream and at its base there is a red flickering light.

As Neville regains consciousness, he is aware of the smell and taste of smoke, acid in his nostrils and throat. It is a taste he is familiar with but not at this intensity, not at an intensity that stings his eyes into tears.

Out of the corner of his eye he sees a flickering; yellow, red, yellow, and his first thought is that he is in a dream, that he is in some vision of hell, an explosion underground or a roof collapse. The pain of a raking cough removes all doubt that this is not fantasy but real, very real, and he struggles to look around through his misted eyes, gasping for clean air, trying to make sense of it all.

He rolls over and tries to rise, his head befuddled with a mixture of pain and alcohol and pushes himself into a kneeling position. From there he reaches out blindly for something solid to hold onto. When his left-hand encounters something hard and vertical he moves his arm upwards, following the surface until his fingers feel the smoothness of the serving counter.

He puts his hand on the countertop and levers himself into a standing position, he is finding it more difficult to breathe, and he sees flames only inches away, relentlessly growing.

In fear now, he staggers and sways, holding on to anything that he can find. Like a man lost in a storm at sea, nothing is stable, nothing is steady enough to guide him to a safe harbour, a welcome shore.

As he gasps, he fights not just for air but for thought; where is he? what is happening?

And then he starts to remember; he is in Alice's fish and chip shop, he can't remember why, but he knows he's there and he needs to get out.

He feels his head aching and he puts his hand to the spot and feels a wet stickiness. Peering further through the smoke, he sees the door and tries to move towards it, but the smoke is too thick, and his lungs are full of it, suffocating him, depriving him of the power of movement, and he slumps back onto his knees.

As he chokes, he cannot believe what is happening, he is too young, he has never thought of his own mortality, not seriously, he has too much to live for… images flit across his mind; his parents when they were young, when he was young, his wife when they first met, his daughter when she was born, and the futility of the anger that has always burnt inside him burns him now as much as his struggle for breath, and he starts to sob. He had not meant to become the man that he is.

Each breath is now a searing pain and almost too much effort to perform. He slips back onto the floor and relapses into a blessed unconsciousness; his last thoughts are those of regret.

When Alice gets home, Sarah asks if there are any fish and chips, but Alice says, 'Sorry love we sold out tonight.'

She says nothing about Neville.

Chapter 31

Later that night, one of the McDonald boys, Kenny, from a family in Third Street, was walking with his girl, Susie, they were on their way to the darkness behind the fish and chip hut, which was as good a private place as any for a little bit of canoodling. When they reached the hut, there seemed to be a light on inside and Kenny said,

'It should be all closed up by now, I'll just take a look.'

The girl hung back, and Kenny went up to the window and peered through. In the far corner, he could see flames dancing, yellow and red.

His face changed from surprise to shock, and he turned quickly back to Susie.

'It looks like there's a fire,' he said, 'you best run home, and I'll run for help.'

Susie ran to the window and peered through, then she turned and started running back down the street. She was not supposed to be out and had clambered out of a back window, dropped into the yard and crept off to meet with Kenny in what she thought was a quiet and secretive manner.

Unbeknown to her, her mother had seen her but decided she was now old enough to look after herself. Kenny wasn't a bad lad, and you had to learn about boys sometime.

Susie didn't know she'd been spotted and getting back home and inside without being caught was her first priority. A fire was one thing, the wrath of her mother was quite another!

Kenny sprinted back to his house, ran inside and blurted out his story. The noise woke up the whole family. His sister, Nora, was wide awake.

'Nora, run and tell Alice, quickly now!' said his mother.

'I'll run to the pit and call out the fire engine,' said his father, pulling on his pants.

'The rest of us will grab buckets and jugs and get up there, there's a water tap at that end of the street and when we get there, we'll see what we can do.'

'Just don't take any daft chances,' said Mr McDonald, running out of the door.

Nobody asked Kenny why he was up at the fish and chip shop well after it had closed.

Alice was awoken by a loud knocking at her door. She opened the window and shouted out. Nora shouted back and Alice leapt out of bed and bumped into Sarah on the stairs. The two of them raced next door and banged on the door. Jenny was first there,

'What's the matter?' said Jenny, wiping the sleep from her eyes.

Alice immediately feared the worst but said, trying to stay calm, 'Nora's just told me there's a fire at the fish and chip shop!'

Sarah stood behind her mother, in the gloom, and nodded.

'Neville's not home so I rushed round here.'

Frank was at Jenny's shoulder.

'I'll go for the fire engine,' he said.

'Dad's already gone,' said Nora, who'd followed Alice round.

'Good,' said Frank, 'then let's grab some buckets and get up there.'

Edward, Grandpa and Jack were not far behind and soon they were running up the street to where the fish and chip shop should be, Frank in the lead, Jenny hurrying as fast as she could, in the rear. Ahead of them they could see an eerie glow, a shimmering yellow against the blackness of the night.

'It doesn't look good,' yelled Frank, without breaking stride.

As soon as they got there, they could see it was already too late. The fire had ignited the fat and now fed on itself as it spread, leaping from fat pan to fat pan, producing more than enough heat to burn anything made of wood.

The windows had already exploded and against the undulating redness, yellow and white, members of the McDonald family were silhouetted, their jugs and buckets hanging impotently in their hands.

The fire was much too intense to approach.

The Lawley's, the Hudson's and the McDonald's merged together, all they could do was watch.

'There's nothing we can do,' said Frank to Jenny.

'I'm so sorry,' said Mrs McDonald.

In the rosy light tears reflected the glow as they trickled down Alice's cheeks, dripped from her chin and wet the white blouse she had hastily thrown on, creating darker patches, indistinguishable, in this light, from blood.

Alice said nothing, just stared ahead. Her daughter, Sarah, squeezed her arm.

Although on the brink of a revolution that would be driven by the internal combustion engine, the colliery fire engine consisted of a coal-fired, steam-driven pump that sat on a purpose-made horse drawn cart.

By the time it arrived, clattering up the street, the fire was leaping up the walls of the hut, fed by the paint, scorching the corrugated iron roof, heating it to branding temperature.

The best that could be done was to connect hoses to the water supply and prevent the fire spreading, dowsing the flames, darkening the night back to black, settling the hut into a smouldering pile.

There was nothing more that could be done that night.

Chapter 32

Alice's mind was in turmoil. She wanted to hope that Neville had got out and crawled away somewhere and that he'd turn up at home or at work.

She didn't care what the consequences would be for her; she just wanted him to appear. She wanted to tell Jenny everything, but she held back, she didn't know why, but she did.

Alice was a nervous wreck, but that was normal under the circumstances, and nobody suspected anything else.

'Neville hasn't come home,' she said, 'I've sent Sarah off to school but I'm worried.'

She was round at Jenny's and clearly hadn't had a wink of sleep.

'I'll look out for him at the pit,' said Frank.

'Do I need to tell the police?' asked Alice, panic in her voice.

'Has he ever stayed away before?' asked Jenny, trying to calm her.

Alice thought for a moment, she wanted to tell everything, but she wouldn't, not yet anyway.

'Once or twice when the drink was on him, but I don't know where he would stay. I don't want to contact the police if I don't have to, it would only make him angry.'

The anxiety was clear to see in Alice's face.

The Police were called in when the body was found.

A death like this was treated as suspicious and the body was identified as Neville's, a gruesome task that Alice had to undertake.

Neville was dead. Alice had seen his charred remains. It was all her fault. She sat in her kitchen with her head in her hands. Sarah came in and put her hand on her mother's shoulder,

'Oh, Ma,' she said.

Alice looked into her daughter's face, she could see traces of Neville's features looking back at her, accusing her. But there was something else, there was love and kindness and worry.

'Don't worry Sarah,' she said, 'I'll get us through this. You just hold on to me.'

Sarah's grip tightened and the tears flowed.

Alice gritted her teeth. Neville was dead, he was never coming back. No matter whose fault it was that was a fact. Her job now was to look after the living, to protect those she cared about, and there was no one she cared about more than Sarah. And, another thought, she must also protect herself, she didn't want to hang! But there was a weak link in her defences, and she must secure it, bind it to the cause of self-preservation and subterfuge. She ran to seek out Tony Sharpe.

He was as white as a sheet and trembling.

'I'm going to the police,' he said, 'I've got to… I can't believe that Neville's dead… did I kill him? Oh my God, Alice?'

Alice grabbed his arms.

'Listen!' she said, 'I don't know what happened. He was alright when I left him, everything was alright…'

'He was unconscious, he was bleeding, how can you say everthing was alright?'

'I mean it wasn't this bad, there was a way back, Neville was going to wake up, come home and…'

'And what?'

'And life would continue.'

Tony bowed his head, Alice shook him.

'Now, look at me,' she said, 'you believe me, don't you? I wouldn't set fire to my own shop on purpose. It was all a dreadful accident.'

Tony looked at her.

'I want to believe you,' he said, and then with growing conviction, 'I do believe you.'

'Good, I would never lie to you, but if the police get told the whole story they'll jump to conclusions won't they, they won't believe the truth, they won't call it an accident, they'll believe it's something else.'

Tony's eyes opened wide.

'Murder?' he said.

It was Alice's turn to shudder.

'So, we need to protect ourselves, do you hear?'

Tony heard alright. This was even worse than he'd thought. He needed guidance.

'Now, did anyone know you were going up to the fish and chip shop?'

Tony strained to think.

'No, I don't think so.'

'Have you talked to anyone since the fire?'

'I've taken time off work; told them I was ill. I just couldn't stand to see anybody.'

'Good,' said Alice, 'Now listen to me, you go back to work, and you say nothing, do you hear?'

Tony nodded.

'But how can I…?'

'All you have to do is nothing. We won't meet or talk, we don't want anyone to get suspicious. If we do see each other, it will just be like normal, nothing special. I won't say that you were at the fish and chip shop, I just won't say, do you understand?'

Tony nodded.

'So, you keep quiet, that's all… and Tony, I'm doing this for Sarah, can you imagine her life if we were accused…'

Tony had thought about no one but himself, and his guilt, and his anxiety, thinking of the effect on an innocent other gave him a focus and steadied his nerve a little more.

'I'll do it,' he said.

Tony was right, nobody had known that he was at the fish and chip shop that night, he had turned up, as agreed, well after closing time and it was dark and the streets had been empty.

If anyone had seen him and remembered it, they would come forward, but that was just a risk they would have to take.

The only reason Alice might have to mention him was to reveal that he had supplied the start-up loan. There was no reason to hide that, the police would probably find out anyway and if she didn't volunteer the information they might think it suspicious.

If they then spoke to Tony, he could confirm Alice's statement, and if he looked ill, then who wouldn't look ill if they'd just seen most of their hard earned savings go up in smoke.

That was all Tony needed to do, nothing more, nothing less.

Tony wasn't happy but then again how could he be. Neville was dead and he felt that he had been complicit in his death. But he was young, he believed Alice that it had all been a dreadful accident, nothing he did or said could bring Neville back, and he needed to carry on, didn't he? No point ruining more lives; his own, Alice's, Sarah's. He had to do what Alice told him, there really was no other way.

But still Tony wanted to tell the police, wanted to explain the whole thing, make it clear that it really was an accident, that neither he nor Alice knew the hut would burn down. After all the fire was against their best interests. The business was a source of income for both of them.

The truth, from Tony's perspective, was that this had all been the result of some kind of horrible misunderstanding.

Tony still didn't quite understand what or why, but in an instant the situation had ignited into violence, a thing that he would never have anticipated nor initiated.

Of course he felt guilty. He could hardly sleep at night and people were starting to ask him if he was alright, he was looking so haggard.

But Alice stayed resolute. If the police did not approach him then he should not approach them. It would only make the situation worse. It would start gossip and rumour, never mind what it might spark in the minds of the police themselves.

It was police officer Dobson who was given the job of interviewing Alice.

Well known about the village, he was generally well liked and trusted, though nobody wanted to find a policeman at their door.

Sitting on opposite sides of Alice's kitchen table, PC Dobson had his back to the fire. He was a large man and his black uniform, with its polished brass buttons and black hardwood truncheon dangling from his belt, gave him an air of authority. Taking off his helmet and placing it on the table beside him, he took out his notebook.

The fire glowed poppy red. Alice sat in silence, her head bowed.

'I'm sorry for your loss, Mrs Hudson.'

Alice nodded.

'But I'm sure you understand, in a case like this, there are questions that need to be asked.'

Alice lifted her head. Her eyes were almost empty. The whole of her life had been thrown into turmoil, she would lose her house, she had nowhere to go, other than protecting Sarah, nothing mattered any more, it couldn't get any worse.

'Ask away,' she said, gritting her teeth. She was determined to hold her nerve.

'When was the last time you saw your husband?'

'When he left in the morning.'

'You didn't see him after that?'

'No.'

'Where did he go?'

'To work, then back home, I don't know for sure, I guess he went to the pub.'

'Was that normal?'

Alice peered at him.

'Do I have to answer?'

'Your husband may have been murdered, Mrs Hudson.'

'Murdered! He is dead, is that not bad enough? Why would you say murdered.'

Her face went from numb to shock, her eyes opened wide, and tears poured out of them. PC Dobson waited for her to settle down.

'He was locked in,' he said, 'he had most probably crawled towards the door in the midst of the fire but couldn't get out. You must understand that we need to know how this all happened.'

Alice Hudson clenched her fists and hung on with a fragile grip to reality.

'My husband is dead, sir, and I have lost my business. I will also lose my home. I have a daughter and nowhere to go, so you go ahead, ask all the questions you want, and I'll do my best to answer them.'

The policeman swallowed hard, no matter the truth of Alice's predicament he had his job to do.

'I was asking about your husband's movements after work. You said he probably went to the pub, was that what he normally did?'

'When he had a bit of money in his pocket it wasn't unusual.'

'Did you know he was seen and that he was probably drunk when he left?'

'No!' said Alice, 'I didn't know that, why would I?'

'I have talked to a number of other people, Mrs Hudson, was there any reason that he would want to get drunk?'

'No reason I know of.'

'Was there any reason that you know of that your husband might be upset?'

'Not that I know of.'

'Was your husband a gambling man, Mrs Hudson?'

Alice sighed heavily.

'He liked a bet,' she said.

'Did he come home?'

'I don't know, I was at work in the fish and chip shop.'

'And when you locked up was everything left safe and sound?'

'It's my business, it is, it was, a wooden building. Fire is, was… my biggest concern, I always check carefully before I lock up.'

'So how do you think the fire started?'

'I don't know. The first I knew was when I was woken up by Nora McDonald. I couldn't believe it. I didn't want to go up there on my own, so I ran next door…'

'I've talked to the McDonalds and the Lawleys.'

'So, you know already. We went up, the place was ablaze, it was terrible!'

'Where did you think your husband was?'

Alice started to shake.

'I didn't know.'

'But you knew he wasn't home.'

'I knew he wasn't home when I got home, yes. I sat up, waiting for him for a bit, but I was tired, so I went to bed. I was trying to get to sleep when Nora came round.'

'What time did you expect him?'

'I didn't know. He should have been home. I was tired after working all day, I tried to sit and wait but I kept dozing off in the chair, so I went to bed.'

'Does he always come in at irregular hours?'

'Not always.'

'But sometimes.'

'Yes, sometimes.'

'Like when he has money in his pocket?'

Alice sat silent.

'Like when he has money in his pocket?' repeated the policeman.

'What do you mean?'

'I wonder if he left you enough money to keep house?'

'I have enough, and I have the fish and chip shop.'

'I wonder if he took that money off you?'

'No, he didn't do that.'

'I wonder if he beat you?'

Alice froze.

Who had he been talking to? What did he know?

'He hadn't come home by the time I was called to watch my business burn,' said Alice, 'he didn't come home afterwards. I didn't know where he was. I told Jenny next door I was worried. Jenny's husband, Frank, told the pit, we were hoping he'd just got drunk and slept it off somewhere and then gone straight into work.'

'I've talked to the pit. I know Frank Lawley was looking out for him.'

'I was waiting to find out, before going for help.'

'You mean before you called the police?'

'Yes.'

'But you didn't have to…'

'No.'

'Because his body was found first.'

Alice started to cry.

'Yes.'

'Were you surprised?'

Alice glared at him through her tears.

'What do you mean?'

'I mean you knew he was dead, didn't you?'

'No.'

'You must have sometimes thought that you'd be better off without him.'

'No, he was my husband.'

'A husband that treated you badly.'

'A husband that kept a roof over our heads.'

'Do you know what I think happened?'

'Nothing happened.'

'I think your husband came up to your fish and chip shop. I think you argued. I think you started a fire. I think you locked him in.'

'No, you're wrong.'

'How did he get in if you weren't there?'

'He has a key.'

PC Dobson knew a key had been found in the ashes.

'Why would he go there? Why would he lock himself in? Why would he start a fire?'

'I don't know, I don't know… I know he didn't like me having a business… I've lost my husband, I'm going to be evicted, why are you persecuting me?'

PC Dobson softened.

'Mrs Hudson, a burned body has been found in suspicious circumstances…'

'It's not a body, it's a person, it's Neville Hudson, father, husband, miner…'

'It's my job.'

'Your job to come into my kitchen and treat me like a criminal?'

Her grief was turning to anger, an anger that was foreign to her nature.

'You've got to admit it's not clear…'

'He's dead!'

'We need to decide whether his death was accidental…'

Alice's anger left her as quickly as it had come, and she sighed heavily.

'He's dead… and I have nowhere to go.'

PC Dobson closed his notebook.

'I'm sorry for your loss,' he said.

'You've got a strange way of showing it,' she said with resignation, 'Have I answered all your questions?'

'For now.'

'Well, you know where I am, for the next two weeks anyway.'

The policeman got up, put on his helmet, pulled down on his tunic, smoothing it around his girth.

'Would you mind leaving by the back door,' said Alice.

'Not at all,' said PC Dobson.

PC Dobson did eventually talk to Tony Sharpe, who freely admitted to being the source of the loan that launched Alice's business although he did not mention that Alice had already paid it back. Such a thing was so unusual that no one would even think to ask that, not even PC Dobson.

The policeman could see how ill Tony looked and commiserated with him on his loss.

'I know Mr Hudson's loss is by far the greater loss,' said Tony, 'but I've always wanted to be a businessman you see, in my own right, and the fish and chip shop seemed like a sound investment. It was a sound investment; it was making money.'

Although PC Dobson could see the pain in Tony's face, this wasn't an aspect of the case he was interested in, and he didn't want other people's matters to distract him from the main issue; was Neville Hudson's death a freak accident or not?

He would leave Tony to sort out the consequences of his loss for himself. He closed his notebook, thanked him for his time, and left.

News that it was Tony Sharpe who had loaned Alice the money to get her business off the ground leaked and spread, as did the fact that his money had been lost when the shed burned down.

'Oh,' said a woman after hearing that, 'of course, that's what they'll have been talking about! Gracious me,' she smiled to herself, 'I always knew it couldn't be anything else, Alice Hudson just isn't like that.'

Pleased with her discovery, she hurried home. She wanted to tell her husband. She was sure that he would be as pleased as she was because, with this new information, she could say to him with conviction,

'It must have been an accident, there was no other reason… oh, thank goodness!'

Chapter 33

Alice Hudson was in the coroner's court. Obviously uncomfortable she was nervously fidgeting, intertwining and freeing her fingers, laying her sweaty hands palm down on the polished oak desk in front of her and then repeating the cycle over and over and over.

When it came to her turn to speak, she answered in such a quiet, trembling voice that they needed to ask her several times to speak up so that everybody could hear her.

She was asked about Neville, what kind of man he was, and on pressing admitted that he could be violent when he had a drink inside him, but that he was not the only man with that weakness.

She had been brought up not to speak ill of the dead and now was not the time to start.

She was then asked to give her account of what happened on the evening of the fire.

Alice told her story over again. She had told and retold it so many times that it had almost become real, even to her. It was easier to lie, she thought, or at least not tell the whole truth, when you're doing it to protect someone you love and anyway, all she was really doing was stopping the police from getting the wrong end of the stick.

Statements were submitted from the MacDonald family and the Lawleys. A further statement was submitted on behalf of the colliery, written by Earnest Weightman, confirming that Alice had full permission to carry out her fish and chip business in the hut and that by the time the colliery fire engine arrived all that could be done was to first contain and then dampen down the fire. In a character statement Neville Hudson was said to be a solid and reliable worker. There was no evidence from any quarter of any reason; feud, argument, or otherwise that might lead to any suspicion of foul play. No reference or statement involving Tony Sharpe was made, why would there be?

After consideration of all the evidence the coroner decided that this had been a tragic and accidental death and that the death certificate could now be completed to reflect that.

After the funeral and the condolences came the eviction notice.

Alice had two weeks to move out.

It was the way of the world in the mining village. If there was no mine wage-earning worker in the house, then the house had to be vacated and transferred to another family who qualified. It was a stark reminder of what underpinned the village community: business, industry, and profit. There may have been sympathy, but there was no alternative to the rules.

Ernest Weightman brought the paperwork around personally.

'I'm sorry Alice,' he said, 'but you know the rules.'

'Yes, Mr Weightman, I know the rules, I always have.'

'Well Alice, if there's anything I can do to help you, if you need the loan of a horse and cart…'

'No, that's alright, Mr Weightman. I'm going to try and sell off my few things before I leave.'

'Well, I'll spread the word Alice,' he said, 'see if I can get you some takers.'

Ernest Weightman did as he promised, and a trickle of people trailed in and out of Alice's house, selecting what they wanted item by item; a set of pans here, a chair there, a cupboard… and paying the little that Alice was asking for them before they left.

Alice was at Jenny's back door.

Frank and Edward were out of the house, on shift deep underground, Jack and George were at school, hopefully learning something, Grandpa was out on his allotment, hopefully growing something.

Jenny was in the house on her own, making the most of the peace and busy preparing the evening meal, scraping potatoes and carrots, a pile of peas waiting to be taken from their pods.

'Can I come in?' asked Alice.

Jenny glanced up, 'You know you don't need to ask,' she said.

Alice sat down at the kitchen table, pulled the pile of pea pods and a bowl towards her and started in on them.

'Ta,' said Jenny.

'Jenny,' said Alice.

'Yes?'

'Jenny, I need your help.'

'I thought this might be more than a social call,' said Jenny.

'I get kicked out next week,' said Alice.

'I'm sorry Alice, there's no sympathy for those who's lost their man in this place.'

'Earnest Weightman came round,' said Alice, 'he's done his best, but he has to follow the rules.'

'Aye, it's the owners who set the rules. It's the same for all of us. We're all helpless. Some of these houses might be damp and draughty, but they aren't ours, they all belong to the company.'

'To be honest' said Alice, 'I need to leave here, there's too much gossip about. I need a fresh start.'

Jenny was surprised, she'd thought that Alice had come round to see if they could put her up for a while, while she found her feet. She'd already been thinking about how she might manage it. To leave immediately sounded too drastic.

'I'm sure there'd be somebody who'd put you and Sarah up for a bit,' she said, 'not permanent, but until you find your feet.'

'Thanks,' said Alice, intuitively understanding that Jenny most likely meant herself, 'but there's no one I'd want to ask. I just want to get away.'

The work continued as they talked, the piles of peelings grew, the peeled were put in water, pea pods separated from peas, a green mound growing in the bowl.

Jenny was puzzled. Alice had surely come round to ask something of her.

'So how can I help?' she said.

Alice stopped the de-podding, reached forward and gently took hold of Jenny's wrist. Then she looked Jenny in the eye,

'I want you to take Sarah,' she said.

'Oh, is that all,' said Jenny smiling, 'she's a good girl, I'd be happy to take her for a week or two. Frank won't mind.'

It would be another mouth to feed, another bed to find, but it was the least Jenny could do. Families were always doing this kind of thing for one another and Jenny recognised the situation Alice was in. She'd be happy to help out.

'No,' said Alice, not letting go of Jenny's wrist, 'you don't understand.'

'What do you mean?'

'I need a fresh start, Jenny, I don't know where I'll end up or how far away I'll be. I'm going to change my name, try and get a job in a shop or a hotel if I can, live in if possible. Start again, Jenny, that's what I want to do, before it's too late, before I'm too old,' she held Jenny's gaze, 'do you know what I mean?'

Jenny knew. She nodded.

'So, you know what I'm asking?'

Jenny stared and then nodded again.

'I'm asking you to take Sarah off me,' said Alice, 'you'd be a better ma than I could ever be, and I can't keep her, Jenny, I just can't. I can't make a new start if Sarah's with me,' Alice paused, 'it's his blood… don't you see, Jenny,' tears sprang into her eyes, 'I've tried to care for the lass as best as I can.'

'She's a good girl,' said Jenny quietly, 'a real credit to you.'

'But sometimes when she looks at me, I see him looking back, or some of the things she does, the way she moves, she's just like him.'

A tear overflowed and rolled down Alice's cheek. Jenny looked away. Tears were something she couldn't cope with, had never been able to.

'I feel so guilty,' said Alice, 'the way I've been.'

'You've always been a good mother,' said Jenny, 'you've nothing to feel guilty about in that regard.'

'I'm not so sure,' said Alice, 'it was a bad marriage, but there's no one to blame but myself.'

Jenny had witnessed the bruising that Alice had suffered, heard her repeated excuses, saw any feelings that she'd had for her husband drain away, to be replaced by a resigned fortitude.

And now, with her husband's death, from whatever cause, her eyes had been reopened. As she looked into Alice's face she could see the desperation, she could begin to understand that this tragedy was also an opportunity.

But Alice had a daughter.

Alice had responsibilities.

Jenny could never imagine walking away and leaving any of her children. They were what she lived for.

'It's not Sarah's fault, it's mine and I know you've lost bairns in the womb, Jenny,' said Alice, 'I know you've always wanted a daughter.'

Jenny could not deny the truth of either of these statements.

'And here's a chance for both of us,' said Alice, 'Sarah needs a mother, and I promise I'll not interfere. I won't be using my married name anymore. I'm going to wipe that slate clean. I'll not contact her. I'll just leave her here, knowing she'll have a better life with you than she could ever have with me. We'll not tell anyone it's permanent, Jenny, just let time solve the problem for us. People will just get used to Sarah being with you, they'll come to take it for granted. After a while you can tell them that I'm dead if you like. Please, Jenny, this is a chance for me, probably a last chance, please…'

Jenny was shocked. She sat in silence for a few moments just staring at Alice. How could a mother do this? How could any mother do this?

'I don't know,' she said, 'do you really mean it?'

'Yes, I do,' said Alice, 'it's my only hope.'

An uneasy silence descended. Alice returned to de-shelling the peas. When she'd finished, she got up to go.

'I'll talk to Frank,' said Jenny, 'I'm not promising anything, let's be clear about that, but I will talk to Frank.'

'That's all I can ask,' said Alice.

She turned to the back door and walked towards it, her feet scraping across the kitchen floor. She walked out into the backyard and closed the kitchen door behind her.

Left alone, Jenny carried on with her tasks, her mind in turmoil. What would she say to Frank? What did she want him to decide? She looked into the mirror that hung above the range.

'There's work to be done,' she said to her reflection.

'What!' said Frank.

Jenny had taken him out for a walk. He'd been immediately suspicious. Jenny had complimented him. His suspicions had increased.

'Come on, lass,' he'd said, 'spit it out.'

Hesitantly at first and then more fluently, Jenny told Frank about her conversation with Alice.

'I knew Neville,' he said, 'he was two different people. Below ground he was a fine worker, but we know there was trouble at home.'

'Maybe we should have done more,' said Jenny.

'Hmm,' said Frank, knowing that they had probably done all that they were able to, 'do you want to take her in?'

'I don't know,' said Jenny, 'I like Sarah, but to take her off her real mother, that's not a good thing to do.'

'What's the alternative?' said Frank, always practical.

Jenny hadn't thought about that, she'd only thought of the choice she had to make.

'What do you mean?' she said.

'If we don't take her, what happens to Sarah?'

'Well, maybe Alice will change her mind and take Sarah with her. But I'm not sure about that, she seems determined to get out on her own,' she thought for a moment, 'and even if she did change her mind, I don't know how it would go... it's a risk for both of them. I don't even know whether Sarah understands how her mother is feeling.'

'Best not to underestimate what kids know,' said Frank, 'however much her mother has tried to hide it from her.'

'I don't like to think about it,' said Jenny, 'it makes me feel like someone should have intervened, kids shouldn't be damaged, they should be protected.'

Frank smiled to himself, he was proud of the woman he'd married, she might show a tough exterior, but she had a heart of gold.

In their wanderings they'd reached a crossroads, forwards was the road out of the village, worn, pitted and muddy after rain, while on either side were smaller tracks leading away across the fields or down towards the beck.

They turned back.

Back towards home.

'Who else would take her?' Frank asked.

'Alice's got no family as far as I know,' said Jenny, 'I guess it would be somebody else in the village, if not it'd have to be the workhouse.'

The workhouse and associated children's home was a last resort for destitute families or orphaned children.

'And would either of those be better options?'

Jenny's pride ruled out the workhouse. As far as Sarah getting better care with any other family in the village Jenny could not bring herself to believe that. She liked Sarah, always had, she'd been the first person Alice had turned to, if anyone in the village was going to take on Sarah, it had to be her.

'Could we manage?' asked Frank.

'Yes, I think so. It'd be a bit of a stretch at first, but with both you and Edward bringing in a wage I think we could just about manage. As she gets older, she'll be able to help around the place more and more.'

'So, you've made up your mind,' he said.

He reached out his hand.

Jenny smiled as she took it.

'Now, Frank,' she said, 'you're not going soft on me, are you?'

Frank looked into her face; her eyes glistened back at him.

'I might be,' he said, 'I might be.'

The next day Jenny went over to see Alice. Sarah was at school and Alice was busy packing.

'I've talked to Frank,' she said.

Alice didn't look up.

'And?'

'Are you sure, Alice?'

'Aye, I'm sure.'

'Then we'll take her,' said Jenny.

Alice still didn't look up.

'I'll bring her over soon as she's back from school,' she said.

Jenny left her to it. Alice waited until she was sure that Jenny had gone and then slumped down onto one of the cases. She hid her face in her hands and sobbed.

Chapter 34

'While your Ma's away we'll look after you,' said Jenny.

Sarah said nothing.

Just stood there, wide-eyed.

'That'll be good, won't it?' said Alice, 'I'll bring the rest of your things over tomorrow and you can sleep here tonight, can't she Jenny?'

'Yes,' said Jenny, 'we've made you up a bed, you'll be sleeping here in the kitchen with Grandpa to start with. It's nice and warm in here and we'll sort out something better after that. I hope you don't mind his snoring.'

Sarah held on to her mother's hand tightly.

'Now, would you like something to eat? Frank and Edward will be home later, and Jack and George are outside in the back lane if you'd rather go with them. Jack's going to bring in some water.'

Sarah slowly let go of her mother.

'I'd like to go and find Jack and George if I may,' she said.

Jenny smiled at the exaggerated politeness. Sarah had been there many times before but always as a visitor or to sew with Jenny, this was like starting all over again.

'Of course, off you go.'

As if released from a tether Sarah ran out of the back door, her feet tripping lightly over the cobbled surface of the back yard.

'There we go,' said Alice.

'Aye, there we go,' said Jenny.

The two women, both strong in their own way, looked at each other and then simultaneously moved forward and hugged. They each had accumulated experience of the world and there were many unspoken words. When the moment had passed, Jenny said,

'I think I understand, Alice, and I wish you well, but I could never do what you're doing.'

'I know,' said Alice, 'and I can hardly believe it myself, but I'm driven to it Jenny. I'm not getting any younger and there's got to be a better life out there somewhere.'

'I hope so, for your sake. We'll take as good care of Sarah as we can.'

'I know,' said Alice.

The two women shook hands, as if cementing a deal, and then Alice left.

A few moments later, Jack, George and Sarah came tumbling in the back door. Jack was carrying a bucketful of water.

'Is Sarah really going to stay with us?' said George.

'Yes,' said his mother.

'Good,' said George, 'we could do with another woman in the house.'

Jenny burst out laughing. The rest joined in, but they weren't sure why.

'Out of the mouths of babes…,' said Jenny.

Sarah was at school when Alice popped in to see Jenny for the final time. She was carrying one carpet bag of belongings.

The kitchen was full of drying laundry and its musty smell.

'Not much to show is it,' said Alice, 'anything I couldn't sell I've left behind; I've no use for it. I've a bit of money in the bank from what I have sold and a few savings from the fish and chip shop.'

'There's been some good times, I'll miss you,' said Jenny

The two women looked at each other. It was a look that carried words; words of fellow-feeling, words of understanding, words of support and hope for the future.

Alice turned and walked away.

Jenny stared at her retreating back.

It did not occur to either Alice or Jenny to speak to Sarah about where she would rather be, or her thoughts on the matter. She was the subject of a transaction, and the two women dealt with it as if it were a piece of furniture that might be leaving one household and shifting to another.

Or maybe that is too unkind, maybe they didn't talk to Sarah because each woman intuitively knew, or believed that they knew, that Sarah was too young to fully understand the situation in all its complexity.

How could she?

Her mother did love her but could not bear to take her along as she left to try and start a new life. It was not Sarah's fault that she bore some resemblance to her father both in looks and mannerisms. It was not her fault that she was a constant reminder to her mother of her suppressed feelings of guilt and complicity.

Alice kept her secrets but every time she looked at Sarah, or Sarah looked at her, she had the fear that Sarah saw through her, saw the truth, and blamed her for her father's death.

And so, the transaction was completed.

A small human being had been identified, packaged up and transferred from the responsibility of one party to the responsibility of another. No money had changed hands; no paper had been signed.

Most of the village just nodded as the news spread, there were more serious and controversial things than this to think about in a community that lived with the daily fear of life and death underground.

It was a small matter, a minor thing, that changed the lives of several human beings forever.

Life had to go on and the ripples caused by Neville's death had to be smoothed over, his absence corrected for, and its impact managed.

The colliery cleared away the ash and charred remains of the shed and put them, with the other discarded materials from the workings, on the pit heap.

One of the significant consequences of Neville's death was that Edward was moved into the same team as Frank to take Neville's place. Someone had to do it, and the underground supervisor judged Edward as good a candidate as any. It was a promotion and came with an increase in pay.

This made Jenny's life easier in a practical sense, knowing that they had to get ready at the same time, cleaning and feeding them when they came home, and a little extra money was always welcome, especially as there was now an extra mouth to feed.

But being in the same team also meant that they would always be in the same part of the pit workings and, if anything did go wrong then both of them would be involved.

Jenny tried not to think about this, but the newspapers were always reporting accidents in the pits and Jenny lived with a constant and helpless worry: she worried when she saw them off, she was thankful when they came back. If she could have taken their place underground, she would have willing done so, but that was not the way of things.

Chapter 35

It was 10 months after Edward was born that Jenny first miscarried. A sudden onset of searing pain. A clutch at her stomach. Alone in the kitchen she collapsed onto the floor. A bloody mess and later, little sympathy.

'These things happen, pet, no accounting for it,' said Mrs Tindale, already a mother of two herself at this stage, her twins waiting for her in the future, 'You just carry on, try not to think about it, and maybe try again in a bit, eh, love, when you're feeling up to it like.'

Soon after it had happened, Jenny and Frank had slipped out into the darkness late one night. They took the remains, wrapped in a dark-stained sheet, and found a quiet spot under a tree. Here Frank took off his cap, dug a hole deep enough to be beyond the risk of disturbance and buried them. Then, with his cap clutched to his chest, he stood back and said a few words,

'I'm sorry we never met you properly, but I wish your spirit well and… we want you to know… that even if you were only so small, you were loved.'

'Yes,' said Jenny, 'I've always wanted a daughter.'

Frank put his cap back on.

'Do you want me to mark the spot?' he said.

'No,' said Jenny, wiping her cheeks dry, 'we'll know where it is, and that's enough.'

Frank took Jenny's hand, and Jenny gripped it hard, it was a rare show of outward affection, and they let each other go as soon as they came back within sight of their street.

Jenny miscarried again after Jack was born but was too young to know what was happening. Edward kept him away and simply told that him that his mother 'had had a bad turn' but she would be alright. That was all Edward knew, and all he'd been told.

Another hole was dug close to the same tree as the first. The same words were spoken. The same hands were held.

These things happened, there was nothing to be done about it, better to be thankful for what you'd got... and keep on going. You could look back over your shoulder if you wanted to but not stop, you had to remember that there was only one direction you were allowed to move in, and that was forward.

In the front of the family Bible Jenny added the names of her miscarriages; May Lawley and June Lawley after the months that they were due to be born.

Now Jenny had inherited a daughter into her well-managed household.

The proggy mats that she'd made early in her marriage still lay on the floor and were both colourful and warm underfoot. Any surface in either of the downstairs rooms was regularly cleaned and dusted. The kitchen range was black leaded once a week to avoid corrosion and the few brasses that had been collected gleamed in the firelight from their regular polishing.

All this was in sharp contrast to the mud and dirt that relentlessly found its way onto the doorstep, the smoke and particles of coal dust that blew over from the mine workings when the wind was in the wrong direction.

Jenny was clear, if you had any dirt on you, you came in the back door. The front door led immediately into the parlour, a haven of relative cleanliness, and the front doorstep was painted white and scrubbed clean.

On entering the back door you took off your boots, any outer dirty clothes were thrown into the wash basket or hung up and, if necessary, you had a wash. No matter how tired or hungry you were, no one was going to sit and eat with dirty faces or hands at Jenny's kitchen table.

Frank, Edward, Jack and Grandpa all went along with it. It was only George who occasionally tried to grasp a piece of bread from the table behind his mother's back and with still dirty hands.

Her physical retribution was instant but not delivered with any force. It always seemed to be softer treatment than Jack had got at that age and he noticed this,

'Why's Ma so soft on George?' he asked his father when they were out on an evening walk.

His father laughed.

'Soft,' he said, 'he seems to get his fair share of clippings as far as I can see.'

But Jack wouldn't let it pass.

'You know what I mean,' he said.

His father walked in silence for a while and then he said.

'Truth of it is son, your mother never found having children easy and George is her last. I think she might take consideration of that in his regard.'

Jack took this in.

Even though he'd pushed, it was unusual for his father to share such confidences. He was starting to talk to him not as a child, but closer to an adult.

The significance of this hit him more than the information that his father had chosen to share. He was a man of few words but what he said was well considered.

'Yes, I see,' said Jack, 'thanks Da.'

And then they walked home in silence, the setting sun turning the sky red at their backs.

Some months later Tony Sharpe resigned from his job at the Co-op and left the area.

He took with him what savings he had, bolstered by Alice's fastidious repayments. He'd found that he couldn't stand to stay in the area, there were too many daily reminders, and he felt both guilty and apprehensive that there would come a moment when he would say something he shouldn't and old wounds would be reopened. He was not a good liar and he did not harbour secrets well.

No one was surprised. Ever since the fire he'd not been the same man. He'd lost some of his spark. He now went through the motions of ordering and selling and explaining the quality of the goods, but he did it without the same lightness of step or the same glint in his eye. The general feeling was that it was probably for the best that he move on.

One lady said, 'It's a shame, I always liked him, never anything other than polite to me.'

When she went home, she shared the same thought with her husband.

Sarah had learnt to wrap herself in insensitivity as a means of self-preservation. If anyone had asked her how she was feeling she wouldn't have been able to say. She missed her father, of course she did, or she missed the father that was quiet and kind. She didn't miss the one that was loud and aggressive and unpredictable.

She chose to believe that her mother would return, but to believe it in the same way she used to believe her father when he said that he was 'done with the drinking'. She would occasionally ask Jenny if her mother was coming to see her and Jenny would put her arm around her and say that she was sure she'd come when she could and that she was probably doing her best to get settled somewhere at the moment.

Jenny was surprised that there were so few tears, but she put it down to Sarah having a 'strong personality'. She didn't want to lie to the girl but thought the truth was too raw to share and hoped that as she settled into the Lawley home she would miss her mother less and whatever grief she was secretly harbouring for her father would fade.

If she just let it, then she believed that time would be their ally and Sarah would settle into new routines. Jenney was a believer in the benefit of routines, not only that but a growing girl like Sarah might progressively lighten her load.

Jack walked Sarah to school, looked after her in the playground and walked her home at the end of the school day.

I say, 'walked her', Sarah was so excited to have Jack all to herself that she would skip, run, and talk non-stop, 'Did you see that boy today, he was wearing odd socks, one black and one blue, just like a bruise, ha, ha, that's funny isn't it? I mean why would he wear different coloured socks?'

'Maybe that's all he had.'

'Oh, I didn't think about that, that's not funny at all is it? That's quite sad, oh, I shouldn't have laughed, oh, Jack, I'm sorry, it was thoughtless of me, but did you see what that girl had in her hair, flowers! I mean, coming to school with flowers in your hair, no wonder the teachers made her take them out, if they hadn't of done we'd all be coming to school with flowers in our hair, wouldn't we?'

'I wouldn't.'

'Ha, ha, Oh Jack, you're so funny, the idea of you with flowers in your hair ha,ha...'

And so on... Jack listened patiently, answered monosyllabically if he could get away with it, succinctly if he couldn't.

Jenny was pleased they got on so well. Jack thought Sarah was a lot more trouble than George who walked to and from school with his own friends and could look after himself in the playground.

But these moments were important to Sarah, short spaces of time when she could just relax and be herself.

When she was in school, she understood the rules of discipline, the rules she was required to follow to receive the learning that was on offer, through repetition, through committing to memory, through doing what you were told when and how you were told to do it.

She understood that the teachers, Mr and Mrs Hughes, knew more than she did and it was better for her to listen and obey than to question.

It was simply an extension of what she had learned when she was living with her father, which had been like living with two different people. In that environment she had learned that, to minimize the risk of trouble, it was better for her to shut her ears to her parents' arguing and pretend that she did not know about her father's aggression.

Over time she had developed her own rules; stay quiet, do not answer back, do what you're asked, pretend to be asleep. Adherence to these rules had served her well, so she carried them with her into the Lawley home where she was quiet, but still attentive and willing to help.

It was only when she was with Jack that she felt safe enough to relax and free to be herself, her true self, the self she kept in a bottle somewhere inside her, somewhere close to her heart.

'We'll put some tatties on to boil,' said Jenny, 'and have them with the ham shank I boiled yesterday. I made some pease pudding as well so that will do. There's plenty of bread and butter isn't there?'

Sarah confirmed there was and set about peeling the potatoes.

With Sarah joining the family there were some rearrangements to be made. The house had two rooms downstairs and two smaller rooms upstairs. After a couple of days sleeping in the kitchen with Grandpa's snoring, Alice was moved upstairs into the smaller room, the boys sharing the larger one.

'Why does she get her own room?' said George grumpily.

'Because she's a girl,' said Edward, who'd been moved out of the smaller room and now had to look forward to sharing with his two brothers.

'Then I want to be a girl,' said George.

'No, you don't, now shut up and go to sleep,' said Jack.

Some people, even some of the miner's wives, felt that formal education was unnecessary for girls. But times were changing, and, like Alice, Jenny wanted Sarah to have every opportunity to learn what she could. She still felt it was important to train Sarah in how to run a household, of course, in readiness for marriage, but she thought that there was nothing wrong with a bit of book learning at the same time.

Jenny felt her own lack of education and she didn't want Sarah to miss out on the opportunities that she had never had.

Sarah loved school and was now always dressed in a clean white cotton smock that covered her from neck to ankle. Although now in Wilkinson Hughes' class she had learned how to knit in the infant's department, guided by Enid Hughes, which had been good preparation for learning to sew with Jenny, and was proud that she had nearly always been allowed to use the pink wool because her hands were clean.

Mrs Hughes encouraged hygiene in her young charges, something that was difficult to maintain when living in a colliery village that had no running water and where it was the working men who got priority use of any hot water that was going.

Sarah did miss her mother, of course she did, but she tried not to show it. It was only on her birthday that she could not hide her sadness. Her mother used to always make her a cake and, as she grew older, she used to help. Sarah used to love using her finger to wipe off the last of the mix from the bowl and lick it clean, the sweet taste and the creamy texture was amazing. On her second birthday with the Lawleys, she told Jenny about this.

'Then we must make you a cake,' said Jenny.

'Can I help?' said Sarah.

'Oh, you can do more than help, you can show me how your mother used to make it, and we'll try and do it the same way.'

Sarah searched her memory, and together they made up a cake mix. When it had been transferred to the tin, Sarah looked at the mixing bowl, there were remnants of the mix left all around its surface.

'What's the matter?' said Jenny.

'Ma,' said Sarah, 'would you mind if I taste the mix?'

Jenny smiled.

'You go ahead,' she said.

Sarah leant forward, stretched out a finger, and ran it around the bowl, the leftover mix built up in a yellowy hump. Then she lifted her finger to her mouth and licked it clean, closing her eyes with the pleasure of it.

'Yum,' she said, and went back for more.

When Sarah thought about her mother, she thought about her being somewhere nice, somewhere clean and without the blackness of coaldust everywhere. She dreamt that her mother was happy and that she thought about Sarah a lot but was just too busy to write or to visit.

'That doesn't mean she doesn't care,' she thought to herself, 'you can think about somebody all the time even if you don't see them.'

She hoped that her mother would come back but she was settled now and wasn't sure she would want to leave, even if it was her mother who came to take her away.

No, when she came to consider it, this was the best that it could be for everybody: her mother was happy, or she hoped that she was, and Sarah was settled-in with the Lawleys.

They fed her, they clothed her, and it was fun, most of the time, to think that she had brothers. Sometimes they were funny, and none of them were unkind.

Edward was like an uncle he was so old; he did everything his father did; worked down the mine, got covered in its blackness, drank at the pub and spoke with a man's voice, deep and resonant. It would be easy to be scared of Edward, he was so tall, but because of his smile Sarah knew that he was alright, and he never shouted at her.

Jack was only a little older than she was, but she looked up to him. He may not know it, but he was her protector, he was the one she would run to if she was in danger, and he would help her, she was sure that he would.

George was another kettle of fish. He was full of mischief and clever enough to get away with most of his shenanigans. She felt protective towards him, and when Jack left school, she would be the one to keep an eye on him… whether he liked it or not.

She liked to go and see Grandpa on his allotment and help him with some of the sowing and planting or weeding and picking. She was a bit scared of the hens, their beaks looked so sharp, and their eyes were scary, but she would feed them if asked and, if really pressed, help clean out their poop from the hen house.

'It's good fertiliser,' said Grandpa.

'It's smelly,' said Sarah.

'That's because it's good, everything that's good has a smell to it on an allotment.'

She didn't like to see Grandpa break their necks though, when their time was up, and they were destined for the pot.

'Mustn't waste anything,' said Grandpa.

And she had to admit that they tasted good.

Frank was clearly the father of the house though he wore that mantle lightly. Sarah did not have a good track record with fathers so she tended to keep her distance.

She was polite of course and, if Frank did talk to her, she thought carefully about her answer before speaking. Frank thought that Sarah seemed timid and therefore tended to leave her alone, she'd been through a lot and he thought that Jenny was better suited to looking after her. So, a kind of comfortable silence built up between them, and they kept themselves to themselves.

Jenny was the mainspring, Sarah had already gravitated to Jenny because of her interest in sewing. With a willing teacher like Jenny, she had learnt quickly and, as she had gained more confidence, had become increasingly skilled.

Jenny would complement her on the neatness of her stitches and her attention to detail. It was the first time that Sarah could remember ever being complemented over anything, and she responded to it by trying harder and making sure she never let Jenny down.

This strong sentiment extended throughout her whole attitude towards Jenny, who was like a second mother to Sarah and Sarah not only needed this but also naturally and instinctively liked Jenny.

She felt that she could say anything to Jenny and that Jenny would take it seriously, not that they didn't have fun together, but when it came to discussing life's problems, and a growing girl's problems, then she felt that Jenny was there for her.

Jenny, for her part, felt that, with Sarah, she had been gifted a chance, although it was a chance that she would not have wished for, the causes were not those that she would have wanted for either Alice or Sarah.

She felt protective towards Sarah and could not understand how her mother could ever have considered leaving her behind. But people were different and Jenny was determined to help Sarah as much as she could.

There was a lot for a growing girl to learn, not just schoolwork but the equally important skills needed to look after a household; how to manage money, what chores needed doing, how often and what kind of routine could ease the burden. Jenny would try and teach Sarah all these things, she was a bright child and deserved a decent future.

Chapter 36

'Grandpa keeps mentioning his time in the army, Ma. Was he away a lot?' asked Sarah one day.

Sarah had come to call Jenny "Ma" and Jenny did not discourage it.

'He was away for long periods,' said Jenny, remembering a childhood that was largely without her father present, 'and then he would come back to visit us. He would be wearing his uniform. I remember that because it made him stand out so much. And he would always fold his clothes and polish his shoes. He'd polish them so bright you could see your face in them.'

She reflected for a moment, they were outside in the yard, Jenny was at work on the laundry, wielding the posser.

'It must have been hard for mother, though she never let on. He used to make her laugh, that's what I remember. She didn't laugh that much normally, but when father was home, she seemed to light up. I guess they loved each other but they never made a fuss. Well, you don't do you? It's not anybody else's business. Anyway, father finally came home permanently, I'd met Frank by then and I moved out shortly after.'

Jenny was talking in time to her possing and was happy to share memories that she had not revisited for some time. In Sarah she had a listening ear.

'I don't have any brothers or sisters,' she continued, 'there was a boy born before me, but he died, and they never really talked about it.'

Swoosh, swoosh went the posser, soapy warm water foaming over the clothes, the water already a dark grey.

'When mother died, father was on his own. He looked helpless. We'd moved here, had a boy then, and we offered him a bed. He sold up what little he had and gave us part of the proceeds. He's been here ever since. He's no trouble really, likes to tell his stories, does his allotment and puts a fair amount of fresh food in our cupboard; potatoes, greens, that sort of thing, and his few chickens, the eggs are always handy. He's well known in the village and likes to talk to the farmers about how best to grow things. He does a few hours labouring for Mr Moore, so one way or another he pays his way.'

The posser rose and fell, squished and swashed.

'Mind, I think he does the labouring so he can keep well in with the farmer as much as anything, cadge a free cartload of manure once in a while, or the loan of a cart. He keeps clear of growing leeks though,' she laughed, 'he knows how competitive that can get and he's keen not to upset anybody. He says he's seen enough upset for one lifetime, what with his time in South Africa fighting the Boer's and all, and now all he wants is peace, quiet, his pipe and something to occupy his body and mind.'

The squishing slowed.

'I know it's another man to look after, but I like having him around. I feel like I've got to know him better now. I don't call him father anymore, I call him Grandpa, just like the boys do. He doesn't seem to mind. You can see he's getting older, but I think he'll do for a while yet.'

Jenny smiled.

'Do you love him?' asked Sarah, taking Jenny by surprise.

She stopped her possing.

'I've never thought about it,' she said, 'he's my father so I suppose I do. He makes me laugh sometimes and although his tobacco is smelly, he's not much bother, but do I love him?' she paused, 'yes I suppose I do.'

'I don't know if I loved my father,' said Sarah, 'I loved the man who taught me how to sing and the man who I can remember talking to me, playing and swinging me round, but I didn't love the other man.'

Jenny dropped her head, could she have done anything more, anything sooner?

'If I were you, I would try and remember the good bits,' she said, 'I'm sure your father loved you, Sarah, so those are the bits that matter the most, aren't they?'

Sarah nodded her head slowly.

'Anyway, you're part of this family as well now, and you and I get along just fine. We'll sort things out, don't you worry.'

'Thank you, Mrs Lawley,' said Sarah.

'Now then, don't you go all polite and shy on me! I know you, Sarah, we're friends already, aren't we? We're partners you and I, and you're going to be a big help to me. There's plenty work to do and these men we're looking after are pretty useless at most things that matter.'

Now it was Sarah's turn to smile. She liked the idea of having people to look after.

It was September and the opportunity for picking blackberries had come round again.

Jenny gave Jack a galvanised metal bucket and sent him and George off with the instructions to 'not pick any red or green ones', and to 'look for those that are shiny black and ready to pop', as well as to 'not eat too many, they'll make you sick', and finally to 'watch out for the thorns'.

Jack knew that for some reason the best blackberries grew on the scorched banks alongside the railway tracks and made straight for a spot where the brambles were thickest, and he'd had success the year before.

They weren't the only people being sent out with buckets though, so they tried to avoid being spotted by following a circuitous route and keeping out of sight.

As they approached the banking, they could immediately see that their luck was in, the berries were black, plump and untouched. Trying to avoid the sharp thorns as much as possible they started to pick, their white hands darting in and out, battling to stop their coats and trousers from becoming entangled.

George could not prevent a number of blackberries from ending up in his mouth.

'You'll give yourself stomach-ache,' said Jack.

George pretended not to hear.

'Who's that?' he said.

'Who's what?'

'Look, there…'

Sarah came up to them. She was carrying a bucket.

'Were you following us?' said Jack.

'Perhaps,' said Sarah.

'We didn't see you.'

'I know, I was careful.'

'This is our patch,' said George.

'There seems to be plenty,' said Sarah, 'I can help.'

'Alright, but watch out for the thorns,' said Jack.

George hmphed.

Once the easy ones were in the bucket they had to increasingly push into the bush and in amongst the prickles to get at the rest, the more difficult they were to get to the bigger and juicier the berries looked. Sarah started to get her smock caught and squealed when her hands were scratched. George fared little better.

'Alright,' said Jack, 'no point everybody getting scratched, find me a stick George and I'll go in and pass the blackberries back.'

Taking his handkerchief and George's he wrapped them around his hands and, with the aid of the stick moved slowly and carefully into the brambles, picking handfuls and passing them back.

'One handful for George and then one for you, Sarah,' he said.

Operating with this kind of 'chain gang', George increasingly following his brother so as to stay within reach, they picked for an hour and then reckoned they had picked enough and walked home together, entering the kitchen with their buckets, flushed with success

Jenny welcomed them back, seemed pleased at the quantity in the buckets and embarked straight away on the task of turning this free foraged harvest into jam.

Soon the fruit was rinsed and mixed with some apples that had been peeled and sliced. Jenny weighed the fruit, measured out the appropriate amount of sugar and all was added to the jam pan with some water. Jenny then asked Sarah to stir the whole thing with a wooden spoon as it simmered its way towards the setting point.

'It'll not set without the apples,' said Jenny, 'it's a bit of an art to get the setting point right, don't want runny jam and don't want jam you have to slice either.'

Jenny tested several times for the set point and when she was satisfied the jam was put into jars, that had been previously sterilised with boiling water and then lined up on the kitchen table to cool.

Jack and George looked at the number of jars appreciatively,

'That was a good haul.' said Jack.

'Hard work,' said George, 'look at these scratches.'

'The war wounds of blackberry picking, and you didn't even go into the thick of it.'

'I would have…'

'I did help,' said Sarah.

Jenny broke in before an argument could start about who had the most scratches, or who had picked the most or who had helped the most. The only thing they could easily agree on was who had eaten the most. George looked sheepish.

'I was testing them,' he said.

'We should leave it to stand really, but I think we'll try some of this tonight,' said Jenny, 'on fresh bread and butter. That will be another test.'

The two boys' mouths began to water. Sarah smiled.

'And we'll see what Dad, Grandpa and Edward think of it,' she continued, 'if its good enough we might give a jar to Mrs Moore, might even see if I can sell a few.'

'Can we try it now?' said George, 'after all our hard work.'

'After all your hard work…hmm, there is a bit left over so you could try it I suppose.'

'Yes please,' said three voices together.

Jack sliced the bread, George brought the butter, Sarah made tea and Jenny shared out the jam scrapings.

They sat silently around the kitchen table savouring the sweet, sharp taste of the jam; George was sure it was the best jam he'd ever tasted, even though it was so fresh.

'Teamwork,' he said, 'that's what this is, thanks to you all for helping me.'

They all laughed, even Jenny, and Jack cuffed George playfully around the ear. He didn't seem to mind and asked if there was any more of his jam leftover. There wasn't.

A life unfolds in chapters, much like a book, but much less tidily.

As Jack got older and more confident in his reading, Wilkinson Hughes increased the level of challenge he set before him. And now he was reaching school leaving age.

Taking him by the shoulder at the end of one school day he led him once more to the limited school library; six long shelves full of books, kept locked behind wood and glass doors, a revered yet eclectic mixture, some of which had been philanthropically donated by the families of the colliery owners, others, like the "Boy's Own Annuals" that were 2 or 3 years out of date, given as they were no longer wanted. But they were like gold dust to enquiring minds that had never held a book before. Jack had read through most of what the shelves held, some twice.

'Look here,' said the teacher, opening the cabinet.

Wilkinson Hughes pointed to a set of five large volumes on the bottom shelf, they looked heavy. On the spine of each was stamped, in gold lettering, "Johnson's Dictionary". He leant in and hefted down the first volume,

'Just had these donated,' he said, 'knowledge is a weighty thing,' and he laid the volume down on a desk and opened it to the title page.

"'A Dictionary of the English language'" he read aloud, 'printed in 1818, almost 100 years ago, and crammed full of wisdom,' he smoothed the page reverentially, 'This is a place to turn to if you're at a loss for the meaning of a word, or in search of inspiration. It has its critics and, I dare say, is not without its defects, but what a wonderful work it is, Jack. I've always wanted a set for the school and now we have one. I imagine that taken together these five volumes contain a rich picture of our language; ordered, systematised, explained, correctly spelled and defined.'

Wilkinson Hughes leafed through the pages until he reached a second title page, "The History of the English Language, by Dr Johnson".

'It would pay you, Jack, to read these pages. It is a treatise on how our language developed, where it came from, its origins in the Greek, the Roman, the Angle and the Saxon, how it came to be the language that we now learn from our cradle. It has its own life, Jack, like a living thing, was birthed, has grown and developed, has reached a fleeting kind of maturity, although we still have many regional dialects and accents, and it forever continues to evolve.'

'But, sir, our words don't change,' said Jack, 'you teach them to us, we write them down, we try to remember them. They don't change from day to day.'

'Perhaps not from day to day,' said the teacher, doing Jack the courtesy of taking his point seriously, 'A potato is a potato from one year to the next, but what of "nowt"? Has that not won out over "nothing" in our local talk, or would those in London know what a "proggy mat" was, or a "stotty"? We all use the same 26 letters, Jack, but look at the multitude of uses we put them to.'

Jack listened.

'The point is, Jack, that very few things are as fixed and unchanging as we might think they are, things change, the earth moves under our feet, and one of those slowly moving tectonic plates is language.'

Wilkinson Hughes smiled.

'Enough philosophising I think, I just wanted to show you these volumes and invite you to dip into them whenever you like.'

'Thank you, sir,' said Jack, conscious that he had been granted a privilege.

'Here I'll show you how. This first volume covers A to C, let's look up "Coal".'

Jack peered over the teacher's shoulder as he turned the pages.

'See at the top of the columns it gives you the first three letters of words. So, what are we looking for?'

Jack thought for a moment.

'If we're looking for coal, sir, I suppose we're looking for the first three letters,' he concentrated, 'C then O then A.'

'Very good,' said the teacher continuing to leaf through the pages, 'CAL... CER... CLA... we're getting closer, ah, here we are, COA. Now let's look down through the columns,' Mr Wilkinson laid his finger on the page and moved it down the columns; '"Coach"... oh no, we've still a little way to go,' he turned another page, 'now, let me see, "Coagulator"... ah, here we are, "Coal", can you see?'

Jack peered in to look more closely.

'Yes, sir, there's a lot written.'

'Hmm, can you see in brackets it compares the word to the Saxon "col", the German "kol", the Dutch "kole", the Danish "kul". Such a simple word, such shared roots. And see? Here is a description, here is an expression "to call over the coals". So, you see, Jack, these volumes contain a wealth of knowledge, too much for one mind to hold, that's why it's written down for people to refer to.'

A while later, Jack took the opportunity of referring to "Johnson's Dictionary". He lifted down Volume 2 with difficulty as it was so heavy. He laid it down and looked up the word "Fart". Once he'd found it, he read:

"Fart (a Saxon word), A wind from behind

Love is the fart
Of every heart
It pains a man when 'tis kept close
And others doth offend, when 'tis let loose
(A verse by Suckling)

To Fart (verb) To break wind behind

As when we a gun discharge
Although the bore be ne'er so large
Before the flame from muzzle burst
Just at the breech it flashes first
So from my lord his passion broke
He farted first, and then he spoke.
(A verse by Swift)"

Jack burst out laughing. He hadn't realised that even up to his last day at school, gaining knowledge could be fun!

He wanted to keep reading; he wanted to keep learning and didn't see any reason why he couldn't. He had only a few books of his own, but when he started earning he would buy some more.

Peter had just left school and joined the university of life full time on the family farm. It was a university he was familiar with, having been born into it and had naturally absorbed its highs and lows, it's quirks and whims.

And now he was worthy of a salary!

He and his father were sitting at the kitchen table. His father scratched his head,

'Well,' he said, 'if we say you don't pay anything for your board and lodging, then I think 7 shillings a week should do it.'

Peter clasped his hands under the table, dug his nails into the flesh trying to hide his emotions, trying not to yell out in glee.

'So, it'll need to cover you for everything else,' continued his father, 'you'll clothe yourself from now on, anything outside of your basic board and lodging'll be down to you. I'll pay you a shilling a day the first week and then weekly at 7 shillings with everyone else on a Sunday.'

Peter knew he had to say something. He said the first thing that came into his head,

'Will me Ma still do me washing?'

His father thought about it.

'That's for you and her to sort out,' he said, realising that to speak for his wife at this juncture was a risk not worth taking.

'You start properly tomorrow, 5:30 am, do a check round and report to me and the Foreman at 6:30 over breakfast, we'll work out the day's work for the men and the horses then.'

'Fine, Dad, and thanks.'

The father raised his eyebrows.

'Careful what you thank me for,' he said, 'you'll be earning your money, that's for sure.'

He stretched out his hand, Peter took it, each had a firm grip, it was like a ceremony; father to son, son to father, man to man.

'I'll go and tell Jack,' he said, 'it'll be his turn next.'

Chapter 37

'They call it "the pit" for a reason, son. It's a bloody deep black hole that they drop you into, and sometimes it's a trap, full of shadows, superstitions and ghosts. Welcome aboard, Jack.'

And now it's time to go underground.

We've waited until it is Jack's time. Frank and Edward and all the other underground workers have been doing it for their own personal amounts of time, as part of their own individual journey. But we have stood back, we have not concerned ourselves with this unseen world. They have left our field of view for a time and then they have re-emerged, tired, hungry and in need of a wash.

They have not talked of their work to those who do not work underground, knowing that they would not understand, that they could not understand, because the world underground is so different that it cannot be explained to those who have not experienced it..

All we've encountered so far is the little bit of the underground that the miners have brought back into the Sun on their clothes and on their skin, all of them keen to wash it away.

How do you describe the smell of freshly mown grass, what words do you use? How do you tell of the feeling you get when you stroke the back of a horse? What do you say to fully describe the taste of milk? Only to those who share the same frame of reference do your words conjure any meaning.

There are others that we will follow down into the earth, but first we must go down with Jack and try to experience it as it might have been experienced then, by a boy, on his first shift.

And so we start on an impossible journey, using words in the best way that we can, to try and join Jack on this auspicious day.

It is dark. It is cold. Outside, the caller has been walking slowly from one house to the other, freely using his wooden hammer to knock on doors, giving out his loud, repeated call to those on the 6 o'clock shift. It sounds like some kind of Gregorian chant rising as it progresses along the street to their door, and then past, the sound receding.

But Jack is still cocooned in his bedsheets, half asleep, wedged in, next to his younger brother George. He is just old enough to start work and his school days are now behind him. As he comes to he feels a mixture of fear and excitement, he is about to cross a line, away from childhood and into the unknown.

His mother has been up for over an hour. She shakes him by the shoulder, trying not to wake his younger brother,

'Get up, get up, get up now, Jack,' she whispers.

Slowly he unravels and washes in the warm water his mother has provided, and dresses in the clothes that she has laid out.

Downstairs his brother and father are already at the table eating their breakfast,

'Don't eat too much, Jack,' says his father, 'its not good to go down on too full a stomach.'

His brother Edward makes pretend retching noises but is silenced by a look from his mother.

Jack is fidgeting.

'You don't have to be so excited,' says Edward, smiling, 'I remember my first day and I can tell you there'll be plenty of new things in store for you underground.'

Frank hushes him.

'When you're down the pit this morning,' he says, 'make sure to follow instructions, stick to what you're told and the patch you're taken to work at. Don't wander off and don't do anything you're not asked to do. If you don't know something, then ask the nearest person for help. They'll likely make fun of you, but don't let that stop you, they will help in the end.'

'You're likely to get plenty of ribbing,' says Edward, 'I remember it well, don't let it vex you, just take it, and you'll soon settle in.'

'You'll be starting as a Trapper, opening and closing your doors as the Drivers come to and fro with the tubs of coal. Stick to your doors, listen to the shouts, it's an important job as the doors control the circulation of fresh air, and we all need that.'

There were two doors that a Trapper looked after forming an airlock between spaces that were at slightly different pressures, ensuring that the ventilation airflow went were it needed to go to keep everybody breathing and not allow the buildup of noxious or flammable gas. It was a simple job, opening and closing doors, and poorly paid, but nevertheless an important one.

'Don't let anybody have your lamp, you keep it,' says Edward, 'I had my lamp taken when I first went down and got in terrible trouble when I came up.'

'And lost pay,' says Frank.

'Aye, that too,' agrees Edward, grimacing.

They talk as they eat, and Jenny listens as she makes up their bait boxes. She wishes that Jack was not going down the pit. To have three people from her house doing it seems too much, but it is the way, son follows father, and there is little other choice. That doesn't stop her from feeling protective towards Jack.

'Listen to this advice, Jack,' she says, 'I've put your bait into this bag, see, just like the others, you'll sling it over your shoulder and take it down the pit with you. Make sure you eat and drink while you're down there.'

Jack has seen his father and brother with their bait bags hundreds of times and didn't need telling, but he stays silent and nods his head.

The three leave the house together, Jack at the back, and make their way down the street, slicked yellow-white by the occasional streetlight, towards the pithead.

It is cold and dark and as they walk, they are joined by other men, their boots scraping on the loose gravel. In the half-light vague outlines of groups of huddled shapes appear and merge into a growing whole that streams towards the pithead.

Inside a long cabin, Jack queues to give his number and receive his lamp. Frank shows him how to test its function and prove that it is gas-proof by blowing around the glass as hard as he can. It is a new procedure for Jack and he follows his father's lead as if he were inheriting the secret of some solemn rite.

On the walk from the lamp cabin to the pit, Jack has to concentrate to stop his lamp from catching on the ground, with the risk of losing the light.

'Be careful,' says Edward, 'you'll need to be a bit taller, Jack, before you can carry your lamp without worrying about it. Keep it up, make sure you keep it up.'

The lamp is heavy; Jack does his best.

Up rattling iron steps file the miners, it seems so high to climb and the steps so many, that Jack loses count.

Once inside he walks past lines of coal tubs, along a gangway and towards the cage that will transport him down the shaft.

Here he joins the queue, a mingling mass of seasoned miners, young men and boys standing huddled and sombre, waiting their turn to go down, each immersed in his own thoughts.

Among so many, there is hardly a sound, who would want to talk at this time in the morning on a cold day, in a gloomy shed, a shift underground in prospect, in dim tunnels and passages, thousands of feet down with countless tons of coal and rock sitting on top of you?

Jack feels the mood and joins the silence, both wishing that this waiting were over and hoping it never ends. His next steps will take him underground and one thing is for sure, there is no turning back now.

The pithead on which Jack stands is a vast structure of iron and steel. Metal joists reach upwards and outwards to the great wheels that turn way up beyond the roof that covers him.

The platform on which he stands is metal and he is surrounded by it; the hardness of it, the smell of it, the sound of it as the coal tipper and tubs rumble and crash, the thick, glistening, greased, steel-spun ropes glide up and down the shaft, and the taught chains emerge, heralding the coming of the metal cage, hauled upward from the dark.

Jack feels as though he has shrunk, that in the midst of this great construction, this great mechanised cacophony, he has grown smaller and at the same time the world has somehow closed in around him, making him feel claustrophobic and alone.

He is scared and apprehensive, but there is also a shard of excitement, a feeling of being on the brink of some new chapter.

A mystery is about to be revealed; a new world opened to him. He has not asked his father or brother to explain it to him, they have not offered, he has instinctively known that no words could have prepared him, that the only real preparation is the experience itself.

As we take these next steps try to keep these images in your mind: imagine that you have moved out of bright sunshine and into a house with all its curtains drawn and only a couple of oil lamps burning. Then leave the sanctuary of this room and move into another darker one further inside with no light. Stop here a moment and then accept the gift of a lit candle that you hold in your hand to see by.

Now add the taste of coal dust to the air and feel the acid prickle as it settles on your face.

Now add the clamour of coal tubs zooming out of the dark and passing within a breeze of where you're standing. Then add the smell of coal, of horse manure, of the sweat of others around you, and hear their voices loud and mixed.

Now enter a room on your hands and knees and push a hundredweight of coal that's piled in a tub ahead of you. Feel the sharp tracks beneath your palms and then reach up and touch the unseen roof, held up by pit props and hope.

Breathe deeply but do not panic, never panic, and turn and bring the coal tub out into the larger spaces, to where the ponies are, and then go back.

Such a surreal work of the imagination may give you a flavour of the world Jack is about to enter.

How do we describe it? Every person, every action, every sound, cannot be considered on the page, we have only a sequential trail of letters to follow, so try and retain some memory of these things as we go on and take our necessarily restricted view as we follow Jack further…

The cage doors are pulled open and closed, arrive and depart, until finally it is his turn and Jack finds himself, with some 40 others, crammed into the restricted space.

The concertina doors are closed and the world begins to fall away as he slides, slowly at first and then faster, rattling down, down, down the deep shaft.

He watches the slimy beams rush past, the black depths waiting for him below.

Or so he thinks.

When the cage slows and then stops, when the metal lattice doors were folded open and he steps out, he is in an area full of yellow light.

Jack's first impressions are those of surprise: the area at the pit bottom is larger and better lit than in his imagination, and it is warmer here than the surface he has left behind.

As he looks around, he can see a number of coal-tub lines and passages spread out like fingers feeling their way into a darkness his eyes cannot penetrate. The idea that all the pit is as well-lit as here disappears almost as quickly as it had materialised in his ever-hopeful mind.

To the miners who go down here every weekday all this is commonplace; the rumbling of the coal tubs, full and empty, the running belts for haulage, the smell of the stables, the echoing voices, the large tunnels where a man can stand that peter out to passages where the tubs scrape along the sides, an overfull tub sticks against the ceiling.

The rules and regulations, some followed, some bent, others broken or ignored, the many jobs of supervision, of cage operations, of horse or machinery handling, of hauling, of setting explosive charges, of hewing and shovelling and filling and doing it all again. All these things contribute, like cogs, large and small, which together make the extraction of coal tick, tub by tub, tub by tub.

Frank and Edward separate, knowing their way. Jack stands waiting.

'You Frank Lawley's boy?'

Jack looks up into a blackened face.

'Yes, sir, I'm Jack Lawley,' he says.

'Sir,' says the man laughing, 'that's a good start. Stay polite and follow instructions, Jack, that'll make the shift go quicker and keep you out of mischief. Do you understand?'

'Yes, sir,' says Jack.

'Alright, let me test your lamp.'

Jack gives his lamp up reticently, the man takes it, tests it and hands it back.

'That's fine, mind you don't knock it out, there's no replacements down here, knock it out and you'll be in the dark for the rest of the shift.'

Jack nods.

The man calls across to another.

'Charlie, this one's your new Trapper, it's his first time down, show him the way will you.'

Charlie takes hold of Jack's shoulder, he is a small wiry man, his grip is strong.

'Come on,' he says, and leads Jack out of the relative light and into the increasing dark, 'Follow me and keep close into the wall, the coal tubs'll not stop for you.'

Jack does what he is told and is soon glad of it, lines of coal-laden tubs roar past, too close for comfort, the wind of their passing brushes his face.

On into the dark they walk for what seems like hours to Jack until they reach the stables, the smell of horses warning of its presence.

Here the light intensifies and steam rises from the pony stalls accompanied by the sound of ponies and the voices of ten's of boys.

One of them recognises Jack from school, he is barely two years older but saunters around like a seasoned worker, face already smeared with black.

'Hey, Jack, welcome to the real world,' he says, 'you look white as a ghost, but a bit of blacking'll quick sort that out.'

'Be quiet and get on with your job,' shouts Charlie, 'there's plenty work to be done.'

Onwards they walk for another half mile until finally they stop at a door that blocks the way.

'These doors are yours.' says Charlie, 'don't leave them unattended for any reason, eat here, shit here if you have to, but stay put and open and close the doors when you're told. It's these doors that control the flow of air and without fresh air we're all fucked. Understand?'

Jack does not understand why opening and closing a door keeps the air fresh but he does understand what his job is.

'And don't think that your job is not important, a young lad in another pit I heard of went and left his door open while he went off to talk to his mate. This led to the build-up of explosive gases and an explosion that killed 41 miners. So you concentrate and do your job, son, you hear?'

'Yes, sir,' says Jack.

'Alright, since it's your first, I'll come and collect you at the end of your shift, but that'll be for the first and last time mind, I've got other things to do, so you remember the way cos you'll be doing it on your own tomorrow.'

'Yes, sir,' says Jack.

Left alone with his lamp Jack has time to think.

He isn't cold, he isn't cramped, the tunnel is too large for that, but he is in a completely unfamiliar world, full of people who all understand it better than he does.

He starts to try and work out how far from the pit bottom he is, because the pit bottom symbolises a kind of safety. Then he tries to imagine how deep below the ground he is, how many tons of rock there are on top of him, but when he thinks about this he can feel his heart pounding in his chest and a trickle of sweat weaves its way past his temples and down his cheek, so he decides to put these thoughts away and concentrate on what he has to do.

And he doesn't need to wait long, the traffic of Drivers with their ponies pulling full tubs away from the face and empty ones towards it, is frequent and endless. Despite the warning he'd had, one of the Drivers takes his lamp.

'Bumped mine,' he says, 'and I need it more than you. Don't you dare tell anyone and I'll give you yours back at the end of the shift.'

Jack could argue, could try to hold on to his little bit of light, a little bit of comfort in the dark. But he doesn't.

For the rest of the shift he sits in his own darkness, opens and closes the doors, watches other people's lights approach and recede, eats the sandwich his mother has made for him, washes it down with tepid water from his tin bottle, which he almost loses when he puts it down and has to grope around in the dark with his fingers to find it again. The water tastes like nectar.

The seconds tick into minutes, the minutes into hours as Jack makes his way through a shift that is filled only with night.

Finally, Charlie comes to collect him.

'What's happened to your lamp?' he asks.

'Knocked it,' says Jack.

'Hmm, we'll see when we match the numbers,' says Charlie.

Together they walk back, Charlie leading. As they pass the stables, Jack feels a tug on his arm.

'Quick, give me my lamp, here's yours, I've knocked the light out.'

It is done in seconds.

'What's that?' shouts Charlie over his shoulder.

'Nothing,' says the boy, 'just giving this young'un a slap on the back, first shift, isn't it?'

'Just leave him alone and look after yourself.'

'I'll do that,' whispers the boy, turning back into the stables to unharness, berth and leave his pony feeding.

As they come to the pit bottom the increased light and space suck them in, and Jack feels both relieved and proud, he has finished his first shift as a miner.

It is a day of perpetual dark for Jack, rising as he had before the sun peeps, red faced, blushing, above the horizon and, by the time he resurfaces, it has slipped behind the hills more than 2 hours since.

Artificial light is his light, oil lamps and gas, and, as he makes his way home with his father and brother, they walk between the stepping-stones of the street lighting, the mediocre light pooling on the cobbles, mirroring their fatigue in its inconstancy, the wind sliding in beneath their clothing, spreading a cold they'd left behind and now return to.

'So, Jack, how was it?' asks his father.

Jack looks up, white eyes from blackened skin and doesn't answer.

His father just nods, and they continue home in silence.

Jack has earned 6 copper pennies for his first hours of graft. When he gets home his mother has a meal on the table and he is third in line for the bath.

Chapter 38

Jack was now a wage-earner.

He earned his meat, and when his brother scoffed at his meager wage Jenny pointed to the table,

'You see the bread and the butter and the pot of tea? Well, Jack's wage paid for all of that.'

Jack smiled and looked at his brother,

'Please,' he said, 'have some more.'

With the little he kept for himself he could now save and buy his own clothes or, if he liked, buy something else: books.

Each shift, filled with claustrophobic darkness, earned Jack a little bit more freedom.

The months passed and Jack learned and established his own routines, he was no longer green, his skin no longer lily-white, and when an opportunity came his way to leave his doors and become a Driver, he grabbed it.

After his job as a Trapper, stuck in one place, repetitively opening and closing the ventilation doors, the job of a Driver seemed much more exciting as it involved leading one of the pit ponies and pulling empty tubs to the face or full ones to the pit bottom or collecting materials and taking them to where they needed to be. It was also much better paid, increasing his salary eightfold to 24s a week. This was a proper job!

The ponies were housed in underground stables for 50 weeks of the year, escaping to the surface for 2 weeks by means of the cage. The stable was divided by wooden partitions that provided comfortable sized stalls and was roofed by thick wooden planks supported by pit props.

When the first shift started, the pony drivers would be there, a blast of air ushering them in, the extra noise, movement and light disturbing swarms of flies and sending the mice scuttling for cover.

A yoke-like piece of equipment hung on a nail at the back of each stall and was fastened to the pony harness and was later used to attach to a tub. The ponies wore a skull pad to prevent injury from a low roof and, when not moving coal, had a variety of harnesses and collars, and wore whichever was most appropriate to the task. The pony was tethered and given a nosebag when it came to the 20 minutes break allowed for feeding.

The ponies were generally beloved by their handlers and had their own ways of getting extra food from the miner's own bait. Some would nip, or even bite, although this was not an endearing quality and was likely to lead to retribution rather than extra food. Some would nudge the pony driver's helmet, asking for a share of his sandwich, others would snort or slobber.

Jack went to the stables to pick up his pony.

The stables were dug back into the wall of the pit. It was lit by lamps hanging off the walls and smelt of horse dung and stale straw.

The Stableman took Jack to one of the stalls above which was a slate chalked with the name "Barney" and standing inside was a brown, or if seen clean and in daylight he would have been brown, pony with a white splash across his head and face. He was a small, stout animal.

'He's a Shetland,' said the Stableman, 'a gelding and no more than 11 hands. You'll be alright with this one, he's good and strong and placid as anything.'

Jack heard one of the other Drivers snigger.

'Take no notice,' said the Stableman, 'come on and I'll show you how to harness him up.'

On entering Barney's stall, the pony kicked out with its back legs. The Stableman moved aside expertly, the kick narrowly missing Jack's chest.

'He's just a bit feisty today for some reason, here give him something to drink.'

Jack did as he was told, moving to the horse's head and trying to slip the water bag over his ears. The pony shook its head from side to side and the water went everywhere.

'Obviously doesn't want a drink,' said the Stableman, 'tell you what I'll show you how to do the harness on the horse next door and then you can come back and do Barney's yourself, I don't think he likes so many people around him.'

The Stableman led Jack into one of the other stalls where a jet-black pony stood placidly.

'This is Archie,' he said, 'one of my favourites, quiet as a mouse.'

Seemingly in agreement with the sentiment there was a scratching and a scurrying in one of the corners, and the straw moved.

'Yep, we really do have mice down here,' he said, 'no idea how they got down here, probably in the hay, but they've established themselves right enough. Now let me show you…'

The Stableman proceeded to show Jack the harness, explain the parts and the purposes,

'…these are the blinkers, they stop the ponies from looking around and getting unnecessarily distracted, keeps them looking forward and keeps them calm…'

Together they put on and took off the harness several times until the Stableman was happy that Jack had got the hang of it.

'Good enough,' he said, 'I've got lots to do so I'll leave you to it. Barney's harness is hanging up in his stall. Just be confident would be my advice, show him who's boss.'

As Jack prepared to approach Barney, he remembered something of what Peter had taught him, and a specific memory flashed into his mind.

They were in the farm's stables, the cart horse in front of them was black from nose to tail, so it wasn't a surprise that his name was "Blackie", and he was tethered in the stall.

'Here,' said Peter, who had passed him a nose bag with oats in it, 'give Blackie something to eat.'

He remembered approaching the horse from the rear and, in what he thought was a friendly gesture, patting him on the rump.

The horse kicked out and missed his head by a hair's breadth.

Peter had laughed. Jack hadn't.

'Animals have feelings,' Peter had said, 'they're not machines. If you're good to them then they'll most likely be good to you. You took him by surprise. He doesn't know you. How would you feel if a complete stranger patted you on the rump?'

Jack remembered feeling like a fool, but before he could answer, Peter had said, 'Here, let me show you.'

He'd taken the nose bag and walked along the horse's flank, talking softly to him, 'Now then Blackie, what's all this, here I bring a friend of mine to see you and you nearly take his head off.'

The horse had strained on his halter, trying to turn his head to Peter, baring his teeth.

Peter had put his arm around the horse's neck and whispered in his ear, 'Now, now, Blackie, here have a sniff of this.'

And he had wafted the nose bag in front of the horse, whose nostrils had flared.

'See, we're bringing you some food, there's nothing to worry about.'

Peter had stroked the horse's neck and when he had settled, he had slipped the nose bag in position and Blackie had started munching contentedly on the contents.

'Impressive,' Jack had said.

'Just got to be kind,' Peter had replied, 'now don't misunderstand me, there's times when discipline's needed, but most of the time a bit of kindness doesn't go amiss.'

And Peter had shown Jack how to be kind, and Jack had learnt and now here he was below ground with another anxious animal.

Jack had no idea why Barney was annoyed but now he went back into Barney's stall, taking a nosebag of oats with him, trying to show more confidence than he actually felt,

'Hello there,' he said, 'I know you don't know me, but I wish you no harm.'

So saying he placed his hand on the pony's back and felt its body tremble in response.

'No, no, it's alright,' he said, and just left his hand where it was, hoping the pony wouldn't kick out. After a few moments he took a step forward, the trembling increased so he took a step back again.

'Don't worry,' he said, 'ssh now, it's alright.'

When the pony settled, Jack tried again and taking a step forward he moved his hand slowly and gently along the pony's back, remembering everything that Peter had taught and shown him on the farm.

In this way, slowly and steadily, he worked his way to the pony's head. It turned and took a nip at him.

Jack laughed, 'I don't blame you,' he said, 'I think I would try and nip me too if I was in your position.'

Jack stood his ground and stroked the pony's scraggy mane. Barney tossed his head up, pulling on the rope that tied him.

Jack kept his hand there and after Barney had tossed his head up and down three more times, he began to settle.

'That's better,' said Jack, 'now after all that you must be hungry.'

He passed the nosebag around the side of Barney's head until it was under his nose.

'There,' he said, 'have a sniff.'

He held the bag while the pony's nostrils flared.

Jack leant in and whispered in the pony's ear.

'Go on have a go, it's not going to kill you.'

The pony nuzzled forward, mouth into the bag, took a mouthful and pulled back again.

'See, it's alright,' said Jack.

The pony did the same thing again and then put its head forward and started eating in earnest. Jack slipped the cord over its head to keep the nose bag in position.

'I don't know what's upset you,' he said, 'but if you don't settle there'll be trouble, and that's no good for either of us, so just you settle down and let's get on with it, shall we?'

The pony seemed to respond to Jack's calm and confident voice and Jack sought out his harness and brought it to him.

'Now you're more experienced at this than I am,' he said, 'you must have had this on and off hundreds of times,' he paused, and leaned in closer, as if confiding a secret, 'but it's all new to me, so you'll have to be patient.'

The pony finished eating and looked at Jack.

'Are you alright now?' asked Jack, 'have you got over your bad temper?'

The pony lowered its head as if in apology.

'Good, well, now let's see if I can do this right.'

Jack put on the harness wondering if he was doing everything correctly. Barney moved around a bit but nothing that Jack couldn't easily counter. Jack knew that it was important to fit the harness properly so that it wouldn't pull unevenly or cause injury. He hoped he'd done it right.

'That's good Jack,' said the Stableman sticking his head in the stall and looking the harness over, 'but you've got to do it a lot faster than that, I thought you'd gone to sleep!'

Jack's job was to pick up some parts from the pit bottom and take them to the face. As he was leading Barney down a rather steep drift road the pony suddenly lay down on the floor and began to roll around in the dust, legs thrashing about in the air, rolling over and back. This had come as a complete surprise to Jack and he didn't know what to do. Had he done something wrong? Given Barney too much food, too little water? Harnessed him incorrectly? Jack reminded himself that there were rules governing horses underground, had he broken one?

Barney stopped as suddenly as he'd started and got up. He looked around as if nothing had happened and carried on following Jack's lead. Another of the Drivers had witnessed the scene and laughed at Jack's consternation.

'They do that sometimes,' he said, 'get fed up of being cooped up in the stables, I guess, and first chance they get they have a bit of a roll about. You'll get used to it, they usually do it in the same spot too.'

Once Barney was allocated to Jack the two of them strove to understand each other, Barney at first taking liberties at Jack's inexperienced expense.

Although technically company property, Jack felt Barney was 'his pony'. Such a feeling must have slowly communicated itself to Barney who seemed to soften and come to recognise and respond to Jack's voice. They even came to understand each other's moods.

Jack looked after Barney's gear, fed him and cleaned out his stall, sending the urine-wet, straw-mixed droppings out and up to the surface where they would be used on allotments or by a local farmer.

As far as the underground world was concerned Jack and Barney were two cogs on the same wheel; Barney was Jack's pony, and Jack was Barney's Driver.

Jack welcomed the increase in pay and found the work less monotonous, transporting parts and materials to where they needed to be in the different sections of the mine. He would pass through the ventilation doors, one of which used to be his, and up to the face, unhook, unload, re-hook and return for the next job.

Doing this job made the time pass more quickly, and he even had somebody to talk to.

Chapter 39

Jim Moore bought his coal from the mine.

He and the other farmers tended to view the miners as 'incomers', people who had migrated in from all different parts to make a temporary home in the mining village.

'The coal will run out,' he explained to his son, Peter, 'and then the mining village will die away again, but the land, ah, the land will go on forever, it'll still be here long after you or I have been forgotten.'

Jim and his family were no incomers, they had worked the same land for generations, with the same neighbours. He was as rooted in the soil as the old yew tree with its leather-leaves and wrinkled bark, that grew in the town churchyard, among the graves.

Before him the Celts had roamed these spaces, the Romans had marched, and the Norsemen had plundered and settled. But these times were long forgotten, only cropmarks left as reminders. But Jim recognised this heritage and felt a part of the extended line of history. At night he would occasionally go out with his pipe and walk under the stars, listening to the echoes in the wind as it chattered through the leaves, speaking many languages, muttering words he could only feel.

And there was a seasonal rhythm to the farmer's life, at harvest time, 20 men would arrive to scythe the corn, and sing as they went, to keep their blades in rhythm. It was hard, sweaty, dusty and thirsty work and they looked forward to the end of it, when the sun cooled and twilight finally called a halt to the day. Then they would wander down to the pub for a welcome pint or two and wash the taste of the dust away.

And there were the permanent farm workers too, surviving on less than a Driver's wage.

Jack and Peter's lives moved on, each in their own predetermined direction.

'The days pass, and the seasons, the years,' said Jim Moore to his son, as they ate their breakfast, 'I know some days seem slow, like standing out in November rain with the icy water trickling down the back of your neck. But most pass quickly, filled with tasks that need doing. There's always something needs doing or needs thinking about.'

He paused and looked at his son,

'And if a family should happen along, well, that only adds to the number of things you need to think about, the number of things that fill up the day to overflowing.'

'But you learn, that's the thing, no year is the same because you've learned, and you do some things differently.'

He paused.

'It takes you by surprise that the years have flown, that your hands don't close as tight as they used to and that there's pain in the joints.'

'It's a good job farmers are not stock or we'd be put out of our misery soon enough or at least put out to grass.'

The farmer laughed and Peter smiled with him. He was beginning to realise how big a job it was to step into his father's shoes.

'The good thing is that a farmer doesn't really retire, he just slows down, gives more advice, welcome or not, and leaves the heavier tasks to younger, stronger limbs.'

'When you can read your land like a book and see whether a horse, or a cow, a pig or a lamb is fit and healthy just by looking at them, then there's always something to occupy you, by Jove there is!'

'Stop being maudlin,' said his wife, 'you're getting worse as you get older.'

Jim looked at his wife and smiled.

'You're right,' he said, and then, turning to his son, 'Now what's our first job of the day?'

The busy periods on the farm were at lambing time, haymaking, and harvest. At these times, there were crowds of people about the place.

With 200 acres of arable land, 20 acres of water meadow, and about 50 acres of pasture to look after the full-time farm workers lived by the farm, carrying out the 'piecework' of hoeing, mowing, ploughing, sewing and reaping as the season dictated. Then there were the stockmen for the horses, the engine of hard labour, the cattle for meat and dairy, the pigs and the sheep. And there were all the others: the blacksmiths, the coopers, the cobblers and the carters, the stone wallers, the mole catchers, the fence makers and, as a last resort, the vet.

At the centre of all of this was Jim and Ella Moore, and increasingly Peter, who had by now worked in each of the various parts that made up the whole, the whole that was the farm.

The foreman, Gareth Price, who, just as his father had always done, Peter would need as his right-hand man, was a man of about 60 who had started work on a farm at about 10 years of age and knew pretty much everything there was to know about the job. He was weathered, ruddy of complexion, broad of shoulder and had a stoical outlook on life. Things were bound to go wrong. They always did. The secret was to notice what was going wrong as soon as possible and fix it.

He was a patient man, but he wasn't going to listen to a young whippersnapper like Peter when he was talking nonsense. For the good of the farm, he would put on a show of listening and then ignore whatever Peter had said. If Peter wanted his respect, then he had to earn it through action and not big words, and that would take a time.

Following one of these episodes, Peter spoke to his father.

'I don't think Mr Price likes me,' he said, not yet confident enough to call him Gareth.

'What do you mean?'

'I talk to him, he seems to listen, and then he does something different.'

His father laughed.

'I don't think it's funny,' said Peter, 'if you want me to…'

'The reason I'm laughing,' interrupted his father, 'is because he used to do the same to me.'

Peter was shocked.

'Yes,' said his father, 'Gareth was first employed by my father, and when I was learning the ropes he gave me a rough time.'

'He must have been a lot younger then.'

'He was, but so was I. He made me win my spurs by learning how to farm this place and proving I was worth listening to. Even then, if he didn't agree with something, if he knew there was a better way, then he would do it behind my back. I wanted to be angry with him but when I saw that he was right I couldn't, I could only smile and learn. My father respected him and when I appealed to him, he would listen and, more often than not, explain to me why I was wrong, and Gareth was right.'

'Didn't you find that annoying?'

'Very.'

'And what happened?'

'I learned the farm. I learned to ask Gareth's advice instead of trying to tell him what to do. It made me a better farmer, it gave me a right-hand man that I've always relied on and can always trust.'

'But he can't always be right.'

'No, that's true.'

'And then?'

'And then you pretend not to notice, talk it out as equals if there's something to learn.'

'And what if you don't agree?'

'If you have the best for the farm at heart, and if you respect each other and can listen to different points of view then you can always agree to choose, there's not always just one right answer.'

Peter thought about this.

'So, what do you advise?'

'Ask don't tell, work on getting to know how to get the best out of each other, not the worst.'

'So, it's my fault not his?'

His father smiled.

'It's nobody's fault, Peter, it's about learning, that's what it's about, running a farm is not easy.'

'I'm beginning to see that,' said Peter, 'you just seem to do things so easily.'

'It's never easy,' said his father, 'but when you've seen the seasons through dozens of times, when you've done things more than twice, then you know what to look out for and what you should do about it. It's time and experience, Peter, there's no substitute.'

Chapter 40

Some of the strongest links in the support network that kept the mining community going were those between the women.

Mothers were the lynchpin of their families, not only did their daily chores support the whole fabric of these isolated communities, but also it was mainly their efforts that kept the families together. There was no more important a tool in this regard than shared mealtimes, and no more important a shared meal than the Sunday lunch.

It was at these times that a whole family would meet around the kitchen table to exchange news, gossip and share information about the week just gone, and the one to come.

Jenny and Sarah now shared the preparation, and the tidying up afterwards. Frank and Edward might go to the pub before the meal was served, Grandpa might go to his allotment with Jack and George in tow, but they would all be back by the time the food was on the table. It was an unwritten law, and none of the men wanted to feel the sharp edge of Jenny's tongue by arriving late.

Jenny loved these occasions; she felt that sitting around the table with her family was her reward for all the work that she had put in. It didn't even bother her that, although Sunday was more or less a day of rest for the men and boys in her life, for her and Sarah it was another day of work.

Children were often born in the home of their parents or grandparents. And daughters, before and after they got married, often took on at least some of their mother's heavy household tasks, and so the mother to daughter relationship was critically important, although not as widely recognised as the father to son progression into paid work.

Jenny tried to treat Sarah as much as a daughter as she could although she was very conscious that she was not her 'real' mother. Her real mother wasn't there anymore, and Jenny did not know where she was or how to contact her. There were many times when she wished that she did.

Women talk to women on women's matters, after all there were things that didn't concern the men. But there were some conversations that Jenny shied away from having with Sarah, conversations that she would have had if she were more confident, or if she had been Sarah's biological mother.

But time does not wait on anyone's convenience.

It was George who rushed in through the back door, 'Sarah's cut herself,' he said.

Jenny was immediately concerned.

'What do you mean?'

'Somewhere on her leg, she won't show me.'

Sarah trailed in after him, her head bowed.

'What's happened, love,' said Jenny.

Sarah glanced up.

'I don't know,' she said.

'She didn't fall down or anything,' said George, 'she was just running and then I saw she was bleeding down her leg.'

'Let me have a look,' said Jenny.

'I don't want you to,' said Srah, clearly embarrassed.

Jenny started to realise. But surely it was too early. Sarah was too young.

'George, go and fill up the buckets with water, and don't come back in until I say.'

George looked bewildered but wandered out to follow his mother's instructions.

'Now, Sarah, tell me what's been happening.'

Now that she was alone with Jenny, Sarah felt more able to explain.

'I've been having some pains, Ma. Just thought it was indigestion or something, and then this happened.'

She raised her dress and showed Jenny.

'Oh, Sarah,' said Jenny.

Sarah started to cry.

'Oh, Sarah, did your mother never tell you about these things?'

'What things?' sniffed Sarah.

Jenny immediately felt a pang of guilt. She should have thought, she should have talked to Sarah about these things, like a real mother would have done. But Sarah was so young, although that was no excuse.

She looked at Sarah and smiled.

'Come here, love,' she said.

Sarah walked across and fell into Jenny's arms. Jenny hugged her and stroked her hair. It was foreign to Jenny's nature to show such open affection, but it felt such a natural thing to do.

'What's wrong, Ma,' said Sarah, 'what have I done wrong?'

'Ssh, Sarah, don't worry, you haven't done anything wrong, you're just growing up, that's all.'

She could feel Sarah trembling in her arms.

'Now first of all, let's get you cleaned up and sorted, and then we'll have a talk. I should have talked to you sooner, I'm sorry.'

There was warm water in the pans on the range. There was always water heating on the range, and Jenny used this.

Mid way through, George was at the back door with more water. He called in to announce his return.

'Just leave them there and go up to the allotment and help your Grandpa,' said Jenny.

'Is Sarah alright?' asked George.

'She's just fine,' said Jenny, 'now off you go.'

George did as he was bid. As he was going out of the backyard he whispered to himself, 'Women!', and then he put his head down and ran off as fast as he could in the direction of the allotments. His Grandpa always had interesting things for him to do.

After Jenny had got Sarah cleaned, changed and sorted, she made a pot of tea, and they sat down to talk.

'Every month?' said Sarah.

'I'm afraid so, it's part of growing up and changing from a girl into a woman.'

'So, I haven't done anything wrong?'

Jenny smiled.

'No, you haven't done anything wrong.'

'And I'm not strange?'

'No, you're not strange, it's really quite normal.'

Sarah sipped her tea.

'So, you'll help me?' she said.

'Yes, I'll help you.'

'And I'm growing up?'

'Yes, you're growing up.'

'Life's full of surprises, isn't it?' said Sarah.

Jenny nodded.

'Do you want a piece of cake?' she said

Chapter 41

It was the start of his shift and Jack stroked Barney's head and whispered in his ear.

'We're in this together, you and me,' he said, and took a carrot out of his pocket and gave it to the pony.

'You're spoiling that horse,' one of the other drivers said, 'he'll start taking liberties, you mark my words.'

Jack ignored the jibe, adjusted Barney's harness, took him out of the stable and hitched him up to a line of 3 tubs that were already loaded with pit props and bars.

Taking the back roads, keeping away from the main routes meant for coal traffic, Jack led Barney towards the face, his lamp in one hand, his pony's collar in the other. On the way he would talk to the horse about anything that came into his head, it kept the horse calm as they proceeded into the increasing dark and Jack liked to believe that he was listening,

'I wonder what it's like in France,' he said, 'or Germany, or Holland? A lot of our coal goes that way you know, out of the ground here, across to Newcastle and shipped from there. I wonder where it ends up and what it's used for? Just think, Barney, the coal my Dad shovels today might be in somebody's grate in a week, maybe a family in Germany, keeping them warm, maybe baking their bread. They won't be thinking of us, that's for sure, and we'll never know them, but they've got us to thank, all of us, including me and you.'

Barney trudged on at a steady pace, his leather blinkers focussing him forwards, helping to ensure there were no distractions. Each time he passed through a set of ventilation doors Jack would nod to the Trapper, some of them looked so young, he thought, wide eyed and scared or eager.

As they got closer to the face, they heard new noises; in the distance the dull thud of an explosive charge freeing the next section of coalface, the clanking of other tubs on rails, the rattling of their chains, the occasional shout of instruction, or warning. Barney ignored all of these and kept up his steady pace.

'Slow and steady wins the race,' muttered Jack, 'slow and steady, that's it Barney, nothing to worry about, you've heard it all before.'

When they got close to the face the tunnel in front narrowed and the ceiling dropped. Jack waited, there was another Driver there too, bringing empty tubs, waiting for the full ones.

'Hello Jack,' he said, 'you alright?'

'Right as rain,' said Jack, 'you?'

'Out with my girl tonight. Hoping for a bit of fun…'

Their conversation was cut short by the sounds of clattering and scraping and loud blaspheming as the Putter emerged. He didn't even look at Jack while he and the other Driver unhitched, turned, and manoeuvred the tubs until the full ones were ready to leave.

'Off you go lad,' said the Putter, 'and hurry back, this seam's cutting well.'

He then turned to Jack,

'Unload what you've got and leave me one tub, I'll take 'em in as we need 'em. Need a hand unloading?'

Jack wasn't sure whether this latter was a question or a challenge, either way he knew that a Putter's job was hard and physical and that the coal they brought out underpinned everybody's pay.

'No,' he said, 'I'll manage.'

The Putter smiled and clapped him on the back.

'That's the spirit,' he said, and turned, checked the chains on the tubs and sitting on the limbers between the new tubs and his own pony, he disappeared back up the tunnel, back bent and head down. The last thing Jack heard was a rattle and a lot of swearing.

It was in the interests of everyone that materials were as near to the face as possible and readily to hand when needed. A coal face could advance six feet a day, and if all the supports were not in place the chance of collapse was increased, the face workers in greater danger, and if the rails were not extended the tubs were more difficult to move.

Nothing stopped the flow of coal, as to do that was to stop the flow of earnings, but the men at the face did not like taking additional risks nor working harder than they had to, so any Driver responsible for a lack of materials was met with short shrift.

Barney stood still as Jack emptied two of the tubs, manhandling the wooden props and crossbeams, the rails and blocks and pegs, some with more difficulty than others, heavy and awkward, and then he unchained the third tub.

He tried to stack it all neatly and off to the side.

By the time he had finished the Putter and Driver were back and repeated their dance of exchanging tubs. When they were done the Putter spoke to Jack,

'That'll do lad, now off you go,' was all he said.

It was one of the biggest compliments Jack had yet received in his working life. He felt he was becoming accustomed to this world and accepted as part of it.

The zinc bath was already full of hot water when Edward and Jack got home, Frank had been temporarily moved to a different shift and Sarah was visiting one of the other houses with a blouse she'd just finished sewing.

The bath sat on the stone fagged floor and steamed in front of the coal fire. Their mother smiled at her sons as they entered through the backyard.

'Take your boots off, and Edward let's get you into this bath before the water goes cold. Jack, don't you bother taking your boots off yet, you can go and fetch some more water and put the kettle and pan on to heating for your bath. I need to be getting on with some cooking if you are to get any tea tonight. Oh, and Jack, keep a lookout for young George while you're getting the water. He should be getting back from school soon.'

Before Jack and Edward responded to the customary string of instructions, they each took their pay from their pockets and laid it on the table.

'And good afternoon to you too mother,' said Edward as he started to strip off his clothes.

Edward's pale white waist and legs contrasted sharply with the ingrained black of his work-worn hands, arms, neck, face and hair.

Jenny took out a small notebook, dog-eared from use, and sat at the kitchen table. Carefully she counted her son's pay twice through to ensure accuracy and then she added this new income neatly to a column of figures.

'I know I'm a bit short this week,' said Edward from the bath, 'but we'll be moving to a softer part of 'Baggy' next week, so I'll make up.'

Jenny nodded and arranged two piles of coins on the table.

'Your money's here when you want it,' she said and rose to lift the lid off a pottery jug, shaped and coloured like a beer barrel, that stood on the corner of the mantelpiece, pushing in the rest of the money and replacing the notebook behind it.

'Where's Grandpa?' asked Edward.

'Your Grandpa's up at his allotment, tending to his vegetables and his chickens, like they were his babies, probably talking to them most like.'

'Telling them stories about the Zulus,' broke in Jack.

'I thought I told you...,' but before she could finish the sentence Jack had raised his hands in surrender, picked up the empty buckets, and turned to leave. Once out of the kitchen door he walked across the cobbled yard, past the privy, and through their green-painted yard door that led into the back lane.

On his way to the street's communal water tap Jack saw his younger brother, George, running home from school. He called over to him.

'Whoa George. Come over here and give me a hand.'

George, who had been slapping his side in pretence of riding a galloping horse, stopped dead in his tracks. Plucked from his daydream he looked around to see who had called him. Seeing it was Jack, his face broke into a broad smile, and he galloped his horse to his side.

'And what was school like today?' asked Jack, starting to fill the first of the buckets.

'Brilliant,' said George, who could not stand still and was prancing on the spot, pulling on the reins of his imaginary young stallion, holding it back with difficulty.

'Brilliant? Well, that's a new one. What made it so good, was the teacher ill?'

'We did lice,' said George, 'Did you know that lice have a Latin name. And I can remember it.'

'Go on then,' said Jack responding to George's enthusiasm, 'You'd better tell me now, you'll of forgotten it by the time we get home.'

'*Pediculus humanus capitis,* and it has no wings and can only live on us humans, sucking our blood.'

'Amazing.'

'And that's not all. Their mouths are specially designed to pierce through our scalp,' said George, gnashing his teeth to drive home the point, 'they're only small and they hide in the shadows keeping out of sight, although they make your head itch.'

'Very nice,' said Jack, filling the second bucket and pausing to scratch his head in sympathy.

'Have you had nits? Dora Heslop's got them. She showed me in the playground. Crawling about they were.'

Jack filled the last of the buckets and handed one that was three quarters full to George.

'I'll get mam to run the nit comb through your head George, and make sure you haven't picked up any unwelcome guests from Dora. Just grab this and let's be getting home, I feel like I'm even more in need of a bath now.'

They walked back down the street side by side, concentrating, careful not to slop or spill any of the precious water, George's stallion had mysteriously disappeared.

'What would you do if you find any?' asked George.

'Oh, just shave all your hair off and paint your scalp yellow with ointment.'

'Ooooooh,' said George, trying hard to keep his hands away from his hair even though there was an itch, aching to be scratched.

He fell silent and, in his mind, he saw himself scalped and yellow and in the playground and being surrounded by his friends who were pointing and laughing. It was not a pretty thought.

'So why doesn't Dora Heslop have her head shaved and painted yellow?'

Jack thought for a moment,

'She's a girl.'

George couldn't argue with this. Dora Heslop was indisputably a girl, and girls were indisputably different in increasingly mystifying ways.

'I don't think I've got nits,' he said and fell silent, concentrating on carrying the water bucket without spilling any.

It took a long time to get clean and Edward was still soaping and scrubbing when Jack returned with George in tow.

'Howdy George,' said Edward over his shoulder and then shouted, 'Mam, George's back.'

From upstairs there was a muffled reply.

Jack re-filled the kettle and pans and put them to the fire to heat, leaning his elbow on the mantelpiece he said,

'Don't ask George what he did at school.'

'Why, what did you do George? You didn't get into trouble again, did you? I was always getting into trouble from Mr Hughes.'

George did not rise to the bait.

'I don't want to talk about it, I'm going to see if I can help Ma,' and he raced off, his feet clumping as he ran up the stairs.

Jack grinned.

'You shouldn't tease him,' said Edward, 'He might be bigger than you someday and then he'll give you a good hiding.'

'I'll take my chances,' said Jack, taking the soap and brush and starting to scrub at Edward's back, 'Are you going down the pub tonight?'

'Does a duck quack?' answered Edward.

'Then get out the bath, and let me have a turn, the fresh water's hot enough now.'

Edward stood up and began towelling himself down.

'Alright, alright, just leave me enough hot water in the kettle for a cup of tea.'

As Jack was getting undressed ready to step into the partially refreshed steaming, soapy, water, his grandfather arrived back from the allotment.

'Hi Grandpa,' said Jack, 'how's the eggs?'

'Not too bad,' he said, taking four newly laid eggs from his jacket pocket and putting them inside his upturned flat cap before placing it on the kitchen table, 'Helps the laying when I talk to them, you know.'

Jack smiled.

Edward had been working down the pit for too long now for the black of his face and hands to be totally removable, no matter how much soap or how much scrubbing was used for the task.

Jack on the other hand was less impregnated and could clean up better. He called for his mother who came downstairs and scrubbed his neck, back and behind his ears as she liked to do. She admired the broad shoulders of her middle son and hoped that her pride wasn't too obvious.

When Jack emerged, George dragged the bath out through the backyard and poured the dirty water away into the gutter that ran down the centre of the back lane. Grandpa then took it off him and lifted it up to hang on the nail on the outside wall ready to be used again on Frank's return.

By the time Edward and Jack were dressed in fresh clothes there were mugs of tea on the kitchen table and the family started to chat about their day. George feared the conversation might get around to nits.

Chapter 42

Jack led Barney to the pit bottom, was shown his next load and instructed where to take it. It was a part of the pit he hadn't been to before.

'There's an incline on the way,' he was told, 'it's long and it's steep, make sure you use the locker.'

Jack hooked the chain from the pony's halter to the first tub and set off.

Although it was a new route for him, he'd used 'lockers' before. These specially made lengths of hard wood were set between the struts of the tub wheels, stopping them from turning and acting as a brake. With metal wheels running on rails coated with coal dust there was little friction so that, even with the lockers in place, the weight of the tubs coupled with the depth of the incline would cause the tubs to move forward, albeit at a slower rate.

Jack knew this, had done this, had talked to other Drivers about the whole 'lockering up' procedure and had watched others as they stopped and put the lockers in place. Needing to brake on an incline held no fears for him.

Jack led Barney through the back passages, keeping out of the way of the fast-moving coal-carrying tubs. When they reached the top of the incline he stopped and quickly secured the lockers in place and, sitting on the limber between Barney's rump and the first tub, urged the pony forward believing that there was now nothing to worry about.

All went well at the start and they moved forward at a slow and steady pace. The tunnel narrowed and, as anticipated, they began to speed up as the angle of incline increased.

It was when Jack heard a sharp crack that he started to worry.

The last of the tubs started to slew and bounce off the tunnel walls, but far from this slowing their progress, they continued to accelerate.

Barney was no longer pulling the load but was now going just fast enough to keep ahead of it, the connecting chains jangling loosely.

They were moving under their own momentum and the one remaining 'locker' only managed to prevent them from being completely out of control.

There was nothing Jack could do.

He felt like a fool.

If he had been standing alongside rather than sitting on the limbers, could he have held them back? There was so little room that he thought not, but it didn't matter, it was too late now, all he could do was hold on and hope that there was nothing in their way.

He felt for Barney, what would happen if he could not run fast enough?

The inevitability of a terrible accident flashed through his mind. And it was all his fault. He had done something wrong.

As back tub screeched, the walls flashed past in a blur, and he thought of his mother, his father and brother, what would they think of him for being so stupid?

Faster and faster they went, Barney now in full gallop. The roof and sides of the roadway raced by only inches away and Jack prayed that no one was coming up the way as it was now only wide enough for a single tub, and they would surely be mown down by his recklessness, the refuge holes cut into the side of the tunnel were too few and too far apart to provide an escape.

Jack's instinct was to jump off, but that was impossible, they were going too fast, the tunnel was too narrow. This was the end; it was only a matter of time.

'Sorry!' he shouted at the top of his lungs, 'Sorry!'

...and then the passage suddenly began to widened and flatten.

They shot forward like a cork out of a bottle, and then, as the ground rose and levelled, the tubs slowed, and Barney began to slow. Matching each other the tubs and the pony now reduced their speed. Jack gulped.

'Come on, Barney,' he muttered, although his voice was lost in the sound of the wheels, the chains, the thud, thud, of his own heart.

…and then the chains tightened… the tubs were being pulled once more, control had been regained.

Barney slowed to a walk.

'Whoa,' said Jack, sweat pouring off him.

Barney obediently stopped and Jack got off the limbers.

Initially he struggled to stand but eventually he moved to the wheels and withdrew the lockers, one intact the other broken in two. The wheels were red hot.

He stood there, gasping. There was no one to talk to, no one to tell him it was alright, no one to celebrate his survival, no one to tell him to take a break.

So he simply carried on.

He threw the broken locker into one of the tubs, thanked God for his life, and took the load to where it was needed, dropped it off and made his way back to the pit bottom to pick up the next one.

At the end of his shift, Jack showed the Stableman the broken locker and told him about his dice with death.

The Stableman smacked him on the head; it was not the sympathetic reaction Jack had been hoping for.

'You stupid or something? You should have checked the condition of the lockers at the start,' he said.

'But…'

'But what?'

'But I thought I had. They're pieces of hardwood, what could go wrong?'

'Checking something down here isn't the same as doing it in broad daylight, shadows hide things, you have to get close, use your lamp, look carefully, and more than once. Maybe somebody rode a tub over one of them. You never know, anything can go wrong at any time. Don't you forget that and always take precautions.'

'Precautions?'

'Like I say, always check your equipment, no matter what it is.'

'But I did,' objected Jack.

'You evidently didn't check it well enough, did you? Always check it twice! Check it more than that if you're worried. Ask someone if you're not sure.'

'But I might get a clip for disturbing them.'

'Better a clip than a coffin! Don't take anything for granted. Don't think that because you've done something time and time again that this time it's going to be alright. Do everything like it was the first time! You could have been killed, you could have killed the horse, you could have killed somebody else.'

'I know,' said Jack, 'I'm sorry.'

'Sorry doesn't turn the clock back, son, sorry doesn't fix anything, the only thing that makes any difference is what you do. Learn Jack, and learn quickly, not everybody gets another chance,' he paused, 'and one other thing, if all else fails, make a lot of noise, let everybody know that you're coming and give them the best chance of getting out of the way.'

'I'm sorry,' he said lowering his head, 'who else do I need to report the accident to?'

His question was partially answered by another smack around the head.

'Accident, what accident? You want me to report that you broke a stick? Don't you think there's more important things for me to be doing? The accident statistics are bad enough without this kind of nonsense,' he paused, 'You've reported it to me, that's enough and, and listen carefully to this, it stays with me, you don't go telling anybody else, you understand?'

'I understand,' said Jack, 'and I am sorry.'

The Stableman softened a little, but only a little.

'You've said that already, you're still alive, nobody's injured, you got away with this one Jack, make sure you learn from it. Now go and get out, it's the end of your shift.'

Jack trudged off towards the pit bottom. The Stableman looked at his retreating back, the slumped shoulders,

'Sometimes I think we start 'em too young, but that's only what I did,' he thought, his hand moving unconsciously to stroke an old scar that ran up his left arm, 'experience is hard earned down here, but there's worse things.'

A series of faces started to appear in his mind, old faces, young faces. He shook his head; there was no time for this. The work needed to be done a shift at a time, and that's how you had to take it, a shift at a time. Learn from the last, survive the present, and let the future look after itself.

Later that night Jack told his father and brother what had happened, he was too full of it to keep it to himself.

'You've been bloody lucky,' they said, but refrained from clipping him round the ear, although only just.

'You're Stableman was right,' said his father, 'learn from it, but at the same time put it behind you, and carry on. Thank God nobody was hurt.'

They were quiet for a moment.

'And it's best not to tell your mother, I think,' said his father.

Jack and Edward agreed.

Jack through embarrassment, Edward because he thought it would only make things worse.

Chapter 43

As normal, Sarah and Jenny were working together in the kitchen.

Jenny was making bread and Sarah was darning socks. They were talking as they worked. Jenny had just been telling Sarah about one of their neighbours. They'd been arguing again, they argued about everything she said, even though they were bringing up eight children and seemed to be managing.

'There's nowt so strange as folk,' said Jenny, 'if you didn't know what a close family they were, and you saw them shouting at each other in the street like that, you'd think they didn't like each other,' she smiled to herself, 'Aye, there's nowt so strange as folk.'

Sarah was quiet for a moment.

Jenny bit her tongue, family squabbles were not something to be reminding Sarah about, she cursed her own thoughtlessness.

The silence dragged and then Sarah said,

'Ma, can I ask you something?'

Jenny's arms were covered in flour; she was knocking back the dough after it had been allowed to rise. She kept kneading, focusing on her task and hoping that she had not unintentionally hurt Sarah.

'Of course you can, Sarah, you know you can always ask me anything.'

'It's about boys,' said Sarah.

'Oh,' said Jenny, trying not to smile, secretly pleased that this was the subject that was occupying Sarah's mind. She was becoming a young woman now; boys were bound to come into the picture.

'How do you know Ma?'

Jenny paused in her work.

'How do you know what?'

'Well, when a boy is for you.'

Jenny left the dough to prove, wiped her arms on her apron.

'That's a difficult one,' she said, taking Sarah's naïveté seriously. In the back of her mind it reminded her of her own younger days and when she'd first met Frank. On that first meeting she hadn't thought him anything special but now they'd been married over 20 years and had three live children and lost two, 'it's different for everybody I think, but for me it was his kindness,' she said.

'His kindness?'

'Yes, I was out one day, on the way to the shops for my own Ma, and I saw two men picking on a smaller one. Frank happened along and he stepped in and stopped the bullying and walked away with the smaller man. I don't think he even saw me, but that made an impression on me. The next time I saw him I decided he was worth getting to know.'

'Is it always like that?'

'I'm not an expert,' said Jenny, 'but seems to me there's always something that gets you interested.'

'Hmm,' said Sarah.

'So, tell me,' said Jenny, 'has a boy got his eye on you?'

'No,' said Sarah, 'but I'm working on it.'

'Oh!' said Jenny, trying to think who it might be and coming up blank. She didn't want to pry but Sarah was as close to her as any daughter, and she wanted to help and protect her if she could.

'Can I help?' she said.

'I think you just have, Ma,' said Sarah.

Jenny wanted to ask more. She wanted to say more. But the bread needed to be baked, cakes needed to be made, clothes needed to be cleaned, water needed to be heated. She made a mental note that this conversation wasn't finished, and she'd look for an opportunity to dig a bit deeper. She knew that girls had crushes and didn't believe that this would be anything too serious. At some point she would need to talk to Sarah about sex, but that could definitely wait for another day.

Chapter 44

Tubs often got derailed and needed manhandling to clear the resulting blockage, which was no easy task.

Rails got twisted and broken and there never seemed to be enough to both extend the lines further in, keeping pace with the progress of the face, and to repair breakages. There were simply not enough new rails sent down into the pit and the Drivers were always on the lookout for disused workings from which old rails could be scavenged for reuse.

'Jack, come with me.'

It was the underground Deputy, Charlie, the man who had first introduced Jack to the stables.

Jack knew better than to argue and walked Barney over to where Charlie was standing.

'Hitch you pony to these tubs,' he said, 'we're going to collect some rails.'

In the first tub were a few tools and a tin water bottle. Jack perched on the limbers, Charlie sat in the last of the three tubs and Barney walked steadily forward, the tubs following the rails beneath their wheels.

They progressed along increasingly older workings until the rails turned away to the right whilst their route lay forward. Jack unhooked Barney from the tubs and helped Charlie to lift them off the rails and to the side so as not to obstruct other traffic. Charlie took a hammer and chisel and the water bottle, and Jack led Barney as they continued on their way, their lamps giving an unsteady though guiding light.

Together they walked on, stumbling occasionally on the uneven floor, pitted by the removal of old rails.

Down increasingly deserted passages they went until they reached a part of the pit that had been worked out.

Jack had never been this way before and found it eerily quiet, the only noise coming from their own breathing and the rattling of Barney's chains. As their lamps swung at their stride the light wavered, lighting a patch here, casting a shadow there.

Eventually they came to the entrance of a narrow passageway with a low roof. Here forward access was blocked by a single wooden plank, splashed with red paint, that denoted that beyond this was a 'no go' area, a closed off and abandoned area in which there was no longer any air circulation.

Charlie stepped forward and, holding up his lamp, examined the wooden spar.

'Come and hold the lamp,' he said to Jack, 'there's some nails here I need to shift.'

Jack did as he was told and Charlie took the hammer and eased the nails from the plank at either end with the claw and then tugged it free. It gave with a creak and he lifted it and put it to one side.

'I don't know how deep we need to go but I do know that there's some rails in here we can salvage.'

Jack looked into the deepening dark. He wasn't so sure.

Leaving Barney at the entrance, they bent to the reduced roof height and entered the passage. At first there were no rails, someone else had been there before them.

So, they went in deeper.

'There are rails in here,' said Charlie, 'we just need to go further in. I'll lead the way. Follow close, watch your lamp, we need all the light we can get.'

Jack was uncomfortable about going further in, there was no guarantee that the abandoned workings were safe as not just rails, but wall and roof supports could have been removed for reuse elsewhere. But he didn't want to show fear in front of Charlie, so he bit his lip and carried on.

They trekked up the passageway in single file. It was immediately clear that it was no longer in the condition that it had been when it had been properly worked. There were areas of partial collapse where the roof had sagged on its supports and the walls had crumbled inwards.

But Charlie would not be put off and they got down on their hands and knees and crawled forward when they had to.

'Come on,' said Charlie, 'it can't be much further.'

They were in about fifty yards before they saw any rails; still lying in their original positions, bearing the scratches and wear marks from the passing of coal tubs, now long gone.

'We'll go in deeper and work our way back,' said Charlie.

They went on a further fifty yards and then bent to set about dismantling the rails. It was slow work getting the rails up. They were laid on wooden bars that themselves were set into the floor with nails hammered home to secure them.

The idea was to raise the rails and then throw them back towards the entrance where Barney was patiently waiting in the pitch black. Jack had faith that Barney was steadfast enough to stand there and wait, but he was worried that if he became too hungry or if his inner clock told him that the shift was nearly over, then he might turn about and start to walk slowly back the way they had come, despite the darkness, searching for a way to get back to the stables. There were plenty of stories in the underground stables of ponies that had done just that and left their Drivers in the lurch. Jack was pretty sure Barney wouldn't do that but there was a lingering doubt, and the longer that he was left alone, the greater the risk. Jack couldn't help but be concerned. He wanted to get back to check on him as soon as he could.

Charlie used the claw of the hammer to extract the securing nails; some gave way easier than others. As they worked they sweated, without air circulation the heat was becoming overpowering and they took a breather every ten minutes or so and then carried on.

Jack told Charlie that he wanted to check on Barney.

Half an hour later, Charlie lifted his safety lamp and held it up to the roof, the yellow flame had a bluish tinge.

'Methane,' said Charlie, 'collecting in pockets. We don't want to stay here any longer than we have to. I think we've loosened enough rails for you to start carrying them back and check your pony. I'll keep working with the hammer, then we can both get out of here. Don't be too long.'

Jack carried and dragged as many rails as he could manage and was relieved when he felt the air cool and become fresher. When he got back to Barney, he put his arm around his neck,

'Good boy, Barney, we'll get out of here as soon as we can, won't be too long now.'

He took a few moments to breathe deeply before splashing some water on his head and rinsing out his mouth, spitting it out into a dark corner. After he'd recovered himself, he returned to the tunnel.

As expected, he soon saw Charlie's light and when he got closer, he called out, 'Charlie, I'm back.'

There was no answer.

'Charlie,' he called again.

Again there was no answer and he made his way forward with increasing trepidation. He soon saw a body slumped next to the lamp. Jack started to panic, he got to the body and shook it,

'Charlie, Charlie,'

The body groaned. Jack slapped his face,

'Charlie, come on, Charlie!'

As he bent closer, he could hear the struggle for breath. Jack got his arm around Charlie's shoulders and started to lift and drag. Charlie was bigger and heavier than Jack and Jack was straining to try and move him.

'Come on Charlie, you've got to help me, come on…'

Jack could feel his own strength beginning to wane, his breathing more of a gasp. Charlie stirred and tried to crawl. Together they made their way out, painful move by painful move, climbing over the stacked rails that they'd thrown in the direction of the exit.

Time slowed and it seemed like hours, the distance seemed like miles, before the first fifty yards were regained and they paused, their backs against the hard surface of the wall, each gasping for breath, and here breath there was, not pure or clean, but purer and cleaner,

'Let's go again,' said Jack.

'Yes,' mumbled Charlie.

And so they did, by a joint act of will, by leaning on each other, they crawled out and past the point where the plank had crossed the passageway, attempting to close it off. Attempting to prevent entry.

Once out they paused again,

'My God,' said Charlie, 'what happened?'

'You collapsed,' said Jack, reaching out to Barney and using his body as a crutch to climb up and regain his feet. He reached out for the tin water bottle and splashed his face and neck, reached down to Charlie and helped him regain his feet, and gave him the water. Although it was tepid, the water was like a salve, and Charlie splashed his face and tried to drink. It made him cough and he staggered to the wall, leant on it, and vomited, an acid reflux splashing onto the floor. He stood bent, splashed and sipped more water, nauseous and coughing. But he was now in fresher air and the air revived him, flushing out his lungs, oxygen recharging his tissues.

Jack stood by and waited. Barney was alongside him, looking on in bewilderment.

'Oh my God,' said Charlie, a splitting headache blurring his vision.

As he came round two thoughts surfaced most strongly,

'Don't ever tell anybody, do you hear me, don't tell anyone!'

Jack said that he wouldn't.

'And I'm not going back without those bloody rails! You'll have to get them!'

'I won't go back,' said Jack.

'I'm not going back empty handed.'

'We've got some,' said Jack, pointing to the few rails he'd brought back.

Charlie gave a laugh.

'That's pathetic,' he said, 'you're going to have to go back and get the rest. If you do it in short bursts, you'll be alright. My problem was the work I put in and the time I was in there. The rails are all loose now, they just need bringing back.'

Jack said nothing.

'Remember who's in charge here,' said Charlie, standing taller and beginning to get angry.

Jack had no choice. Charlie was a Deputy, he was only a Driver. What a Deputy said, a Driver did.

Without saying anything else Jack started towards the passageway.

'Shout if you need help,' said Charlie, 'here, take the water.'

Jack re-entered the tunnel.

He tried to shut out everything else from his mind and focus purely ahead and, move by shuffled move, he made his way to the furthest of the loose rails, turned, grabbed them one at a time and hurled them as far as he could in the direction of the exit.

Then he moved onwards, now in the direction of the exit, his light wavering, not looking at whether it was purely yellow or not, until he felt the next rails, as black as the ground they lay in, and repeated the process, occasionally hearing the clang of rail hitting rail in the darkness ahead.

Then he moved forward again, feeling the sweat trickle down his neck, and paused to regain his breath, taking a little water, swilling it around his mouth, spitting it out, splashing a little on his wrists and neck, realising that his breathing was becoming more laboured, and then he threw again, more rails this time, the number accumulating.

Jack repeated this process 5 more times, stooping to crawl where the roof was at its lowest, trying to ensure the rails did not hit the weakened roof or wall in their flight and dislodge anything.

After this amount of exertion, Jack squeezed past the pile of rails, took a few and returned to the entrance where Charlie was waiting. He seemed much recovered and was standing more steadily.

Jack dropped the rails at Charlie's feet and leant against the wall breathing in deeply the sweeter, but by no means fresh, air.

'I'll take these back to the tubs,' said Charlie, 'then I'll go in and get the rest.'

Jack shook his head.

'I think I'm through the worst of it,' he said, 'I'll go back in and finish the job.'

Charlie just nodded. He understood, and, lifting the rails, he disappeared down the passage towards the tubs, his light swinging from side to side with his steps.

Jack leant against Barney's shoulder and stroked his mane.

'I'm beginning to understand how you feel,' he said, 'you must think we're all crazy.'

The pony nodded his head up and down.

'I'll just give it a couple of more minutes then I'll go in again,' said Jack.

And after those few minutes, he hitched up his belt, took his lamp, leaving Barney in the dark, and entered the narrow passage again.

This time he only needed to go in sixty or seventy yards to reach the growing pile of rails, squeeze past them and throw them one after the other towards the entrance.

Then again, and again, the accumulation of rails getting closer to the entrance, the air getting less bad, reaching up to the point where rails had previously been removed and feeling relief in the knowledge that others had been in this far, and then taking another rail, moving it forward,

'Almost done,' he said to himself, 'almost done,'

After another twenty minutes of effort, he heard Charlie shouting.

'Jack, I can hear you now, stop a minute, I'm coming in.'

Seeing Jack's light Charlie was soon there,

'It's wide enough for the two of us now,' he said.

And together they lifted and threw and recovered, the two men looking at each other but not speaking, and going again; throw, move forward, throw, collect, making short work of the last twenty yards.

Once all the rails were outside of the abandoned passageway, Charlie hammered the plank back into place, re-closing the tunnel.

'If anyone asks, I'd strongly advise against trying to recover any more rails from here,' he said, 'it's too dangerous.'

Jack thoroughly agreed but said nothing.

Over the next forty minutes they shifted the rails to where the tubs were, some laid across Barney's back as Jack walked him back and forth.

'Is that the last?' said Charlie.

'Yes.'

'Alright, let's go.'

Jack attached Barney to the chains, sat on the limbers, Charlie made enough space to get into one of the tubs.

As they rumbled on, at Barney's walking pace, Jack wondered whether it had all been worth it. The rails would be welcomed, he was sure of that, but wouldn't it have been better to fix the real problem? The problem that not enough rails were being sent down to match the speed at which the workings were advancing.

This lack of materials was the reason that rails had become so valuable a commodity underground and Jack had heard stories of rails that were piled up for use in one section being stolen for use in another.

It was becoming common practice to hide rails in a darkened corner somewhere for future use. The Drivers would get into real trouble with the face workers if they failed to provide the materials they needed when they needed them, even though it might be through no fault of their own.

There were even stories of fights breaking out, and that didn't help anybody. Put under such stress, one Driver had even gone so far as to rip up already laid rails en route to his own section but away from the face.

This was a cardinal sin and the culprit was severely dealt with as an example to others. But that didn't stop Drivers being on permanent lookout for materials that could be of use in their sections, and there was no honour among them where rails are concerned.

Jack didn't know if anyone knew about what they'd been doing, and he wasn't going to ask. When Charlie told him not to tell anyone about their efforts, he got his answer. But what would they have done if the air had been more noxious, if they had both been overcome?

They returned slowly, and Jack was too exhausted to think about it.

In fact, he was too exhausted to think about anything and left Barney to carry them on their way without giving him any directions, which didn't seem to matter as the pony walked through the more and more familiar passages steadily and confidently.

When they reached one of the doors, the Trapper recognised Jack,

'Hello there, Jack,' he said, 'been reading any good books lately?'

Charlie, who the Trapper hadn't seen, called from behind,

'I don't have time for idle chatter, just open the bloody doors!'

The Trapper was stunned into silence and although Jack tried to give him a reassuring nod, he leapt into action without another word and they continued on their way.

After dropping off the rails at the section Charlie directed them to and hiding a number in a hollow that was cut into one of the walls, they made their way to the pit bottom and collected more, and cooler, water that they both drank as if it were the best thing they'd ever tasted.

Leaving Charlie and the now empty tubs at the pit bottom, Jack made his way back to the stables, fed Barney and relieved him of his harness.

When his father and brother asked him what kind of shift he'd had, Jack just said that he'd been busy helping Charlie and that the time had passed quite quickly.

'Ah, the Deputy,' said his father, 'he's got a reputation for taking chances he has, not afraid to bend the rules double over. Didn't have you doing anything fishy did he?'

'Oh, no,' said Jack too quickly, 'of course not.'

Edward and Frank glanced at each other; they both knew when it was better not to ask any more questions.

Chapter 45

At shearing time families in their horse drawn caravans would appear, park up in the designated field and do a hard day's work for cash in hand.

At night, if the weather was kind, there would be a blazing fire using branches salvaged from the adjacent wood, and in the yellow-red flickering light there would be eating, drinking and loud talk, and on more than one occasion there would be music, singing and perhaps the swirl of dance.

Peter and Jack would slip out, when they could get away with it, on nights like this and sit in the shadows watching, the heat flushing their cheeks.

Over his visits, Jack was becoming more and more aware of the difference between their lives.

Mr Moore did not shave every day and was often found with stubble on his chin. Frank, Jack's father, shaved every day believing that, by doing so, he was reducing the number of places where the coal dust could settle, though, from the colour of his skin when he got home, it didn't seem to make that much difference.

Jack's life as a miner was dictated by the clock, irrespective of rain, hail, snow or sunshine there was only one season underground and you got there and stayed there for your allotted time.

Jack worked to bring out coal and put nothing back. A mine would open, be worked until it was no longer worth it and other mines would be dug ready to replace it. According to the geologists, there was nothing to worry about, the supply of coal in the area was limitless.

Peter's life, on the other hand, was dictated by the seasons, one day never the same as the last, each day bringing both familiar and 'surprise' tasks, either welcome or unwelcome. They had a clock in the farmhouse, but it was only a guide, not a master.

Peter worked to give and take in equal measure, dealing in birth and death, sowing and reaping, aiming to ensure the farm remained sustainable for generations to come.

'Look at this,' said Peter, 'here on the back of this cow.'

Jack went closer and looked.

On the back of the cow was something that looked like a large boil, in the centre of which was a white spot.

'Looks painful,' said Jack.

'Look more closely,' said Peter

Peter put his fingers either side of the swelling and stretched the skin. The cow moved uncomfortably.

'Steady girl,' said Peter, 'we'll soon have you sorted.'

Jack bent his head, the white in the centre seemed to be larger now and, when he looked more closely, it seemed to be moving. Jack looked again, yes, it was definitely moving.

'Yeugh,' he said, 'what's that?'

'It's a grub,' said Peter, 'nasty things, they hatch out as ugly looking flies if you let them: large, hairy, brown and orange, almost look like a bumblebee, only nastier. They don't feed and don't live very long but mate and lay their eggs on the hairs on the cow's lower legs. That's why we call them "heel flies".'

'If they lay their eggs down there then how…,' Jack paused, 'oh, no, don't tell me…'

'Yes, I'm afraid so,' said Peter, 'when the eggs hatch the larvae burrow into the skin and eat their way upwards through the muscles.'

'That sounds horrible.'

'Spend months wriggling around inside,' said Peter, enjoying Jack's discomfort, 'and then they come up towards the surface and produce these swellings, that's how you know they're getting close to hatching.'

'So what are we going to do?'

'We're going to break the skin and get the little buggers out.'

Jack wasn't keen.

'Why don't we squash them?'

'If we squash them under the skin, it can cause an infection, better to get them out, even if it leaves a hole or a scar.'

'They're horrible but do they do any harm?'

'Damages the meat, can affect milk yields, so they're not good news. Here you stretch the skin.'

Jack did what he was told and when Peter scratched the skin a yellowish-white maggot about an inch long emerged.

'Yeugh,' said Jack for the second time.

'Now we squish it,' said Peter, taking it between his finger and thumb and squeezing.

The maggot burst open, its milky insides making a mess.

'Yeugh!'

'Now we look for others on this cow and then inspect the rest,' said Peter.

'Great,' said Jack, 'what a nice way to spend an afternoon.'

Bathed in the afternoon sun, the sounds and smells and sights of the farm surrounding them, they found several more and dealt with them in the same way.

Chapter 46

Depending on his work schedule, Jack would sometimes eat his bait at the stables and occasionally the Stableman would join him.

He was also an avid reader and as a consequence took to Jack and liked to talk to him about life underground and some of the things he'd experienced, or been reliably told, during his time.

'Some ponies can be very clever and learn from experience,' he said, 'If a tub is travelling too fast on an incline for the pony to gallop ahead of and stay safe, a clever pony will use its hind quarters and lean back a bit to slow down the tubs before they can pick up too much speed. I've even known a pony to kick out its hind legs and uncouple the chains from the tubs so they can swerve off to one side and let the runaway tubs carry on without them.'

'What about the Driver?' asked Jack, alarmed.

'Just got to hold on until the tubs slow down. If he's got lockers in place properly, it's not as dangerous as it sounds.'

'Unless they break,' muttered Jack.

'What's that?'

'Nothing,' said Jack, 'nothing at all.'

'In one section,' continued the Stableman, 'where the weight of the roof had lowered it so that in a few places it was lower than a certain pony's hindquarters, this clever animal, that I knew, would go down on its front knees and walk like that for the few steps needed to get under the lowest part of the roof. There's no end to the talents of an intelligent pony, but they're not all like that unfortunately, some can be pretty stupid.'

'I think I've got a clever one,' said Jack.

'Clever and strong willed,' said the Stableman, 'but as I say, they're not all clever and, although I didn't witness the event itself, I've been involved in some accidents were the pony was so stupid it seemed to have a death wish.'

'Really?' said Jack, 'I would have thought that any animal's first instinct would be to survive.'

'You'd think so wouldn't you. The pony I mean was called Stanley, he was young, inexperienced, and headstrong, and whenever he could he would get the bit between his teeth and take off in a headlong gallop.'

'Normally, as you well know Jack, whenever a pony gets the bit between its teeth, no amount of pulling on the reins will make it come to a stop, and no Driver could ever stop Stanley from doing this.'

'Well, on one shift, Stanley broke into a gallop and his Driver could see ahead of them that there were lights being swung from side to side giving a warning of some kind of trouble. But Stanley wouldn't be slowed and as they got closer and closer to the lights the Driver had no alternative but to save himself and jump out of the way, which he did.'

'As it happens, the obstruction was due to some derailed tubs. The tubs were full of coal and there were men battling to try and move them back onto the rails. Well, even though Stanley must have seen them he ran headlong into the back of them. Other ponies would have at least tried to move to one side of the tubs; it was a main passage and there was room.'

'When the Driver picked himself up and reached the scene, Stanley was lying on his side panting and couldn't stand up.'

'The Supervisor was told and the area vet was called for. The Driver blamed himself, but there was little he could have done with a runaway horse at full gallop.'

'He went to his pony and did his best to calm him. The pony was clearly in pain and the Driver kept talking to him. He even took out his bait tin and offered Stanley a sandwich, but he showed no interest in eating, which was very unusual. He then brought over the water bottle and tried to get Stanley to take a drink, which he did, but only a little.'

'The news got back to the stable and about half an hour later I arrived with another pony pulling a flat-bed which I'd hoped I wouldn't need.'

'Once I'd examined the pony, I was pretty sure the injuries were serious, and I told the Driver, who broke down in tears.'

'When the pony urinated, it was a discoloured brown colour, a sure sign of internal bleeding, so I was confirmed in my fears. Although I thought that the humane thing to do was to put the pony out of its pain, I didn't have either the equipment or the authority, and the poor animal had to endure its suffering for two more hours until the vet arrived.'

'When the vet had examined the pony, he pronounced that there was one broken fetlock, another that was seriously damaged, and internal injuries that were more difficult to diagnose under the conditions.'

'Without any further consideration he extracted a humane killer from his equipment, placed the gun against Stanley's forehead and pulled the trigger.'

'The horse was killed instantly. The body was then put onto the flat-bed, it needed four men to lift and manoeuvre it, and then it was taken to the pit bottom, its Driver accompanying it, the body still warm.'

'The Driver even talked to the dead horse on the way, I could hear him, he cursed the pony for being a fool, told him he had tried his best to hold him back, that there was nothing more he could have done to prevent the accident, and then he told him how sorry he was.'

'I looked away because there were tears streaming down his face. Once we reached the pit bottom the body was taken up the shaft and into the daylight.'

'That's the thing about working with animals,' said the Stableman, 'it doesn't matter how stupid they are, you still get to know them, they become an extension of yourself, and if anything happens to them you still feel it.'

Jack thought about Barney, and how he would feel if an accident like that ever happened to him. Barney was not stupid, but working underground was a dangerous pursuit, and accidents could happen to the best of them.

He finished his bait and got back to work, making sure Barney had eaten his oats and giving him a drink. He put his arm around Barney's neck and whispered in his ear,

'I'll do my best to look after you,' he said, 'you deserve it, you're a grand lad.'

Barney neighed softly and began to turn, he knew it was time to get back to work.

He was a clever pony.

Chapter 47

Sarah was a good help to Jenny and willingly took on responsibility for as many of the household chores as she was increasingly capable of.

Without saying anything Sarah won her way into Jenny's heart through her willingness to turn her hand to anything that was asked of her and by her open, generous and kind nature.

If Jenny picked fault with anything that she did, however gentle the criticism, Sarah would bow her head, listen carefully, and vow to herself that she would do better next time. Pleased to have a home, she was desperate to make herself useful and Jenny was happy to admit that when it came to sewing, darning, knitting and the making or repair of clothing, Sarah was a natural.

One afternoon while Sarah was out at a neighbouring farm, Jenny said to Jack, who was with her in the backyard,

'She's a good lass that Sarah. She must have been very unhappy before, though she never talks about her father's temper after a drink. I've never seen anyone take on chores so easy and do them so well,' she paused, 'but I don't want you telling her I said that, you hear.'

Jack nodded his head. He knew that such praise was hard won from his mother's lips. He'd never really thought about Sarah as a person before, just as another body occupying the same house as him. Maybe he should pay her more attention.

Jenny and Sarah had built up a local reputation for making copies of dresses that they would see in the dress shop windows of Newcastle or Sunderland, at almost equal quality and significantly lower cost.

Sarah, in particular, was good at remembering the shapes, colours and patterns and then making similar looking items at home. Indeed, Jenny and Sarah would plan occasional visits to Newcastle or Sunderland for things that were best bought there and would make sure that they left themselves enough time to look around the dress shops before they got the train home.

'I sold that dress to Mrs Moore, and she told her niece about it, and she came knocking, asking if I had anything else made up,' said Sarah.

'Oh well, we'll have to get something started then, folks are wanting more ready made from us these days,' said Jenny.

'I've been thinking for a bit now that we might consider buying a sewing machine. It would speed the making up,' said Sarah.

Jenny had to admit that ready-to-wear seemed to be taking over from made-to-measure clothing now that the factory system was in full flow and sewing machines were becoming more readily available, but it was still expensive to buy clothing from the High Street.

'Yes, but how much does a sewing machine cost?' asked Jenny, always conscious of not over-spending.

Sarah didn't know.

'Well, maybe we can look into it. I might ask Mr Denby when he comes around next.'

Although Jenny was averse to the unsettling nature of change, she knew that it was important to keep up with what her customers wanted. If she were seen to be becoming 'old fashioned' then people might simply go elsewhere for their clothes, and the extra income dressmaking gave her was important enough not to want that to happen.

Jenny and Sarah also altered clothes to fit the prevailing fashion, for example, by adding new neck collars, or enhancing the detail on a skirt.

They had always done this to their own clothes as, although they both liked to keep up with the prevailing fashion, they couldn't afford to buy brand new dresses that could be considered a luxury, and not strictly due to the ravages of wear and tear.

Although she looked after the pennies, Jenny would often make items of clothing for the least well-off families without being asked and without payment. She couldn't bear to see children 'shabby' as she called it and, as long as she had some 'spare' material, then she was happy to use it.

As she prepared the vegetables, Jenny gathered the peelings and put them to one side for Grandpa to take to the allotment. She put the potatoes into a pot and placed that onto the iron grill of the range, directly above the red glow of the perpetual coal fire. The kettle, heavy with the water that Sarah had brought in from the communal standpipe, was on the hot plate coming to the boil.

Sarah arranged the plates and cutlery and brought out the boiled ham, pease pudding, and bread from the pantry.

'You'll make some young miner a fine wife,' Jenny said to Sarah, her thoughts becoming words before she had time to stop them.

Sarah blushed.

Jenny thought about the things Sarah must have witnessed between her own parents. She regretted her words, even though they were meant lightly. She was too strong a character to back down now though.

'A woman needs a roof over her head and a wage coming in,' she said, 'and there's not many other ways than finding a good husband that I know of.'

'But there's not so many good husbands going begging is there?' said Sarah.

Fortunately for both of them there was the sound of hobnail boots in the yard outside. The back door opened and Frank and Edward walked in.

'Get your dirties off and wash yourselves,' said Jenny, 'I'll get your house clothes. Sarah empty that kettle and the bucket into the tub, will you. Then re-fill the kettle and set it back on the range. The soap's on the windersill and I'll bring the scrubbing brush and the towel. I'll scrub your backs, you do your own heads, front, arms and hands. Hurry up now Frank, Edward's got to follow you, and the tatties are on and I don't want them getting over boiled or going cold. Sarah, you go outside now, and I'll give you a shout when they're decent. Then get the butter and put it on the table.'

'We better do what we're told,' said Frank.

'You're right there Da, there's more instructions here than we get down the pit!'

Whenever he could Jack would bring down an apple or a carrot for Barney, with the idea of keeping it until sometime during the shift when they both needed a breather.

This well-meant plan was hardly ever executed successfully however as Barney had a nose for these treats and when he'd decided which pocket it was in, would repeatedly nudge until Jack could stand it no longer and gave over the prize, which was immediately consumed.

'If you keep behaving like this, I won't bring you anymore,' Jack would say into the pony's ear.

But both he and Barney knew he didn't mean it. Jack saw Barney as a pal as well as a workmate, and the pony responded to his kindness.

'There was one horse that I can't forget,' said the Stableman, 'Sam was his name, he was a horse of great strength. Dapple grey he was, larger than a pony. He worked at the pit bottom where the work requires a horse of great strength, any of the ponies, although strong for their size, would find work like that too demanding. It was not unusual to see him pulling twenty tubs all in a line. Sam always rose to any task.'

As he spoke it was as if the Stableman was talking about a son of his, the pride in his voice was so evident.

'He worked for years at the job, he was such a fine looking and friendly horse and was everyone's favourite. Lots of the men brought him a carrot or an apple or other treats.'

His voice dropped as he continued.

'On one shift, a shift we thought was just like all the others, a number of tubs 'ran away' and hit and trapped Sam and he fell to the ground. He was obviously badly injured and the area vet was called down from the surface. When he arrived he diagnosed a seriously injured back, said the horse could not be saved, and that he would put Sam out of his misery.'

The Stableman swallowed hard at the memory.

'I asked if there was any hope, if I could take Sam back to the stables and try and save him. The vet told me I was on a loser but, because I had the support of the ring of onlookers who knew how special Sam was, he reluctantly gave his permission for me to try and, though he prescribed a course of painkillers for the horse, said that if the horse was in severe pain then he should be called back and he would see to it that Sam was humanely killed.'

The Stableman paused to wipe a fleck of coal dust from his eye.

'There was no shortage of helpers as we manhandled Sam onto an open sided buggy and took him to the stables where I managed to put together some slings and harnesses and, with help, haul Sam back onto his feet.'

'Later I made a further set of, I suppose you could call them cradles, and strung these from the roof. I managed it so that Sam's legs were touching the floor but most of his weight was supported.'

The Stableman supped on his cold tea. Jack sat and listened, conscious that bait time was nearly up, but he wanted to hear the end of the story. He had lots of questions he wanted to ask but knew that any interruption would slow the telling, so he just sat quiet and listened.

'It took a few months, Sam never let his head drop, although there were times I thought we'd have to call it a day, but then slowly there were signs that he was beginning to improve. It was a miracle really, made possible because he was a strong horse, in mind and spirit as well as physically.'

'Slowly but surely I was able to loosen and then remove his supports, feed him up and watch as he came back to fitness. The funny thing was that, in all the trauma and everything, when it came time to put a harness on him again, something he'd had hundreds of times before the accident, he shied away and I had to retrain him all over again, just as if he were a new horse. He'd also forgotten how to listen to and follow instruction and how to pull tubs. It took a time but eventually Sam was good as new, head held as proud as before, and pulling the same weight, with the same ease.'

The Stableman stopped.

'You saved his life,' Jack said.

'Didn't do anything that he didn't deserve,' said the Stableman, 'now I've blathered on quite long enough, let's get back to work.'

That evening, Jack repeated the story to his father,

'That's all true,' said Frank, 'I remember that horse, I think anybody in the mine at that time would remember Sam, and not without affection. But he didn't tell you the rest of the story?'

'Is there more?' Jack feared the worst.

'There is,' said Frank, 'Sam did not end his days in the dark. After the years he'd put in he was brought up to the surface one last time and was taken on by one of the farmers and lived out his days like any retired miner should, in the daylight and on lighter duties.'

'Really?'

'There's even a bit more,' said Frank, 'Sam was such a good looking horse that he was shown at some of the local fairs, and won many a prize in his category. He was even featured in the newspaper with a report on all his rosettes.'

'That's some life,' said Jack.

'Better than a lot of others,' said Frank.

Some girls were taught the way to a man's heart by their mothers.

For others there was no such conversation.

'They might be stronger than us but they're like big kids,' said Jenny one day as she and Sarah were doing the laundry out in the back yard, Jenny adding the soap and getting at it with the posser, Sarah fetching the water and heating it up. There were plenty of dirty clothes and it would take more than one tub full to get it all done.

'Give them a welcoming home to come back to, a good fire in the grate, and food on the table. That's what they like, to be fed and looked after.'

At least the 'fire in the grate' was made easier by the weekly deliveries of free coal from the pit, a perk of the miner's job. But it still needed managing to make sure it didn't run out, and the fires needed tending and the ashes needed raking out, to use in the privy or on the allotment.

'But what about love,' said Sarah.

Jenny stopped pounding the clothes for a moment and looked at Sarah.

'Aye, it helps if you like each other,' she said, 'makes life a lot easier.'

But Sarah had started this now and she wasn't going to be put off.

'But how do you know, Ma?' she said.

She'd asked the same question of Jenny before. But this time it seemed to go deeper.

Jenny was all too aware of the turbulent household that Sarah had been brought up in and the mysterious death of her father. Sarah must have already seen many things that were better not seen.

'With me an' Frank,' said Jenny, 'it weren't no instant thing, he kind of grew on me, he made me laugh, he still does, and he and me seemed to have the same attitude; work hard, find some good things along the way,' she paused, 'And we have found some good things, our three boys first among them.'

She almost said, 'and you,' but she didn't.

Sarah was listening closely.

'And how did he make you feel, Ma?' she said.

Jenny smiled.

'Ah,' she said, 'I see.'

Sarah blushed.

'He made me feel soft,' she said, 'when he touched me it was like nothing I'd felt before.'

Jenny paused, then said,

'My mother never told me anything about love making. But there's things that are best known, and ways that are good to know about.'

'I'll get some more water,' said Sarah, hurrying away.

Chapter 48

Most of Jack's shifts were uneventful.

He harnessed Barney, went where he was told, pulled loads from one place to another, ate his bait at the stable or in the near darkness of the pit, moved some more loads, unharnessed Barney, kept him fed, bedded and watered, and arrived and left via the pit shaft, trading darkness for light, or darkness for moonlight, depending on the season or shift timetable.

Once Barney got to know Jack and trust him, he was docile, and would respond to his voice, stopping and going without the need for the rein. Jack was proud of the way he handled himself and was sure that Barney knew the job at least as well as he did. Barney was never uncontrollable and he did not kick out or try to bite any of the other ponies like some of the others did.

Jack was now used to harnessing him up and his confidence transferred itself to Barney, who would move himself in ways that assisted the process. Jack was also no longer surprised by Barney's roll in the dust and actively encouraged it as he could see how much his pony enjoyed the experience.

After hooking Barney's halter to two tubs of wood props, Jack made his way towards the face, dropped them off, and then prepared to return to the pit bottom with the empty tubs to pick up his next load. They'd done this so many times that it had almost become automatic for Jack and he got careless.

Going around a particularly tight bend his lamp smacked against the wall and went out.

Jack was sitting on the limbers and ordered Barney to stop. It was alright to be confident of your whereabouts when you had a little light but complete darkness was a different thing altogether. There were many twists and turns along the way and obstacles to be avoided and Jack didn't want to risk an accident or take a wrong turn. The safest thing to do was to stay put and wait for somebody else to come that way.

Jack inspected the lamp with his fingers, but in the dark he couldn't identify any damage and anyway he had no way of re-lighting it.

Jack sat for what seemed like hours, but wasn't, and felt Barney begin to get uneasy.

They were in the middle of a passageway, in complete darkness.

Jack considered how well he knew the way and wondered if he could slowly find his own way out in the dark by following the rails by touch and hoping to find a light ahead.

This was more risky than staying put, but it might be a few hours before someone else came that way, and he was letting down the supply of props to his section of the face and knew very well what the face workers would think about that, especially when it was his own carelessness that had got him into this situation.

His pride stopped him from calling out, he didn't know whether anyone would hear and if they did it would become a funny story that would get passed around and he'd get teased about for some time to come.

With Barney shuffling his feet and eager to proceed, there was one other possibility. He had heard that some ponies could 'see in the dark', perhaps Barney was one of those. As long as they went very slowly there was little to lose from giving it a go.

'Go on then, Barney,' he said, 'take us back to the pit bottom.'

Straight away Barney began to pull, not at a slower more careful pace, but at his normal working pace.

Jack contemplated pulling on the reins, it felt very strange moving forward in total darkness, but Barney seemed to have total confidence and this confidence transferred itself to Jack, and he let the pony continue as it wished.

They travelled on, Jack holding his breath, Barney in complete calmness.

After 10 minutes Jack felt Barney move round at a right angle and pull himself and the tubs after. He also felt a lesser current of air and knew that they were now moving towards a pair of air-doors.

Even if the Trapper was on the wrong side Jack was sure that Barney would stop if he bumped into the door and that there would be no serious damage done, the tubs were empty and their pace was steady but not fast.

Jack felt Barney begin to slow and then heard the noise of the pony pushing with his head onto something. It could only be the air-door and Barney was opening it!

Jack could not believe that Barney could possibly see the door, he must have somehow sensed it.

They went through the door and as they approached the next the Trapper approached, his light a very welcome sight.

'What the…' came the young voice.

'Lamp went out,' said Jack, 'I'll take…'

He thought back to his first day, the Driver who had taken his lamp, the miserable hours he'd spent in darkness.

'How long have you been on the doors?' he asked.

'This is nearly the end of my first week,' said the voice proudly, white eyes and teeth showing from a blackened face.

'Alright, well carry on,' said Jack.

Once free of the doors, Jack whispered in Barney's ear,

'It's easier from here, just keep going.'

And easier it was, soon there were more lights about and more lit areas. When they reached the pit bottom Jack was relieved and made sure to get a replacement lamp before he did anything else.

Jack talked to one of the older miners about his experience. He didn't seem surprised,

'Some ponies have a sixth sense which we just can't understand,' he said, 'I've heard of some that refuse to go into an area where miners have been killed. I remember one that I drove as a lad, and I'm going back twenty years or more, who refused to pass a certain point slowly, he always broke into a gallop well before we reached it, and when we were past it, he would slow down and resume his normal pace. I could never work it out. When I finally told the Stableman about it, he told me that a horse and driver had been killed at that point. The deaths had happened years before my pony had even been born but somehow, he knew. Yes, stranger things than we understand have happened and are still happening down here. Don't treat your pony like a fool, that's always my advice to any new Driver, because they aren't. They know things we don't.'

With an even greater respect for his pony and all this talk of a sixth sense, Jack was keen to share his experience, but when he did so, as a kind of passing pleasantry, to the area Deputy he got a very different response,

'You stupid bugger!' he said, 'You've risked your pony, and what would have happened if another load had been coming in the opposite direction? You wouldn't have been able to signal your presence, and someone could have been killed.'

'But I would have been late with my next load of props,' said Jack, and immediately wished that he hadn't.

'And who's bloody fault was that? Who bashed his lamp? Tell me, which stupid idiot was to blame!?'

Jack bowed his head, he was to blame and whichever way he looked at it he would have been in trouble with somebody, either with the face workers for making them short on props, or from the Deputy, for taking the risk of moving in the dark.

There was nothing he could say, he deserved this telling off.

'Think of all the forms I would have had to fill in, the reports I'd have had to write.'

He stormed off.

Jack had really annoyed him, and he needed to cool off or he might have hit him.

Jack realised that he hadn't thought things through. He should have at least paused to consider the eventualities and probably should have stayed where he was. That was, most likely, the safest solution. His actions had been headstrong and foolish and were probably driven by his uncomfortableness at sitting impotently in the dark, and thinking how he was going to explain away his lamp going out - a cardinal sin for a Driver.

'Wait a minute,' he thought, 'the Deputy didn't even consider that I might have been injured as well,' he paused in his thinking, looking into himself, and then concluded, 'but then again I'd have deserved it.'

When, later, he confided in his brother, Edward, he got even shorter shrift,

'That's stupid, Jack, you don't take unnecessary risks underground. If the face workers berated you then that's because you'd have deserved it, but if you'd caused a bad accident...'

He didn't even bother finishing the sentence. He didn't have to.

Chapter 49

Jack and Peter were standing in the farmyard, Jim Moore and Gareth Price joined them.

'I've told Peter a lot of what I know about cattle,' said Gareth Price, 'There seems to be a lot of watchfulness in a bull's eye, like he's watching patiently, waiting for an opportunity to make his point. Never get stuck between a bull and a hard place, that's the golden rule, but even so,' he said, chewing on a piece of grass, 'even the experienced can make a mistake.'

'It was a lucky escape,' said Jim Moore.

He shook his head.

Peter just stood by, listening to his own story.

'Nasty buggers when they feel like it,' said Jim Moore.

'I was needing the bucket,' said Gareth, talking to Jack, the others listening, 'the bull was in the byre, and he was tied up. I went in to get the bucket and the damn bull backed me into a corner, the rope obviously gave him too long a tether, and he started leaning on me, crushing me between his arse and the wall. The wind was knocked out of me, I can tell you, but I had time to think how stupid I'd been.'

'I saw what was happening,' said Peter, 'and I rushed over and pulled on the bull's rope. It's tied to a ring that goes through his nose. The bull didn't want to move but I just kept pulling. He wasn't happy, tugged back and raised his head and bellowed.'

'The main thing,' said Gareth Price, 'was that the big bugger moved a little. Moved just enough for me to wriggle free and flop over the wall before the bastard's back legs kicked out and took a chunk out of the wall where I'd just been standing.'

Jim Moore took Jack to look over the restraining wall and pointed.

'You can still see the marks on the wall.'

'Wow,' said Jack, 'that was one hell of a kick.'

'I tell you it was a lucky day for me. Maybe I'm not as smart as I think I am, it was a child's mistake.'

'Everybody makes them,' said Jim Moore, 'important thing is you got away with it.'

'Thanks to your son,' said Gareth, then he turned to Peter, 'Peter, in front of your father and your friend let me admit that I've been hard on you. I thought you had a lot to learn, and it seems you're not the only one.'

'That's not a problem,' said Peter, embarrassed by such an open-hearted confession from such an experienced man.

'Well, I owe you,' said Gareth Price.

Jim Moore smiled.

This was a breakthrough.

He would never have wanted such an incident to have happened. It was too close for comfort. But he knew that Gareth Price was a man of his word and now that he'd said he would support Peter, then he would, and the farm would be the better for it.

'What are you going to do with the bull?' asked Jack.

'Do with it?' said Gareth Price.

'It nearly killed you, it's obviously got a bad nature, are you going to keep it?'

The three farmers glanced at each other.

'Bulls are valuable,' said Peter.

'It's a good bull,' said Gareth Price.

'It's a bull,' said Jim Moore.

'You've got to respect a bull,' said Gareth Price, 'if you don't then you get what you deserve. It was my mistake not the bull's.'

Time marched on.

Now that he and Gareth Price were working well together, Peter was stepping more and more into his father's shoes. It was a team effort, his father would be around for a while yet, a long while he hoped, and Gareth too, although at 60 he wasn't sure how many years he had left in him. He was due a fine retirement but he would be a difficult man to replace. Peter's hands were more work-worn now, his shoulders' broader and his face more weathered. If you saw him on the street, you would take him for a farmer.

Both Frank and Edward were Hewers and as such among the highest earners underground.

Jack was accepted into manhood, settled as a Driver but ambitious to step up to the job of Putter. Up top he'd joined the colliery football team and was now old enough to join his father and brother on their visits to the pub. Peter also joined them occasionally.

George was still at school, though he was becoming more and more independent.

Grandpa was satisfied with his allotment which gave him the opportunity to contribute to the family table, and he loved the odd days he worked on the farm and the farmyard manure he got by the cartload in part-payment. He also enjoyed the allotment way of sharing produce, swapping onions for carrots, eggs for strawberries.

Jenny was Jenny and was at the centre of the household. She enjoyed her sewing and the smiles it brought to others; the extra money didn't hurt either.

Sarah was the one who was feeling increasingly unsettled. She seldom thought of her mother these days, enjoyed working with Jenny, was proud of her dressmaking and alteration skills and pleased that people paid her money for her efforts. But she was a young woman now and wasn't sure that what she had was all she ever wanted to have.

It was Jack's fault.

He had loaned her books and shown her things and talked about more. If she was going to do something different, what could it be? She could look for a job in town, at one of the factories, or one of the clothes shops, or maybe she could go 'into service'.

It was in the kitchen, whilst doing other chores, that Jenny and Sarah would put the world to rights,

'It's not fair,' said Sarah.

'What's not fair?' said Jenny.

'I was in town the other day, and you see all these people in their fine clothes, they're no better than we are, and yet the way they look at me…'

Jenny smiled.

'Aye,' she said.

'Look at Frank and Edward and Jack, they go down the pit each day, they don't even know if they're going to come up again!'

'Don't say that,' said Jenny.

'But it's true, isn't it?'

'Doesn't bear thinking about, put it out of your mind love, just take everything a day at a time, that's what I do.'

'And they work so hard, Ma. I can only imagine what it's like down there, all dark and sweaty and dirty.'

'I'm sure it's all those things, love, but don't go thinking that they don't have time for joshing and talking, you'll not hear Frank say as he hates it down there. They're all in it together it's like a boy's club. I'm not saying it's easy, he still needs the grime scrubbing off his back when he gets home.'

Jenny paused,

'And don't go thinking that what we do is any less hard work… only difference is we don't get paid for it!'

Sarah carried on with her cleaning while she thought about this,

'But down in the dark, Ma, I'm sure I wouldn't like it down there.'

'I'm sure lots of people wouldn't, Sarah, but it's what puts this roof over our heads, the food on our table, now then, what were you saying about your visit to town?'

'Oh, it's just that coming from the pit village you're labelled as being inferior and I don't like it.'

Jenny slid the bread into the oven, clapped her hands together to get rid of the majority of the flour before wiping the rest off on her apron.

She remembered when she'd been Sarah's age. All she'd wanted was to settle down and wrap a warm, secure home around herself. If she thought about it now, which she rarely did, she'd done quite a good job of doing that.

The youngsters of today though, they were so different! Why did they always want something better than they'd been born into? What was wrong with what they'd got? On the other hand, having a dream was no bad thing, as long as you didn't let it eat you up from the inside.

'We are at the root of the tree,' she said, remembering something her father had said and, taking the kettle from the range, she started the ceremonial process of making tea, 'and just like a root, we can never hope to become a branch, or a leaf or a flower, but without us, the tree would not be fed, it would not grow, there would be no branches, there would be no flowers, there would be no seeds in fact, there would be no trees and no new trees spawned. Best to be happy that you're in amongst the roots and know your place, know that you're part of the tree and that what you do counts.'

Sarah scowled.

Jenny had the tea in the pot and was letting it mast.

'Anyway,' she said, 'can you imagine our Jack in a shirt and tie and a bowler hat sitting on the top of his head.'

The image brought lightness back into Sarah's expression.

'He would look awkward wouldn't he,' she said, 'with polished shoes and creases in his pants…'

'And talking all posh…'

'And with an umbrella under his arm…'

They both laughed and Jenny poured the tea, putting milk in the cups first.

'I bet they took your money alright,' said Jenny.

'Oh, they did that and no mistake, couldn't get it into their tills fast enough. Served the posh people first, of course.'

'"The wealth of the few comes from the sweat of the many", as Grandpa always says,' said Jenny, blowing on her tea to cool it, 'But if there wasn't the sweat there wouldn't be the wealth, no coal to keep them warm and feed the engines, no stocks worth buying, no investments, and we'd all be back in the Stone Age. Aye, they have a lot to thank us for, and they'd do well to remember it every once in a while.'

'Here, here!' said Sarah raising her cup in mock salute, 'we'll be getting the vote soon, then we'll see what happens.'

'And pigs might fly,' said Jenny returning the salute, 'now if you're interested, I might have one or two scones left over?'

'I'll get the butter and jam,' said Sarah.

But the idea of 'something better' did not leave Sarah.

It was worth thinking about.

One of her friends was called Mary Jones, someone she had run through the streets with, scraped knees on cobbles with, tumbled out of trees with and now Mary was 'in service' in Sunderland, in the house of a Mr Archer, a Solicitor, and his family, and only came home occasionally. When she did come home, she was well-dressed and chalk-white clean. Sarah was envious of her appearance and when she was next home for the weekend, she paid her a visit.

When Sarah arrived, Mary's father was on his shift and her sister was visiting a friend.

'As you know she was always a bit of a tearaway at school,' said her mother, 'so I'm pleased she's found something and settled down a bit.'

'Ma!'

'Although she's so far away I don't really know what she gets up to.'

'Ma! I work very hard.'

Her mother smiled.

'Mary brought us some preserves and cold meats and cake,' she said.

'Cook gave them to me,' said Mary.

'Then you must thank her, they were all very welcome.'

'I'll tell her, she's nice really but she has a sharp tongue, you wouldn't want to get on the wrong side of her.'

'Well, I think it was nice of her,' said Mrs Jones.

'I suppose it was; she feeds us well.'

'You get your meals?' said Sarah.

Mary laughed.

'Yes, of course, all of them, three meals a day.'

Sarah couldn't believe it, getting her meals cooked for her at her age, that was ridiculous.

'Hmm,' said her mother, 'well it's me that cooks the meals here so I'll leave you girls to chatter for a bit, I've got work to do.'

When they were alone, sitting drinking tea out of china cups in the front lounge, Mary started talking about her day,

'It's not easy,' she said, 'up at 6.00am every morning, getting the fires going, cleaning the boots and emptying the chamber pots.'

'Sounds like Jenny,' said Sarah.

'Yes, but Jenny, just like my own Ma, does it to her own routine, I have to follow somebody else's,' she said, 'and Mrs Archer can be very demanding, let me tell you, and no matter how rude she is to you, you have to always be polite. Then it's on to tidying and dusting and polishing the furniture and running the sweeper over the carpets in the downstairs rooms. And all this before I get any breakfast!'

'You mean your breakfast if cooked for you?' said Sarah, incredulous at this luxury.

'Yes, the cook, she's a large woman called Phoebe Proctor, runs the kitchen with her kitchen maids. Nobody dare interfere with the kitchen, and breakfast is nothing special, maybe a bowl of porridge, a cup of tea and bread and butter.'

'But still.'

'If you want to know what a good breakfast is, it's the one served up to the Archers, they get eggs, sausages, perhaps a pair of kippers, fruit, or maybe devilled kidneys.'

'That would put me to sleep,' said Sarah.

'Then I bring in the coal and kindling to keep the fires going and prepare a bath for Mrs Archer and, if she asks, help her dress and do her hair. We're only a small staff so we have to do a bit of everything, I have to keep washing my hands to keep them clean, we've got running water of course. There's a nanny for the two children.'

'A nanny! They don't even look after their own children?'

'Of course not, the master and mistress have much more important things to do.'

'Like what?

'Well, Mr Archer is a Solicitor and even though I don't know what solicitors do, I can see that its very important from the serious looks he and his clients always have on their faces and the amount of papers that he has on his desk.'

'What about Mrs Archer?'

'Oh, she has to tell us all what to do, tell us what she wants and when, and she must always look smart and be ready to hold polite conversation with any of her husband's clients or friends, or their wives. Appearance and reputation are everything to a Solicitor; I've learnt that much.'

'It sounds like a completely different world,' said Sarah, thinking of the team of people that the Archers had at their beck and call.

'Do you ever get out of the house?'

'Oh, yes, after I've cleaned the bedrooms, I quite often get sent on messages, to the shops or to deliver a note.'

'What about the laundry?'

'Oh, somebody else does that.'

Sarah thought about all the hours that she and Jenny spent doing laundry, 'somebody else does that' resounded in her head like some kind of impossible dream.

'I normally stop for a cup of tea at 11 and have lunch at 12. The family eat at 1 o'clock and its always a three-course meal.'

Sarah gasped. This glimpse into other people's lives was an eye opener.

'I check the fires at 2 and then, if I'm lucky, have a couple of hours to myself. At 5 the family take tea, and quite often have guests. At 6 I eat supper, a smaller meal than lunch, and the family and their guests have a five-course meal at 8, with wine.'

'With wine! I've never tasted wine.'

'I've tried a little, I'm not sure I like it. While the family are eating dinner, I clean up the bedrooms, pick up any clothes, draw the curtains, and lay out the night wear. Then when they've gone to bed, I just check that the fires and everything are alright, and then I go to bed, its usually about 10:30 by the time I'm finished.'

'How many of you are there?'

'Household staff you mean?'

Mary counted on her fingers.

'5 I think, yes, 5, we all have our own jobs and then sometimes we do things together, if carpets need beating, that kind of thing.'

To Sarah this all sounded amazing.

'As well as the running water, we've got gas to the lamps and a telephone.'

'A telephone?'

'Yes, it's attached to the wall in the hall. I'm not allowed to use it of course but Mrs Archer can call some of her suppliers and Mr Archer uses it quite a lot for business. I don't think it's as good as talking to somebody face to face though. We might get electric lights soon from what I've heard, there's always something new happening.'

'And you get paid?'

'Of course, wouldn't do it otherwise. I get all my board and food, a half day off a week and £4 every quarter.'

'£4…'

'Yes, you don't get paid in advance, so it was a long wait for my first money but once you get started its alright. I've even got a bank account, and I send some money home and try and save some as well. When it comes to getting paid the Head Housekeeper, Mrs Charlton, sits opposite you with a cash box beside her and an accounts book, sometimes Mrs Archer sits in the room just to hear what goes on. Anything personal you've bought, like shoes or underwear, is listed in the accounts and gets deducted from your pay, whatever is left is counted out and given to you. If either the Head Housekeeper, or Mrs Archer want to say anything to you, if they want you to change anything or improve anything then this is another opportunity for them to tell you. I just sit quietly, listen, and wait for my money. They say I'm quiet and polite but really, I just don't want to make a fuss.'

'You weren't always quiet and polite at school,' said Sarah.

Mary laughed, 'I've grown up since then.'

'Since when you put that spider down Vicky Oliver's neck, you mean?'

'Ooo, you remember that.'

'I think Vicky does too.'

'On my half day off, I get together with some of the other girls in the neighbourhood and we go strolling along the promenade. That's when we might meet some boys.'

'Boys!'

'Well men really, I shouldn't call them boys, they wouldn't like it. There's this one called Tom…'

Mary told Sarah about Tom, how smart dressed he was, how he worked in a shop but wanted to start his own, how he bought her presents, even when it wasn't her birthday, how they'd held hands and…

It was just at this point that Mary's mother came in. There was an immediate silence.

'What you girls talking about?' asked Mrs Jones.

Sarah glanced at Mary.

'Mary was just telling me how invigorating the sea air is in Sunderland,' said Sarah.

Mary giggled.

This reaction was not lost on her mother.

'Invigorating is it,' she said, 'best make sure you wrap up tight then, you never know what nooks an' crannies a breeze might blow into.'

She looked at the girls who were studiously avoiding eye contact, then she smiled.

'There's nowt wrong with a bit of fun, but you mustn't let it go too far.'

'It's only a breeze, Ma,' said Mary

'Aye, an' ye can never be quite sure how strong a breeze might blow, can ye?'

The two girls looked at each other and then all three started to laugh.

'Now enough about breezes,' said Mrs Jones, 'I've got some jobs need doing and you girls can give me a hand.'

That night and for days afterwards Sarah's head was full of thoughts of running water, gas lighting, telephones, no cooking, no laundering, clean hands and getting paid. It all seemed very attractive compared to all the work she did for no pay, and little appreciation, and the little she earned from her sewing.

She decided that if she could, no not if, when she could, she would pay Mary a visit in Sunderland and see for herself.

Chapter 50

Frank was a simple, straightforward man.

He worked hard, kept his nose clean and expected nothing more than a fair day's pay for a fair day's work. If he could keep a roof over his family's head, food on the table and clothes on their backs then he was satisfied.

Always a family man at heart he had no real ambitions of his own. He and Jenny had come south as newlyweds in search of work and a home. It had been a time when new shafts were being sunk in the colliery, creating new jobs, with free housing, and they grabbed at the opportunity. If his own heart was anywhere other than wherever his family was, it was up north where he was born and raised, where granite hills rose from river cut valleys and you could breathe deep, feeling the space under the sky.

When Frank did think of this northern world the sun was always shining, the sky was always blue. When not working underground in the safety lamp lit murk of the coalface, he would willingly help Grandpa with a bit of manual labour on the allotment and the chickens' clucking, head jerking antics would always make him smile. They never seemed to quite know where they were or where they were going to and each time they raised their heads to look around they seemed to be startled, seeing the place for the first time, wondering how they got there.

When in need of peace he would take himself off on long solitary walks, away from the grime and into the surrounding green, climbing up to gaze at far horizons whose distance stretched further away with his increasing height.

Atop a summit he would simply sit, eat the bait Jenny had prepared for him, and look up at the sky, watching the clouds float by.

He would return home refreshed and ready for another day. He would never talk to anybody about these walks. There was nothing to say.

Frank had his own prejudices when it came to recognizing the difference between owners and workers and was not shy in repeating them around the kitchen table.

'It's the bosses have the big houses, with lots of servants needed to keep them going. And their missus's got to have their fur coats and jewellery. I feel sorry for them; they'll never know what a real day's work is.'

'But you'll still touch your cap to them in the street won't you Dad,' said Edward.

Frank rose to the bait, 'Got to keep a roof over our heads don't I, and food on the table. Stand up to them individually and they just break you, next thing you know you're out on the street, no house, no food, no job. If you're going to stand up to them you need to do it as part of a crowd, that's where the Union comes in.'

Edward rolled his eyes; he wasn't in the mood for another of his father's well-ploughed rants on the Union and the merits of membership.

'When will we know about the job cuts?' he asked.

'God only knows, they normally save it up for just before Christmas to get us in the festive mood.'

'Can't you talk about something a bit more cheerful,' said Jenny, starting to clear away the dirty dishes.

'You coming to watch me play football?' asked Jack.

'Would like to son,' said Frank, glancing across at Jenny, 'but me and your mam have got something else on this afternoon. Hope you have a good game though, and don't get yourself injured. Can't afford the loss of pay.'

'Thanks for caring dad,' said Jack.

'Me and George'll come along,' said Grandpa, 'swell the crowd a bit, give you a cheer.'

'I'll come to,' said Edward.

'You better score a goal or two,' said George, 'give 'em a good hiding.'

The field used for the inter-village football game was at the back of the school, alongside the allotments. The seriousness with which the game was taken was apparent in the precision of its measurements; a regulation 100 yards long and 50 wide, the goalposts 8 yards apart, the bar 8 feet from the ground.

The woodwork was newly painted a brilliant white by dedicated supporters, using paint that had somehow materialised from the colliery storehouse. There was no net.

Jack played on the right wing for the colliery team, with Adam Thompson centre forward.

The nearby village of Langley Mill supplied the opposing team and there was intense rivalry between them. To prevent any overly home bias, about which there had been many pub-grumbled accusations after previous games, the referee was also from Langley Mill and was expected to know better than to attempt to too obviously favour his own team if he wished to return home from this hostile territory in one piece.

Indeed, he was roundly reminded of the fact by some of the rougher factions of the noisy crowd as the teams ran out onto the pitch to start the game. The referee took it well and waved back, but the worried look on his face showed that he'd understood the point.

The crowd lined the pitch-side, opposing supporters on opposite sidelines, giving off a smell of stale ale and smoke. Only a very few of the women were in attendance and they formed a cleaner clique near one of the goals.

Sarah was in amongst these, trying not to be embarrassed by some of the foul language that was shouted out so loudly and so liberally by the men.

The home team goalkeeper was a tall, cool, clearheaded player who could be relied upon not to be bullied by the opposing forwards. The two full backs had been selected for their pugnacious strength and resolve. As part of the last line of defence in front of the goalkeeper they were under clear instructions to play it safe, do nothing fancy, and not to worry about where the ball went as long as it flew out of the danger area as quickly and effectively as possible.

More centrally the three halfbacks' game was to follow up as their forwards advanced, or to tackle back as the opposing forwards attacked, winning back the ball and feeding it onwards to their forwards hoping to encourage wave after wave of offensive play and grind the enemy into submission.

The forwards would be the glory boys, working together to get a shot on goal, getting the ball to the centre forward when he was in a shooting position. The wide players, with Jack on the right, would stay out on their wing, stretching the game, running with the ball, dribbling down to the touchline and delivering crosses into the penalty area for one of the three more centrally placed forwards to head or hammer into the goal.

The men knew that they had to play together as a team and had come to know each other's strengths and weaknesses, and each tried to play to those strengths and cover up the weaknesses.

The team had trained and practised when they could, shifts and weather permitting.

A football injury was a serious thing, leading to time off work, loss of pay and wrath and lack of sympathy around the kitchen table. Once a game had started however this did not prevent the men from playing hard, holding nothing back.

Thus were the positions, thus the tactics.

In the back room of 'The Stackyard', Earnest Weightman, who helped with the training and the management of the team, would make it all seem so easy, their plan so perfect, with no margin for error.

They were an unstoppable force, an invincible army. No one could stand against them. They had the best players, all previous disappointments were simply learning experiences.

It was impossible to imagine that the Langley Mill team might win, even though they had won, home and away, on the 7 previous occasions that they'd met.

Today was different.

Today marked the beginning of a new and glorious chapter. The Langley Mill team did not stand a chance; they were lambs to the slaughter.

But as Earnest Weightman stood on the sidelines and looked at the strength and fitness of their opponents his words of invincibility seemed a bit premature and, as the whistle blew to begin the game, he was not so sure of victory, a victory that had seemed so certain when they laid their plans in the backroom of 'The Stackyard'.

The pitch was heavy with recent rain and the surface cut up badly under Jack's half inch studs, sending pieces of green and brown flying in all directions and leaving furrowed scars behind.

When Jack first got the ball, he was immediately scythed to the ground by the opposing full-back, a vicious brute, short, stocky, built like the proverbial shit house. As the ball flew out for a throw in, he tugged on Jack's shirt and growled into his face.

'I hope you've said your bloody prayers mate; I'm taking no fucking prisoners.'

Jack smiled back,

'We'll just have to see about that won't we,' he said.

Grandpa, Edward and George stood on the sidelines shouting encouragement. Sarah had her hands to her mouth.

As the game progressed Jack was repeatedly and unceremoniously upended each time the ball came to him, often after being tackled from behind in blatant, but un-penalised, flagrance of the rules of the game. He winced as he picked himself up again and again and limped on.

'I'll take your fucking leg off next time,' was all the sympathy he heard in his ear.

Jack shouted at the referee that he had been fouled again and was supported in his claims from the sidelines.

'Are you bloody blind as well as daft,' bellowed Edward at the referee, unusually animated.

Beyond this private duel the game flowed evenly from end to end, the home goalkeeper being forced into a number of brave saves.

Whether influenced by the verbal chastisement or not, the next time that Jack was chopped to the ground the referee awarded a freekick and shook his finger theatrically from side to side in the direction of the offending full-back, who just smiled back unabashed.

The freekick was about 20 yards from goal and the opposing team formed a wall of three players 6 yards from the ball. Instead of shooting Jack chipped the ball into the centre of the penalty area where Adam Thompson rose to head confidently into the top corner scoring the first and only goal of the half.

Sarah knew what she wanted to do and, as the half-time interval would only be five minutes, she knew she had to do it quickly.

As inconspicuously as possible she made her way over to where the opposing team were gathered in a huddle. Sidling up to the offending full-back, she whispered something to him. Startled, his mouth fell open, but before he had time to collect his wits sufficiently to respond, Sarah had turned her back and walked away.

The second half brought an early equaliser, the ball played long into the penalty area where it was chested down and, leaving the goalkeeper with little chance, dispatched firmly into the goal.

The opposing fans cheered, jeered and booed as the two teams locked horns and the game swung first in favour of one and then the other.

Both teams played for all they were worth and played well. It was a fast game, and running to a close finish when, much to the exasperation of all, the game was suspended for a short time to clear an escaped chicken from the pitch, an embarrassed Grandpa disappearing with the offending bird in the direction of the allotments.

Throughout the second half the full-back continued to play a strong game but did not make the unfair and vicious challenges he'd made in the first. Occasionally he would steal a glance in Sarah's direction, and she would nod back at him.

With only minutes of the game left, Jack, buoyed up by the much easier time he was having, centred to Adam who hammered a shot goalwards, beating the goalkeeper but not the bar, the ball crashing against the woodwork, knocking it off and rebounding onto the thigh of the full-back from where it bounced tamely back over the line.

The referee looked around uncertainly, but as the ball had clearly entered the goal well under the normal level of the bar he had no alternative but to award the goal, an own goal.

Although the referee then allowed an unprecedented number of extra minutes at the end of the game, Jack's team held on and secured the win!

On the touchline Earnest Weightman let out a huge sigh of relief. Honour had been restored; a miracle had occurred.

After the game Edward, who had noticed Sarah's actions during the half-time interval, asked her what had happened. Sarah confided that she had approached the man and said,

'I know what you're up to, and if you don't play the game more fairly, I'll tell your woman all about it.'

Edward was flabbergasted and asked how on earth she knew the man's secrets.

Sarah replied that she did not know him, had never set eyes on him until today, but that she had thought that the kind of man who would cheat so blatantly on the football field would be very likely to also cheat off it.

From the man's reaction she had clearly been right.

Edward laughed. He thought it was a great story.

'I'd better watch out for you,' he said.

Elated by this reaction, Sarah sought out Jack and told him the same thing.

Jack's reaction was very different.

'I already have one mother, I don't need another one,' he said.

Jack felt his manhood had been challenged. That somehow, his ability to cope had been questioned. He was a man and didn't need this kind of help from a girl.

Sarah was very upset by Jack's reaction and immediately tried to apologise and explain, but Jack would not listen, he turned his mud-smeared back and walked away.

Edward caught up to him and, putting an arm around his shoulders, calmed him down.

'You're my brother Jack, and I love you,' he said, 'but you're also an idiot.'

As they stormed off in their different directions, Sarah was still annoyed.

'I was only trying to help,' she thought, 'but if you don't want my help, Jack Lawley, then I'll show you!'

After this incident Sarah was even more determined to go to Sunderland and see what being 'in service' might be like.

Jenny and Frank had not been at the game.

They were standing side-by-side with heads bowed towards the foot of a tree around which wildflowers grew.

'I've never been very lucky with daughters,' said Jenny, wiping her eyes on her apron.

There would be no more children for Jenny.

They talked about how they had moved down from Scotland, the pull of the work, the new shafts that were being opened, of how they had resettled, made a home and started a family.

All their children had been born in the village. They couldn't remember the last time they'd been back to Scotland.

Maybe they would never go back.

They stood together in what had become an act of annual remembrance.

Chapter 51

Jack was lucky.

A hundred or so years earlier girls and young women had been employed as Putters and it wasn't that long ago that the job of pushing or dragging the tubs of hewed coal from the face through the low passages, in the dark and the dust, to the places where the height and the width increased and the Drivers could hitch up their ponies and take them away to the pit bottom and thence to the surface, was done by two boys working together, sharing the earnings, sometimes equally and sometimes not. Or there was the 'trace and chain' method, where a Putter was chained to the tubs, a leather girdle worn around his waist, a chain attached and passed between his legs.

Whichever way you looked at it, it was arduous, dirty work, described by some as 'modern slavery'.

Putters had had to strain to get overthrown tubs back on the rails, fight their way up inclines, and slow the tubs on the down slopes. When pulling their load through low places they had often been forced to go down on all fours, and had rubbed the skin off their backs, shoulders and arms on the low roofs and narrow walls.

Thankfully, by the time Jack became a Putter, the methods and techniques had been somewhat improved, and ponies were used to assist the Putters in Jack's mine. At only 11 hands, Barney was small enough for this job and Jack was pleased to take him along with him. The larger animals of over 14 hands and up to 17 were too big for the small tunnels the Putters worked in and they were used for other haulage jobs, including moving the coal tubs, full and empty, from the Putter's sidings to the pit bottom.

I said that Jack was lucky, but as he twisted and turned in the near dark along the narrowing passages that made their way to the ever-moving face, the ceiling closing in on him, he didn't feel very lucky.

It was a job that needed physical strength, ingenuity and perseverance, and when Jack asked a more seasoned Putter why he did it, he said it was because he was 'daft', but even as he said it, the wry smile that accompanied the remark showed an underlying sense of pride in his ability to do what was probably the most difficult job in the pit, and stick to it.

Jack and Barney took the tubs to the face, took the full ones away, brought in materials; pit props, roofing, tools, whatever was needed. They were the butlers to the 'Lords of the face', the Hewers, supplying their needs, keeping the work moving along.

To be a Putter was to work your shift with your head between your knees, cooped up on the limbers between a pony's backside and the first coal tub in a narrow, dark, passageway, lit only by a glimpse of light, where the timber holding up the roof creaked and groaned and the tubs scraped along the top and sides.

Jack would sit with his shoulder against Barney's rump, his hand gripping the tub handle as together they swirled along the narrow track, guiding the tubs around each turn, going at a pace that kept up with the coal extraction at the face, always aware that it was the coal in those tubs that paid the wages of everyone at the pit.

Barney and Jack were a team, their days of Driving had formed a bond of mutual trust between them, a confidence in their separate abilities. Jack would sweat and swear when he scraped his arm or banged his head. Barney would splutter and stop for a breather every now and then, immovable for a few minutes, and then ready to go again. Jack would keep a couple of carrots in his pocket if he could and feed them to Barney when he thought he needed a treat. Barney would nuzzle up to Jack when Jack put his arm around his neck and whispered one of their shared secrets into his ear.

It was a hard job, no doubt about it, but Jack liked it better than Driving, he felt more like he was his own man in this job, although he couldn't let his concentration drop; that's how accidents happened.

Back at the stables at the end of one of his shifts, Jack could immediately feel the tension and asked the Stableman what was wrong.

'It's Alan Taylor,' he said, 'one of the lads attending a door had heard a cracking sound, and he reported it, as he should.'

The Stableman lowered his head, 'There were two Putters nearby and they were told to have a look. One of them returned, saying he couldn't hear anything, but Alan was in there, looking at the roof when a stone, 9 feet long by 3 feet wide, broke from the roof and fell on him.'

Jack gasped.

'He's been killed instantly. We've managed to move the stone enough to get him out and he's back on the surface now.'

'Poor Alan.'

'Aye, he was around 30 I would guess, wife and three children. He was an experienced miner. It happened so fast. It could happen to anyone. It was nobody's fault.'

Jack turned away and removed Barney's harness and gave him something to eat and drink. He whispered in his ear,

'There but for the Grace of God, there but for the Grace of God.'

As he was leaving the Stableman said, 'There'll be an investigation, maybe some improvements in roof supports, but his wife'll need to be told, and she'll be evicted of course. That's the way it is, it was nobody's fault, these things happen, we'll repair the tunnel tomorrow and carry on. That's what we do Jack. Always remember that. We carry on. The mine doesn't stop for anyone.'

The Stableman slapped Jack on the back, it was as if he had been talking to himself more than anything but just doing it out loud, and Jack had just happened to be the one there to hear it.

Frank and Edward had also heard of the accident, and the three of them talked about it on the way home.

'Don't make too much of it to your Ma,' said Frank, 'she worries enough already and if there's things she can do, then I'm sure that she'll do them.'

'Could have been any of us,' said Edward.

Jack said nothing.

'But it wasn't,' said Frank, pausing to cough and spit out black onto the pathway, 'we live to fight on another day. It's a reminder to take nothing for granted.'

Jack's walk from his front door to the pithead was always the same but never the same.

Dressed in flat cap, white scarf, grey overcoat, and waistcoat, a white collarless shirt, long trousers with short trousers underneath, woollen socks and leather boots, his own bait bag slung over his shoulder, he walked towards the towering metal skeleton of the winding gear.

It was always the same route; down past the row of houses, the washing lines and street lights, down to the end of Second Street, then left onto Main Street, that lead directly to the colliery gates, past the wooden fences on the right that separated the road from the allotments, past First Street on the left with its line of identical houses, and then, once inside the colliery gates, the familiar greetings as the new shift converged on the lamp room where they picked up their lamps, tested and locked, and took their two pit checks.

Then outside again and across the yard to the iron staircase that chimed to the sound of the tens of boots that climbed steadily upwards towards the winding wheels and into the Onsetter's territory, handing over a pit check token to be hung on a board, evidence of who was underground, keeping the other token tucked in his boot so that, if the worst did happen, his body could be identified and counted off.

Then into the cage, hearing the rattling of the doors as they were pulled to, pressed in like sardines in the small space that started to rattle and rumble as it fell away into the earth, taking him down, down, into his underground world of work.

But at the same time this trek was never the same. The changing seasons brought different colours to the verges, the lengthening and shortening days brought different levels and tones of light, the weather brought wet or dry, grey or bright, and along the way there would be the cooing of pigeons from the lofts, perhaps the clucking of hens, the odd sighting of one of the pit's cats, creeping through the grass after a night of ratting.

Then there were the varying smells from the allotments, newly fertilised with cartloads of manure procured from nearby farms, or with shoots showing, or full of green growth, or flowers that the bees buzzed among.

The washing lines were strung out like flags, pegged clothing fluttering like bunting in a warm breeze or women rushing out to take it in and protect it from heavy rain.

And amongst the footfall, were the new, the maturing, the changing faces, the sleepy greetings, the hunched shoulders.

Every day was different in smaller or larger ways.

Each day Jack would hope his routine would not be broken by the sound of the klaxon sounding out for an accident, or worse. Such a sound could precipitate a less orderly reaction of rescue teams, of ambulance services, of families and mothers waiting for news.

After a few weeks Jack had his new routine set; reach the face, swing the empty tubs into a small, rough, siding, hitch up the full ones, get back on the limbers, and off you go, fast enough so as not to cause production delays, or keep anybody waiting.

Jack knew that it was the Putters who controlled the speed of coal production, and they were paid well as a consequence, Jack bringing home 36s a week on average, a really good wage.

He and the other Putters' tubs dripped from the face sections, joined into rivulets, then rivers of tubs that rumbled, unstoppable towards the pit bottom, from where the newly-hewn coal rose up, up, and out into a world not glimpsed for 300 million years.

Jack learnt from experience.

The job was tough but straightforward until a tub slipped off the rails.

Then Jack's work really began. His attempts to lift a full tub were bad enough, but if one side had got snagged against a prop, or the roof was so low that the wheel was still an inch below the rail when he'd strained to lift it, that's when it got difficult. And it was up to him!

He could call for help but that was frowned upon, his job was to keep everything running and fix any problems that might occur.

So, he would twist and wrestle and scheme and then drop it all and think again. Sometimes he would get the front end back on the rail but couldn't get round to sort out the back end, there not being enough space for even a mouse to get past the tub, never mind Jack.

Then he would sit and ponder.

A Putter was a weightlifter and a problem solver, an unraveller of puzzles, an eel, and a lifting crane. Soaked in sweat, and almost exhausted, he knew he couldn't give up, and most of all he knew he must keep his head.

The Hewers were waiting on him, the Drivers were waiting on him, and he'd get no credit from any of them for all his efforts, but he'd get a damn good telling off if he held any of them up.

Jack and Barney worked together to sort things out. Sometimes Jack wouldn't even know how they'd done it in the end, but that didn't matter, all that mattered was that the interrupted flow was interrupted no more, until the next time, and the next puzzle to solve.

Jack had heard of other Putters, all strong men, in the dark and on their own, who had cried out with passion, shouted at the tub as if it were a purposefully awkward sentient being, or thrown things at it, both sour words and rocks, in their frustration.

Jack came to understand all this.

Chapter 52

Sarah was becoming increasingly unsettled, her talk with Mary had done nothing to put her off the idea of moving away.

What was she waiting for? She was earning a little money from her sewing, the sewing machine proving to be a big help with both the speed and consistency of her work, and she had learnt an awful lot from Jenny, and before that from her own mother, about what it took to run a household. But was that it? Was that all the future held, helping Jenny and making and altering clothes?

It did not seem enough.

Was she waiting to be married? The idea seemed ridiculous, but there were so many of her former schoolmates doing just that. It seemed so contrived somehow, like some kind of transaction, and that wasn't good enough for her.

She wrote to Mary and got a positive response, 'Of course she could visit and see what the place was like'. As the time passed, and letters were sent and received, increasingly clear plans were laid and she was looking more and more forward to her visit to Sunderland.

To get to Sunderland, Sarah had to change trains in Newcastle Central Station.

She didn't think that this would be too difficult even though she wasn't used to travelling on her own. Thousands of other people seemed to be able to manage it and anyway she had a tongue in her head, didn't she, she could ask for directions if she had to.

On the journey to Newcastle the train rattled past fields filled with waving crops or lazily grazing animals, the landscape peppered with tens of towering winding gears, the wheels turning, the metal ropes moving. Then on, into and out of stations with visible rows of terraced houses leading away from the railway lines, large in comparison to the miners' cottages, then past the train yards hissing with steam, and through the confused spiderweb of tracks that disappeared in all directions.

By the time she stepped onto the platform at Newcastle Central Station her nervousness had increased, the confidence she had started out with had all but disappeared like the wisps of steam that issued from the idling trains.

The place was so big with its 12 platforms, its cathedral-like span of metal and glass above, its busily milling passengers clattering about below, its whistles, its hissing steam, and the clanking of metal wheels on metal track.

There seemed to be thousands of people, all moving about haphazardly, determinedly going about their own business, dodging hundreds of pieces of luggage stacked in random piles.

Sarah knew she would need help.

Going up to the kiosk she purchased her onward ticket to Sunderland and asked when the next train would leave. The ticket clerk was very helpful and pointed her in the direction of Platform 8.

The train was on time, cost 1s and took 35minutes to get to Sunderland.

Sunderland was a busy seaport, an export outlet for coal with an important shipbuilding industry. It had a population of 160,000, much smaller than Newcastle, and lay at the mouth of the River Wear.

An electric Tramway crossed the lofty Wearmouth bridge to the suburbs of Monkwearmouth and Roker, which was a popular seaside resort and had a long pier. Coal was never far away though, and the nearby Pemberton coal mine was said to be the deepest in the world at almost 2,300 feet.

As she walked out of the station, she consulted the letter she'd received from Mary that gave her the address and directions of how to get there.

It was only a short walk downhill to Front Street and she hunted out the correct property.

A brass plaque on the wall by the front door confirmed she had found the right place and she rang the bell.

It was her friend who came to the door. She was wearing a housemaid's uniform.

'Oh, Sarah, you should have come to the tradesman's entrance, I must have forgotten to tell you. Go round the back and I'll meet you there.'

'Who is that?' came a sharp voice from inside.

'Someone come to the wrong house, ma'am, I'm just sending them away.'

'Then hurry up about it and bring me some tea.'

It was due to be Mary's afternoon off.

'But I have to wait for permission,' she said, 'I can't leave until I'm told I can, and anyway it has to be after lunch and that can go on a bit if there's guests.'

'So, what should I do?' said Sarah.

'Come to the kitchen with me and I'll ask the cook if she can give you something to eat.'

Mary introduced Sarah to Phoebe Proctor, the cook, and then left to carry on with her chores, they would all have to be finished to the Housekeeper's satisfaction before she'd be allowed to go out.

'So, you're a friend of Mary's,' said Phoebe, talking as she worked, making preparations for lunch, watching over the kitchen maid.

'We went to school together,' said Sarah.

The cook smiled as she moved vegetables into the pot for boiling, a salmon was on the table waiting to be filleted.

'So those were the days, eh, no responsibilities, times are different now, aren't they? Got to look out for yourself now.'

Sarah thought of her mother, Alice, she hadn't heard from her for years, but then she thought of Jenny and smiled to herself, she wasn't alone, there was always someone she knew she could talk to.

'I'm not sure what I want to do,' she said, 'and Mary made working here sound like a good idea.'

The cook laughed.

'I don't know if it's a good idea, lass, but it's bloody hard work that's for sure.'

Sarah was surprised at the language and blushed.

'Anyway, you go over there, there's bread and butter and cheese and some cold meat in the cupboard, cut yourself some of that.'

Sarah was surprised at the cook's generosity, and by the look on her face, so was the kitchen maid.

'She's taken a liking to you,' she whispered, as Sarah was following the cook's instruction, 'she's not normally so nice, let me tell you!'

'What you talking about?' said the cook.

'Nothing,' said the kitchen maid.

'Well, stop talking nothing and get on with your work, this lunch isn't going to prepare itself.'

'See,' whispered the kitchen maid, and hurried over to the salmon and picked up a sharp knife.

'Can I make you both a cup of tea?' said Sarah.

'Of course you can,' said the cook, 'you'll find the tea, milk and sugar over there,' she pointed, 'and you can fill the kettle for yourself, the sink's got running water.'

'Running water,' thought Sarah, so it was true.

Mary was released at 3pm with instructions to be back by 7.

'We need to hurry,' she said, 'I want to take you to the seaside, to Roker promenade.'

'Why?'

'I want you to see the sea and meet a friend of mine.'

They took the tram and made their way to a tearoom. There was someone there already, sitting at a table by the window, a slim man, clean shaven and in smart clothes. He stood up as they approached.

'You're late,' he said.

'Sorry, Tom,' said Mary, 'you know what it's like.'

Tom smiled.

'And this is Sarah,' she said, 'we went to school together.'

'Nice to meet you, Sarah,' said Tom, 'now would you ladies like a cup of tea, and perhaps a slice of cake.'

When Tom had gone off to place the order, Sarah said,

'He's a man!'

Mary smiled.

'He's handsome, isn't he? Works in a shop, I met him that way, he's very ambitious, you know, wants to open his own shop someday, selling clothes.'

This was all too much for Sarah.

'So, you're friends?'

Mary coloured.

'You could say that,' she said.

Tom returned, closely followed by tea and cake. They sat and chatted. Sarah's head was in a whirl. This was a different world.

Afterwards they walked along the promenade and looked out over the sands, out to the white horses of the breaking waves.

There were plenty of people about, though Sarah felt increasingly that she was in the way and said that she would like to explore the place on her own for a bit. Mary pretended that she wouldn't hear of it, but was secretly delighted, and so they agreed to meet back at the tram stop in an hour.

As Sarah walked around, she could taste the salt in the air, the fresh sea breeze on her face. Was this a place she could move to? Was this a life she could get used to?

Her steps took her along the promenade, past shops and to a fish & chip shop. She went in and bought a portion. It was splashed with vinegar, sprinkled with salt and wrapped in newspaper.

Sarah found a bench that looked out over the sea and ate with her fingers, appraising the quality,

'Our fish was better,' she thought, 'the batter was definitely crispier, and these chips, they're nice but not as good as ours.'

In her mind she had automatically used "our" and "ours" and now she paused,

'Oh, Ma,' she said softly into the breeze, 'you did so well, I enjoyed helping you, your fish & chip shop was such a good idea, and you worked so hard,' she paused, the salt air had brought tears to her eyes, 'I miss you,' she said.

They met up at the tram stop as agreed. Mary looked happy and flushed. Tom gave her a peck on the cheek on parting.

'He seems nice,' said Sarah as they made their way back.

'He's alright I suppose,' said Mary, and then she leaned in close, 'he's very handsome isn't he.'

'He seems quite sure of himself,' said Sarah.

'And quite good looking,' said Mary.

Sarah laughed.

'And quite good looking,' she paused, 'if you like that kind of thing.'

'I do,' said Mary, and they giggled, 'he's got plenty of nice friends, you know.'

'I bet he has,' said Sarah.

'If you were in Sunderland, you might meet some of them.'

Sarah blushed. They both laughed.

It was 5 minutes to 7 when they were back, standing outside Mary's place of work.

'I'd better go in,' she said.

'It was nice to see you,' said Sarah.

'You must visit again,' said Mary.

'Perhaps I will,' said Sarah.

'Please tell my Ma and Da that I'm doing alright.'

'I will.'

'But don't mention Tom.'

'I won't.'

They hugged briefly and then Mary went off in one direction and Sarah headed back to the station.

Chapter 53

David Goodwin and Jack were working in the same section.

The coal at the face was cutting well and tubs were flying to and fro with a regularity that was hard to keep up with.

The two men wriggled and twisted in a fog of black dust. Naked to the waist, the sweat on their bodies acted like a kind of glue and their bodies were caked in black. Head between their legs under the low roof, they worked with their ponies to move, lift, manhandle, tub after tub, each of which held 14 hundredweight of fresh-hewn coal.

They saw each other as flickering lights and heard the movement, pony and man in tandem, back and forth, back and forth, moving easy coal to a low price market, more coal needed to make the same pay.

'Doesn't seem fair,' said Jack, as they sat eating their bait, 'coal's as good, probably better than most, but we get less for it.'

'Supply and demand,' said David, 'basic economics.'

'That's the thing isn't it? Mathematics ruling our lives, some strange equation somewhere that nobody understands determining how much bread we can buy…'

'Or beer…' David paused, and then said, '"To toil like slaves for little pay".'

Jack's ears pricked up, he knew that, like him, David Goodwin loved books.

'Go on,' he said.

David smiled.

'William Henry Davies,' he said, 'A Welshman, a tramp, a traveler, a pipe smoker, a writer and a poet. I've just been reading some of his poetry. He sounds like one of us, speaking for us.'

Jack waited, he knew there'd be more.

'Now let me think,' said David, 'see if I can remember a few more lines…'

His brow furrowed as he searched his memory.

'Ah, here we go,' he said, '"Peace makes more slaves than savage War, and we who toil like slaves for little pay, make human moles, that sweat and slave down in the dark",' he paused, 'I'm not sure that's correct, but you get the gist.'

'You can hear the Welsh lilt in it can't you, the driving rhythm of a passionate heart.'

David laughed.

'Whoa, Jack, you're getting all literary on me and all I'm getting is coal dust in my tea.'

'Say it again,' said Jack.

And David did as he was bid, and got it as close as his memory would allow.

'That's the value of poetry,' said Jack, 'a lot said in few words.'

'Rather than very little in a lot!' grinned David, '"While the proud rich they, without our cares, in comfort live, and masters, who hate Liberty, can in their height of power and greed, force weaker men to serve their need",'

Jack's eyes opened wide, two pools of white in a black face, 'That's true,' he said, 'owners and miners, we live in different worlds, and they're the richer for it. Is that the same man?'

'Not just the same man, but the same poem.'

'It's powerful stuff.'

'Aye, worth thinking about, if it don't make you too sullen. You've got to accept that we live in a world where "One Tyrant, though not right, is strong, can punish thousands for no wrong"!'

'Hmm,' said Jack, 'we can't be having too much of that, can we? A man can only put up with so much injustice before he is pushed to take some action.'

'Unions, Jack, working collectively, knowing our worth, that's the way we fight our corner. Now, talking about knowing our worth, it's high time we got back to work, this coal isn't going to shift itself.'

David got to his feet and clapped Jack on the back; the coal dust flew.

'It's good talking to you, Jack,' he said.

Chapter 54

Sarah returned from Sunderland full of ideas.

'It's an interesting life,' she said to Jenny, 'three meals a day and your uniform cleaned and ironed, running water, can you imagine that Jenny, running water and gas lighting in every room.'

'You'd be always at somebody else's beck and call,' said Jenny, 'always told what to do, when and how.'

'And paid £4 a quarter. I could open a bank account, imagine that. I could send you some money.'

Jenny immediately rose to this.

'We don't need your money,' she said, 'with Frank, Edward and Jack all earning good money, we've never been so well off.'

And Jenny was right. With 2 Hewer's wages coming in that averaged 41s a week and Jack's Putter's pay at 36s they were much better off than most households. Jenny knew it wouldn't last though. With Frank's cough getting worse and with boys that were sure to move out one day this hefty income would soon disappear. For this reason, and without telling Frank, she was putting to one side all that she could safely afford, building up savings for the inevitable rainy days ahead.

Sarah immediately backtracked.

'I didn't mean you needed it,' she said, blushing, 'it's just that I would be able to.'

'Able to or not we wouldn't want it. Any money you make, you can keep, and that includes from your sewing and alterations.'

Jack came in. He immediately felt the tension in the room.

'Everything alright?' he said.

'Everything is just fine,' said Jenny, not meaning it, 'Sarah is thinking of leaving, and going into service in Sunderland.'

'Oh,' said Jack.

'I'd come home,' said Sarah, quickly.

'With half a day off a week and the odd full day, how would you do that? Look at Mary Jones she sees her mother once every three months if she's lucky.'

'But Ma, she's making a life for herself, and anyway you could all come and see me.'

'For part of your half a day? For a walk along the promenade? For a cup of tea and a cake?' said Jenny, feeling she was losing another daughter.

'Ma,' said Jack, 'you and Dad have always said we have to make our own way, just like you two did…'

This hit home.

Jenny and Frank had moved, moved away from family to where the work was, made this life for themselves, brought up a family, and they'd hardly ever gone back, they'd more or less lost touch. Maybe that was wrong or maybe that was just what Sarah was planning to do. Jenny's ruffled feathers smoothed slightly.

'Yes, of course, Sarah, you must do what you think is best. We'll all support you, won't we Jack?'

'Of course,' said Jack, 'whatever you choose, we'll support you.'

He'd known Sarah just about all his life, but her not being there any more didn't really sink in. He was just thinking about it logically.

'All right then,' said Sarah, 'I will think about it. And I might just do it!'

She turned on her heal and stormed out the back door, buckets scraping across the yard as she went to collect more water. The back gate slammed behind her.

'She doesn't seem to be very happy,' said Jack.

'Growing up is never easy,' said Jenny, wishing she'd handled the conversation better.

Chapter 55

Frank, Edward and Jack would talk of their day's work and everyone in the house would know and understand the mining terms they used. To an outsider their language would have seemed indecipherable but to the initiated, and that meant everybody in the mining village regardless of sex, age or position, it was as clear as day.

Often Frank, who liked to keep abreast of the news and always read his daily paper, would look up in pleasure or exasperation and blurt out what he thought about this or that; the Prime Minister's latest speech on education, the working week, fair pay, or how Newcastle United were doing in the League or Cup. Increasingly he was becoming worried about the prospect of war in Europe and the possible effects on the coal trade. Jenny didn't want to listen to this kind of talk, they had enough to be going on with without worrying about things that probably would never happen, and she would tell him to 'shush', which he would do, but only after he'd had his say.

If I were to attempt a balanced, clear and straightforward account of the economic and social conditions in the early years of the 20th century from the information I have gathered the result would only succeed in demonstrating two things: my ignorance and the untrustworthiness of my sources.

In these early years of the century about 150,000 people were employed directly in the Durham Coalfields. Growth in demand for the high-quality coal attracted workers from all parts of the country who wished to benefit from the ready employment and comparatively good pay. From the over 120 coal mines in active operation about 40 million tons of coal a year were lifted back into the daylight to fuel the massive social and economic engine that powered this phase of the Industrial Revolution.

And in this period of growth and common, though misbalanced, purpose, the Durham Miners Association (DMA) was founded in 1869, and came to sit at the same table as the owners and their representatives to agree on basic conditions that were applied across all of the Durham mines. Their remit included the all-important 'sliding scale' that linked the rate of pay per shift of the Hewer to the average realised price of a ton of Durham coal on the open market.

But such attempts at 'fairness' and standardisation were fraught with difficulties because the conditions in the different mines varied considerably as well as there being significant variation between the working seams within a single pit.

Some seams were thin, others thick, some pits were dry and easy to work, others were wet and difficult, some seams were predominantly sources of gas coal, others of simple grades of ordinary household coal.

It was the gas coals of Durham that were held in particularly high esteem both locally and in the London area, often accepted as being amongst the best, if not the best, in Western Europe.

With all these complications, there could be considerable differences in the tonnage and the realised price per ton from pit to pit and therefore considerable differences in the earning power of the Hewer. And if the Hewer's pay was affected, then so was everybody else's.

At the advice of his father and elder brother, Jack joined the Union.

Jenny, Frank, Edward and Jack were all in the kitchen, George was out playing somewhere, Sarah was out with her sewing and Grandpa was on his allotment. The coal crackled in the grate, glowing red at the centre.

'The Union is important because it aims to do two things,' said Frank, 'it tries to protect us, its members, and negotiate the best possible conditions across the whole of Durham, and then it tries to recognise individual differences between pits and work out ways to individually compensate for them.'

'Sounds almost impossible,' said Edward, 'in my view it's always the owners that come out on top. Look at the size of their houses, you don't see them covered in coal dust.'

There was no refuting Edwards's point, you just had to use your eyes to see the proof of it, so Frank chose to ignore it and carry on with his own theme, sucking on his pipe, tapping the stem on the arm of his chair in time with the ticking of the mantle clock.

'These differences,' he said, 'shift over time, a good seam runs out, poorer ones are left, the market price goes up or down for reasons completely out of our control… so I'm a supporter of the Joint Committee. It may not be perfect but without it there'd be even more friction than there is.'

'Joint Committee?' said Jack, 'what's that?'

'It's a lot of men talking instead of working,' said Jenny.

Frank shook his head slowly.

'It's a committee that has an equal number of miners and owners represented on it,' he said, 'Durham is divided into districts and each has its own committee.'

'More blather than sense,' said Jenny, 'and no women to knock some sense into them.'

Her sons smiled.

'Now however that may be,' said Frank, 'and I'm not saying that it's not, these committees meet every few weeks and if we have a grievance it's a place we can take it to.'

'For all the good it does,' said Jenny.

Frank squirmed uneasily in his seat, his pipe stem tapping to a faster rhythm.

'Now Jenny,' he said, 'don't get too het up. Remember when we said the price for the hewing was too low? And they agreed to increase it.'

'Eventually.'

Frank wasn't willing to give up on this success.

'And paid us back money.'

'Was that really the Joint Committee?' said Jenny.

'Yes, it was.'

'Would probably have been better sorting it out locally, directly with the owners. Earnest Weightman could have done that, I'm sure, he's a good man. This committee of yours probably slowed it all down.'

'And the back pay… you welcomed that didn't you? We wouldn't have got that except through the Committee's rules and regulations.'

Frank failed to mention the occasions when the Committee decided pay should be reduced. He wasn't stupid.

'The backpay was useful,' conceded Jenny. 'but if this committee is so good why's there so many strikes?'

Jack and Edward watched on. They found this kind of tussle between their parents very amusing, even if the subject was crucially important to their wellbeing.

'The committee can't always agree, but if it wasn't there there'd be even more strikes. Nobody wants their pay to go down, even when there might be reason…'

'Humph.'

'…might I said, might, and so there'll be times that we have to make a stand.'

'Aye, and lose money while you're out, and still expect me to put meals on the table.'

'Jenny…'

'I'm just saying, you don't always think about family and the women when you…'

Frank put up a hand,

'I always think about you and the family,' he said.

Jenny stopped in her tracks.

'You do,' she said, more softly, 'but a lot don't and when it comes to striking, its mob rule.'

'Majority rule,' said Frank, 'majority rule.'

'And when the fighting breaks out?'

'It's a serious thing, people have strong views…'

'You don't see the women fighting, and we have strong views.'

'Yes, you do,' said Frank, looking up affectionately at his wife, 'and I love you for it.'

Jack and Edward winked at each other. Jenny brushed her hands down her apron front.

'Right, well then,' she said, 'meals don't make themselves; Edward put the kettle on, Jack go and get some more water and find George, I'll be putting the food out.'

'And Dad?' asked Edward.

'Your father has Affairs of State to mull over, you leave him to his paper for a few minutes.'

The boys laughed. Their mother scowled at them. Each went about their business.

Chapter 56

More letters passed between Sarah and Mary. Jenny went to talk to Mrs Jones.

'It's not easy, Jenny,' she said, 'but we have two girls and only the one income and he doesn't make a Hewer's pay, like your husband.'

In fact William Jones had suffered an injury at the coal face and because of permanent damage to his shoulder he was no longer fit to work underground. Earnest Weightman had taken up his case for compensation with the Joint Committee.

The doctor's report prepared by the Union was presented alongside that prepared on behalf of the colliery owners. There were distinct differences between them in their assessment of William's injuries but eventually a compensation payment was agreed and Earnest managed to find him a surface job; a blow to his pride and significantly less money, but it meant he could keep the house.

In comparison Jenny recognised their own privileged position. They'd worked for it, but nevertheless they were in a good position. Until the boys moved out that was. Boys! In her head she still called them that, 'her boys', to anybody else they were men.

'So, one way or another there'll come a time when we can't keep the house on,' said Mrs Jones, 'William's shoulder is getting worse, even though he's moved to a surface job. We're looking at those new retirement homes at the moment, trying to find out what they're all about. Earnest is helping us again with that.'

Jenny had heard about these miner's retirement homes but hadn't really thought about them. They were a relatively new idea and one of the good things to come out of the work of the Union. She didn't realise that Mr and Mrs Jones were already considering this as their future, they weren't that much older than Frank and her.

'The girls need a future. Martha is courting Adam Thompson, and he's a good lad, so I've high hopes there. But Mary never struck up with anyone special, so going into service seemed a good solution. As you can see, she looks good on it and even sends a little money home.'

Jenny understood how different their circumstances were.

'But don't you miss her?' she asked.

Mrs Jones smiled.

'Course I do, just imagine what a help she could be around the place,' she paused, 'though her sister, Martha's, very good too.'

She thought for a minute.

'You see, Jenny, none of my girls took to anything like sewing that might bring in some money, they just learned the basics, that's all the start I could give them. Of course I miss Mary, but I'm happy she's building herself a life in Sunderland, much better than wasting away here. There was no choice really.'

No choice! Perhaps that was the way it was for Jenny too. Sarah had to decide for herself, and Jenny had no choice but to go along with it.

Later, she shared her thoughts with Jack.

'No choice,' he said, 'Sarah's a strong woman, she'll do what she wants in the end.'

Chapter 57

About 1 in every 10 miners suffered from some kind of disability: 40% due to accidents and 30% to industrial diseases such as pneumoconiosis and chronic bronchitis.

A miner's earning ability depended largely on his skill and physical capability. The pieceworkers at or near the coal face were the highest paid and had the highest status, their work being the most physically exacting, their output determining the pay of others.

Other underground and surface workers were paid a day wage and cutting across these functional divisions were the stages of a miner's 'life-cycle'; a boy out of school may work on the surface or as a Trapper underground, then he could perhaps 'graduate' to Driver, then Putter and finally, perhaps in his early 20s, to Hewer.

After a time, the arduous work at the coal face would become too much, or injury, or illness would cause the miner to retreat and take a lower paid job either underground or on the surface.

As well as the miners, there were the craftsman; Fitters, Electricians, Bricklayers… trained and qualified to work underground and, at the supervisory level; the Shot-firer, the Deputy, the Under Manager, most of whom were ex-miners, and beyond them the specialist Engineers, the Finance Managers, the pushers of paper.

For all that the miner's work was hard and dangerous it was also a source of quiet pride and satisfaction. They did not see their work as meaningless. They were not minor cogs in a machine whose ultimate purpose was beyond their ken. The pit was self-evidently there and their job of extracting and measuring and sending off the coal, without which the new engines of society would grind to a halt, was important and clear to all.

Underground the men got to know each other by sweating together, they got to know each other's strengths but also their weaknesses.

They were working to a common purpose; to earn money. A group in conflict with itself was not conducive to achieving this goal and therefore, the men tried their best to get along, especially as a miner's safety, should he get into trouble or have an accident, could well depend on whether he got help from his workmates and how quickly he got it.

Putting it another way, the presence of physical danger led to both a high level of continual concentration on the work, a strong sense of individual responsibility, and an unspoken inter-reliance between the miners.

Miners therefore attached great importance to working as members of an established group made up of known and trusted workmates.

And the miners had a sense of their own inheritance. For many, their fathers and grandfathers had been miners and had talked to them about their experiences underground, this 'pit talk', which reached back generations, morphed partly into a kind of inherited mythology, made real through the retellings.

To a miner, his work was his obsession. Whether he loved it or he hated it, whether he was fascinated by it or repelled by it he bore a form of pride towards it; it was difficult and he did it.

For most it was also difficult to leave this work behind them, and when they met in the street, talked over the garden fence, or over a pint in the pub, one of the enduring topics of conversation would always be the pit. In fact, if a man wanted to escape from the pit and from pit-talk for an hour or two it was best he find an activity that did not involve other miners.

The Putters were known to be an independent, physically fit and strong-minded bunch. These characteristics were virtues in the dark tunnels, when coal needed shifting, but sometimes, when they had grievances that they thought were not being taken seriously, these same characteristics led to obstinacy and trouble. Sometimes the grievances themselves were serious and sometimes they were trivial.

It was as if the pressure built, like pop in a bottle, and just had to be released.

But once it kicked off it was difficult to stop.

At such times the Putters, who would range in age from about 17 to 32 years of age, would hold a meeting of their own.

No one but Putters were allowed in.

David Goodwin would sometimes act as chairman, and the meeting would be carried off in a fairly business-like way.

If collective action was agreed by a majority, then everyone was expected to go along with the decision.

On one such occasion the grievance was that food and water for the ponies was not always brought forward at the right time and the Putters understood that this was because pit props, tools, and keeping empty tubs moving was seen as more important.

When they got no immediate satisfaction, they decided to stop the pit.

This was a serious misdemeanour and they were all charged and taken to court over it.

On their day in court, they each insisted, as they'd agreed earlier between themselves, that they were not willing for the case to proceed as a group action as each of them had their own reasons for doing what they'd done, and therefore the Magistrates must take each case individually on its own merits, with each Putter conducting his own case.

There was not much the Magistrates could do to prevent this as each Putter had the right to ask for an individual hearing and to represent himself.

All the Putters, getting on for 50 of them, were in the courthouse and the first case was called. It was David Goodwin.

David had, all of a sudden, developed a hearing difficulty, and when the Clark asked him his name, he asked him to repeat the question and when the charge was read out he asked for it to be read again, but this time in plain English.

Then he proceeded to question the Magistrates on their ability to judge on such a case as his own when none of them had ever been down the pit.

When these obstacles were overruled he asked if any of them had ever read "Moby Dick" or such other sources of knowledge that might give them an understanding of the strong link between man and animal and said that it was not too far-fetched to suggest that the moral inherent in that great work of literature hitherto referred to could be but reversed such that the strong emotions Captain Ahab displayed for the White Whale might be seen as no less fierce than the love a Putter has for his pony.

There were cheers from the gallery, and several times the Clerk had to call for order and quiet. Eventually the Magistrates took an adjournment to discuss this situation between themselves.

Whilst they were away the Putters started to sing "Cushy Butterfield" and, as the court officials had been given no rules for a situation such as this, and even if they had there was little hope of enforcing them, they just left them to it.

On returning to the court the Chief Magistrate announced that hearing each case individually was a waste of court time, that at this rate it would take more than a week and they had other important matters waiting their turn, that if they were not careful they would all be held in contempt of court which could result in a jail sentence, but that, if they all agreed to go back to work immediately, as, after all, nobody gained from a stopped pit, then they would each be fined a shilling, and the court would see to it that getting the pony's victuals to where they needed to be would be placed as an order on the owners, one of whom was a magistrate and had already shown his willingness to accept this simple solution.

On behalf of all assembled David Goodwin thanked the court, and in respectfully accepting its decision said, 'That's all we were asking for,' and proceeded to enquire where and how he could pay his shilling.

Jack was cock-a-hoop, but was brought down to earth by his father

'You've taken money out of everybody's pockets, you've taken a risk that you might end up suspended, fired, or in jail, and, by some, you're all looked on as fools. Don't think the owners will forget about this, or who was involved, now you'll have to keep one eye looking over your shoulder, you might have won today, but tomorrow...'

He didn't need to finish.

Jack went outside with his tail between his legs; he needed some air.

Why was everything always so complicated?

Chapter 58

'You make really nice cakes.'

Jenny looked up, while keeping the rhythm of the wash tub posser going. They had two tubs as they had lots of laundry and were doing it together.

'I just make cakes like I've always made them.'

'They're really nice. I wish I could bake cakes like you do.'

The swoosh of the soapy water punctuated their conversation, as in unison their arms were raised and then lowered, raised and then lowered, in the perpetual motion of a never-ending task.

'I was just wondering,' said Sarah.

'Yes?'

'If you would help me bake a cake. I was thinking,' she continued, the words pouring from her, tumbling over each other, 'a sponge cake perhaps, with a jam and cream filling.'

'Jack's favourite, you mean?'

'Oh, is that so. What a coincidence.'

'Yes indeed, Sarah, what a coincidence.'

The splodging continued in silence for a while. Sarah's face was flushed, presumably from the exertion.

When the water was a soapy dark grey and gritted with coal dust they lifted the washing, water-wet, heavy, from their tubs to be rinsed and mangle-squeezed dry for hanging.

'Better ask Grandpa if we've got enough eggs,' said Jenny, 'I've got some nice home-made jam, and you can go get the cream.'

Sarah could hardly contain her excitement.

'I'll do that as soon as the washing's strung up,' she said, 'and perhaps it can be ready by the time Ja…, I mean the boys, are all home.'

'Perhaps it can my girl, perhaps it can,' said Jenny, 'but like lots of things it doesn't pay to rush sponge cake. Too much haste, and it's likely to fall flat.'

The heat rose to Sarah's cheeks, and she turned away, her arms full of dripping clothes, so that Jenny could not see her face. But Jenny did not need to see. She knew.

Memories of her own youth crowded in upon her and she could not prevent the smile that spread across her face.

'So do you like Jack?' said Jenny, 'I mean especially.'

'Especially?'

'Yes, especially.'

Sarah coloured. 'I do like Jack, but I can't say that I like him especially.'

'Oh, that's all right then,' said Jenny.

'What do you mean?' said Sarah, a little worried.

'Just that I can put his mind at rest,' said Jenny.

'What do you mean?'

'That I can tell him.'

'Tell him what?'

'That you don't like him especially.'

Sarah was flustered now, her fingers fidgeting.

'That's alright isn't it.? That is what you said.'

'But…'

'But?'

'Well, I didn't think you were asking so that you could tell him.'

Later, the two women were on their knees in the kitchen. Their arms were smeared to the elbows, they were blacking the kitchen range, a dirty job, covering the hard surface with blacking and raising sweat by polishing it to a shine.

'You wouldn't mind though, would you pet?'

Sarah was polishing more violently now, her breathing heavier.

'Mind?'

'If I told Jack.'

There was a long pause.

'I'd rather you didn't,' said Sarah.

'He's just like his dad was, you know.'

'How do you mean?'

'As observant as a brick,' said Jenny, and they both laughed.

'I know what you mean,' said Sarah, relieved now.

'You'll have to take a sledgehammer to crack his nut,' said Jenny.

Putting their backs into their task they fell silent. But Sarah's mind was spinning more violently than even the vigour she displayed in her polishing. She had to decide, did she go to Sunderland, or did she stay here? She'd thought it over carefully and there was only one unanswered question … and that was Jack … and he probably had no idea!

Sarah baked the cake, and everybody enjoyed it. Jenny asked Jack if he'd liked it and he said it was 'nice'.

It was the Sunday after pay Saturday and Jack had some free time. He had a book in his hand, a smile on his face and he was about to set out on his walk.

His mother caught him on the way out.

'What do you think about Sarah moving to Sunderland?' she asked.

'Not really thought about it, I guess she'll go if she wants to.'

'Will you miss her?'

This simple question was like a bolt out of the blue. Jack had known Sarah all his life as neighbour, at school, and now as a sister… well, not a real sister, but she was part of the family, so that's what it felt like.

And what would it feel like if she wasn't there anymore? Jack struggled to imagine it. Rationally and logically, he would support whatever decision she made, of course he would, but how did he feel… that was a different thing altogether.

'Erm, I think I will,' he said.

'She's not a girl anymore,' said Jenny, trying to pierce through Jack's tough hide, 'she's a young woman, a capable, good looking young woman. I wouldn't be surprised if she was snapped up by some young lad in Sunderland.'

Capable?

Yes, definitely.

Good looking?

She was Sarah, he'd never really thought about it. If he did pause to think, then yes, he supposed she was good looking, she always kept herself very clean, and dressed nicely…

He paused and thought about himself, what would anyone think of him?

He tried to keep himself clean, but the coal dust had a way of burying itself in your skin and becoming unshiftable. He tried to keep his hair cut and combed, but his clothes weren't new and that showed.

Compared to him, Sarah definitely came out on top.

'Snapped up?' he said.

'She's not going to be short of admirers, in fact there's some around here…'

Jack felt his hackles rise, but he didn't know why.

'Is there?'

'Oh yes, you've just got to use your eyes, Jack.'

This thing, this thing that was only hypothetical and in the future, had just become very real.

'Do you think she'll go?' he said.

'Why not,' said his mother, 'after all, what's keeping her here?'

Already disoriented, on his way out for a second time, he bumped into his brother Edward.

'Off out?' he said.

'Yes,' said Jack.

'I thought you might be walking your girl out, it's a nice day for it.'

'What girl's that? I don't have any girl.'

'Jack, you're as blind as a bat if you think that,' said Edward, 'and twice as daft.'

Jack said nothing, only frowned.

Finally escaping the house, the sky above him was blue and flected with clouds.

His steps took him away from the pit-head rather than towards it. Today he would not leave the light behind him for the darkness beneath, today he would have the sun on his back all day.

After walking for half an hour, he stopped and breathed in deeply.

The fresh morning air that filled his lungs was exhilarating and he could smell flowers, he could hear the twittering of busy sparrows, they didn't get a day's respite.

As he continued on his walk Jack took in the colours in all their brightness, the smells, the sounds, and wondered if anyone other than a miner could ever appreciate it as much as he did. The contrast between his working world and the glory of this one on such a Summer's day had sent his senses into overdrive and he both reveled in it and struggled to cope with the avalanche of sensory signals that his body was receiving.

He walked slowly, all his work underground had earned him this day and before long he was out in the fields, away from the familiar colliery rows.

The thick green of the grass was mixed with the yellow of celandines, dandelions and buttercups, a lark rose and climbed up into the sky, spiraling upwards until it was only a tiny dot in the blue, its presence betrayed by the trail of its song that followed its flight, reaching a peak before parachuting back to earth. Black and yellow striped bees droned and moved greedily from clover to clover, and, from a short distance, came the munching, tearing sound of feeding cattle.

Jack arrived at a stile, climbed over and sat down with his back against a dry-stone wall. The air was fragrant with the scent of new mown hay from some unseen field. He sat there quietly, thinking nothing, feeling everything.

A weasel, with its chestnut back and creamy white throat and belly, scurried along a hedge line, a hare went loping through the long grass of the open field, and Jack felt an observer's sense of dreamy restfulness that soothed both his body and his mind as his thoughts drifted with the tops of the long grass in the gentle breeze.

He moved on a little further and then lay down in the grass, almost hidden by it, everything shut out but the green around him and the blue above. He lay there, boy like, daydreaming and at peace.

But he didn't stay like that for long, he'd agreed to meet up with Peter so they could eat their lunch together out in the open and, as he rose to his feet he could see Peter's distinctive outline approaching from the direction of the farm.

When Peter arrived, there was a whiff of cow dung about him.

'Sorry,' he said, when he saw Jack wrinkle up his nose, 'can't smell it meself, been in with the cows all morning.'

'I can tell,' said Jack.

Peter laughed.

Jack showed him the book he'd brought out with him, it was called "The Hound of the Baskervilles" and was written by Arthur Conan Doyle,

'It's a Sherlock Holmes story,' he said.

'Oh, I've read some of the short stories,' said Peter, 'they're like puzzles and only Sherlock Holmes is able to see through them, what's his partner called again?'

'Doctor Watson.'

'Oh yes, that's right,' he paused, 'hold on a bit, is this an old story? I thought Sherlock Holmes had been killed off in the last one.'

'He had; he's been brought back to life.'

'That's the thing about being a writer, you can just make impossible things happen whenever you feel like it.'

Jack laughed.

'It's about a family curse and a giant hound that lives out on the moors, and murder of course, that Holmes and Watson have to try and solve. I've just started reading it and it's very good.'

'It sounds interesting, can I read it after you?'

'Of course, I'll bring it over when I've finished, after all you helped me build my small collection of books.'

'Not me, my father.'

'But you didn't stop him.'

'I can't stop him from doing anything,' said Peter.

Peter and Jack both had sandwiches and cold tea. Neither dared comment on the other's food as they knew their respective mothers had made them and any comment about one outshining the other was too dangerous a territory to enter.

Their talk drifted around to Sarah and the possibility of her leaving.

'That would be a shame,' said Peter, 'I've always liked Sarah.'

Jack was surprised.

'You've never told me that,' he said.

'Thought I'd better keep it to myself.'

'Why's that?'

'Always thought she was your girl.'

'My girl!?'

'Yes, it's pretty obvious from the way she looks at you.'

Jack was beginning to think that everybody knew something that he didn't.

'From the way she looks at me?'

'Yes, and the things she says. I bet she'd even bake you a cake!'

Jack stopped in his tracks.

'She did bake a cake,' he said, 'but it was for everybody.'

'And?'

Jack thought about it.

'And it just happened to be my favourite.'

Peter laughed.

'There you go then… and what did you say?'

Jack wracked his brains trying to remember.

'I think I said it was nice.'

Peter laughed again.

'Jack, my friend, sometimes the things most difficult to see are those right under your nose.'

After Peter had gone, Jack walked on until he reached the banks of a stream. Here he watched the flies as they rose above the water, circling and flocking in murmurations, while below them a fish rose to the surface and a ripple spread out its concentric rings.

Being still, he could hear the mellow call of the thrush, the drone and buzz of insect life, the soothing rustle of the wind. For a moment he felt as though he was suspended between a world that was and a world that could be, and that he, Jack Lawley, was a very small piece in a miraculous whole.

He only had to turn his head to see, in the distance, the pit-head winding gear standing stark, housed in its towering, sharp-angled metal lattice. Alongside, the great chimney smoked lazily, and below and beside he could imagine the long rows of colliery houses, arranged like a regiment in line, his mother at the front of one of them, perhaps scrubbing the front doorstep to recover the white.

In these moments of peace, Jack tried to examine his own feelings.

He liked Sarah, she was one of his closest friends. Now he came to think about it, she was the only real female friend that he had that was close to his own age.

He'd never chased after girls. He'd kissed a few but there wasn't anyone special.

Or was there?

Was Sarah special without him realising it?

Why did he feel an ache when he thought about her not being there anymore? Why did he feel his blood rise at the thought of her being 'snapped up' in Sunderland?

And anyway, what did she really think about him? Others had told him that she liked him but what if they were wrong? What if she was just being polite, or worse, what if she was scared of him?

This last thought made him wince, after the treatment she'd had from her father that would be terrible. There was only one way to find out. He would have to ask her.

As soon as he came to this conclusion, he knew that it was right. What surprised him was the associated feeling of nervousness.

Jack walked back up his street.

His boots scuffed the gravel, kicking up particles of coal dust that rose as if in irritation at being disturbed, before falling as gently as black snow and resettling in amongst their multitudinous comrades.

Men were sitting outside their houses in their trousers and shirts, some had their sleeves rolled up, others bared their chests in response to the unaccustomed warmth of the day. Jack was given a wave, a nod or a greeting as he passed by each one and he returned the favour.

All the doors of the houses were open for an airing, the numbers chalked on them a stark reminder that this was but a short interlude between work and more work, the marks informing the morning 'caller' whether to knock the men in the house up at 3 o'clock or at 5 o'clock in the morning.

But today they were free to sit in the Sun.

When Jack walked through his front door he was immediately met by two things; one was a shout from his mother telling him to take his boots off, she'd been cleaning all day and didn't need him treading in muck, the second was the sizzling sound and unmistakable smell of bacon frying.

Jack hadn't realised just how hungry he was until he smelt the bacon. With the long walk and his deep thoughts to fuel it, he was not going to let the offer of fried bacon with new-baked bread, butter and a large mug of sweet tea pass him by.

His mother must have seen him coming when he was a way off, he thought. He smiled, he'd always thought his mother had eyes everywhere.

He put his book down, and, as he sat down at the kitchen table to eat, he looked around at the pile of cleaned clothes, the scrubbed floor, the burnished range, and realised that while his day had been one of relaxation, contemplation and leisure, his mother's had not.

His brothers, father and grandfather were all out and after he'd eaten, Jack took the opportunity, unmolested by his mother who was now out in the back yard, to go into the front room, where he was allowed to keep his small, but growing collection of secondhand books.

They sat nestled together in one corner of the room, stored in a makeshift bookcase made from orange boxes that his grandfather had painted a uniform blue and had lined the 'shelves' with brown paper.

The books were organised in categories: History at the top, Fiction in the middle and Poetry at the bottom. He put his book back on the middle shelf. He would read it later, his mind was racing too fast to concentrate on reading now.

He looked at his books with affection, they were like old friends and the faded gold-lettering on their spines brought back flashes of memory of the stories inside. If he could ever be tempted to part with any then he would give them to his old school, in appreciation of the encouragement he'd received from his teacher, Wilkinson Hughes.

A couple of them had been shifted around, he shifted them back. Even though he told nobody to touch them his mother must have done it when she was tidying up.

Two were new additions and as such represented uncharted territory, lands yet to be explored, wonders yet to be discovered.

He picked one of them out, opened the cover and smelt that unmistakable smell of old books that was like a 'welcome mat' to Jack.

At this point his mother glanced in,

'Did you see Peter?' she said.

'Yes,'

'How was he?'

'Smelling of cow dung,' said Jack.

His mother laughed.

'Yes, his mother tells me he's really taking to the farm work, they're very proud of him.'

Jack replaced his book and wondered fleetingly if anyone was proud of him.

'Ma?'

'Yes?'

He was going to talk to her about Sarah, perhaps ask her advice, but in any case, to let her know he was going to talk to her. But before he could get started the family began to return, his father and elder brother chattering from the pub, his Grandpa, who was immediately told to take his muddy boots off, with an armful of vegetables and a pocketful of eggs and. George full of stories of climbing trees and swinging across streams. And then Sarah returned. Draped over her arm was the dress she was working on. She was returning from a fitting and her head was full of the small alterations she needed to make. She didn't seem to notice Jack, but he looked at her in a different way, as if she were almost a stranger who he was meeting for the first time.

'Have you all enjoyed yourselves?' said Jenny.

There was a barb in her voice and it produced an immediate silence.

'I've only been working all day,' she said.

The others looked at each other, they knew it was true.

'I'll get some more coal in,' said Jack.

'I'll put some paper in the privy,' said Edward.

'I'll get some water,' said George.

'Would you like to go out for a walk?' said Frank.

'I'll have some peas shelled and vegetables peeled by the time you get back,' said Sarah.

Grandpa raised his hand, 'And I'll collect the peelings and clean my boots.'

'Outside!' said Jenny.

'Outside,' said Grandpa.

'Then,' said Jenny, untying her apron strings, 'I would love to go out for a few minutes' walk on this fine day.'

Frank reached out his hand, Jenny took it, and they left through the front door.

Chapter 59

The problems Jack encountered as a Putter were unpredictable, each solution unique, and there were worse things than tubs slipping the rails.

Sometimes Jack would be Putting by himself, but not always, there were other times when he was working with two or three others, all according to the number of Hewers at the face.

When this happened the Putters generally agreed to cooperate, pool their earnings, and each take an equal share. This prevented any rivalry that could undermine each other's safety.

On one of these occasions Jack was trying to lever a full tub back onto the rails. At just the wrong moment, with the tub off the ground, Jack slipped and the lever broke, trapping Jack's foot under the tub.

This was no time to be a hero, and Jack screamed for help.

Luckily for him David Goodwin was nearby and rushed to Jack's assistance. David was a strong man amongst strong men and immediately took a hold on the tub,

'When I lift you pull your bloody foot out... and do it fast, I won't be able to hold it long.'

Jack clenched his teeth and nodded.

'Alright,' said David, 'here we go... one... two... thhhhreeee...'

As soon as he felt the weight lift Jack pulled out his foot. He rolled away, twisted into a foetal position and started to shake. A shower of coal particles rained down as David dropped the tub. He was sweating and gasping for breath.

Recovering himself he went over to Jack. Barney was nosing him gently in the back as he lay, curled up in the black dust.

Jack had been caught like a rat in a trap. The shock of not being able to extricate himself, and the immediate pain had caused him to panic. He wasn't proud of it but as his trembling subsided, he unwound himself. David brought him some water.

'Thanks,' he said, 'I think I forgot there were others here. I was thinking I was helpless and trapped.'

'I can understand that,' said David, 'it can happen to any of us. Now how's your foot?'

Jack tried to stand but couldn't put any weight on his foot, he grimaced, it was too painful.

'Let's get you to a doctor,' said David, and called over to a Driver who had just arrived with some empty tubs.

'Hey, you, take Jack back with you. We'll cover for you here, Jack, as best we can.'

Jack knew that there could be a reduction in coal production for the rest of the shift because of his absence.

'I'm sorry, David,' he said.

'We all have our moments, let's just hope nothing's broken.'

'I'll take myself back,' said Jack, his foot ached but there was no sharp pain unless he tried to put it down. Now that his panic had subsided he felt a lot better but he knew he'd had a narrow escape and if he'd been stuck in a tunnel on his own and the weight in the tub had shifted just a little, which it was prone to do, then the result could have been a lot different, 'Barney knows the way.'

David was surprised but Jack insisted.

After Jack got to the surface, the doctor examined him,

'Your foot has been saved by your boot,' he said, 'must have clamped down on the sole. You're very lucky, Jack Lawley, very lucky. There's nothing broken and, if I support it with a bandage, you should be able to walk, although it might be painful for a few days. Let's see how it goes over the weekend, you might even get away without missing a shift.'

'Thanks, doctor, but I don't feel lucky, I feel stupid.'

The doctor had been working at coal mines for over a decade and he wasn't shy in using shock tactics to get his point across.

'Somewhere in this country,' he said, 'every working day in the coal mining industry, four people are killed. You shouldn't feel stupid, you should feel fortunate.'

'The lever snapped at exactly the moment I slipped,' said Jack, 'it all happened so quickly.'

'No recriminations, Jack, learn from the accident, warn others, that's the ticket.'

Jack told his mother.

She didn't say anything, she just wrapped him in her arms and he felt a hot tear on his cheek.

The shame and stupidity he felt at the accident, and his reaction to it, put any thoughts of talking to Sarah out of his head. Nobody would want a coward like him.

The next day Jack was in the kitchen with Jenny, Frank and Edward,

'You know,' he said to his mother, twisting his foot this way and that, realizing it felt a lot better after a night's sleep, 'if there was any justice in the world, and if there was such a thing as a good life, a life with permanent freedom from insecurity, a life filled with the thirst for knowledge and the pursuit of leisure, then the men who do the world's dirty, sweaty, toilsome, risky work,' he looked at his mother, 'and the women who share that life with them, ought to be the first in the queue for it. But when I look around, you can see that such people, such people as us, are not first in line, but last. In fact, the further you get away from the real work, the better life you have!'

Jenny sighed.

'You might be right, and you might be wrong,' she said, 'but you know what I've learned.'

Jack stayed silent.

'I've learned that it's best to make the most of what you've got, take up your rightful grievances when you must but don't believe that the world is going to get any different anytime soon, make the most of it, Jack, there's people a lot worse off than us.'

'I'm proud of the work I do,' said Frank, clearing his throat and spitting black into the coals of the fire, where it sizzled to nothingness, 'it might be dirty, but it's good work, important work, the whole country is running on the coal we bring to the surface, if that flow stopped then everything would stop.'

'Then perhaps we should stop,' said Edward, 'so that everybody comes into that same way of thinking.'

Frank glowered at him.

'That sounds like a game with no winners,' he said.

Frank was one of the many who developed the miner's cough. Down in the mine, especially at the pit face, the black dust hung in the air and entered, felt and tasted, into the mouths and noses of the men and passed down into the stomach or the lungs.

The larger pieces did not enter the airways, and the smallest pieces were breathed out, but the dust that was neither small nor large came to sit and accumulate within the men's lungs. Some of it would be coughed up and spat on the ground later or be the cause of the unwelcome raking cough that was the morning trademark of an waking miner.

Frank had the cough, Edward would retch, cough, and spit and Jack had yet to be noticeably affected.

When Frank coughed, Jenny shuddered. Although the Old Age Pensions Act gave some security at seven shillings and six pence for a married couple, you had to be 70 years old and proven to be of good character before you could start collecting it. Underground workers seldom got anywhere close to reaching that age.

The rate was set deliberately low in order to encourage people to make provision for their old age and not to give up work too easily.

The idea of saving money for the future was just not possible for most mining families although the Lawley household was one of the few that could do this, and Jenny was putting a bit aside each payday without bothering to tell anyone.

However, the prospect of a pension and the advent of accommodation for retired miners, was a vast improvement from the times when the elderly or infirm had no alternative but to rely on their families to take care of them or, if they didn't have any sons or daughters who could, or would, agree to look after them, find themselves in the workhouse.

'I hope I live long enough to get me old age pension,' Frank had said to Jenny when the Bill was passed.

'Well, even if you do you still might not get it, if they have to look into your character,' said Jenny.

Frank smiled before turning away and returning to his newspaper. The print was small but at least he still had eyesight good enough to read it.

Although Jack had escaped serious injury, he kept the bandage on for a few more days and limped when he felt twinges of pain although that didn't stop him going to work.

Back underground Jack saw the slim wraith-like figure of David Goodwin, back bent, shovel squealing against the hard stone floor, levitating wayward lumps of coal back into the tubs. As he worked, he chanted poetry, not always accurately, but always with his words booming in those restricted spaces.

Alfred, Lord Tennyson was a favourite, or Rudyard Kipling, Thomas Gray or Robert Burns… and so in these low, gloomy, dusty, working places, no more than 5 yards wide, and 4 or 5 feet high, more than a thousand feet below the sunlit surface, images of green fields or rippling streams, of battlefields, of Crimea, India or Scotland, of distant hills or tim'rous beasties…would be conjured up and talked about as they sat to take their bait, their sweat-soaked shoes and dust-caked bodies propped against a convenient wall.

It made the work seem a little easier, it made the time go faster.

Jack was earning a good wage, paid for by a body bent double most of the time, or squirming like a contortionist to clear a blockage or right a tub. Barney was his stalwart companion, steady, strong and trustworthy and Jack would pat his neck or rump occasionally, just to show his appreciation, although it was when an apple or a carrot appeared that Barney really felt appreciated.

Jack used his half gallon tin bottle of water, always lukewarm, sparingly. Mainly he would gargle the dust out of his throat and spit it into the dark recesses. When he drank, he would only take a little, as he'd learnt from harsh experience that to take too much too quickly could produce painful stomach cramps, and they were no help to the work that still needed to be done. Instead, he would pour a little onto his wrists and neck in an attempt to keep his body temperature down.

Back home his mother would have a bath and a hot meal waiting, perhaps a pot pie, and then he would go to the pub with his brother or spend a few precious hours in the parlour with his books and a chair by the fire.

On this particular evening, as Jack and Edward made their way to the open door of "The Stackyard", Edward asked,

'Whose round is it tonight?'

From inside the lights shone bright and they could hear the boisterous singing. On the threshold Jack paused and rubbed an almost invisible scar above his eye, appearing to suffer intense pain at the touch.

'Alright, I'll buy the first one,' Edward laughed, 'It's a bloody expensive scar you've got there and no mistake.'

They settled at a table and as they sipped at their pint glasses Edward told Jack that he had heard a good story and asked whether Jack would like to hear it? Always one for a story, Jack said yes.

'So there's this guy,' Edward began, 'and he goes for an interview for a job down the pit, there's two of them waiting and the first one goes in. Once he's got sat down the interviewer says,

"To work down the pit we need to make sure you've got your head screwed on, so I'm going to ask you some questions."

"OK, sir," says our man.

"The first question is; if someone put one of your eyes out what would be the effect?"

Our man thinks this a very strange question, but he needs the job, so he says,

"I wouldn't be able to see very well, sir."

"That's correct," says the interviewer, "now then, what about if someone put both your eyes out?"

Our man is not happy with these questions, working down the pit is dangerous enough without this kind of questioning, but still, he needs the job, so he says,

"I wouldn't be able to see at all, sir."

"Correct again," says the interviewer, "you've shown me that you've got a good level of common sense… so you've got a job and can start tomorrow."

"Thank you, sir," says our man.

On the way out the other man takes him to one side and asks him how it went.

"They ask you some daft questions," says our man, "and if you get them right, they give you a job."

"Oh," says the second man, "come on then mate, tell me the answers. I'll buy you a beer or two later."

"OK," says our man, cos he's got nothing to lose, he's already got a job for himself, so he may as well help, and get a couple of free beers in the process, "the answer to the first question is, 'I wouldn't be able to see very well', and the answer to the second question is 'I wouldn't be able to see at all'."

"Right," says the second man, "to the first question I answer, 'I wouldn't be able to see very well', and to the second question I answer, 'I wouldn't be able to see at all', is that right?"

"That's right," says our man.

"OK, I've got it."

So, when he's called, the second man gets up, takes off his flat cap, puts it in his pocket, spits on his hands, smooths down his hair, and goes in.

It's the same man doing the interview and when the second man is sat down, he says,

"To work down the pit we need to make sure you've got your head screwed on, we don't want anybody who's a liability to himself or his workmates working down there, so I'm going to ask you some questions, to make sure you're up to it."

"OK, sir," says the second man, confident he knows what to say.

"The first question I want you to think about is; if someone cut one of your ears off, what would be the effect?'"

Our friend thinks that this is a very strange question, but he's delighted that he got a steer from the first man because he too needs the job, so he answers with confidence,

"I wouldn't be able to see very well, sir."

"What's that you say?" says the interviewer.

"I wouldn't be able to see very well, sir."

"Hmm," says the interviewer, "let me just ask you one more question: what about if someone cut both your ears off?'"

The man is feeling really confident now, he's sure he's got the answer, so he says,

"I wouldn't be able to see at all, sir."

"Really?" says the interviewer, "are you sure?"

"Absolutely, sir," says the man.

"Well…" says the interviewer shaking his head. But before he ends the interview, he decides he's got to ask.

"So, if you got one of your ears cut off, you wouldn't be able to see very well, and if you got both of them cut off you wouldn't be able to see at all… is that right?"

"Absolutely, sir, that's right."

The man says this with such confidence that the interviewer scratches his head and then he says,

"If you got one of your ears cut off, you wouldn't be able to see very well, and if you got both of them cut off you wouldn't be able to see at all… how do you make that out?"

"Well, sir, if someone cut one of my ears off then me cap would drop over me eye and I wouldn't be able to see very well, and if both me ears were cut off me cap would drop down over both me eyes and I wouldn't be able to see at all!'"

Jack laughed, But Edward wasn't finished.

'Later on, the two men meet up in the pub.

"How did it go?" asks the first man.

"Well, they were very strange questions," says the second man, lifting his cap high enough so that he can scratch his head.

"They were that," says the first man.

"But I gave the answers you told me."

"Aye?"

"…and I not only got the job, but I've been marked down as Foreman material!'"

Edward roared with laughter at his own joke.

'That is a good one!' said Jack, smiling.

Edward chuckled,

'It's your round now,' he said.

When they got home, they were still laughing. The rest of the family were sitting around in the kitchen.

Sarah looked straight at Jack.

'I got a letter from Mary Jones today; there's a vacancy in Sunderland for a kitchen maid.'

Jack stopped laughing.

Chapter 60

On the following Sunday afternoon, Jack took Sarah out for a walk.

They walked away from the colliery, the pithead at their backs. As they walked Jack named the flowers that littered the verge with vibrancy and life; the daisy, the dandelion, the 'love me, love me not' yellow sun-trapped buttercup, and the less common ones; the Bird's-foot-trefoil, with its red-flushed yellow flowers buzzing with bees, the purple flowers bunched on the long stems of the tangled Milk Vetch, the branched flower head, the tight white flower bunches of the patches of Cow parsley, the red-purple thistle-like florets of the Knapweed.

Sarah listened quietly, butterflies fluttered around them. Jack named these too; the Red Admiral, with its black wings slashed with red, splattered with white, waving like flags, the deep orange of the Peacock with its large false eyes ringed in black and blue and white, the humble Cabbage Whites, and the Tortoiseshell with its black, white, and orange epaulettes.

Eventually Sarah stopped him.

'You're very clever, Jack, to know all these names and such…'

Jack smiled at the compliment.

'…but does everything have to have a name?'

Jack was surprised.

'What do you mean?' he said, the concept of something not having a name foreign to him. He spent his spare time reading, accumulating knowledge, and knowledge of things started with knowing their names.

'Well, I was just thinking,' said Sarah, 'take that butterfly over there.'

'The Red Admiral…'

'Yes, I suppose so, but would it look any different if we called it a…' she paused thinking of a suitable alternative, '…a 'Black Lady' for example?'

'But it's not a Black Lady, it's a Red Admiral.'

'It doesn't know that does it,' said Sarah, 'it just knows what it must look for to eat, how to find a mate, where to lay her eggs, it hasn't decided to have wings that colour, they just are, and it gets on with it… it's like we're given two legs, we didn't ask for them, they're just there.'

Jack laughed.

'Good job,' he said, 'it would be more difficult to walk if we only had one!'

She looked at him sternly.

'Are you laughing at me?'

Jack was immediately thrown off balance.

'No, no, I'm not, honest I'm not, I'm just surprised by some of your ideas.'

'Are you?'

'Yes,' he said, and then, 'it's one of the things I like about you.'

'Only one, Jack Lawley, we'll then, there's hope for me yet!'

She laughed.

Jack laughed, but he wasn't sure why, he was just being carried along by her presence.

As they continued their walk, Jack stopped showing off his encyclopaedic knowledge of the naming of things, and their talk moved on to other subjects, many and varied. Sarah proved herself more than a match for Jack's tendency to jump from one thing to the next as ideas, grasshopper like, occurred to him and then flitted away.

Sarah avoided talking about those areas, though there were many, where she knew Jack was ignorant; the 'time of the month', the period pains, the blood, the secret laundering and then there was the essential though underrated tasks; the cooking, the sewing, the family laundering, the perpetual cycle of cleaning… all the things that his mother did for him automatically and invisibly, things he didn't purposely take for granted, it was just that they never crossed his mind.

'I remember when I was at school,' she said, 'sitting alone in a corner of the playground crying. I felt like I was shunned. I felt dirty. All the other children, even those I thought were my friends, just let me be, they probably couldn't understand, just thought I was strange, and didn't know what to do, but you must have seen me and you just ran over, grabbed me by the hand and pulled me back into the middle of a game of "Drill Sergeant".'

'You of course were the lead and stood in front of a line of twenty or so of us. You told us that we had to carry out your instructions, and to show, to the best of our ability, what a well-drilled squad we could be. "Do as I do" you instructed and "No laughing or giggling or sniggering, or you're out." and then you proceeded to do the silliest things; standing on one leg, hopping in a circle, pulling funny faces.'

'We all tried to do the same thing and keep serious, but it wasn't long before we were being sent out one by one for laughing. When half the squad had been eliminated the remaining half ran and jumped on their backs and got a piggyback ride round the playground.'

'You carried me on your back. I knew you cared. You looked after me. I think I've liked you from that moment.'

And he had liked her. Of course he had, why else would he have talked to her, why else would he have always kept an eye out to see where she was and make sure she was alright?

So, it had been there all along and the reason he hadn't noticed was because it was so natural, it was just there, it was a part of his normality. It was only with the threat of losing it that he'd noticed it at all. What was it Peter had said, "Sometimes the most difficult things to notice are those that are right under your nose". And he'd been right.

Sarah's words stopped Jack in his tracks.

He had been wondering how to talk to her and been gabbling and not knowing what to say or how to start. But she'd done it for him. Everything he'd known but not realised slotted neatly into place.

Her brown eyes overflowed.

Jack put a protective arm around her.

They walked and talked for the rest of the afternoon.

It was getting late.

'Look, what a sunset,' Jack said, and they gazed together at a sky that was smeared with red and flecked with streaks of yellow and orange.

'Isn't it beautiful,' said Sarah.

They sat together, gazing, until it was quite dark, and the night chill brought them closer together.

When they returned home nobody said anything. Even George refrained. Sitting around in the kitchen, drinking tea, nothing had changed.

But everything had changed.

Chapter 61

Sarah was sitting at the table, pen in hand, a blank piece of paper in front of her. Jenny walked in from the backyard. Sarah sighed.

'Everything alright, pet?' asked Jenny.

Sarah twiddled the pen in her fingers.

'I'm trying to write a letter to Mary, in Sunderland, normally I just tell her the local news and gossip, but this time I just can't seem to get started.'

'I see,' said Jenny, knowing that this was an important letter, 'I suppose you'll be organising a trip over there?'

'For an interview you mean?'

'Yes, I think that's what I meant.'

Jenny felt like she was walking a tightrope. On the one hand she wanted to know what Sarah was going to do, but on the other she didn't want her words to push her into making a hasty decision, one way or the other.

'I'm not sure I'm cut out for it, Ma,' said Sarah, 'it's not the work, and the food, the clothes, the cleanliness, the running water which are all very nice, it's the idea of always being told what to do, to have my day all set out from waking to bedtime.'

'Routines are good,' said Jenny, then bit her tongue.

'I suppose what you do Ma is in the service of the family, I'd be working for a stranger.'

'At least you'd get paid for it,' said Jenny, 'and there'd be some time off.'

She wondered why she was finding herself putting arguments that sounded like they were in favour of Sarah leaving. If she'd had time to think about it, she'd have realised that she knew intuitively that if you manipulate somebody into making the decision that you want them to make they can hate you for it later, she'd seen it happen, and she liked Sarah too much to put their relationship in such jeopardy. But she didn't have time to think and was acting without thinking, in the way her nature dictated.

'I like the idea of having my own money, I mean, I have a little now but not enough to live on, I'm reliant on your support.'

'You're part of the family, Sarah, and anyway you pay your way. If I didn't have your help then, with three men working underground and a boy at school, I'd have to pay somebody to come and help me.'

'Could we afford that?'

'With three good wages coming in we could, but with your help I don't need to.'

'But if I wasn't here…'

'Then I could get by.'

'Hmm,'

Sarah picked up her pen,

'I did get another letter, a postcard actually, with a nice photograph of Roker Beach on the front, only today.'

'Oh, yes?'

'Yes, Mary sent it because she was in a rush but wanted to tell me the news.'

'Oh, is she getting married?'

'No, no, if she got married, she'd lose her job. No, it was just to tell me that the kitchen maid position has been filled.'

Jenny's immediate reaction was to want to shout for joy, to want to run over and give Sarah one of the biggest hugs she'd ever had. But she restrained herself and said,

'That's a shame.'

'I don't know,' said Sarah, 'I don't know what to say about it, that's why I'm struggling to get started.'

'Well, you just sit there, and I'll make us a cup of tea, and I've got a couple of scones that need eating.'

'It seems like you're stuck with me for a while yet,' said Sarah.

'Oh, I think I can cope,' said Jenny.

Jenny was full of the news but knew it was for Sarah to say something.

Jack came home early, at this time his shift finished two hours before Frank and Edward's. Sarah was out and Jenny was scrubbing his back.

'You've got some new scratches here,' she said, 'I'll clean those with a cloth and then put some of that ointment on that Elsie Walton recommended.'

'It hurts like hell,' said Jack.

'Don't use that language, and anyway, if it hurts it shows that it's working.'

'Must be very good stuff then.'

'It's important that they don't get infected.'

After his bath the tea was poured, and Jenny couldn't hold back any longer.

'Sarah has some news,' she said.

'Oh,' said Jack, sure that he was about to hear it.

'It's about Sunderland.'

'Oh.'

'If I tell you then when Sarah says something you have to pretend you didn't know already.'

Jack smiled.

The complexities of female communication had always baffled him.

'Alright,' he said.

'It's about that position in Sunderland, it's been filled, so she won't be moving out after all.'

'Oh.'

'You don't sound very surprised.'

'That's because she's told me already.'

'How did she do that, she only found out today?'

'She was waiting for me at the colliery gates.'

'Oh,' said Jenny, 'I see.'

She paused.

'Do you want a scone?' she said.

Chapter 62

Adam Thompson, who was walking out with Martha Jones, was a Newcastle United supporter like Frank.

They were both in the pub and Frank called him over. With a broad smile on his face Adam offered to buy Frank and Edward a drink and handed them each a cigarette. Such generosity indicated Adam wasn't short of a bob or two at present and Frank assumed that he must have been working one of the softer sections of the 'Baggy' seam the past few weeks.

Frank got straight to the point of common interest.

'You ready for the game tomorrow?'

'Going to be a tough one,' he said.

'Oh no,' said Edward butting in, 'You guys are going to get boring about football now. I'll leave you to it,' and he started to walk away towards the piano, 'Dad, I'll catch up with you later, we'll walk back together.'

Edward liked to sing and had a rather rich untrained baritone of which he was justifiably proud. The men gathered around the piano made room for him. Edward knew most of the words to the music hall song they were singing and joined in the chorus enthusiastically,

I was holding me coconut,
when a lady winked at me,
I see you've got it with you,
she shouted out with glee.
Up came a policeman,
he threw me in the cut,
the only thing that held me up,
was holding me coconut.

Singing always made him smile.

This is a diversion. And I make no apology for it. Frank and Adam would understand.

This is exactly what you are told not to do when you're writing a book, you are supposed to stick like a limpet to the story arc, the development of the main characters, the progression of the plot. But Newcastle United had never won the FA Cup, they'd been finalists three times previously, and lost all three…

As Newcastle fans, Frank and Adam were used to disappointment, the 'nearly's' and the 'almost's' and the 'not again's' when it came to the FA Cup.

They could get to the final alright but just couldn't win being beaten the last time by Everton, 0-1. The finals were played at the Crystal Palace ground, which was becoming known to all Newcastle fans as the 'Palace of Doom'.

A year later they won the League again amassing 51 points over 38 games, the League having been extended the previous year to 20 teams.

Although they were unbeaten at home in the League all season, they surprisingly lost at home in the first round of the FA Cup to Crystal Palace 0-1. Another example of the supernatural Palace jinx.

Gaining the top spot by the end of that year they did not relinquish it and showed the whole country what worthy Champions they were, also winning the Charity Shield at the Craven Cottage ground against a good amateur team, Corinthians, 5-2.

But the early exit from the FA Cup left a bad taste.

The following year they were beaten finalists yet again, this time losing to Wolverhampton Wanderers 1-3. Bedevilled by injuries to key players at key times it was starting to feel like Newcastle were subject to some kind of supernatural power that was interceding to stop them ever winning the Cup.

It should have been different this time after a convincing 6-0 win in the semi-final. But by the time the final came around they were on a losing run, it had rained all day, and Newcastle were 2 nil down at halftime: the first goal being deflected, the muddy ball skidding through the goalkeeper's hands, the second coming while they were still reeling from the shock of the first.

It felt like the Newcastle jinx was alive and kicking.

In the second half they got one back and chased the equaliser but pushing forward meant leaving gaps at the back and Wolves scored a third.

A tsunami of disappointment and frustration flowed along the telegraph wires all the way from London to Newcastle and the groans of 'not again' were loud and widespread.

The next year they won the League again!

Winners for the 3rd time with 53 points over the 38 games, they secured the title with 4 games still to play, although there was a blemish along the way when they managed to lose 9-1 at home to arch-rivals Sunderland and 1-3 away, although they did knock them out of the FA Cup, beating them in a quarterfinal replay.

Again they won the Charity Shield, this time against Northampton Town at the Stamford Bridge ground 2-0.

But it was at the Bramall Lane ground, Sheffield, that Newcastle met Manchester United in the semifinal of the Cup and, with key players missing and a key player badly injured during the game, they had an off day, and Manchester United scored the winner late in the game.

Dreams of a double were dashed and the more familiar feelings of disappointment, misery and grief returned.

So, in the next season expectations were tempered by past history, whilst there was also a degree of intrigue associated with one of Newcastle's key strikers, a man who was, unknown to him, about to become a hero and a legend.

Albert Shepherd had unaccountably walked off the pitch in Newcastle's game against Woolwich Arsenal and was then dropped for the FA Cup semifinal.

Rumours ran riot around the town, with much vague and unsubstantiated gossip about Shepherd's apparent friendship with some of the local bookmakers.

Whatever the truth, and we shall never know it, he was back in the forward line for the final.

Newcastle's fourth attempt at glory was again played at the Palace ground, London, where Newcastle were yet to win and, in front of a crowd of nearly 78,000, Barnsley played a 'man first, ball second' game.

This brutally physical approach disrupted Newcastle's style of play while Barnsley played a simple game of sending long balls up the pitch for their forwards to chase.

These tactics paid off and Barnsley took the lead 10 minutes before half time, Tufnell toe-ending the ball just inside the post.

In the second half Barnsley continued to defend strongly, and Newcastle found it impossible to either breakthrough or even mount an effective attack.

It was well into the half when Shepherd scored what he thought was the equaliser. He, his teammates and all the Newcastle supporters were already celebrating when the goal was ruled out for offside.

From then on it looked like a repeat of previous finals, Newcastle clearly being the better footballing side, but it not being their day…again!

However, in the last 15 minutes of the game, Newcastle abandoned their normal style of play and reverted to launching ball after ball into the Barnsley penalty area. With only 8 minutes to play Wilson picked up a cross-field pass from Veitch and charged down the wing before crossing the ball into the centre where Rutherford, who had just got himself going again after being injured, leapt into the air and headed the ball home. Barnsley claimed offside, but the referee did not agree.

Newcastle had equalised.

Although both sides kept pressing, the match ended in a draw.

The jinx of the Palace ground had not been completely assuaged but at least Newcastle hadn't lost and there'd be another chance in the replay

Incredible as it may seem Newcastle then had to play two league games in the 5 days between the final and the replay, both of which were away from home, the second of which was in Birmingham, the afternoon before the replay, which was in Liverpool!

For both of these games Newcastle unashamedly put out reserve teams, winning one and losing the other, concentrating all of their efforts on the replay.

Maybe this, at last, would be their time?

The newspaper reports tell the story:

"Yesterday afternoon, on the ground of Everton football club, Goodison Park, Liverpool, Newcastle United and Barnsley met in the replay of the English Cup Final.

Despite the wet, a huge crowd had assembled of fully 60,000, with gate receipts of £4,166.

Half an hour before the kick-off, the pressure of the crowd broke through part of the railings and people swarmed onto the field. Mounted constables slowly drove them back onto the terraces again. Still, the crush was very great, and once, during the game, 2-300 people once more broke through.

Play, however, was not interfered with.

There had been rumours that Newcastle would probably make two changes to their team. It was known, of course, that Carr was playing instead of Whitson, who had been injured on Saturday, and, in the event, with that exception the teams turned out as in the first match.

It soon became apparent that the state of the ground would seriously affect the play as, in the slush and mud, a firm foothold seemed impossible, and the difficulties of the players were great in trying to control the ball and take passes on the run.

A great pace was set from the start, and tremendous vigour and earnestness was imparted into all that was done, and from the kick-off there was not a dull moment.

Barnsley scarcely derived any advantage from winning the toss, but were first to attack, McCracken having to clear a centre from

Bartrop. After that, Barnsley indulged in long passes, while the Newcastle forwards varied their work, and more than once got into dangerous positions by dribbling and short passes.

Newcastle did most of the pressing with remarkable skill, considering the conditions. Howie had a shot intercepted, and from the resulting rebound Shepherd forced a corner.

From the corner Higgins charged the Barnsley keeper, Mearns, who was hurt and so incensed by this treatment, that, when he had recovered, he rushed after his opponent in a threatening manner and had to be restrained by the referee and his colleagues.

Still Newcastle attacked, Howie heading just wide from a centre by Wilson.

Barnsley were often in danger, Low tried to score with a long shot that was luckily intercepted, following which Rutherford centred, and a corner resulted.

Newcastle enjoyed one escape when their keeper, Lawrence, ran out to clear and only just got back in time to fall and stop a shot from Bartrop although Veitch and McCracken, both standing under the bar, were also covering this dangerous situation.

Even more exciting events occurred in the Barnsley goal. Downs and Ness often cleared, but Downs was hurt in stopping a hard shot by Wilson, who then beat Glendinning and shot, Mearns kicking out to Rutherford, who lifted the ball high over the bar.

On another occasion Rutherford raced past Ness and, with Mearns coming out, got nearest the goal but could not steady himself on the greasy surface and, as he centred, Mearns threw himself over and managed to push the ball behind.

Nothing came of the corner, and then Barnsley enjoyed another wonderful escape; Wilson centred, and Shepherd went straight for goal, Mearns rushed out, but fell, and the ball looked to be going into the net when Ness rushed in and just managed to kick it out from the goalmouth.

Remarkably, half-time arrived without any score.

The sun shone when play resumed, but water still stood on the ground, and the conditions had in no way improved.

For a brief time, it seemed that the great exertions of the first half had taken the wind out of both sides' sails. Newcastle controlled the play as before, but there was not the same dash in the game until Rutherford set up an attack, back-heeled cleverly to Howie who was strongly challenged before he could shoot.

With play opening up, Low met a long kick and volleyed across to where Higgins found a way to pass the ball forward to Shepherd who raced through and shot, low and into the net, as Mearns rushed out in vain.

So, seven minutes after the change of ends, Newcastle were 1-0 up.

Tremendous cheering greeted this successful effort.

Long after Barnsley had kicked off again the roar of the Geordie crowd continued to enliven the proceedings.

Just once Barnsley broke away, Lawrence, having to save from Bartrop, but almost all the attacks were on the Barnsley goal.

Mearns saved a great shot from Rutherford, who had raced clear of the opposition, and then he punched away an equally good shot from Wilson.

Again, from a centre by Rutherford, Barnsley's defence was beaten, and Higgins found the net only for the goal to be disallowed for offside.

Downs received an injury that necessitated his being carried off the field, but he soon returned to the game.

Barnsley now seemed a beaten side. They had lost their pace, could scarcely get past midfield, and were constantly in danger.

For a clear trip on Shepherd, who was dribbling through on goal, a penalty was awarded.

In taking the kick, Shepherd shot hard and low into the net, making Newcastle's lead two goals, with 20 minutes left to play.

Barnsley were still playing rough, and, for unfairly tripping Rutherford, who was going clear on goal, Utley was spoken to by the referee, and shortly after Newcastle almost scored again, a shot from Howie being turned against a post.

Barnsley although seemingly beaten still managed a breakaway, Bartrop forcing a corner. Nothing came of this however and the pace of play slackened, with Newcastle holding their own and playing well within themselves.

Lawrence had a long shot from Bartrop to clear, and then the sun emerged and shone more brightly than it had ever done in any other part of the match.

With only 10 minutes remaining, the issue was beyond doubt. Barnsley could do nothing but try to stop their opponents, and the Newcastle men had no reason to make special efforts. Much of the play was now scrambling, with Newcastle showing some clever work and retaining their lead easily.

When the final whistle blew, Newcastle had gained their victory, a victory that was greeted with the utmost enthusiasm.

After the game, there was a remarkable scene in front of the stand, the crowd swarming forward and half filling the pitch in order to see the presentation of the Cup and the medals. The cheering was loud and prolonged, and only slowly subsided as the great crowd reluctantly departed.

The Local Newspaper reports were equally clear:

Overall Verdict

Newcastle United gained a well-deserved victory over Barnsley by two goals to nil and so secured possession of the Football Association Challenge Cup for the first time in their history.

Whatever may have been their shortcomings in their previous struggles to win the cup, the Newcastle men showed that they are a great side and in dribbling, passing, and general tactics, they outplayed the Barnsley men completely.

Scenes in Newcastle

Large crowds assembled at the newspaper offices in Newcastle upon Tyne to gain tidings of the Cup final replay.

The no score at halftime was received with mixed feelings, but when the news came later that Newcastle had scored, and then scored again, there was great enthusiasm.

The announcement at the finish that Newcastle had won two to nil, and that the Cup had come to Newcastle at last, created a furore. Congratulations were expressed on every hand at the success of the Tynesiders and there was dancing in the streets and singing late into the night."

'Neville would have loved this,' Frank said, as he put down his paper with a satisfied smile.

'Sssh,' said Jenny.

But it was too late, Sarah had overheard.

'You're right, my dad was a big supporter of 'the Toon', he took me along once you know, taught me to sing.'

'To sing?' said Jenny.

'Oh yes,

Oh me lads ya shoulda seen us gannin
Gannin along the Scotsford Road
To see the Blaydon Races...'

She stopped, embarrassed.

'That is right, isn't it?'

'Yes,' said Frank, 'perfect.'

Sarah smiled.

Later, when they were in bed, Jenny whispered,

'You know Frank, I don't think you need to have been a good man to be remembered, you just have to have done some good things.'

'There's still hope for me then,' said Frank.

Jenny smiled and dug him in the ribs.

'Go to sleep ya daft lump,' she said.

Chapter 63

Edward VII died at the age of 68, after only 9 years on the throne, poor in comparison to his mother's 63 years. The new king was George V, and mourning was turned to celebration at his coronation.

There were firework displays on cricket fields all over the country and bunting and flag waving. The celebrations in the colliery village were more low-key.

'I don't know what difference it makes who the King is,' said Edward, 'our lives are no different.'

'Shh,' said Jack, 'you'll get yourself locked up for treason.'

'Never mind treason,' said Edward, 'it's your round isn't it?'

More important than any coronation was the Miner's Gala.

Whether you were connected with the pits or not, an annual pilgrimage to Durham showed that you belonged to the community. And Durham itself was a social melting pot due to the rapid development of the coal field during the 19th century and the immigrant workforce that was attracted by the work and which arrived from all parts of the British Isles.

Although everyone would come to think of themselves as 'Durham people' their parent dialect or accent would remain a reminder of their place of origin and there was a combination of Lancashire, Cumberland, Yorkshire, Staffordshire, Cornish, Irish, Scottish, Welsh, Northumbrian and Durham accents, dialect and languages heard in the streets.

At six o'clock in the morning, the people of Jack's village congregated beside the pit and marched through the village behind the brass band before making their way to the railway station, the numbers increasing as they went, to board one of the special trains to Durham.

The northern railway companies liked to claim that the Durham Gala was the largest single annual gathering in the world.

Trains came into Durham from all directions and once assembled each party took their turn to march through the city and on to the racecourse.

The Lawley family gathered with everyone else connected with their village and fell in behind the band ready to march through the city streets that were lined with thousands of people, cheering, chatting, laughing, shouting and waving flags.

Down the steep road from the station they went, along North Road and over the River Wear, for the first time, on Framwellgate Bridge, then on, past the shops; the Bakers, the Jewellers, the Secondhand Bookshop, the clothes shops that were scattered between the pubs and into the Market Place, that was already packed with people.

'We're going to pop off for a quick pint,' said Frank to Jenny, 'before the pubs get too packed.'

'You don't think they're packed now?'

'It's not as bad as it's going to be.'

'Alright, we'll go on to the racecourse and bag a spot as close as we can to where we were last year.'

'Fair do's, we'll only be half an hour.'

'Really?'

Jenny led Sarah and George away through the crowds in one direction and Frank, Edward, Grandpa and Jack shuffled off in another. As they climbed up one of the steeper streets Frank coughed.

'That cough's not getting any better,' said Grandpa.

'Goes with the job,' said Frank, 'I'm not the only one.'

Grandpa led them away from the main streets to a pub that he hoped would be a little less congested.

'I'll get them in,' said Edward, 'Jack, you give me a hand, I'll not be able to manage all of them.'

'I'll miss on this round,' said Jack, 'I want to go back to one of the shops we've passed, I'll see you back here.'

'Don't be long,' said Frank, 'I promised your mother…'

But Jack had already headed off and was soon lost from sight.

'I'll bet you he's going to buy a book,' said Edward.

Grandpa laughed.

'You won't get very good odds on that one,' he said.

By the time Jack was back they were just finishing their pints.

'It's a good local brew,' said Edward, 'shall we have another?'

'Better not,' said Frank, 'the clock's ticking and I don't want to upset your mother.'

'Well, you've missed out here, Jack, and no mistake,' said Edward, 'you're going to have to go dry, and you've missed one of Grandpa's war stories.'

'I'm sorry about that,' said Jack.

'What,' said Edward, 'missing the pint or missing the story?'

'Any success?' said Grandpa.

'I went back to that bookshop we passed,' no one was surprised, 'and I got this.'

He lifted a book from his coat pocket and showed it around.

'It's a guide to the Roman Wall. I'd like to go visit it someday.'

'So, you're still keen,' said his father.

'I am,' said Jack, 'I thought I'd plan it as an outing, and this book will help me do that.'

'Good idea,' said Frank, 'as its about 80 miles long it's a good idea to know which part you're going to.'

'Maybe I'll come along,' said Edward.

'Errrm…'

Grandpa laughed.

'I think Jack's got other ideas,' he said.

The four of them made their way on towards the racecourse, crossing the Wear for the second time via Elvet Bridge and marching down Old Elvet. With such a big crowd in boisterous mood there was lots of money spent, and money made, and shops and stalls were open for business. As they made their way they were surrounded by banners and brass bands.

Unfortunately, a number of the nearly 200 banners that were paraded across the whole of the city were draped in black, in memory of fatal accidents that had occurred at that colliery during the previous 12 months.

With some difficulty and much amiable pushing and shoving they located Jenny, George and Sarah, who were sitting on the grass.

Sarah looked up at Jack. He winked.

'Half an hour?' said Jenny, raising her voice above the hubbub.

'About that,' said Frank.

Jenny smiled. Everyone else relaxed.

'I've got some pork pies, some sandwiches and bottles of ginger beer,' she said, 'and you've arrived just in time to hear Earnest Weightman's speech.'

There were lots of speeches and Earnest Weightman was giving one on behalf of their colliery village.

'Oh, good,' said Edward.

'I hope it's short,' said Frank.

Jenny glowered at them.

'Earnest Weightman is a good man and it's important we hear what he has to say.'

There were makeshift stages dotted around the racecourse, some for speeches, some for brass bands.

Earnest Weightman climbed the few steps to a nearby stage. He had a good voice and natural projection.

'I am honoured to have been asked to say a few words...'

'They all have to say that,' said Edward.

'Shh,' said his mother.

'I know that what we all want is a fair day's pay for a fair day's work,' said Earnest.

Shouts of 'You're right there!'

'And that linking pay to output and market prices puts us all in a state of perpetual insecurity. Not to mention the differences that exist between mines, between seams, and between the quality of coal, most of which is entirely outside of our control.'

'Here, here!'

'So, it is my belief that what we need is a minimum wage! A wage that would at least give our families a grounding in security.'

'Just another way for owners to pay us less!', 'It's too complicated already without this!', 'Who would set it?', 'How can it be managed?', 'How much?'

'Thank you, thank you, all good points that I do not have the time to answer here…'

'No answers!', 'Booo!'

'I will just repeat that it is my view that the current system is too cumbersome, to complicated and can too heavily penalise the miner, a minimum wage would at least give some baseline of security,' he held up his hand, 'but I want to move on to something just as important as money and that is our working conditions.'

'Go on then!'

'Let me start with shorter working hours; eight hours working for men and boys underground is long enough and is a principle that can be applied to pits north, east, west, or south. It is a principle that can apply whether the coal is ten yards thick or is two feet thick. It is a principle that can apply to any pit.'

'And what about our pay, does that get shorter too!', 'Yes, what about that!'

'A number of owners and employers said it was impossible, that it would bring ruin upon the world! But that is not true, they must abide by the law, and what we see is that the commercial and economic sides can adjust themselves without panic. Working ourselves to death is no solution, an eight-hour shift underground is enough for anybody! Not only that, but it is practicable, it can be done!'

'He's got a good point about not working yourself to death,' said Jenny looking at Frank.

'Now I must turn to a sadder subject. There are too many accidents in our pits, and too many men and families who suffer the consequences. Although there is the Workmen's Compensation Act, which can provide money to the home after the breadwinner has gone, although it is only a few shillings a week, we must continue our efforts to improve safety and reduce accidents. This is the one question that I think we may all agree upon, and all our collective efforts should continue to be brought to bear to try to mitigate these accidents.'

'Here, here, but I don't know how!', 'I agree!'

'For our Union, I cannot conceive of a greater work than to seek to save human life, to protect it against injury, and I do believe that much can be done, including by the Government of our country.'

'I also believe that great possibilities lie in the future, and we must use our collective powers wisely and well. While preserving our own interests, we must also remember the interests of other workers whose living depends on coal. Unity is our strength, and our Union could set an example and, as a result, both protect more men's lives and gain a greater recognition from the wider public of the arduous and dangerous duties that we perform on their behalf.'

'Not in my lifetime!', 'You must be joking.'

'And there I will end and will conclude by saying that the changes we seek to bring about should be done in a spirit of collective collaboration and honest negotiation and that calling a strike should not be a first course of action but rather the action we reluctantly turn to when all other alternatives have failed.'

'Now it only remains for me to thank you for your attention, and hope that you enjoy the rest of this glorious day!'

And so saying Earnest Weightman left the stage and made his way over to his wife, who was standing with her arms folded, but with a smile on her face.

'He's a good speaker, I'll give him that,' said Grandpa, who'd heard most of this before, sometimes in different guises and in different circumstances.

'He says a lot of sensible things,' said Jenny.

'Worth thinking about,' said Frank, 'strikes only make us all poorer.'

'It went on too long,' said Edward.

Jack and Sarah had been secretly holding hands and hadn't really been listening, so they didn't say anything.

'Is there any more ginger beer,' said George.

Because Jack wanted to go into Durham Cathedral, they decided to separate on the way back; Jack, Sarah and George, as chaperone, making one party and everyone else making their way towards the station.

As they approached the solid oak doors, studded with metal, that gave entrance to the cathedral, Jack pointed out the knocker to George. It looked fearsome and gargoyle-like.

'That's the Sanctuary Knocker,' he said, 'in the olden days if people were after you, maybe trying to kill you, you could run to the cathedral and grab hold of this and knock and shout "sanctuary", and the monks would let you in and because inside is holy ground, whoever was after you couldn't get you.'

'Ooo,' said George.

'And then what?' said Sarah.

'And then you were safe,' said Jack.

'But you couldn't stay in there forever, you had to leave sometime.'

'Perhaps they waited until it was very dark,' said George, who increasingly displayed an active imagination, 'a night with no stars and no moon and then they would creep out the back, jump on a fast horse and ride away.'

'And where did they get the horse?'

'Friends,' said George.

'Shall we go in,' said Jack.

Once inside, the massive, vaulted, grandeur of the space held them silent for a few moments, even George.

Oak bench pews spread out either side of a central aisle, massive, spiralled stone columns supported the vaulted roof that hovered high above while the sunlight streamed through stained glass windows and lay, multi-coloured, on the stone-flagged floor.

A choir was practicing in the stalls and the sound of their collective voices resonated around them.

'Wow,' said George.

'Wow, indeed,' said Jack, 'that's why I wanted to pay a visit, this place is always impressive.'

'There's nothing like this in our village,' said Sarah, 'if people can build places like this then why can't they build better houses around coal mines?'

There was no answer other than economics, labour, profit and efficiency and they all seemed out of place at a time like this.

'Let me show you St Cuthbert's tomb,' said Jack, and led them along, outside and past the choir stalls and on to St Cuthbert's Shrine.

'He was originally buried at Lindisfarne but because of Viking raids…'

'Vikings!' hissed George.

'Yes, St Cuthbert was around when the Vikings were raiding and looting and setting fire to things.'

'And worse,' said Sarah.

'Nice,' said George.

'To protect his body the monks removed his remains and took them in search of safety. They passed through several places before St Cuthbert's body rested in a place called Chester-le-street, so-called because it was originally a fort built alongside a Roman road…'

'Romans!' said George, 'I thought you said Vikings.'

'I was just saying… never mind, let's stick to the Vikings and the story of St Cuthbert's remains. They lay in a church in

Chester-le-street for about a hundred years before there were more Viking raids and they had to be moved again. Finally, they found their permanent resting place here in Durham, and the cathedral was built up around them.'

'How do you know all of this?' asked Sarah.

'Reading.'

'But is everything you read really true?'

'It's all I know.'

'So, we've got the Vikings to thank for Durham Cathedral?' she said,

Jack thought about it.

'I suppose you could put it that way, although I'm not sure "thank" is the right word.'

'I think I like the Vikings,' said George.

'They eventually settled,' said Jack, 'so maybe we've got a bit of Viking blood in us.'

'I hope so,' said George.

'I hope not,' said Sarah.

'I just want to show you one more thing,' said Jack, and took them round to the Chapel of Nine Altars.

'You see those pillars there,' he's said, pointing.

'The black ones,' said Sarah.

'Go and look more closely.'

Sarah and George went to look. On closer inspection the pillars seemed to have pieces of white frozen in them; some circular, some cylindrical, some with marks and stripes and spines.

'That's Frosterly Marble,' said Jack, 'it's a limestone really and those pieces it's stuffed with are the fossilised remains of coral and marine life from over 300 million years ago, it's pretty much the same age as coal.'

George scrutinised each one saying, 'Look at this bit', about every five seconds or so. Eventually they dragged him away and left the cathedral.

'That's a special place,' said Sarah.

'It is,' said Jack.

'Vikings and fossils, wow!' said George, having already forgotten everything else.

On their walk back to the station they passed several pubs. As it was getting late in the day, a few of the customers were showing signs of overindulgence. Most of it was good natured banter, although the language was flowery, but as they turned a corner, they witnessed an argument that had turned into a fight.

Rather than stepping in to stop the fight most of the onlookers were roaring them on. It was nothing more than a commonplace example of the thin line between mirth and mayhem that is fuelled by alcohol.

Sarah immediately shied away and looked frightened. Jack guided her past and away from the mass of swaying drunks.

'I'm sorry,' she said, 'it's just…'

'It's alright Sarah, I understand.'

George took hold of her hand.

'Don't worry,' he said, 'I'll look after you.'

When they got home, George told everybody that he enjoyed his trip into Durham Cathedral, and that if they wanted to be saved all they had to do was knock on the door, that the Vikings had built it, and that it was over 300 million years old.

Sarah smiled.

Jack shook his head. He couldn't imagine what Wilkinson Hughes would think if George blurted out his version of things in one of the History lessons at school.

Chapter 64

It wasn't unusual for the pit to lay idle at times, when stocks were high and trade was slow.

Being laid off meant no money, and some of the men would go over the moors to see if they could get a few rabbits for the table. Mr Moore and the other local farmers would generally turn a blind eye to this.

'As long as they leave the fish alone,' he used to say, 'then I won't miss a few rabbits.'

During a layoff, that were usually of only a few days duration, the produce from Grandpa's allotment rose in importance.

'I can't make the hens lay any faster,' he said to Jenny on one of these occasions.

'Well, maybe you should get a few more.'

'I thought you didn't like hens?'

'I don't, but I like their produce.'

Jack would go and give Peter a hand on the farm, and Grandpa was up for a bit of labouring if there was any. They wouldn't get paid for this but would normally return with some form of farm produce that was a very welcome addition to the table.

The miners always blamed the owners.

'All they ever care about is their profits and not their workers,' said Edward.

The colliery owner did not live anywhere near the pit, hardly visited it, and made no attempt to keep in touch with what was going on day to day. He left the running of the mine to his agent and colliery managers. What most owners were interested in were profits and shareholder returns and they were keen to be regularly appraised of the numbers, the life left in the seam, and the progress made in the search for the next one.

Their priorities were straightforward; find coal, get it out, and sell it and always make sure you take in more money than you spend. Such were the laws of business and the owners cared for them as dearly as they cared for their own families or, as some might say, even more dearly.

The first shift back was always the worst. You had to ensure that nothing had shifted while you'd had your back turned.

As a Hewer, like his father, Edward worked at the coalface in a damp, dark, sweaty environment with little light from his safety lamp and was paid by the weight of coal he and his team got out.

As the coal seam was inconsistent in depth and quality the Hewers would rotate positions on a weekly basis to ensure equal opportunity for earnings. On average a Hewer would remove 3-4 tons of coal on his shift.

Edward stripped down to his sleeveless rough cotton vest for the work; a routine of hacking and blowing and clearing and hacking again.

First, he cut out a layer of coal from the base of the seam, swinging his pick in the semidarkness, conscious of the dangers of gas, flooding, ceiling collapse and dust explosions.

He cursed when his pick hit a stone and produced a glittering shower of dangerous sparks that cascaded around him.

Having undercut the seam, holes were drilled into the higher level of the coalface and packed with black powder explosive. A pricker was then inserted and the hole sealed with clay. The pricker was then taken out leaving a hole into which a squib was inserted.

Now came the most dangerous moment.

The pit face was cleared, the squib was lit and shot into the hole igniting the rest of the powder, the explosion freed the coal that then fell away.

It was an unpredictable process, and Edward was always relieved when it was over.

The air around him swirled in the finest black fairy dust that glittered and sparkled in the light from his lamp. But this fairy dust was sharp and malevolent and settled on his clothes, his exposed skin at face and neck, arms and hands. It entered his body when he breathed. It choked and gagged him.

As he worked, the sweat trickled down from his hairline and created tributaries of comparative clean streaks amidst the black. His body worked to a rhythm, a routine, the repeated work of hewing, hewing at the seemingly unending coal face.

A lifetime later, the cage creaked and rattled into the light. Double metal doors were dragged complaining apart and the men were disgorged in a tumbling, mumbling rush.

The movement, accentuated by the accidental collisions of the clumsy compression of men as they fanned out from the pithead, disturbed the coal dust from their hair, from thick woollen jackets, from trousers and grandfather shirts.

Shaken free the black dust floated in the air and was caught in the ripe sunlight from which it had been born millennia ago. In this light it glittered, swirled and danced around the men, a halo of sharp silver stars, before joining the layers of black snow that covered everything, always.

'Thank fuck that's over,' said Edward to himself.

Chapter 65

'My mother never told me anything about love making,' said Sarah bashfully.

'I'll put the kettle on,' said Jenny.

There were few things that could knock Jenny off her stride, she'd seen too many things in her life, both good and bad. But with Sarah sitting wide-eyed in front of her, a surrogate daughter and possibly a prospective daughter-in-law, asking her advice on sex, she had reached a limit.

Uncomfortable by nature in entering into this kind of conversation, being put in a position of supposed expertise on the subject was too much of a stretch, even for her.

The noisy entrance of George clattering through the back yard, home from school, gave her an escape route.

'Erm, we can't talk about this now, Sarah,' she said and saw the confusion and disappointment in Sarah's eyes, it must have taken a lot of courage for her to broach the subject.

'Talk about what?' said George.

'Never you mind,' said his mother and, turning back to Sarah, 'but we will talk about it, pet, don't you worry.'

Over the next few days, it was Jenny that worried about it. It was not her place to have this conversation with Sarah; their relationship was far too complicated. What if she said something wrong? What if something went wrong later and it was her advice that had contributed? It didn't bear thinking about.

Like everything else Jenny thought it through. This was one of the few problems she couldn't talk to Frank about, even though he sensed that something was bothering her.

'Don't worry,' she said to him, 'I've just got a tricky bit of sewing I'm doing for Mrs Tindale, but I'll sort it out.'

Frank was content with that; he didn't know anything about sewing.

The mention of Mrs Tindale was not without purpose. She was no stranger to childbirth and such and Jenny supposed her experience of men's ways and methods of conception was no less extensive. She went around and talked to her.

Mrs Tindale laughed when she heard the suggestion.

'Well, I never,' she said, 'send her round, I can tell her a thing or two.'

The following afternoon Jenny, after explaining the situation to Sarah, delivered her to Mrs Tindale's back door.

'Come in, come in,' she beamed, 'sit yourself down Sarah, and Jenny here's them clothes that need a bit of a seeing to, thanks for your help.'

Jenny took the bundle in her arms and turned to go.

'Now don't you worry about a thing,' said Mrs Tindale to Jenny's retreating back, 'I'll send this young lady back to you with a smile on her face.'

When Sarah did return, she was a deep red colour. She staggered over to the kitchen table, pulled out a chair, that screeched on the stone-slab floor, and sat down heavily.

'Oh my God!' she said.

'Would you like a cup of tea?' said Jenny.

'Is there any of that brandy left over from Christmas,' said Sarah.

What nearly caused the accident was Jack's lack of concentration.

Jack knew that he had to keep focussed, but his mind was full of Sarah. There was something happening that was completely unexpected, and he was struggling to cope with it, to push it out of his mind and to concentrate on what he was doing,

'Hey, Jack!' yelled David, 'watch out for that wall!'

Jack's row of tubs swung dangerously as he battled to regain control and avoid a collision. At the last second they obeyed his command and Jack slowed Barney and they came to a safe stop. Jack wiped his brow with a trembling hand.

'Sorry, David,' he said, 'my mind isn't on it today.'

'Well, you had better get yourself sorted out. Take a short break, have a drink, and pull yourself together. Better to be a few minutes late than dead!'

Jack dropped his head. David's voice softened.

'You know how important it is to keep your mind on the job,' he said.

Jack knew and took a few minutes to himself, his arm around Barney's neck. He tried to put Sarah out of his mind and concentrate on the job.

For the rest of his shift, he more or less managed it.

Later, when he was back in the stables putting Barney into his stall, removing his harness, giving him something to eat, he lent forward, and whispered into his ear.

'Barney, I don't know what's happening,' he said, 'I know you've got it tougher than me, stuck down here 50 weeks a year with only two weeks in the sun. I wish that when I go up in the cage, I wish that I could take you with me, but I can't.'

The pony munched contentedly, seemingly soothed by Jack's caring words.

'But I feel like something's got to happen, or I'm going to explode!'

The horse gave a shudder.

'What's going on over there?' shouted the Stableman.

'Nothing,' replied Jack.

'Well get your nothing finished with and get to the pit bottom; your shift's over and you're due back on the surface.'

Jack turned back to Barney.

'Well, Barney,' he said, 'I'd best just let nature take its course. I guess there's nothing else left to do. I cant carry on like this we either move forward or...'

Barney grunted into his nose bag.

Jack's hand slid across Sarah's chest.

Carefully, slowly, their eyes locked into each other's, their minds following every touch, every nuance. Jack fumbled with buttons and Sarah smiled at his haste and lack of expertise.

Jack smiled back with his eyes, they were like two children playing, two grown-ups learning to dance as partners. Sarah did not raise her own hands to help him but neither did she move to stop him. Willingly compliant she allowed him to take the lead at this many times half imagined moment.

Fingertips manipulated buttons through buttonholes, Jack's hand moved through the remaining cotton layers, peeling each away from the centre, unwrapping, feeling the increasing warmth, moving in time to the heaving of Sarah's chest, the beating of her heart. When the last layer of cotton fabric was encountered and overcome and Sarah's flesh met his touch Jack stroked his fingers sideways, brushing the rubber hardness of a nipple, fondling and cupping a breast.

Sarah sighed.

A line had been crossed.

A step that could not be retraced had been taken. Whatever the future held it would now be different as a consequence of this moment, these actions.

Their mouths came together, dry with anticipation, moist with emotion, and they pressed their lips together and kissed properly for the first time.

Jack was approaching the colliery gates. He had just finished a shift. Sarah was half turned from him as he approached, although he knew he had her full attention. He felt like a small boy who was not sure whether his behaviour warranted praise or punishment but was about to find out.

'Are you … alright?'

'Yes… I am,' she said, 'and you, do you think less of me?'

Jack was startled.

'Do I …?'

'Do you think less of me? Just tell me, it's alright, I just need to know,' she said, the shadow of a frown wrinkling her forehead.

Jack paused, Sarah's brown eyes were moist as she gazed into his. He smiled.

'No Sarah, I don't think less of you.'

'That's alright then.'

There followed a pause, a taking stock, a subliminal assessment each of the other. Jack broke what was becoming an uneasy silence.

'In fact,' he said, 'I think more of you.'

'You do? You mustn't tease me Jack, please don't tease me.'

'I'm not teasing, I can't stop thinking…'

'Me too,' she said, her voice on the verge of a giggle.

'Over and over..'

'.. and over.'

She spun around in a circle, her dress billowing outwards and brushing against him.

'What are you doing?'

'I'm dancing.'

'We're in the middle of the street. People are looking.'

'I don't care, I don't care,' she said and spun herself around again.

'You'll make yourself dizzy.'

'I am dizzy,' she panted.

'You're mad.'

'I am mad. And you?'

He laughed.

'I'm mad too, I suppose.'

'You suppose?'

Jack straightened himself, trying to regain composure, reminding himself that he was not a little boy, he was a man and he should be acting like one. He tugged at the corners of his coal-dust covered jacket. Pulled his peeked cap forward on his head and addressed Sarah with solemnity.

'Miss Sarah Hudson.'

'Yes Jack, that is my name.'

'Sarah sssh, let me finish, don't tease.'

Sarah stood in front of him with an almost-serious expression on her face.

'Pray continue,' she said.

Jack ignored the playful tone.

'Miss Sarah Hudson. It has come to my attention that I have not, as yet, fulfilled my ambition of visiting the Roman Wall and I was wondering if you would do me the honour of accompanying me on an expedition.'

Sarah screwed her face in mock thought, stroked her chin with her fingers.

'Hmmmm' she said, 'how romantic, a trip to see an old relic.'

Jack waited.

'Mr Jack Lawley,' she said, 'I have carefully thought through your proposal, which you have properly and politely laid before me.'

'And?'

'And I do believe that it would be possible to lay aside any alternative social engagements that I may have planned.'

'What does that mean?'

'It means yes, stupid. Yes, yes, yes. When are we going to go?'

'You're mad,' said Jack.

'I know, isn't it wonderful. Are you mad too?'

'I must be,' he said.

Chapter 66

'There's been another bad accident,' said Frank, lifting his head from his paper.

'Is it local?' said Jenny.

'I'm afraid so,' said Frank, 'they were using electricity to drive cutting and haulage machinery. It looks like there was some kind of overload that sparked off the coal dust and produced a fireball underground.'

He put the paper down.

'Oh my God, Jenny, a fireball. They didn't stand a chance.'

Jenny wiped her hands on her apron and came to stand behind her husband. She put a hand on his shoulder. There were tears in her eyes.

'Was there a reason?'

He looked at the article again.

'Just a normal day as far as I can see, operating the same machinery, in the same way, just like they must have done hundreds of times before.'

'How many?' she asked.

'They set up a temporary hospital by the pithead and cleared the debris sufficiently to get a cage operating down one of the shafts in less than 12 hours.'

'How many?'

'Rescue teams brought out 26 alive,' he said.

'How many?'

He paused. He couldn't hide the truth.

'I'm afraid it's over 160.'

'Over 160 miners dead!'

'I'm afraid so, Jenny.'

Her body sagged and she moved away and sat at the kitchen table.

'Men and boys,' she said.

Frank didn't reply. He knew what Jenny was thinking. He knew what was coming next.

'Men just like you, and Edward, and Jack…'

'We don't use electricity,' he said.

'But you will.'

Frank couldn't argue against that, electrification was coming, it was seen as a big improvement for lighting and power underground.

'We've got our safety lamps, it's the gas, the firedamp, mainly methane, that can collect in pockets or be released at the face. What we do, Jenny, is make sure there's no sparks or other sources of ignition, we do our best to stay safe.'

Frank could see Jenny's anxiety and although it was justified, there was no use her worrying, worrying made no difference whatsoever.

But Jenny was too het up to let it go.

'I thought you said it was the coal dust.'

Frank knew better than to lie or ignore his wife. The truth, however raw, was the best policy.

'There's always coal dust, Jenny, you know, we come home covered in it. But it's safe as long as there's no spark.'

He chose not to mention what happened when a pick hit a rock.

'More than 160 men and boys went out to work, they'll have been seen off by their wives and mothers, their bait would have been in their bags, they'll have been thinking about what they'd do after their shift, taking for granted that they'd come home.'

'Jenny, please…'

'No, wait, let me finish… and then they don't come home, and the wives and the mothers rush to the pithead and wonder if their son or their husband is among the dead or the living, and what they'll do…'

'Jenny…'

'Whether they'll lose their home, how they'll afford to live, the futures of their children…'

'Jenny…'

'No, Frank, that's how it is every day, every day when you leave, I don't know if any of you are coming back...'

Frank got up and came over to her, she stood up and fell into his arms, sobbing on his shoulder.

'More than160,' she said, '160... all those families.'

Frank just held her and gave her time. Secretly he wondered whether not coming home was a better ending than where his cough was likely to lead him, but he dare not ever say that to Jenny.

After she had pulled away and wiped away her tears on her apron he said,

'There'll be an investigation, they'll find out what went wrong and make sure it can't happen again.'

'Makes no difference to those that are gone, or those that are left behind,' said Jenny.

'There'll be a relief fund I'm sure, and compensation...'

He knew that his words sounded hollow.

'Compensation!' she said, her hackles rising.

'I know,' he said, 'I know...'

She looked at him, sorrow and fear in her eyes.

'It's a good job we're alone. Everybody thinks you're so strong.'

'I am,' she said, straightening.

Frank paused.

'You're my rock.'

Jenny smoothed down her apron.

'You've got to make the most of every day,' she said.

Frank smiled.

'I'd love a cup of tea,' he said.

Chapter 67

While Frank, Edward and Jack were working their shifts underground, disturbed coal dust swirling around them, a Luncheon was taking place in Newcastle. The meal had just been completed, the food complimented, and before the cigars were brought out a local industrialist had been invited to say a few words, he rose to his feet,

'I thank my hosts for this opportunity to talk to you about the critical industrial problem that faces us at this present moment,' he said, in such a confined space and with such a strong voice, used to public speaking, there was no problem hearing his words in all corners of the room, 'You all know that we are confronted by an outbreak of strikes more numerous, more sudden, more widespread than, I am sure, the oldest amongst us here tonight, can ever remember. Such discontent is all the more remarkable as it is not confined to this country alone but is being displayed worldwide and is even more prevalent in those places where industrial and social conditions are most advanced.'

'I cannot promise to give you precise conclusions or guaranteed solutions, but I am willing to share with you my own findings, after having looked at the questions involved so much as I am able, from my own perspective.'

'It is relatively easy to consider the singular causes of a particular strike following its conclusion, but to pronounce upon those factors underlying the whole phenomenon is more difficult, even if, as I believe, there must be some general cause or tendency apart from the particular difficulty in each case. There must be the influence of some general tendency upon the minds of the men, leading them to have a predisposition to strike. It is not easy to discover what this general cause is. Probably not even the men themselves know it or are, at best, only half conscious of it.'

'There can be no widespread strikes and unrest without widespread discontent. What is causing this discontent? Is it that in this present day there are abnormal hardships? I believe that the hardships are less today than they were 50 years ago; certainly, much less than they were 100 years ago. Therefore, I do not believe this is a satisfactory answer. These are not strikes undertaken by men driven to it by unemployment; these are strikes undertaken by men who are in full employment.'

'Thus, the underlying cause cannot be the condition of labour or work, or that suffering is greater today than it was in yesteryear; so that the cause must lie in the hopes and expectations of men that are now greater than they were in previous generations.'

[General nodding of heads.]

'Disappointment has increased, and this has raised the temperature of the industrial world; and this disappointment has increased not because hardships are more than they have been, but because hopes and expectations are greater.'

'The total wealth of the country is increasing, though the connection between wealth and happiness is not a simple one to suppose. The desire for greater equality, or a belief that greater equality may somehow be possible, has gained ground. This has been followed by greater expectations of the pace at which conditions may change. It is inevitable, from the history of politics, that this should be so. The theory of political equality has been accepted and, consciously or unconsciously, this has created the expectation of greater economic equality and has stimulated the demand for it.'

[Some uncomfortable shuffling.]

'The trade unions have done a great deal for the men; and the men are conscious of that, and they now stand by their unions as much as, or more than, ever. At the same time, especially among the younger men, because they have obtained less than they expected, there is a rising disposition to displace the current union officials and to take power into their own hands.'

'Any attempt in this direction, if it is recklessly continued, must lead on, not to the assertion but to the negation of unionism, not to organisation improvement, but to chaos. Part of the restlessness and impatience that is unsettling the industrial world is due to the great hopes and expectations on the part of the wage-earning classes, combined with the consciousness of power, and with dissatisfaction at the results hitherto obtained, and a determination to achieve a more effective means of using that power.'

'The industrial situation is in many ways disquieting. We could not have made the trade of this country what it is, or support the enormous population it now contains, without the stimulus of individual enterprise and the pressure of competition. But it is necessary that men should understand the best methods of using their power and realising their hopes which, even if they have failed to achieve all that they had hoped, would yet make sure of obtaining something that is possible. Order and organisation are essential to such methods.'

[Muted 'Hear, Hear' from some quarters]

'In collective bargaining, it is essential that there be no disorganisation of business, and it is as essential that men who have voluntarily made a bargain with their employers should carry out that bargain, as it is that the employer should carry out their contracts with other firms, otherwise a union becomes a mob and a mob has only the power to wreck and destroy, but not to build up or to conquer.'

'It is an ignoble motive to attempt to set class against class, and to espouse the gospel of hate. These things have never built up anything. Employers and employed must arrive at a mutual undertaking and a reasonable settlement; but the difficulty is to make the settlement seem reasonable to those outside of the negotiation room, to make them understand that their representatives have emerged not weaker but wiser than they went in. It is essential that men should stand by their unions and organisations. I am not pessimistic. I believe that the people, men and women alike, have now as much public spirit as any generation which has proceeded them.'

'Men should build up industry, not to enrich themselves, but to enrich the State. There is no doubt a great increase of wealth in individual hands, but much of the profits do not go into their own pockets, for their own exclusive use, but are used for increasing business and providing more employment.'

[Calls of 'Hear, Hear!']

'If anything can be done to give people a greater feeling of security and make them feel they have some insurance against the risks of life, then this must be the stability and security of our industrial condition. The current situation has many disquieting features, but in times of danger, common sense and reasonableness has risen to the top in the past and I believe that these qualities are still present, in undiminished degree, in the majority of the British people at this present time. There are doubtless pigheaded people among employers and among the employed; but, when things become serious, it is the common sense and reasonable men that come in and the others that are pushed aside.'

'The main movement of public life, I believe, is that of internal industrial development and social progress, and not foreign affairs. There is economic interdependence between the great nations, and the nations that are the most prosperous are the nations that have the largest armament.'

[Muted whisperings.]

'Some people talk of war; but I see no need for war, and I do not expect it. The first country that has a successful war, unless it is a war of defence, will follow conflict abroad by social upheaval at home.'

'What we need is men who can understand these complexities and, without class prejudice, help us find a way forward that is to the benefit of all. And having said my piece, it only remains for me to thank you for your attention and for a most enjoyable luncheon.'

[Loud applause as he retakes his seat.]

The speech was reported verbatim in the newspaper and after he'd read it Frank said,

'It's easy for him to say, he's not stuck down a hole 8 hours a day, hoping that the roof doesn't cave in.'

'Fine words,' said Jack.

'No conclusions,' said Jenny.

'Pleased they had such a good lunch,' said Edward.

'You complaining about the food?' said Jenny.

'Dangerous ground,' whispered Grandpa to Edward.

'Not a bit of it, Ma, the men underground are always trying to nick my bait.'

'Nice recovery,' whispered Sarah.

Chapter 68

The long awaited and carefully planned expedition to the Roman Wall was finally underway.

Jack and Sarah were sitting in a 3rd Class carriage, and Sarah was gazing out of the window, watching the landscape rushing by.

The train was running at 60mph on its rails, metal to metal, coal fired, steam powered, twice the speed of a galloping horse.

'Without trains we couldn't do this in a day,' said Jack, 'there's progress for you, the world is getting smaller.'

'Costs though,' said Sarah.

'One penny a mile,' said Jack, 'and I got a cheaper return rate so it was only 5 shillings each.'

'10 shillings!' said Sarah, 'do you know how much cloth I could buy with that, or worse, do you know how much sewing I would have to do to earn that much?'

'It's my treat,' said Jack, 'the coal's been kind for the last few weeks and I've been able to save a bit.'

'And now you're wasting it on this,' said Sarah, and then added in exasperation, 'it might have been raining!'

'But it's not raining,' said Jack, 'it's a nice day, and it looks like it's going to stay that way, and I've always wanted to visit the Wall.'

'Well why didn't you go on your own, it would have been much cheaper?'

'Because I wanted to take you,' said Jack.

Sarah immediately softened, 'Did you?' she said.

'Of course,' said Jack and leaned across to kiss her on the cheek.

'Jack!' said Sarah blushing, 'people are watching.'

'Let them watch,' said Jack, taking hold of Sarah's hand, 'I'm going to enjoy today.'

'I think I might too,' said Sarah.

After leaving home, they'd travelled up through Birtley. past the farms and the collieries, the green fields and the spoil heaps, past the towns with their smoking chimneys, under bridges, over streams, past church spires, through Low Fell and Gateshead, past the Workhouse, the smoking rows of houses, across the Tyne on the railway bridge, a ferry steaming on the river underneath, the river black with runoff, ships moored, and into Newcastle Central Station.

Then across platforms busy with people and a change of trains and out of Newcastle on the Carlisle line, following the north bank of the river, out of the city with several stops, then back across the river at Wylam and along the southern bank, past Prudhoe Castle and Riding station and Corbridge, then parallel with the line of a Roman road to Hexham, the town in the distance with its gaol and Abbey, then back across the river once more at Warden, and on past collieries, mills, stations and farms, following the valley, the hills on either side, criss-crossing rivers on railway bridges until finally they arrived and alighted at Bardon Mill.

Here there was a large station house and a long, white, timber building that ran parallel to the tracks. When Sarah saw it, she gasped,

'Look, Jack,' she said, 'it's built just like Mam's Fish and Chip shop, same colour as well.'

Jack didn't know how best to respond.

'There's lots of white wooden shacks about Sarah, although it is a bit like …'

'No, I was just remembering how happy Mam was when she was running the shop, that's all.'

'She was happy wasn't she.'

'I wonder where she is now.'

'I don't know,' said Jack.

'I hope she's happy,' said Sarah, wondering why she didn't hear from her. Her own mother was more a distant memory now, but every now and again something would remind her… and she would wonder, just wonder, with no deep feelings of sadness or rejection. She had a new family now and was no longer a child, she was making her own way in the world, and that's how it should be.

'It's an hour's walk from here,' said Jack, consulting his map and hoping to change the subject, which he found awkward, 'maybe two, so we'd better get started.'

'How much did the map cost?' asked Sarah.

'Not that much.'

'How much is not that much?'

'2 shillings.'

'2 shillings!' exclaimed Sarah.

'I thought it was important to know where we were, where we were going, and not get lost.'

'We could ask people.'

'But we don't know anybody here.'

'What does it matter if you know them or not, as long as they're willing to help?'

'I didn't know how many people would be about.'

'We're not going into a desert, are we?'

'Alright, I've done it now anyway… look this is where we are and this is the road we need to follow.'

'You mean this road in front of us?'

'Yes.'

'You mean the only road that leads out of town this way?'

'It's better to be safe than sorry,' said Jack, folding the map up and putting it in his backpack.

'So, let's go,' he said.

'Lead on,' said Sarah.

As they walked, they were passed in both directions by horses and carts with people riding in them. Jack talked about the Roman Wall, keen to pass on what he'd learnt from his book "The Hand-Book to the Roman Wall" by J. Collingwood Bruce, that he'd picked up cheaply in Durham.

'After the Romans left Britain there was over a thousand years of silence about what they'd left behind,' he said.

Sarah smiled.

'Sometimes, Jack Lawley, you talk like a poet.'

Jack blushed.

'I like it,' she added quickly and laughed.

'Well then,' continued Jack, 'in the late 1500s William Camden included some observations on the remains of the Wall in his book "Britannia", a book that was so popular that it was updated and republished over the course of the next two hundred years, imagine that, a book that was so well respected that people took the trouble to do that. Anyway, as it was updated so were the observations on the Wall.'

The sun shone on them as they walked.

'You're making it sound quite mysterious,' said Sarah, 'like in a storybook,' she paused and looked around, there were hills and trees and rivers that where wholly unfamiliar to her, 'by the way, are we on the right road?'

Jack consulted the map just to make sure.

'Yes, this seems right. Now, there were a number of other historians over the years who also recorded their observations.'

He paused to get a piece of paper out of his canvas backpack.

'I made a note.'

'Of course you did,' said Sarah.

'What?'

'I said, "that's good",' she said.

'The main ones seem to be Horsley's "Britannia Romana" of 1732, Warburton's "Vallum Romanum" in 1753, Stukeley's "Iter Boreale",' Jack struggled with the pronunciation, 'in 1776, Brand's "History of Newcastle" in1789, and, one of the most interesting I think, William Hutton of Birmingham who, in 1801, at the age of 78, walked the whole length of the wall and was so upset when he saw so much of the Roman stone being robbed out and taken away to be used elsewhere, that he stopped one of the local farmers who was busy doing just that and tried to explain to him how important history was and how magnificent an inheritance the Wall was and implored him not to destroy it, and to tell others the same. In the preface to his book "The History of the Roman Wall" he says, wait a minute I've written it down here, "...perhaps I am the first man that ever travelled the whole length of the Wall, and probably the last that will ever attempt it... Men have been deified for trifles compared with this memorable structure."'

'How do you know all of this?' said Sarah, 'you can't possibly have read all these books, I've seen your bookcase, you don't have these books in it.'

'It's all summarised in this one,' he said, getting out Bruce's Hand-Book and tapping the cardboard cover, 'somebody's done all the work for me.'

'So, it's a bit of a cheat really then,' said Sarah, 'anybody can read one book.'

Jack decided to ignore this jibe and carry on regardless. From the look on her face, Sarah seemed to be finding it fun.

'The Reverend John Hodgson published an account of the Wall in 1812 and in 1816 the Lysons' "Magna Britannia" had something in about it,' Sarah yawned, Jack carried on quickly, 'with the patronage of the Duke of Northumberland a detailed survey of what remained was made in the years 1852 to 1854 by Henry Mac Lauchlan.'

'You've got to remember that for each of the generations that rediscovered the Wall over these last 400 years or so, for those who uncovered its buildings, ditches, roads, those who found coins, glass, and pottery, it was like discovering a lost civilisation under their own feet, and was no less miraculous than the first discovery and recognition of fossilised dinosaur bones!'

'Hmm,' said Sarah, 'when you put it like that... so we're not just going to see a pile of stones and ruins, we're going to see where real people, people like us, lived two thousand years ago.'

'Exactly!' said Jack.

'Ooh, that does sound more exciting. Jack, you are so clever,' she paused, 'and interesting.'

The land around them rose and fell, green moorland with coverings of purple and brown. The road wound through the landscape, avoiding too many leg-sapping ups and downs. More horse drawn carts passed them, one of them asking if they wanted a lift to the Military Road that ran parallel to the Wall, for sixpence. But Jack declined saying that they wanted to take their time and enjoy the landscape. Sarah didn't look so sure about this decision, but Jack was too engrossed to notice.

When they reached the top road they could see, rising in front of them, the top line of Sewingshield Crags.

'Look,' said Jack, 'right at the summit, can you see it, I think that's the Wall.'

Sarah looked as hard as she could but wasn't sure.

'Let's climb up and take a look,' said Jack, 'if it is the Wall we should be able to follow it along until we get to the fort.'

'You mean, just walk straight up there, from here?' said Sarah, 'but there's no path.'

'There's a few tracks,' said Jack, 'I'm sure it'll be alright.'

Not wanting to quash his enthusiasm, Sarah followed his lead. There wasn't really a track but they found their way between tussocks, sheep droppings and molehills.

But then they reached a mound followed by a steep ditch that was boggy at the bottom. They had to step carefully to prevent their feet from getting wet.

After they'd clambered out of the ditch there was another mound to get over. The ditch seemed to run away to either side of them.

'Great idea, Jack,' said Sarah, thankful she'd managed to keep her feet dry.

And then it got steep.

Jack could see that Sarah was starting to flag.

'I'm not used to walking so much,' she said.

Jack took her hand and together they bent their backs to the slope and slowly made their way upwards. Near the top it started to flatten out a bit and in front of them, on the edge of the escarpment, there were three or four courses of stone.

'It is the Wall!' said Jack, pulling Sarah up the last few yards.

When he reached the Wall, he put out his hand and ran his fingers along it, feeling the crevices between the blocks, still filled with Roman mortar.

'Look how thick it is,' he said, 'must be 5 or 6 feet. Imagine, Sarah, nearly 1800 years ago people were starting to build this. I bet they never imagined bits of it would still be here 1800 years later.'

Sarah was getting her breath back. She was listening to what Jack was saying but, after all, it was only a wall.

'Just imagine having to cut all these blocks without any explosives to help you, with nothing more than hammers, chisels and wedges… and making the mortar, there are lots of lime kilns around here,' he turned around to take in the scene, 'there's some down there I think, see their shape, it's like a bottle.'

Sarah was in fear that Jack would want to walk down the slope and show her, so she said yes, she could see what Jack was pointing at and yes, she could make out the shape and yes, it was very interesting.

They sat for a little while to take in the view.

They'd made it.

In front of them lay the rolling hills and the way they had come, over the other side of the Wall was a vertical fall of hard, sharp, whinstone.

'The Romans had already occupied Britain for some two generations before their emperor Hadrian, who had been emperor for about two years, visited the island in 119AD. He didn't stay long…'

'Probably couldn't stand the rain,' said Sarah.

'…but he gave instruction,' said Jack, carrying on regardless, 'for a wall from one side of the country to the other and left it to his deputies to get the work done.'

'No difference there then,' said Sarah, 'bosses say things must be done, but never do it themselves. Can I have some water?'

Jack passed the bottle to Sarah who took a drink and passed it back. Jack took a swig, and then carried on,

'It must have been a mammoth task, employing tens of thousands of labourers and lots of skilled craftsmen; carpenters, stonemasons, surveyors, blacksmiths, plasterers… because they finished the first version in less than 5 years, over 70 miles of it, I don't think we could do anything like that now, even with our steam engines and machinery.'

'Must have been slavery,' said Sarah, 'only way you can get so many people labouring, must have been horrible conditions.'

'Worse than working underground?'

'I've never been down the pit, so I don't know.'

'You don't want to go down there either.'

'But at least you have a choice,' said Sarah, 'the people who did all the labouring, building this,' she patted the Wall, 'probably didn't.'

'You think I have a choice?' said Jack, 'what choice do I have?'

Sarah changed the subject.

'Why did you say, "first version"?'

'Because the Wall wasn't just a wall, it was part of a complex military system that involved roads, forts, milecastles, turrets and on the north side a ditch and on the south side another protective ditch with banked earth mounds on either side, called the Vallum.'

'So that's what you dragged me through?'

'It would have been deeper in their day, and probably more sharply banked with higher mounds on both sides.'

'It was bad enough, thank you very much,' said Sarah, 'and anyway I thought the Wall was to give protection from the north not the south, what do you need another ditch for?'

It was a good question and Jack had no clear answer.

'I said "first version" because it was endlessly modified. Some of it was first built in turf and then later rebuilt in stone, and there must have been lots of changes. The Romans used it for 300 years after all and it was attacked in places so it must have been damaged and repaired, damaged and repaired lots of times, riding the waves of not only the tidal turbulence of the times in Britannia but also the consequences of the turbulence in Rome that swirled across the wider Empire.'

'Sometimes…' said Sarah.

'And then the Romans finally left us in 446AD,' Jack said quickly.

From their height they looked down on the road they'd walked up.

It now looked a long way away, the few horse-drawn carts and carriages, walkers and cyclists, looked small and separated.

Together they walked eastwards along the line of the Wall, following the track as it rose and fell with the lie of the crags. For most of the way the Wall was still 4 or so courses high, with hardy grasses growing along the top.

'Look at how they've used the landscape,' said Jack, 'just look at the view to north and south, nobody could get close without being seen, and I guess the Romans patrolled along the top of the Wall all the time.'

'Except at night,' said Sarah.

'What?'

'Except on a moonless night, or in a fog for that matter, you couldn't see for miles then could you.'

Jack hadn't thought about that.

'It's still a good position,' he said.

'And up here you'll get the wind as it whistles along the tops, bashing into the crags, driving rain into your face, not to mention the icy cold, the snow…'

'Alright, alright,' said Jack.

'It's a man's idea of a good spot,' said Sarah.

'Well, what would you have done?'

Sarah thought about it, protected as they were by the shade of the Wall as they walked along.

'I'd have built the wall,' she said, 'but I'd have put windows in it. Make the most of the shelter and not trudge along, exposed to the weather, on top.'

Jack was flabbergasted. On the one hand it sounded ridiculous, on the other he wondered why the Romans hadn't thought of it.

'It would have made the soldiers soft,' he said, 'better to keep them hardened to their place, they'd be more ready to fight at any time then.'

It seemed a bit of a lame argument. There must have been months, perhaps even years, without fighting, and the fighting, when it did come, would only last a few hours. It seemed a large price to pay.

'It was a deterrent,' he added.

'A what?'

'If you saw Roman soldiers armed with swords and spears and shields walking about all over the place you'd think twice about causing any trouble, wouldn't you.'

He was more satisfied with this answer.

'Can't have been very popular.'

'You didn't become a Roman soldier, and they came from all over Europe, not just Italy and Rome, to be popular. Maybe you'd be forced to join, maybe you did it for the pay, the food and the roof over your head, maybe you even did it for the adventure!'

'Sounds like becoming a miner,' said Sarah.

That shut Jack up and they walked in silence until they reached a portion of Wall that had the remains of other buildings attached to it.

Jack consulted his handbook,

'We're less than 500 yards from the fort we're aiming for and this is the remains of a milecastle.'

Sarah looked puzzled.

'500 yards isn't a mile,' she said, 'why is it called a milecastle?'

'Milecastles were built along the length of the Wall and were a Roman mile apart. It didn't matter what else was in between.'

'Bit daft.'

'Well maybe the milecastles were built first because they're smaller and easier to build and then the forts were added later on, in what they considered was the best place for them.'

'So, like you said before, we see all these things laid out together but they might have been built hundreds of years apart?'

'That's right,' said Jack, pleased Sarah had been listening.

Sarah smiled.

'Jack Lawley, sometimes you're…'

'Please don't call me "interesting".'

'I wasn't going to.'

'Well, what were you going to call me?'

'I'm not going to tell you now,' said Sarah.

Jack shook his head, he didn't understand women.

The milecastle had been built on rocky, uneven ground and when they went inside they could see some of the bare rock protruding through the grass.

Jack stood in the middle and read from his handbook,

'The north wall of the milecastle is formed by the Roman Wall itself and still stands up to 14 courses or 9 feet 6 inches tall.'

Sarah went and stood flat against the north wall and looked up,

'It's certainly tall,' she said, and then stood back and counted the courses,

'14 all present and correct.'

'From west to east it is 57 feet 7 inches wide and from north to south 49 feet 7 inches. The thickness of the walls on the east and west is 9 feet, the thickness at the north gateway is more than 10 feet. The southern angles are rounded externally but are square on the inside.'

'Sounds like you're measuring a dress,' said Sarah.

'Would have to be a very big one,' said Jack, 'and imagine how much work went into making walls that thick.'

They walked around a bit, just to absorb the atmosphere.

'It's a bit creepy,' said Sarah.

'You can see that the north gateway has been narrowed,' he said and consulted his book, 'yes, the original opening was 10 feet, but it was reduced to 3 feet 9 inches.'

'Why did they have to reduce it by so much?'

'Easier to guard I suppose, or maybe there were less men available at the time.'

'What does your book say?'

'Here we are; when this milecastle was excavated they found evidence of buildings that had been forcibly thrown down and burnt. Not just once either, and each time they rebuilt it, they just cleared and levelled the old and put a new set of buildings on top.'

'Sounds like this was a dangerous place.'

'Maybe this is a dangerous stretch, maybe that's why the fort's here.'

'Or close to here.'

'And maybe the new buildings were built on top of the old because it was faster, maybe it was more important to be fast than to take the time to do a thorough job of clearing out all the debris before starting again. This was a way through the Wall, maybe they'd underestimated the wrath of the locals and the strength of opposition to putting a wall here, cutting off traffic between north and south.'

'Yes,' said Sarah, 'just imagine some strangers coming along and drawing a line on a map and then building a wall along it. There might have been families split apart, lands that had been owned by the same people for generations and then, all of a sudden, there was a wall across the middle of it, and you had to ask permission of these strangers, who were rough and unpleasant to you, each time you wanted to go between the two sides.'

'Maybe you had to pay,' said Jack.

'There's reasons the locals would have got upset,' said Sarah, who was joining in with Jack's imaginings, they were like two children set loose to play, 'Here real people lived, cooked, gossiped, and fought.'

'And died,' said Jack.

'Lots more people than there are here today.'

'Yes,' said Jack, 'in this quiet, peaceful and deserted spot, bathed in sunshine there lurks in the shadows so many people's stories, people whose language we wouldn't even understand, people whose stories are buried with them and the best we can do is to make some wild guesses about what they were really like, and we'll never know whether our guesses are right or wrong.'

Sarah gave an involuntary shiver.

'Sometimes, you sound like a book,' she said, 'I wonder what people will say about us in1800 years time?'

She paused to think.

'I didn't even know my Grandparents, never mind trying to picture people from this long ago.'

They clambered onto the top of the Wall.

'Is this allowed?' asked Sarah.

'Don't see why not,' said Jack, 'we're going to be careful aren't we.'

The views both north and south were spectacular; to the north towards the Cheviots Hills and to the south towards their home, the far distance peppered with chimneys emitting wisps of smoke.

They walked slowly and in single file, Jack leading, through a copse of trees that took no heed of the Wall that cut through its heart, and out the other side to where they could see their objective; the remains of the Roman Fort of Borcovicium, or Housesteads as it was commonly called.

Carefully they dismounted the Wall, Jack lending Sarah a hand, and made their way to what remained of the west gate and entered together into what remained of this city of the dead.

Still in their minds were the lost peoples and the turbulent times of the milecastle, but this was different, this was on a much grander scale, this was a fortress and a town.

'There were families here,' said Sarah softly.

'It was built for soldiers,' said Jack, 'maybe as many as a thousand, and their horses, and their weapons, and their stores and the craftsmen that made and maintained everything they needed.'

'There were women here,' said Sarah, 'women and girls, they're probably not as well remembered, but they were here, I can feel them.'

'Sarah,' said Jack, 'it's seems it isn't just me that can get poetic.'

Sarah smiled.

'I have my moments,' she said.

They walked around the remains, there were a few other people there, but other than a 'Good day' they did not talk to them. Some seemed, from their dress and demeanour, to be of a separate class, but they left Jack and Sarah alone, and Jack was thankful for that. They'd asked no permission and paid no entry fee and Jack was not sure whether they'd broken any rules, so they kept to themselves and, handbook at the ready, they started to explore the fort.

The form of the fort was rectangular, attached to the Wall on its northern side, rounded at the external southern corners, its greater length being from west to east, lying on a basalt shelf, the rock protruding through the soil layer in several places, the whole shelf sloping gently to the south.

Jack and Sarah walked to the centre, the remains of a main street could be made out, crossing the fort, joining the north gate to the south.

'This was a big place,' said Sarah.

'Imagine it all built up,' said Jack, 'it must have been full of people and noise and strange smells.'

'Strange smells?'

'All those horses, wood burning, privies…'

'Alright, that's enough, I get the picture!'

They looked over a fence at the uncovered stone skeleton of a central building and when they turned around, they could see that another wide road lead down to the east gate.

Jack referred to his handbook, feeling that it had been money well-spent at the secondhand bookstore.

'There is evidence of 18 other buildings all running west to east, 10 seem to be barrack blocks for 80 or so soldiers each.'

They walked down the length of one of them, seeing the size of the individual compartments.

'They had less space than us,' said Sarah, 'it looks very cramped.'

'I suppose they were out most of the time; patrolling, working, doing what they were told.'

'Must have been smelly,' said Sarah.

'Again, evidence has been found of the fort buildings being destroyed, by accident or design, and then rebuilt, on top of the ruins.'

'Just like the milecastle,' said Sarah.

'Yes, maybe at the same time, after repelling the same attack?'

He paused.

'Just imagine the battle, the fire, the screams, the blood…'

'I'd rather not,' said Sarah.

Jack and Sarah then turned their attention to two buildings that lay side by side in the northern half of the fort. They looked very different; both having raised floors and buttressed walls.

'Granaries,' said Jack, 'each of them is 78 feet long and 18 feet wide, massive buildings, just shows how dependent the whole place was on grain and bread.'

'So, these are the real engine rooms of the fort,' said Sarah.

'I suppose you could say that, it's a good example of how important farming was, animals and crops, to the whole thing. There must have been acres and acres of farmland and hundreds of farm labourers that we have no trace of now, and the harvesting, threshing, carting and trading, it must have been a whole parallel world, no less important than making swords.'

'More important, you've got to eat.'

Partway along one of the granaries was the remains of a kiln for drying corn.

'Here's an example of the layering of history,' said Jack, 'after the Romans left, these buildings were too good not to be taken over and used by others. According to the handbook, this is not a Roman kiln but a design from 1,000 years later, when this whole area was in dispute between England and Scotland, and families would raid families to steal livestock or in revenge for some past wrong. At that time a place like this, made out of stone must have felt safe. There's other evidence here of Roman buildings being used as living quarters or byres for cattle, or hearths where they cooked and warmed themselves.'

'That feels so strange.'

'Yes, by that time the Romans would have been forgotten, or a distant memory, remembered locally only through folk tales and remains like this.'

'And now we're here.'

'But just as visitors.'

'Aren't we all?' said Sarah.

Jack looked at her,

'Sometimes Sarah you're…'

'Don't you dare call me "interesting"!'

'I wasn't going to.'

'Well, what were you going to call me?'

'I'm not going to tell you now,' said Jack, grinning widely.

'Men!' said Sarah.

Jack and Sarah walked to the east gate.

'This was probably the main gate in Roman times,' said Jack, 'Like all of the other gates it was reduced in width at some time during the Roman occupation. When the southern section was closed up, the guard chamber belonging to it was converted into a dwelling room and when it was excavated in 1833 nearly a cart load of coals was found in it.'

'Coal!'

'But we don't know who put it there or when.'

'Just makes it feel like this place isn't so ancient after all.'

Jack pointed out the holes in the stone where the pivot for the doors would have slotted into place and the stone in the middle against which the gates would have closed.

They left the fort by the east gate and walked down towards the point where the Knag Burn passed through the line of the Wall.

Between the fort and the burn there were bumps and mounds indicating the presence of the remains of suburban dwellings lying beneath the turf.

'There must have been shops and pubs and families here,' said Sarah, 'although it's now all just bumps in the ground. I think this is as important as anything inside the fort.'

'And it's all inside the "military zone", marked by the Vallum to the south and the ditch on the north of the Wall,' said Jack, pointing, 'there's the line of the Vallum down there.'

'So, the so-called military zone wasn't just for soldiers then,' said Sarah.

'Apparently not, maybe it started off like that and then, over time things got a bit more friendly, the line between the Roman soldiers and the local people more blurred.'

'The Romans would have married the local women,' said Sarah, 'why not? Men need women and here there were lots of men.'

'You might be right,' said Jack uncomfortably, he seemed to remember that a serving Roman soldier couldn't get married, but that didn't necessarily stop them from having a family, and having them close by seemed like a sensible option. You couldn't expect men to stay celibate for 25 years, which was their length of service should they survive it.

When they reached the burn, they followed it through to the other side of the Wall. They followed it along until they found a quiet spot. Here they sat, with their backs against the Roman stones, shaded from the slight breeze, and started on their bait.

As they ate their sandwiches, Jack, looking north, said,

'I'm sure we're seeing all the way into Scotland; it's a great view from here.'

'I've never been to Scotland, and probably never will.'

'I'd like to travel,' said Jack, 'the world is so vast and the books I've read have given me only a taste of it.'

'I'm happy where I am,' said Sarah, 'there's plenty to occupy me right here.'

'Me you mean?'

Sarah nudged him in the arm.

'You're so arrogant, Mr Lawley. No, I did not mean you, I meant...'

Jack gave a forlorn look. She nudged him again and laughing said,

'Alright just a little bit you, just a little bit mind.'

Jack perked up immediately.

'I like you, Sarah Hudson, I like you a lot.'

'Jack sometimes...'

'No,' he said, reaching into the canvas backpack, 'don't you dare...'

He took out a small package and handed it to her.

'What's this?'

'Take a look.'

Slowly she opened the package, something fell into the palm of her hand.

'So?' said Jack.

'What?'

'Will you?'

'Will I what?'

'Miss Sarah Hudson, will you marry me?'

'But we've been arguing all day!'

'Not "arguing", "discussing".'

'Oh, Jack.'

For the first time he started to worry, had he misjudged everything?

Sarah had tears in her eyes.

'Are you sure, Jack?'

'Yes, I'm sure.'

'Then I am too. Yes Jack Lawley, I would love to be your wife.'

They embraced. In a place steeped in history, they were making some of their own.

'Where did you get the ring?'

'Durham.'

'You mean during the Gala?'

'Yes, there's more than just bookshops in Durham.'

She looked at the ring and then turned to Jack,

'It's lovely,' she said.

The rest of the day was a blur.

Sarah was thinking of all the things that needed to be done.

Jack was reveling in her animated happiness that mirrored his own.

He hadn't been sure whether he should propose today, he wasn't even sure if he could. But the weather had been kind and he had enjoyed having Sarah with him, and the way she'd increasingly got involved, fed off his interest and enthusiasm, and hadn't made fun of him… much.

Now it was done, he was pleased he'd done it.

They walked down the steep bank, and up an equally steep climb that took them south of the fort and back to the road.

Arm in arm, Jack could see how tired Sarah was after all this walking, and other excitements.

They stood at the roadside to catch their breath. Jack approached a cart driver and when he returned, he told Sarah that they didn't have to walk back, they could ride.

Sarah was very thankful and after Jack had helped her on he took two silver shillings from his pocket, the King's head on one side, a lion astride the crown on the other, and handed them to the driver. They glinted in the afternoon sun.

'That's about 4 hours' work underground, that is,' he said, as he passed the money over.

'A man's got to make a living,' said the Carter smiling.

They rode back to Bardon Mill, the Wall high on their right to start, wending its way along the ridge, and then they turned south and left it behind them.

Sarah took the ring off before they got home.

'Let me tell Jenny,' she said, 'and don't tell anybody else until I've told her.'

Jack would have preferred to have been the bearer of the good news, but he readily agreed.

Chapter 69

Jack did is best to clear the way and eventually Sarah and Jenny were alone in the kitchen. Sarah was fidgeting,

'What's wrong?' said Jenny, 'it's like you're sitting on hot coals.'

Sarah had planned in her head lots of ways to say it, but in the end, she just blurted it out,

'Jack wants to marry me,' she said.

Jenny looked up; she didn't seem that surprised.

'What did you say?' she asked.

'Well, I said I'd think about it,' said Sarah, 'what do you think, Ma?'

Jenny smiled, 'I think you're a kind, hardworking girl and Jack should count himself lucky,' she said.

'Oh, Ma!' said Sarah.

'Now don't you be getting all soft and teary,' said Jenny, 'and I have to say straight away that I think engagements are funny things. I always think folks thinks it entitles them to things.'

'What do you mean, Ma, entitles them to what?'

'Well, if you get engaged, that might make you want to do something you would normally wait until after you're married to do,' said Jenny.

Sarah blushed.

'Oh, I think I see what you mean,' she mumbled, embarrassed, 'I might just tell Jack that we'll get married as long as we don't have a long engagement.'

'You're not in a hurry, are you?' said Jenny, changing tack.

'No, Ma, but Jack thought it might be a good time now that he's earning a steady wage and all.'

'Well, I think a short engagement might be for the best, then we can just get on and organise the wedding,' said Jenny, wishing she'd had the opportunity to talk to some of the other girls in the village like this.

There was little shame associated with pregnancy before marriage provided matrimony followed fairly rapidly.

Family reputation was a vital asset, particularly amongst those who saw themselves as 'respectable' members of the community. Jenny and Frank were respectable, they did not owe too much money, were members of the Co-op and went to church regularly.

If pregnancy was involved the risk was that, if anything happened to the prospective husband before the wedding day, the increasingly obviously pregnant wife would be left to fend for herself. Unlike pregnant brides, unmarried mothers were frowned upon and, if their family or friends refused to support them then they might well find themselves on the road to the workhouse.

For these reasons, Jenny was not in favour of long engagements. And there was one other reason, a reason related to why she and Frank always added an extra year to their married life if ever they were asked how long they had been married; a small correction made in consideration of Edward's age.

Frank was at first surprised and then delighted. He had seen Jack and Sarah more as brother and sister rather than man and wife. But the friendship between them was obvious and friendship was a good basis for a long marriage, he thought.

Edward was only surprised that it had taken Jack so long to get round to it. Sarah's affection for Jack had always been obvious to him, and he was happy for his younger brother and a little envious at the same time. He took Jack down the pub at the earliest opportunity in order to celebrate and spread the news, he even bought the first round willingly.

George got the idea that this was good news but couldn't really understand why boys and girls felt the need to do this kind of thing. He was quite happy on his own, with his playmates at school and down the rows, running around and having adventures.

Grandpa took Sarah to one side,

'You're a fine girl, Sarah, and I think Jack will make a good husband, just don't let him ever think about becoming a soldier.'

No matter what momentous decisions were being made above ground, the work underground never stopped, and never got any easier.

Before Jack could get to the farm and tell Peter his news he had another shift to complete. Concentrating on the task at hand somehow became easier now. Although there were lots of new things that needed doing, his mind was more settled. During his break he told Barney his news and gave him not only an apple, but half a sandwich as well. Barney seemed pleased.

As the cage rattled its way skywards at the end of his shift, Jack raised a black-smeared hand to protect his eyes and gazed up through a narrow gap that he set between his fingers. Edward stood beside him.

The small overhead circle of light grew steadily as the cage clattered and groaned its way out of the darkness. Inside the human cargo was squashed together and, much to the frustration of the pit management, the cage traveled at a slower regulated speed than when it lifted tubs of coal. There was no direct profit in lifting men in and out of the ground, the pit's economy was regulated by the number of fully laden lifts of coal that could be got out in a day, every day. The sooner this expensive equipment could return to its more profitable work, the better.

The whiteness of the men's eyes contrasted sharply with the blackness of their faces as they chattered and jibed their noisy way upwards, the journey punctuated by the occasional flash of laughter or teeth.

Finally the cage broke the surface and came to a grinding stop. The buzzer sounded a safe arrival and the wrought iron metal gates scraped and creaked as they were hauled back, disgorging the men into the greater light in a tumbling, mumbling rush, their shoulders stooped, squinting into the unaccustomed brightness. The noise of the buzzer echoed in their ears as a clarion call to a comparative, though fleeting, freedom.

The men fanned out from the pithead, jostling and colliding in a sleepwalking mass as their eyes became accustomed to the new levels of light, and their pupils shrank to a surface-dweller size.

Following his usual superstitious ritual Edward said, 'Thank fuck that's over,' and turning to Jack, patted him on the back, raising black fairy dust.

'You told your pony before me!' said Peter.

Jack realised that being too open and honest wasn't always the best policy.

'I came out to see you as soon as I could,' he said.

'Well, I'm happy for you,' said Peter, looking tired, 'we had a difficult calving last night so apologies if I don't seem awake, I was helping with a breach at 2 o'clock this morning.'

Jack didn't want any more details of the birthing process.

'I want to make sure you come to the wedding,' he said.

'You try and stop me, free food and drink! When is it going to be?'

'I don't know yet, Ma wants it quickly.'

Peter nudged him.

'There's not a reason is there?'

Jack coloured.

'No, there's not a reason! Ma just doesn't believe in long engagements.'

'Fair enough, only asking.'

Jack laughed.

'And how are you doing?'

'I'm doing what my father did, and what my grandfather did before that, I'm learning how to farm,' he paused, 'and making lots of mistakes along the way.'

'That's like me with mining, when it's all you know, when it's the world you've grown up in, then it just seems natural to do the same thing.'

'Me on the surface, you underground,' said Peter.

He looked up at the sky.

'I think I might've got the best of it,' he said.

Jack laughed.

'At least I don't have to lose sleep over cows giving birth.'

Peter laughed.

'You're right, come on, before I fall asleep, let's go and tell my Mam and Dad the good news.'

When Jack returned home his arms were full of cheese and chutneys, his pockets full of eggs.

Jenny had news.

Under these new circumstances, she had got herself worried about the family sleeping arrangements.

'Everybody will know soon, and we've got our reputation to think about,' she said, 'and yours.'

She had already talked to Mrs Jones, Mary's mother, and arranged for Sarah to sleep over at their house for a small fee.

Jack was shocked.

'She'll still be here most of the day,' said Jenny, 'just at night she'll go over to Mrs Jones'.'

'What does Sarah think?'

'She doesn't know yet, I've only just made the arrangements.'

Sarah was surprised. The rest of the family was amused. They hadn't realised Jenny could be such a prude.

'It's for the best,' she said, looking at her husband for support.

'I think we'll all get used to it,' he said.

'I'll happily sleep over at Mrs Jones',' said Sarah, 'but I'll pay my own way, Jenny, I've got money from my sewing I can use.'

'No, Sarah, it was my idea, it's only right I pay.'

Jack was in the middle of two strong-willed women wondering what to say. He decided to say nothing.

'It's me who'll pay,' said Sarah, 'I should have thought of how it looks now that we're engaged. I will pay.'

Jenny was beaten.

Jack was proud.

'You're going to need all your money for the wedding and after, so I'll let you pay as long as you promise to come and ask me for help if you come to need it.'

Sarah thought about this.

'Alright, Ma,' she said, 'it's a deal.'

Jack gave a sigh of relief.

Both women looked at him.

'Something caught in my throat,' he said hastily, and gave a little cough.

'Alright?' said Sarah, looking at Jack.

He shrugged his shoulders.

'Alright,' he said.

His world was changing faster than he'd anticipated.

The arrangements for the wedding were left to the women.

The food would be prepared by three or four willing helpers and served back at the Lawley's home. The dresses for the women would be made by Jenny and Sarah. Jack had already applied for a house of their own following the wedding, and it looked like there was one available on Third Street. Earnest Weightman was looking into it for them.

The banns would have to be read; extended family told the good news and invited to attend.

Sarah had chosen dark blue for her wedding outfit, in a style that could be worn again later. She knew what she wanted, and Jenny and Sarah had it cut out all ready to sew.

The skirt had a frill of gathered material around the bottom to provide some detail, but the accompanying white blouse made it special. It had leg-of-mutton sleeves, which were popular, a high neck with the same detailing as the frill on the skirt. Sarah planned to wear a cameo brooch that her mother had given her before she left, on the neck of the blouse.

They had tried, and failed, to contact her mother, Alice. Sarah had not heard from her, and there was no address to write to. It was a sadness that her mother would not be there to see her married, but Sarah thought that perhaps it was for the best as it might awaken memories of her own wedding and a marriage she would rather forget. Still, they put a notice of the wedding in the paper in the hope that Alice might see it.

Jenny's blouse was made out of the same material as Sarah's, and she would wear a long black skirt to go with it. There were two bridesmaids whose outfits contained aspects of the bride's outfit and were all beautifully made by other skilled dressmakers, and all hand sewn.

Jack wanted a new suit for the wedding and wanted to buy it from "Denby's".

Mr Denby was Scottish but represented a Newcastle warehouse. He visited the village every fortnight, on a Friday. He was a tall, smart man and liked his tea. He had lots of customers in the village and brought his catalogue of what was available to buy on credit, or 'tick' as it was known.

Each significant order required a deposit of five shillings, and then Mr Denby would call each fortnight to collect his dues until it was paid off.

He would travel from village to village, taking his orders, delivering his goods and collecting the payments.

He knew he had to be good value for money because he was in competition with the Co-op, that sold just about everything and had the advantage of being able to offer a dividend on purchases. Mr Denby always ensured that the garments he supplied were of good quality and Sarah was happy for Jack to order a suit from him.

'I can't believe you want a new suit,' Jenny had said, always conscious of not spending too much, 'there's nothing wrong with your Sunday suit. You look good in it.'

'Yes, but that's just it, Ma, it's what I always wear,' said Jack, 'I want something different to be married in and I'm going to go to Newcastle and order something direct from Mr Denby's. Sarah's agreed and we'll go in together. She needs some stuff of her own anyway.'

'But what's the matter with the store?' insisted his mother.

'This is my wedding, Ma, and I'm going to Newcastle to order a suit and that's that. I'm not a child anymore, I can make my own decisions.'

Jack and Sarah travelled to Newcastle by train and the shopping trip was a success. Jack came home proudly telling everyone that he had ordered a blue three-piece suit and a new bowler hat from Mr Denby's warehouse.

Jenny took Sarah to one side.

'Sarah, I don't know what you were thinking, letting him get a blue suit. I ask you, what will folks think?' she said.

'But, Ma, I couldn't stop him. He got it into his head that he wanted this blue material, and I couldn't talk him out of it. Mr Denby is going to bring the suit the next time he comes, I think it might be alright, it's a deep blue!'

Jenny shook her head, 'I should have come with you,' she said, 'what a waste of money. How often does he think he's going to need a blue suit?'

Other than Jenny's largely unfounded concerns about the cost and the colour of Jack's suit, plans for the wedding were going well; Jack and Sarah were going to get married, the expense was affordable, and everyone was relatively healthy… what could possibly go wrong?

Chapter 70

The vast majority of men at the colliery belonged to a trade union, the Enginemen's Union, the Mechanics Union or the main Miner's Lodge. Being a union member was by now a natural part of life at the pit, the running of them being left to a handful of trusted men.

There was always the risk of stoppages, layoffs or strikes mainly because of the vagaries of the coal market and the complexity of the 'sliding scale' that adjusted the pay of the Hewer, whilst taking no account of any local rise in the cost of living.

The owners used this approach to their advantage as a means of 'sharing the pain' of market volatility and as a means of retaining profitability for themselves or, as they would have it, to protect the means of future investment that was a necessity for all.

The acrimony resulting from the perceived arbitrary and too eager reductions in pay compared to the laggardly approach to increases, built up an increasing resentment. In simple terms the miners, who were recognised as carrying out both dangerous and arduous work, felt a growing sense of unfairness when they were tasked to do the same work, and take the same risks, for less reward. Any gain that they had enjoyed in the 'good times' was forgotten and overshadowed by the losses they suffered in the 'bad'.

After a year in which miner's pay had fallen yet again, while the cost of household goods had risen, the bubble finally burst.

A dispute that began in Derbyshire spread through the union lines and area after area voted to join the strike until it finally became the first national miners' strike.

After the vote Edward was trying to explain it to his mother,
'We've got no choice, Ma, you know how things have been going; lower wages, higher prices, it couldn't go on forever.'

'But a strike means no pay,'

'Hopefully it'll be over quickly,' said Frank, 'nobody wants the country to run out of coal.'

'Well, if it has to be done,' said Grandpa, who, as an ex-soldier, could not contemplate the armed forces ever going on strike, no matter how bad the circumstances, and he'd encountered some bad ones.

'I know families that are barely making do,' said Edward.

Jenny couldn't argue with that, she knew better than any of the men how difficult some of the women of the village were finding it to make ends meet.

But a strike!

Would that solve anything?

'Nobody cares about the miners,' continued Edward, 'we've tried resolving this locally but it's just not working. The Owners have too much power. We produce the coal that the whole country relies on but we get no recognition for it. The only thing left for us to do is to take the supply away. Then maybe it won't be taken for granted anymore… and then let's see what happens.'

Silence followed these words. There was undoubted truth in them, but there was also risk.

'It's a last resort,' said Jack.

'And the wedding?' said Sarah.

'We'll keep on with the preparations, pet,' said Jenny, 'but we might best wait until after this is sorted to fix the ceremony.'

Jack bowed his head, he hadn't thought about that when he cast his vote. He'd been carried along by the logic and passion of Earnest Weightman's arguments on behalf of the Union. Even if he'd voted against it, it wouldn't have mattered, the majority was overwhelming.

Just before the pit stopped working there was a rush on coal, private purchasers paying double the price, 25 shillings per ton instead of 12 shillings and 6 pence, to stockpile what they could.

'Unity is Strength' was the union motto and it had never been held so dearly, nor seen so clearly, than at the start of this nationwide strike.

Not everything stopped though, the school remained open. George continued to attend and Mr and Mrs Hughes continued to teach.

'I see no reason why the children's education should be interrupted,' said Wilkinson Hughes to Earnest Weightman, 'I hope you can convince the Owners that it is in nobody's interests to close the school. It is not the children who are on strike, it is their parents and older siblings.'

'I'll do what I can,' said Earnest.

'I intend to keep these doors open,' said Wilkinson.

Enid stood alongside him and nodded in full agreement.

Tempers in some of the households were already fraying.

'Are you sure going on strike is the right thing to do?' said Jenny.

'They're bound to settle soon,' said Frank, his head in the newspaper, reading the reports from all parts of the country.

'I'm not going to believe that,' said Jenny, 'we're all going to move on to "strike rations" and spread everything out as thin as we can, that way we'll last a bit longer. I've bought some provisions; butter, cheese, tea, a sack of flour and one of potatoes to keep us going.'

'Oh, Ma, you're worrying too much,' said Edward.

'And you men will get yourselves out from under my feet,' she said, her eyes set so that nobody felt like arguing.

'I'll go over to the farm and give Peter a hand, there's always work to be done over there,' said Jack.

'I'll go with you and stop off along the way at the allotment,' said Grandpa.

'I'll collect George from the school gate and take him off somewhere, keep him out of your hair for a while,' said Frank.

'Wrap up warm all of you,' said Sarah, 'it's cold out there.'

'It's cold in here' whispered Edward as he made a hasty retreat.

'And Edward, no drinking down the pub, we can't afford it.'

'Wouldn't dream of it, Ma, wouldn't dream of it.'

When he'd voted for a strike he hadn't thought that he was voting to go without beer!

Grandpa didn't make it as far as the farm, he could see work that needed doing on the allotment, and that was more than enough for him to be getting on with.

'Your Ma's right,' he said to Jack, 'better to assume the worst, there'll be others carrying on as normal, burning up all the coal in their bunker, they'll be sorry if this doesn't get settled quickly.'

Because of this uncertainty, and with no immediate agreement in sight, the pit ponies were brought out of the pit and distributed around the local farms for care and shelter.

Barney was taken in by the Moores.

Jack was doubly pleased for Barney, pleased that he had time in daylight and breathing clean air, and pleased that it was the Moore's farm that would be caring for him. He knew Peter loved horses and there would be no better place for Barney.

When he reached the farm, Jack immediately sought Barney out and patted his neck and whispered in his ear,

'I know this will be like a holiday for you,' he said, 'and I don't know how long it will be for, but remember that our job is underground, enjoy your break but don't forget your work.'

Barney nodded his head and then nuzzled one of Jack's pockets, he could smell carrots. Jack gave in easily.

At the end of the first week of the strike the last pay was drawn, short of course and with the uncertainty of when the next might be, but it did mean that families still had some money in their pockets.

The general feeling was positive, and the men were treating the strike as if it were a holiday. Most of the women were also supportive at the start as it was a refreshing change to have their menfolk at home and not to be subject to the demands of the shift timetable that normally dictated their waking, feeding, washing and laundering, especially the laundering.

Mr Denby delivered Jack's wedding suit and Jack tried it on,
'It fits well, I think,' he said.
'I like it,' said Sarah.
Jenny inspected it carefully, especially the colour, it was a very dark blue.
'It's not as bad as I feared,' she said.
With the strike bringing more to worry about than what shade of blue a suit was, Jack got away with it, and it was never again raised as an issue.

Nearly one million miners were now out on strike.

Time soon started to pass slowly for many of the miners.
Their bodies and minds were attuned to long periods of manual labour and they were finding it difficult to cope with having nothing to do. Kicked out of the house because they were disrupting their wives' routines, they gathered on corners or strolled around the countryside.
Those who had hobbies took full advantage of the time, improving their gardens, working on their allotment, breeding their pigeons or, like Jack, reading.
Jack's small library had grown and, although he was finding it increasingly difficult to concentrate, he perused his unread titles; "The Pickwick Papers", "The Jungle Book", "Kidnapped", "The Adventures of Huckleberry Finn" and picked out the first one, it was a thick volume and he thought it would keep him going for some time.

When they could escape Jack and Sarah would walk out together, although Jenny would annoyingly send George along as 'chaperone' whenever she could. Both Sarah and Jack liked George and his mischievous, energetic personality but there were moments when they would try and send him off to do some errand or other.

The arrangements for the wedding were progressing despite the strike and Earnest Weightman had indicated that there might be a house available for them to move into when they were married.

This was one of the things that was affecting Jack's concentration.

The idea of leaving home and setting up house with Sarah was both exciting and worrying in equal measure.

'Imagine,' said Sarah, smiling, 'our own home, our own tables and chairs…'

'It'll be a lot of work,' said Jack.

'Don't you worry about that,' said Sarah.

Her determination reminded him of his mother.

Jack visited Barney and whispered to him his news and concerns. Barney seemed to understand and his docile nature gave Jack some reassurance that everything would be alright.

He gave him an apple, brushed his coat and stroked his mane. Jim Moore had been watching,

'You'll spoil that horse if you're not careful,' he said.

Jack hadn't seen him and jumped.

'He works hard below ground, Mr Moore, just thought he needed a bit of a brush up.'

Jim Moore smiled, he was no stranger to loving animals and loving some more than others.

'Peter's out in the sheep fields, there's lambing going on. Why don't you go and see if you can give him a hand?'

For Mr Moore to invite him to help was a mark of confidence indeed.

'How's the strike going?'

'Still going I'm afraid, and from what Da is reading in the papers, we're no closer to an agreement.'

'Well, sooner it's over the better,' said Mr Moore, 'no guessing what people might be thinking if they start running out of food.'

Peter was in the sheep fields, it was all hands to the pump, round the clock, at lambing time.

'You've got to keep an eye on them,' he said to Jack, 'though Gordon Armstrong's a good shepherd and he's in charge. I'm giving him a hand. A lot of the ewes look after themselves and birth no problem.'

'Oh, good,' said Jack, who had decided he was a bit squeamish. Peter smiled.

'In those cases, you'll see the ewes lick their newborns clean and then watch as they stagger and stumble to their feet looking for a teat and a first feed. Very important those first few minutes. If you see a lamb struggling to breathe you can clean out its airways and if it's a bad or a first-time mother you sometimes have to make sure she gets a good sniff of her lamb so she doesn't reject it.'

'Sheep reject their own lambs?'

'Sometimes, out in the fields there's a lot of lambs, and a lot of ewes, they need to know which is theirs, they won't feed any other, they'll push it away. If you want to help then have a walk around the field, walk slowly and steadily, you don't want to spook a heavily pregnant ewe. See if there's a lamb or a ewe that's limping, or if they're stuck somewhere, sheep are experts at getting stuck, or if a ewe's on its side and seems to be struggling. Rescue stuck sheep straight away if you can but otherwise come and get me or Gordon right away.'

Jack did as he was told. The far corner of the field was boggy and a sheep was standing in the middle bleating, unable or unwilling to move.

Jack felt like this was an easy job and his plan was to find a stick and prod the sheep's behind with it to encourage it to move.

He found the stick easily enough but found it more difficult to get into position on the treacherous ground. The ewe didn't like losing sight of him and was twisting around and bleating loudly.

The act of turning must have broken the suction, and the ewe raised its two front feet and kind of hopped out, moving at just the moment that Jack was in mid-prod and causing him to lose his balance and fall face-down into the cold mud. The ewe ran off.

On his way back Jack was grumbling to himself and not really paying attention. A kind of grunt made him look up as, with a sploosh, a lamb was born not 20 paces away from him.

Jack froze, he didn't know what to do.

But the new mother did. With a rasping tongue she licked the yellow from her lamb's face, clearing the airways to breathe, and carried on down the length of the lamb's body. The lamb sneezed, a sneeze that shook its whole body, and then lay quietly, being licked.

After a few minutes the lamb turned so that its legs were beneath it and in a few more minutes, that felt like anxious hours to the watching Jack, it pushed itself up on its knees and then fell back.

Jack wondered if he should intervene, but he didn't know whether he should or not so he did nothing and just stood and watched without moving.

The newborn lamb persisted; half up, then down, half up, hold it, then down, and so it went until it was up, and hold it, and with slightly splayed legs, stood, and staggered and, its mother still licking it, unsteadily made its way towards the teat.

Jack moved away.

The new mother looked up at him.

Following Peter's advice, he moved slowly and steadily and gave mother and newborn a wide berth.

'What have you been doing?' said Peter when Jack re-appeared. He tried desperately not to laugh at the caked mud while the shepherd gave a grunt and muttered 'Townie', he'd seen nothing like this for a long time.

Jack told his tale.

'You miners,' said Peter, 'you just can't stay out of the dirt.'

'Ha, bloody ha,' said Jack and then told them about the birth he'd seen.

He had their attention.

'And what did you do?' asked Peter.

Jack was sure there was something he should have done but he had to be honest.

'I didn't do anything,' he said.

'Well done, lad,' said Gordon Armstrong, smiling at him for the first time, 'that's the thing about lambing, you have to know when to leave well alone, and when to interfere. By the sounds of it, you made the right choice, well done.'

'If you'd spooked the sheep,' said Peter, 'she might have left her lamb before they were properly bonded, that would have been a real problem.'

Jack felt he'd been lucky rather than clever.

'We'll make a shepherd of you yet,' said Peter.

'No thank you,' said Jack.

Peter laughed.

'If you go back to the farmhouse, I'm sure Ma will help you get cleaned up,' he said.

'Shame we don't have a sheep to lick you clean,' said Gordon.

Mrs Moore did her best, but when Jack got home he got another telling off.

'I don't expect you to come home giving me more to do because of the mess you're in,' said Jenny.

Jack was pleased his mother hadn't seen him before he'd got partially cleaned up.

Sarah sniggered.

'You may as well have gone down the pit,' she said.

Coal, desperately needed for the railway and shipping industries, was now in short supply and both were badly affected. Train timetables were increasingly disrupted and services cancelled.

Chapter 71

Three weeks was longer than most people expected the strike to last, but agreement seemed no closer.

The weather was cold, and it wasn't long before the absence of a steady supply of coal began to be felt.

Food supplies were also getting low, and money was running out.

To try and keep flagging spirits up, Earnest Weightman and others from the union organised events.

In "The Stackyard" a singing contest was held.

The place was packed out. There were two judges and the first prize was five shillings worth of groceries, the second prize was four shillings worth of groceries, the third prize was three shillings worth of mutton, and the fourth prize was three stones of potatoes and half a pound of tea. The groceries on offer were of a perishable nature and on the verge of being unsaleable.

Edward's rendition of "Cushy Butterfield" won him fourth place and when he got home Jenny was delighted with the surprise additions to their larder. She told Edward to take a stone of potatoes round to Mrs Tindale and asked him who had won the other prizes,

'First was Adam Thompson who sang "The Lambton Worm", I have to admit he's got a good baritone voice, the other two I can't remember, I was too engrossed in conversation with the landlord.'

'Why was that?'

'Well, Da had reminded me that beer goes off if it's not drunk.'

'That's true,' said Frank from his seat by the range.

'Tastes horrible, has to be thrown away,' said Grandpa.

'So, I was asking the landlord whether he'd like to pour his beer down the drain or whether he'd rather relent on his rule and let people buy one or two pints 'on tick'.'

'And?' said Jack, too enthusiastically for Sarah's liking.

'He said he'd think about it,' said Edward.

'In that case, let's have a cup of your prize tea to celebrate,' said Frank.

The next day there was a race around the colliery streets, the racers being cheered along the way.

The day after there was a football match. When one miner made too rough a tackle he was surrounded by players of both teams,

'Hey!' Adam Thompson said, on behalf of all, 'we're here for a bit of fun, anybody gets injured now they're not going to be able to work once the strike's over. You can tackle, but go easy or it'll be your pay we'll be taking for compensation.'

The rest of the game was played in good spirit; the final score was 5-5.

Strange to say in a mining village, but coal was becoming scarce, and people were scratching through the spoil heap to get what they could and carry it home in whatever form of conveyance they could muster, from sacks to carts, from barrows to boxes.

At the Lawley house, what was left of their coal allowance was being moved out of the coal bunker and into the house, there were too many stories of midnight pilfering to do anything else.

'Can we really not trust our neighbours and workmates?' said Jack.

'If you've got a big family that needs food and warmth, what would you do, blood's thicker than water,' said Edward.

'You mean the Tindales?'

Edward shrugged.

'I'm saying nothing, I'm just saying…'

'Better safe than sorry,' said Frank.

Jack knew that if Barney spent too much time in the open air he'd be unlikely to be happy to go back underground. Come to think about it, Jack was also getting a taste for daylight irrespective of the cold and the rain and he wasn't much looking forward to going back underground either.

The problem was that that was the only way he knew of making a living and now he was on the verge of married life, making a living was more important than ever.

To keep himself occupied he continued to help on the farm. Jack, Peter and Gordon were in the barn where a number of pens had been set up for the lambing time.

Gordon Armstrong was marking the new lambs and keeping the records. Most sheep had a single lamb, though some had twins. Unfortunately, not all of the births went well and Jack witnessed a stillborn that he found difficult to cope with.

'It's the job,' said the shepherd, 'you do your best, but sometimes…'

'There's one ewe had triplets,' said Peter, 'so what we're going to do is take one of them and get it accepted by the ewe that's lost her lamb.'

Gordon was already getting to work.

'What's he doing?' said Jack.

'Acceptance is all about smell,' said Peter, 'he has to quickly skin the stillborn lamb and wrap its skin around one of the triplets, tying it in place.'

Jack realised that this was not a job for him but watched in fascination as the shepherd introduced the fake child to the bereft mother.

'Surely she'll be able to see something's not right,' said Jack.

'She'll be suspicious of course but she wants to be a mother, she'll have milk in her teats, the urge is strong and it'll be the smell that settles it.'

Jack watched as the lamb bleated and moved towards its foster mother.

'A ewe can't easily cope with triplets, so by doing this, if it works, we'll be sorting out two problems in one go.'

The ewe pushed the lamb away with its nose.

'It's not working,' said Jack.

'Just watch,' said Peter.

The lamb persisted and the foster mother-to-be was uncertain. She sniffed and licked the fleece of her stillborn, tied with twine onto the stolen triplet. It was an uneasy few minutes, she was obviously trying to decide, and then the lamb found the teat and started to suck, and the ewe did not push it away. Soon they were nestling together in the pen.

'Great,' said Peter, 'they've bonded, we'll leave the fleece tied on for a few days and then it'll fall off or we'll take it off and, because they'll be properly bonded by then, the ewe won't mind.'

'Sometimes we have to rub the ewe's nose on the fleece,' said Gordon, 'if she's reluctant that is, this ewe was easy.'

Jack was amazed, what he'd seen was like a grizzly kind of magic, but it confirmed him in his view that, with all its difficulties, he was better suited to the work of a miner.

Chapter 72

As he'd promised, Earnest Weightman took Jack and Sarah to see an empty house on Third Street.

'The family left in a hurry,' said Earnest, 'suffice it to say that it was probably for the best. Before we go in, I think it's fair to say that there's good and there's bad. Leaving so quickly has meant that they've left quite a lot behind, which you'd be welcome to inherit if it was any help to you.'

Jack hadn't seen anything yet, but it felt like Christmas. He squeezed Sarah's hand. She squeezed back.

'If that's the good, then the bad is that they didn't really look after the place and you'll see there's a lot of work needs doing to get it back into good order. With it being a colliery house then there will be some help with that; craftsmen, paint, ladders, that kind of thing, but it will be a lot of work.'

'Can we have a look?' said Sarah.

'Certainly,' said Earnest, and he led them to the front door, over a step that should have been white but wasn't, and into the front parlour that smelt damp and musty.

'It's not been properly looked after for a while,' he said, 'my advice would be to not look at it as it is but rather try to see it as it could be.'

'What a mess!' said Jack.

'I did warn you,' said Earnest.

The first thing they saw, standing by the door, was an aspidistra that was looking very sorry for itself.

'Poor thing,' said Sarah, 'all it needs is its leaves wiping and a bit of cold tea and it'll be as right as rain.'

Earnest Weightman smiled.

There was a big couch along the wall to their left.

'I can't guarantee that there are no mice living in there,' he said.

Sarah shuddered, mice scurrying about her feet was not something she liked the thought of. Jack saw her reaction.

'I could get that lifted outside on a dry day and have a good look, then decide what to do,' he said.

Directly in front of them was a large, heavy, piece of furniture that was divided into two sections, a chest of drawers below and a set of open shelves above. It was sturdy but filthy. One of the drawers was missing a handle, one of the shelves was broken in two. Jack gave it a look over,

'I think this will clean up,' he said, 'the shelves could be for books.'

'Oh, yes, of course,' said Sarah, 'books, and the drawers for my sewing things.'

Earnest Weightman smiled at the sparring, they were acting like they were married already,

'I'll leave you two to look around,' he said, 'make a list and let me know. If I can help I will. Here's the keys, bring them back to me with your list.'

In the kitchen there was a table, it was black with ingrained grease and surrounded by chairs that were each badly damaged in different ways.

'I think I can get the table clean,' said Sarah, running her fingers over the surface.

'We need new chairs,' said Jack.

The range, that was full of grey ash, showed rust and a lack of care. In front of this was a rocking chair. Two oil lamps stood on the stone-slab floor that was black and covered in grime.

As they went upstairs, they were assaulted by a bad smell that only got worse. They soon found the reason. Hiding under the larger of the two beds were unemptied chamber pots. They could not believe that they had been left like this!

'Yeugh!' said Sarah.

'I think we should carry these out immediately,' said Jack.

'You go first,' said Sarah.

They carried them downstairs with great care and out into the back yard.

'I'll charge the privy with ash and put them down there,' said Jack.

As he went about that, Sarah finished her list; they might be able to use the bed frames but would need new horsehair mattresses. There was a flour sack-backed proggy mat that could be recovered but they would need new curtains, and repainting and re-papering throughout was essential. In the backyard the coalhouse and privy needed new doors and the privy needed scrubbing out with disinfectant.

When she looked in the cupboard under the stairs, she found a useable poss tub and a mangle. Pots, pans, utensils and dozens of other things would be needed, but none of it was impossible.

The house was filthy from top to bottom, and it was all Jack could do to stop Sarah rolling up her sleeves and getting on with it straight away. She turned to face Jack,

'We can do this,' she said.

'Are you sure?' he said, 'we can wait for a house that's in better condition.'

'And when will that be?'

'I can ask Mr Weightman.'

'I can make some patterned curtains, we can get help, with the strike on you've got time.'

'That's true,' said Jack, 'I'd just have to tell Peter I wouldn't be able to help him on the farm.'

'I'm sure he'd cope,' said Sarah.

It was harsh but true. Peter was more than capable of managing without him.

When Jack delivered the list and returned the keys to Earnest Weightman, Earnest could see that he was overwhelmed.

'I'll tell you what,' he said, 'as there's a lot of idle hands about at the minute why don't I see if I can get the work started. The house needs the work doing, no matter who moves into it next.'

'Can you?' said Jack.

'Yes, why don't I do that and then we'll see.'

The lack of coal had now brought the pottery industry to a standstill as there was no fuel for the kilns.

A soup kitchen was opened in the village, next to the school. Children were offered a breakfast of tea, currant bun, and bread and butter for 2d.

George was amongst the first in the queue.

A new Bill to give women the vote was defeated in Parliament. The result was that suffragette action became more violent, shop windows being smashed and acts of vandalism, including arson, were on the increase.

'If the Minimum Wage Bill is defeated,' said Edward, 'then there'll be a lot more violence than that.'

'It is in difficulty,' said Frank, 'I read in the paper that the Owners are lobbying against it and the voice of the Union is hardly heard. There's a move to get the Police involved and force us back to work.'

Jenny shuddered.

'That wouldn't work,' said Edward, 'we've gone too far and risked too much to stop now.'

'Just please let there not be violence,' said Jenny.

Sarah nodded. Grandpa shook his head. Jack stayed silent, he didn't know what to say. Along with Sarah he was hoping for the future and holding on day by day.

'As long as nobody starts breaking the strike, as long as we can stick together, then I think it'll be alright,' said Frank.

'There's families suffering, there's pressure to go back to work,' said Jenny.

'And there's reasons not to,' said Frank.

By the fourth week things were getting serious.

The Owners and the Unions were deadlocked, households were paying double or triple for their coal if they could get it at all, and industry was running out of it. The consequences of the strike were spreading wider and deeper by the day.

The Liberal Government, with Herbert Asquith as Prime Minister, was getting more and more jittery, the idea that, under their watch, the economy was being brought to a standstill was bad politics, and unlikely to go down well when it came to the polls.

Edward, like a growing number of others, was scouring the spoil heap for the pieces of coal that had been thrown away. He had a sack with him that had contained flour. After an hour's toil he managed to fill the sack with poor coal, whose burning qualities he doubted.

'We'll mix it in with the good stuff we've got left,' said his father, 'that'll make it go further.'

'This is beyond a joke now,' said Jenny with her hands on her hips, 'I can't cook properly, we're going cold at night, it's time you went back to work.'

'We can't give in now,' said Edward, 'if we give up now everything will just go back to how it was and the strike will have been for nothing.'

'There's something got to happen,' said Frank, an edge of desperation in his voice, 'Owners have no coal to sell, their shareholders are unhappy, even when they have coal, transporting it is difficult.'

'And that's a good thing?' said Jenny, 'that the misery is spreading.'

'It's got to get worse before it gets better,' said Edward.

Jenny bit her tongue.

'William Jones' shoulder's no better, they'll need coal like the rest of us but he won't be able to collect it, so, Edward, when you've emptied that sack why don't you go and fill it again and take it round to them. Sarah is sleeping there after all.'

Edward started to say something, but his father caught his eye and he swallowed the words,

'Yes, Ma, of course,' he said, 'I'll do that.'

'After that, I'll buy you a pint,' said Frank.

He looked at his wife, 'Thanks to Edward, the pub is letting us buy on tick for a bit, better to sell it than let perfectly good beer go to waste.'

'Hmm, then only one,' she said, 'you have to pay for it sometime.'

That night, Grandpa caught a couple of boys on his allotment. They were like moving shadows.

'Hallo, there,' he said.

The shapes stopped dead.

'I can see you,' said Grandpa.

'Sorry,' said one of the shapes, 'is this your allotment? Must have got mixed up in the dark.'

'You can take two eggs,' said Grandpa, 'but not all of them, a couple of leeks, parsnips and a cabbage. But that's all mind, don't hurt the hens…'

'But Ma sent us out for…'

'Shhh!'

'You do what I've said and we'll forget all about it. Don't do it again, come ask me if you're in need and I'll be fair with you,' he paused, 'if you don't do as I say then I'm going to have to tell on you, do you understand, there's a lot of people struggling that still don't like thieves,' he paused again, 'do you understand?'

'Yes,' said the smaller shadow.

'Yes… and thanks,' said the larger shadow.

Grandpa smiled, a smile he was sure they couldn't see, and then he turned and trudged off home.

'You're back early,' said Jenny.

'Got distracted,' said Grandpa.

'Where's the veg?' said Jenny.

'I'm going to pop out for it in a minute,' said Grandpa, 'any chance of a cup of tea first?'

'I suppose so,' said Jenny.

'Anyway,' said Grandpa 'everybody knows that leeks are best picked close to midnight.'

Jenny knew she was missing something but this was her father and if he didn't want to tell her, then she didn't want to know.

'No,' she said, 'actually I've never heard that!'

Earnest Weightman had somehow organised a team of men to work on the house on 3rd Street. With so little to do the men were pleased to get the work.

Jack had put the chamber pots in the middle of the back yard and covered them with sacking.

'We'll not be using these again,' he'd said, 'and we can start making a pile of things we just want to throw away.'

'That's a good idea,' said Sarah, 'and you can start with that couch.'

'It's heavy, I'll ask Edward to help,' said Jack.

As Edward and Jack approached the couch, they saw movement and heard scratching sounds.

'I think you've made a good decision,' said Edward.

As they lifted the couch two or three mice fell out of the bottom and raced around the floor.

'Better get this outside quickly,' said Edward, 'then we can come back and deal with the runaways.'

When they'd dropped the couch outside, Edward said,

'I hope you don't have to leave this here too long, the house'll be invaded, the mice'll come in for the warmth.'

'There is no warmth at the moment,' said Jack, 'but Earnest Weightman's sending a horse and cart round later today to take away our rubbish.'

The broken kitchen chairs followed, together with the horsehair mattresses, a number of items of clothing and other personal effects.

'They must have left in a hurry,' said Jack, 'what a mess they left.'

Earnest Weightman arrived with the Carter and supervised the loading.

'If there's more later then I can send the cart back,' he said.

'How did the house get in such a state?' asked Sarah.

'I'm not going to break any confidences by telling you what happened,' said Earnest, 'but I'm sure the neighbours will tell you something if you really want to know. My advice is not to ask and concentrate on giving this house a fresh start. There'll be two men round tomorrow, they'll do a bit of painting and papering, I think you should get all the windows open while you're here, the house needs a good airing.'

Although they'd done what they could to chase out the mice Sarah was not convinced and borrowed a cat from an old school friend. The cat was reputed to be a 'good mouser'.

For a few days they kept the cat indoors and found the 'gifts' of body parts and whole bodies left for them, and then nothing.

Sarah returned the cat with thanks and the promise of a new blouse.

'Maybe we should get a cat,' said Sarah.

'Let's get in first,' said Jack.

Sarah got to work.

She wiped the aspidistra's leaves and added cold tea to the pot.

On her knees she scrubbed the kitchen floor twice with hot water and Lifebuoy soap, mopping, wiping and squeezing the dirty water into a bucket.

A man came round to sweep the chimney and check and clean out the congealed soot and ash from the range. Sarah was pleased but the additional mess had her cleaning the floor again!

Once the metal surfaces of the range had been cleared, scrubbed and blacked, she lit a fire with the scarce coal that somehow Earnest Weightman had managed to conjure up.

The proggy mat was soaped and washed and hung up to dry, the colours rediscovered.

George came over and helped bring in more water. The water tap at the end of the back lane had a corrugated metal surround 12 inches in diameter, a bell type dome on the top and a grid to rest your bucket on. According to George it was easier to use than the one on 2nd Street.

Men, sent round by Earnest Weightman, brought their own paint, paper and ladders and got on with the job, only stopping when Jenny arrived with fresh scones that she had baked from her dwindling supply of flour, and a pot of tea.

They even repaired the drawers and shelves on the sideboard in the parlour.

Sarah, helped by Jenny, set about making new curtains from material they had to hand.

Sarah and Jenny also completed making the outfits for the wedding that they were responsible for. When there were no men about, they tried them on,

'That looks good, Sarah,' said Jenny.

'I like yours too,' said Sarah, 'I think we're ready.'

'All we need now is a wedding.'

When it came to doing work for others, Jenny and Sarah had to accept delayed payment for some of their completed garments. As they trusted all of their customers, they much preferred doing this rather than not doing the work and letting people down.

Bartering across the allotments and between households became the norm; eggs for bread, coal for cheese.

There was less travelling outside of the local area now and in terms of transport the horse had returned to its preeminent position.

Hundreds of pounds locally, and millions of pounds nationally, were not available to spend and all the local retailers that relied on the mining communities as customers were suffering.

The Co-op was selling 'on tick' and all retailers of perishable goods were forced to do the same.

Sentiment outside of the mining communities was turning against them as town's people struggled to understand the causes of the strike and the failure to return to work, whilst being directly and adversely affected by its consequences.

As a mark of good faith Mr Denby even allowed Jack to defer a couple of the payments on his suit.

Nobody was winning but neither side wanted to give in. The strike had become a trial of strength. The price of any remaining coal stocks soared, even well-to-do families in the towns and cities were starting to feel the effects.

The conversations in smoke-filled rooms were becoming more acrimonious, each party blaming the other for intransigence.

In the mining village the soup kitchen was busy and, even though she was not short of things to do, Sarah volunteered some of her time to help.

Nobody thought it would go on this long.

A National Strike such as this was unprecedented but unfortunately lit a flame for the future.

Every corner of Society was affected, every space that needed coal heating, every steam engine that needed firing up.

The comforts of home, train travel, shipping, every industry that needed coal; iron and steel, the potteries... all were imploding.

When a structure is built on one brick it is vulnerable to collapse when that brick is loosened.

Unemployment, soup kitchens, social unrest, political panic – the strike had to be stopped!

In the colliery village tempers were rising. Jenny wanted an end to the strike. Some Owners thought they could starve the men back to work.

Frank was following the news in the daily papers.

There was an increase in poaching and in stealing produce from farms.

Jim Moore no longer went out at night without his gun.

'We've always got along, the farms and the mines,' he said to Jack, 'but it isn't me that's decided to go on strike, and I don't want to be stolen from, I work too hard for that.'

The Owners had underestimated the stamina of the Union and their members but, at the same time, the Union was coming close to overplaying its hand. If the unrest grew, if the strike was broken by an enforced return to work, then the whole collaborative structure that had been built up over decades would collapse ... with no obvious alternative to fill the vacuum.

The Liberal Government stepped in.

Not unanimously but after many thousands of words had been expended and by majority, and in haste, by men who could wax lyrical about the working conditions of the miners but whose lives were as foreign to the experience of working underground as they were to the experience of walking on the moon.

The Coal Mines Minimum Wage Bill made its disputed way through Parliament and into Law. The Government hoped that this would be enough.

After 37 days of strike action, the Unions put to ballot a proposal for a return to work: "Are you in favour of resuming work pending a settlement of the minimum rates of wages in the various grades by the district boards to be appointed under the Mines Minimum Wage Act?"

The result of the vote was a straight majority in favour of continuing the strike, but Union rules required a two thirds majority and so the miners, by default, accepted a return to work.

News of the settlement spread quickly.

'Told you it wouldn't last forever,' said Edward.

'It's been too long,' said Jenny, 'and what have we gained?'

'A minimum wage, Jenny, something we've never had before,' said Frank, 'at least that gives us some security, something we can depend on.'

'And what is it, this minimum wage? In shillings and pence, what is it?'

'We haven't completely agreed on that,' said Frank.

'At least now we can go back to work with our heads held high… we won, Unity is Strength,' said Edward.

'Did we, did we really, how much of our savings have we spent over the last 5 weeks? How many bills have we built up? How long will it take us to recover from that?'

Grandpa, Jenny's father, intervened,

'Jenny,' was all he said.

'But…'

'Jenny, it's time to look forward,' said Grandpa.

Jenny's shoulders sagged, her father put his hand on her arm, it was a rare gesture.

'We can start getting back to "normal",' said Jack.

Jenny moved to the range and put the kettle on.

'Alright,' she said, 'I've got lots to do if you three are going back to work tomorrow.'

The first thing the miners did was deliver coals to themselves. The lines of coal shed doors hung open, protruding into the back lanes in welcome anticipation.

Jack told Peter the strike was over,
'Thank goodness,' said Peter, 'it's been increasingly like being under siege here. I'll miss your help but I'm pleased it's over.'

The pit ponies were moved back underground.

Sarah was looking around their house with Jack,
'Shame it didn't last another week,' she said, 'we were making really good progress on fixing up the house.'
Jack laughed.

The men went back to work.
Underground some walls had moved, some roofs had sagged, it was a dangerous time, the miners had to reaccustom themselves to their old haunts.

The Coal Hewer's minimum wage was fixed at 5s 6d per day. Frank and Edward were earning 7s 1d per day, an increase of $3\frac{3}{4}\%$ over their pre-strike pay. At this rate, if all had remained stable afterwards, which it didn't, then it would have taken about 3yrs to recover the pay they'd lost during the strike.

'There is one thing though,' Peter said to Jack, 'that pit pony, Barney. Father and I have been talking, when it comes his time to retire, we'd like to buy him and give him a home on the farm.'
This shook Jack to the core; it was so unexpected. Barney retiring! He'd never even thought about it. Barney was his trusted partner and friend underground. The thought of someone just buying him as if he were a piece of furniture was shocking.

As the thought sank in however, he understood how generous the offer was. Barney had a secure future whilst so many other pit pony's road led only to the abattoir.

'Thanks,' he said.

Less than 10 days later the RMS Titanic, the unsinkable ship, sunk in the Northern Atlantic Ocean. Struck by Nature in the form of an iceberg, Nature won out over metal and steam and more than 1,500 lives were lost.

Frank handed his first new pay packet over to Jenny,
'I think it was all worth it,' he said.
Jenny was less sure,
'Let's not do it again,' she said.

3 months later an explosion in a pit in Yorkshire killed 38 men. Later the same day a rescue party went below ground, another explosion occurred, killing 53 of them.

Chapter 73

The wedding day came round with both the icy slowness of an advancing glacier and that of a runaway train.

Jenny was grateful that she could help with the preparations and wasn't shy to call in the assistance of friends and neighbours when she thought it necessary.

Most weddings were happy events, though some were rushed, and people were pleased to get involved, it gave them something different to think and gossip about.

On the day before the wedding Jenny had insisted on photographs, and the family had gone to the photographer's studio in the nearby town.

It was an additional expense but she wanted photographs to remember the day and knew it was important as she treasured the few photographs she had of her own life.

She had always regretted not being able to afford photographs of her children when they were babies but felt that for this occasion it would be money well spent.

George was the problem.

He didn't feel comfortable in his outfit, and couldn't sit still, and when he was sitting still, he was pulling a face.

The photographer did his best but it was his father's stricter approach that finally won the day,

'George, sit still and smile,' he said, 'if you don't then you're not coming to the wedding.'

The idea of missing something so exciting, including scrabbling around for the pennies that Jack was going to scatter as he and his new wife left the church, was too big a penalty. He gritted his teeth and obeyed long enough for the photographs to be taken.

Sarah's wedding outfit was topped off by an elegant blue straw hat with a brim, and a flower on the side.

Jenny and Sarah had agreed that the clothes worn at the wedding would be serviceable so that they could be worn regularly after the event.

Sarah looked very smart, as did Jack in his three-piece dark blue suit, tie, polished black leather shoes and bowler hat, which he would obediently remove as he entered the church.

Sarah's hair was put up on the morning of the wedding, rising upwards from the face and worn high over the forehead. This was a very popular style and Sarah had seen it in an advert during her shopping trip to Newcastle with Jack. Once the decision had been made, she and Jenny had made practice runs so that on the morning of the wedding they were sure to get it exactly right.

The weather on the day was unusually mild for the time of year. The wedding party left their colliery houses and walked to the church. Jack had arranged for a horse drawn farm cart, driven by Peter, to take him and Sarah to the church and then back to his parent's house, which would be their first journey together as man and wife.

Mrs Tindale stayed behind to set out the food on the Lawley kitchen table and make sure that the kettle would be on the boil by the time the family and guests arrived.

The ceremony itself was a blur, and after all the 'I do's' had been said in all the right places, Jack and Sarah were pronounced man and wife. It was a strange feeling that so much planning, so much anticipation and so much pent-up anxiety had all come to a head in such a straightforward moment.

As they left the church, George ran ahead and took up a strategic position. Jack put his hand in his pocket and brought out a collection of coppers; farthings, halfpennies and pennies, and hurled them up and away into the air, and in the opposite direction to where George was standing. Waiting children ran after them and stooped to pick them up.

'Aww!' yelled George.

Jack put his hand into his other pocket and drew out more coins and this time threw them away and over George's head. George turned around in glee and was soon on his hands and knees searching through the grass.

'Good job we had the photographs taken yesterday,' said Sarah.

After the ceremony had started, a slim figure had quietly entered through the open door and moved quickly to stand at the back. Wearing a pale blue dress, long sleeves, buttoned at the neck, a hat whose brim shaded her face, she waited until the church was empty before she slipped out and walked away.

'Alice?'

The figure stopped but did not turn, stood for a moment, and then continued to walk away.

Jenny hurried to catch up and laid a hand on her arm.

'Alice,' she said, 'I'm pleased you came.'

The figure turned, there were tears in her eyes.

'I meant to stay away, but I couldn't. When I saw the announcement in the paper I had to come.'

'Come over,' said Jenny, 'talk to Sarah.'

Alice pulled away.

'I can't,' she said, 'she's a woman now, I don't want to get in her way.'

'But you...'

Alice gently raised a hand, 'No, Jenny, I've seen her and I wish her and your son every happiness, but I must go.'

'At least tell me,' said Jenny, looking at Alice earnestly, 'Are you well? Are you alright?'

Alice smiled, 'I've started again, Jenny, I'm happy in my new life... I have my regrets, of course I do, but I have to believe that I did the right thing... the right thing for both of us... and if it was the right thing then, then it still is.'

'Are you sure?'

'Yes, Jenny, I'm sure. Thank you for what you've done.'

'I don't need thanks; Sarah is a credit to you.'

Alice bowed her head, turned and walked away. Jenny watched her retreating back until she turned a corner and was lost to sight.

Chapter 74

The catering for the reception at the Lawley's house had been organised by Jenny and put together with the help of several of her neighbours and friends.

Mrs Tindale had set the food out, it was a lavish spread of sandwiches, pies, meats, cheese, pickles, cake and scones.

Jenny used the plates, bowls and other items of china that she had inherited from her mother and usually stood only on display. After the event she would carefully clean them and tidy them away to await the next special family event.

There was as much tea as the guests could drink, although Jenny also had some ginger beer or lemonade, but nothing stronger. If the men wanted anything else then they were welcome to go down the pub after they'd eaten and contributed sufficiently to the polite conversation.

There would not be any alcohol on offer to those in Jenny's house, not even to celebrate Sarah's wedding, what alcohol there was would be kept safely in the cupboard.

As soon as Jenny allowed them, Frank and Edward left the clearing up to the women and made their way to 'The Stackyard' for a celebratory drink.

Later, when Sarah could escape the congratulations, she asked Jenny,

'Who was it you were talking to?'

'What do you mean?'

'After the service, I saw you talking to someone, someone in a blue dress, pale blue.'

'Oh,' said Jenny.

'You seemed to be talking together very seriously.'

Jenny looked into Sarah's eyes.

'She was an old friend,' she said.

Sarah staggered, reached out for Jenny's arm. Jenny nodded and the two women hugged each other.

Jack was watching from a distance. This was so out of character for his mother that he was immediately worried that something was seriously wrong and hurried over.

'Are you two alright?' he asked.

The two women took a step apart, both with their own understanding.

'Can't a mother-in-law congratulate her new daughter-in-law on her wedding day?' said Jenny.

'Can't a daughter-in-law allow her new mother-in-law to congratulate her on her wedding day?' said Sarah.

Jack raised his hands. He knew when he was beaten. When the two most important women in his life ganged up on him, then he knew he had no chance.

'Alright,' he said, 'I was just wondering whether my new wife would like me to bring her a drink.'

The two women relaxed.

'That would be very nice,' said Sarah, 'perhaps some ginger beer.'

While Jack was out of earshot, Sarah asked,

'Is your friend doing alright? Is she happy?'

'She told me she was happy and she said how proud of you she was.'

Sarah caught her breath and coloured, trying hard to keep her emotions in check,

'Oh, good,' she said, and then, 'Thank you, Jenny, thank you.'

Jack arrived, glass in hand.

'Good timing, Jack,' said Sarah, 'I am thirsty, I could really do with this.'

'I could do with one too,' said Jenny.

Jack looked surprised; his mother never drank anything other than tea.

Before she was allowed to safely escape to her own house, that she had worked so hard on, cleaning and setting it to rights in the days and nights leading up to the wedding, Jenny led Sarah into the parlour and to the table where the family bible was open and waiting.

'You're part of our family history now,' she said to Sarah, 'and I'd like you to add your name to our family bible.'

Sarah realised how important this was and the pen trembled in her hand.

'It's alright,' said Jenny smiling, 'take a few moments if you like, after you've written your name in there, I'll add the day and the month and the year.'

Sarah took a deep breath and signed her name as neatly as she could, with Jenny watching over her shoulder.

'Very good,' said Jenny, 'now off the two of you go and we'll see you sometime tomorrow. I'll finish up and tidy up here.'

Sarah wasn't completely sure but she thought that Mrs Tindale winked at her on the way out. Whatever the case Sarah turned bright crimson as she left, hand in hand with her new husband.

Frank and Edward returned from the pub sometime later. Frank, in particular, had celebrated hard and was a little the worse for wear. This was unusual for him and he was heard before he was seen as he came down the middle of the back lane supported by Edward and singing 'Cushy Butterfield' at the top of his voice.

'That's never Dad,' said George.

'Yes, lad, I'm afraid it is, he's drunk,' said Jenny, 'I'll go and get him and hopefully he'll just go straight to bed.'

The back gate banged open. The singing stopped, but they could hear Frank talking in a loud voice.

'Come on then! Come on then...'

Jenny picked up the oil lamp from the table, opened the back door, and looked out and into the yard.

By the light of the lamp she could see Frank with his fists up, circling the mangle. Edward was laughing.

'What on earth are you doing?' said Jenny.

'I'm letting this fella here see that I can still look after meself,' said Frank.

'But there's nobody there,' said Jenny.

'He bumped into the mangle,' laughed Edward, 'he thinks it attacked him!'

'Mangle?' said Frank, 'what mangle? Where's that big fella gone? Run off has he!'

Edward took his father by the arm and maneuvered him in through the back door, past his scowling mother.

George burst into a fit of the giggles,

'Da was trying to fight the mangle. Wait until I tell everybody tomorrow,' he said.

'Don't you dare,' said Jenny, 'get to bed and keep this to yourself.'

Chapter 75

Like children they lay together.

Jack reached over and gently touched Sarah's breast that lay tantalisingly pliant beneath her cotton nightdress. He looked deep into her dark brown eyes.

'Hello husband,' she said.

Jack smiled; it sounded right.

Sarah reached out her own hand and with the tips of her fingers traced the rough line of the old scar above Jack's eye. Slowly as they touched and moved together they explored each other sensitively, taking their time, each putting their trust in the other, each enjoying the feeling of a melding, of a ceasing to be a distinct being, of being instead a Jack&Sarah, a something else, a something that had no name but was greater than either of them, no longer conscious of where their own body ended and the other began.

All their senses were more alive than they had ever been before, each pore was tingling, they were like an irresistible force of nature, a tide that could not be turned, a river that strained to flood.

They lay together on their new mattress, between their new sheets, in their new home, yellow and blue honey-scented flowers in a vase on the windowsill, curtains drawn, they lay there for what was both an instant and an eternity.

In these moments they each knew that their lives would never be the same.

Words that Jack had heard but had never before known the proper meaning of came to his mind and flew to his lips, without effort, impossible to restrain.

'I love you,' he said.

She smiled, 'And I love you too, Jack, I think I always have.'

They kissed, tasting each other, their lips moving slowly and carefully exploring each hill and dale, each undulation of flesh and skin. They touched as if each part of their body had discovered a new sensation. They saw each other as if for the first time, seeing as well with eyes closed, as with eyes open. They heard the sound of their own hearts beating, the sound of their breathing and the feeling of warm breath on their skin, a feeling of hope, of life, of youth, of renewal, of a future that now rushed towards them, ready to be drunk to the full.

Sarah was determined to run their home as best she could.

Their income should be sufficient and her ambition was to have a little left over in order to build up a few savings that they could fall back on when there was a need.

She talked to more experienced women like Jenny, Mrs Tindale and Mrs Jones and wrote notes on what she thought important to remember.

One evening after Jack had cleaned himself up, he caught her at her writing and asked her what she was doing. She explained sheepishly but was encouraged when Jack showed both interest and curiosity.

'Would you like to know what I've learned?' she asked.

Jack smiled.

'I would,' he said, 'perhaps I could listen better with a cup of tea.'

'You and your tea,' said Sarah, 'I'll put the kettle on, you get the cups.'

Soon they were seated at their kitchen table, tea by their side,

'Right,' said Sarah, 'this is what I've learnt so far… firstly, pay for everything in cash, don't put things on tick unless you really have to, debt is to be avoided.'

'I completely agree,' said Jack, 'although we had to buy the clock, chest of drawers, mattresses and whatever else on instalments, we had no choice.'

'Yes, but we set a budget of no more than £5, a lot of money I know, and we'll pay it back at 2s a week. You have to do that when you're just starting out, but we'll try and pay cash whenever we can.'

'Agreed,' said Jack.

'Second, draw up a list of necessities and allocate amounts of money to each, do not overspend on things you don't need.'

'Third, learn how to buy cheaply, I'm good at that, and how to cook wholesome and tasty food. Use everything, including any leftovers, do not waste scraps of meat for example, make a stew or a soup with them.'

'That makes sense to me,' said Jack, 'I don't mind eating leftovers, a stew with bread and butter to dip in it is good for me.'

'It would be good if we could grow some of our own food, maybe I can try carrots in the front garden.'

'Don't do too much,' said Jack, 'you're doing a lot already.'

'Fourth, make your own clothes.'

'You're expert at that,' said Jack, 'and I'd rather have you doing your sewing than growing carrots.'

'Sixth, don't spend too much on beer and tobacco!'

Jack laughed.

'That's me told then. I don't smoke but I understand about the beer. I do like to go down the pub occasionally though.'

'Moderation is fine,' said Sarah, a memory of her father's weakness flashing through her mind.

Jack saw the worry on her face and guessed the cause.

'Moderation it is, Sarah, you can give me the money we can afford, I'll not buy beer on tick.'

Sarah relaxed a little.

'You should write a book,' said Jack.

'Don't make fun of me,' said Sarah.

Jack put his arms around her.

'I didn't mean to,' he said, 'it's just that I'm so proud of you.'

'Are you?' she said.

'I am, I really am,' said Jack.

The tea was left to go cold as Sarah led him upstairs.

Chapter 76

As a married man, Jack felt his new responsibilities and asked advice from Earnest Weightman,

'I want to make sure Sarah will be alright if I get sick or injured,' he said.

'A wise man,' said Earnest, 'I wish there were more men thought ahead like this, it's much better than assuming that nothing can or will happen to you.'

'I've seen too much,' said Jack, 'although some accidents are down to mistakes others are just down to chance.'

'Have you talked to your wife about this?'

'I don't want Sarah to worry about the risks underground,' said Jack, 'her worrying won't help anything.'

This was a common approach; the men did not like to talk to their wives about what it was truly like underground. In this regard Jack was just like his father.

'Well,' said Earnest, 'as you know the National Insurance Act gives you some protection; sick pay and access to a doctor for free, but does not protect your wife if she gets ill or injured. If you want that extra protection I, on behalf of the Union, would suggest the Permanent Relief Fund, that we recommended strongly before the NI Act came in. It'll cost you a bit of money but it could put your mind at rest.'

'I think I'll do that,' said Jack.

'I'll get you the details, the money will be taken directly out of your pay.'

When Jack told Sarah what he'd done she said,

'Do we need that extra expense? Can we afford it?'

'Can we afford not to? We need to look after each other.'

'Sometimes, Jack, you are sooo… ooh come here!'

The payments began to be made within the week.

Sarah kept track of her weekly expenditure:

Co-op repayment	2s
Bread and Flour	3s
Meat and Dripping	4s
Tea and sugar	1s
Butter and Cheese	2s
Potatoes and Vegetables	2s
Soap, Candles, oil	2s
Clothing	4s
Jack's beer	1s
Other needs & payments	12s
(Coal – free allocation)	
Savings	3s
Income	36s

And she'd added a note as a reminder: "Don't spend too much on beer, at 2d a pint we're paying as much on beer per week as on tea and sugar!"

She tried to explain to Jack.

'The "other" is so big because a pair of boots, for example, could cost 10s, or I might need some material, or you might need some tools, there's lots of unknowns and I've tried to use an average, some weeks it will be more, some less.'

'And my pay will vary,' said Jack.

'There's that too,' said Sarah screwing up her nose, 'it's all so difficult.'

Jack smiled.

'I think you've done a good job,' he said, 'I can go down the pit knowing that when I come back up again I can still afford a beer.'

She dug him in the ribs.

'Be serious.'

'I am, I think your list makes good sense and I'm very pleased that we seem to be alright, a lot of households have much less than us to live on and more mouths to feed.'

For breakfast Sarah made sure there was always tea, sugar, milk, bread and butter and, every now and again, fried bacon with bread fried in the fat that was left in the pan or eggs; fried, scrambled, poached or boiled, sometimes dropped off by Grandpa from his allotment. Jack didn't want too big a breakfast before starting his shift so whatever the breakfast was, the portions were small.

For lunch Sarah made Jack a bait of sandwiches and cold tea, a lump of cheese or a meat pie.

For dinner there might be boiled beef and carrots or a piece of roast beef or scrag of mutton boiled with turnips, or soup, or cold meat leftovers from the day before, or shepherd's pie, or stew, or beef sausages with boiled or mashed potatoes and vegetables.

For supper there was a cup of tea, bread and butter, or perhaps cheese, or picking at leftovers.

Sarah liked to tell Jack what she'd learnt whether he really wanted to know or not. When the evening meal was finished, cleared away and cleaned up, when the coal and the water was brought in for the next morning, then Sarah would do her sewing and Jack would sit in the rocking chair by the range reading a book or the newspaper.

It was then that Sarah would share how she was feeling and Jack would listen.

'It's the time it takes,' she said, 'and you have to keep an eye on it, you can't walk away, that's a recipe for disaster. If you're roasting, boiling or baking. A pound of beef, mutton or lamb takes 30 minutes, if it's 2 pounds it's 45 minutes. For cooking vegetables its 20 to 30 minutes for potatoes, cabbage, spinach, and sprouts, 40 to 60 minutes for carrots, you've got to know all of these things, that's why the mantle clock's so important…'

'It also gets me to work on time,' added Jack. Partly to prove he was listening.

'...and the tricks, like toasting a crust to nearly black and putting it into the water you're boiling cabbage in to prevent that very unpleasant smell you'd get otherwise.'

Jack did listen, he was not expert in any of these things, his mother used to look after him and now his wife did. He knew how to lead a pit pony in the near dark, how best to put a coal tub back on the rails, but he didn't know how to boil a potato.

'And the soot,' said Sarah, 'if it gets on your kettle or pans then they don't boil as fast and the same with the range, if the soot builds up then nothing heats up like it should.'

'Anything else?' asked Jack, wanting to get back to his book.

'You know the grease left on the pans? Instead of getting rid of that you can use it on the sticks we use to light the fire, it makes them burn up much quicker and ignite the coal much better.'

'That's a good one,' said Jack, genuinely interested, 'I'd never have thought of that, but it makes a lot of sense.'

Like Jenny, Sarah also hated dirt, she believed that anything dirty could make you ill and a dirty larder was worst of all. She was also influenced by Elsie Walton and spent extra to buy Lifebuoy soap and use it religiously to disinfect her larders, cupboards and shelves, believing its claims that it destroyed germs and made everything "sweet and wholesome". She used Sunlight Soap for washing pans, knives, forks, dishes as well as for the laundry and in Jack's bath when he came home.

'I use my scales a lot,' said Sarah, 'I don't like to guess the weights, I'm happier if I've weighed things out, even if it takes me longer.'

'I can understand that,' said Jack, 'we're always checking and re-checking things that we do underground, walls can shift, roofs can sag, it's always better to be safe than sorry.'

Sarah thought that weighing out a pound of flour rather than guessing the quantity wasn't as important as what Jack had just let slip. She knew his work underground was dangerous but, like most of the miners, he preferred not to talk about it.

As one of her recipe books put it; "guesses produce nothing but messes".

And time passed and rains came, and sunshine. Routines were established and shifts completed. There were more smiles than tears.

Jack stuck to his work underground, Barney by his side. The coal was cutting easily and was of good quality. At least once a week Sarah and Jack would go around to Jenny's for a meal and would always take something with them, even though Jenny would always say that they didn't have to bother.

Sarah still made time for her sewing, and it was one of the reasons that she would go around to see Jenny, to make use of the sewing machine.

Jenny would ask her how things were going and Sarah would readily tell her stories of what she and Jack had been up to. Jenny thought that she now knew more about what Jack was doing than when he'd been living at home!

Sarah took a blouse she'd just completed around to one of the houses on First Street.

The couple, Mr and Mrs Proctor, had no children and instead kept a dog. It was a wiry haired, sturdy, grizzle and tan border terrier that gloried in the name of "Scrap". It was difficult to call it a pet as it was very much its own master. The couple would talk to it as if it were a child and the dog would listen patiently, but how much he actually understood was anyone's guess.

Small and muscular Scrap had earned his name from his attitude to conflict. He would never back away from a fight no matter how uneven the contest seemed to be. It didn't matter if the opponent was larger or heavier, if it had made the foolish decision to test Scrap's mettle, then it was in for as shock.

As evidence of his temperament one of Scrap's ears, which were black in colour, was torn and hung down. The old saying "his bark is worse than his bite" did not apply to Scrap whose approach to battle escalated in clearly defined stages.

The first warning was a low growl along with the baring of teeth, sharp teeth, set in a muscular jaw. If this deterrent did not suffice, then barking would follow, increasing in intensity, and more likely than not accompanied by lively movements back and forth, his eyes focused on the source of the threat.

If that still did not do the trick then the fight would be engaged and Scrap would give no quarter. He was never the first to back away and many was the time that he had to be grabbed by the collar and lifted, kicking and screaming his discontent, back to his owners.

He was well known in the village and, despite these forays into violence, well liked, for he was friendly with children and docile, though protective, in the home.

If he took a dislike to somebody it would not be kept a secret and Mr or Mrs Proctor would have to remove him to another room and firmly shut the door.

When Sarah visited however, Scrap fussed around her, licking her hand.

'He doesn't take to everyone,' said Mrs Proctor, who was trying on the blouse and looking at herself in the mirror, 'but he's certainly taken a fancy to you.'

'He's such a softy,' said Sarah, scratching Scrap behind his one undamaged ear.

Mrs Proctor laughed.

'A softy! Well, well, that's a new one.'

She took off the blouse.

'Thank you, Sarah, the blouse is perfect, it fits very well.'

She left the room and then returned with the money in her hand.

'You know,' she said, as she handed over the coins, 'Scrap is normally suspicious of strangers.'

She thought for a moment.

'You're not pregnant are you? A dog knows, you know.'

Sarah blushed.

'Oh, no, Mrs Proctor, I don't think so.'

When she got home, she felt nauseous and was sick, she thought it must have been something she'd eaten.

About a month later, Sarah was sure, and she told Jack.

'Wow!' he said.

'Are you pleased?'

'Pleased? I'm…' he stopped, 'I don't know what I am, come here…'

After he'd let her go, she said,

'I'd like to be the one to tell Jenny.'

'Of course,' he said.

Jenny was in the kitchen when Sarah told her she was pregnant.

'That's good, pet,' she said knowingly, 'I was wondering.'

'I am a bit worried,' said Sarah, 'I've been a bit unwell lately.'

Jenny looked at her seriously.

'It's your first, you're bound to be a bit worried, and a bit of sickness is nothing to be concerned about.'

She smiled at Sarah.

'I'll look after you, don't worry, I'll look after you.'

Sarah would have loved to tell her mother, Alice, the news, but she had no idea where she was, so that was impossible.

One of the immediate impacts of the news was that Jenny started knitting, aiming to provide the baby with plenty of clothes, blankets and shawls on its arrival.

'It's important to keep a young baby warm,' she said.

Frank, Edward and Grandpa speculated over the gender.

'There's both girls and boys on my side of the family,' said Grandpa.

'Mainly boys on mine,' said Frank.

George, who had just run in from the yard, contributed his penny worth,

'I think it will definitely be a boy or a girl,' he said.

'That settles it then,' said Frank.

The question of gender was not unimportant, a boy was a prospective wage-earner, a girl could be a help around the house. Children in general played an essential part in the smooth running of a family household. There was so much work to do that, as soon as they were strong enough, they were required to help; fetching water, carrying coal, running messages, not only for their own families but also for those small number of households that had no children.

Sarah was sitting at Jenny's kitchen table, pen in hand, her condition was not just noticeable now but becoming uncomfortable. The back door was open to let in a little more air, cool air. Sarah heard a noise from that direction and turned her head.

'Scrap, what are you doing here?'

The dog hung back, unsure whether he was welcome in this strange kitchen. His head was down, tail dragging.

Sarah looked at him and smiled.

'Oh, all right then, come here.'

The dog's head immediately came up, his tail began to wag and he trotted over to sit alongside Sarah's chair, his wet nose nuzzling onto her lap. She started to scratch the top of his head affectionately.

'You understand, don't you love,' she said, 'I don't know how, but you understand.'

Jenny left them to it and went off on her errands.

When she returned, she found Sarah asleep in the chair, Scrap curled up on her lap.

'Well I never,' she said, knowing of Scrap's reputation.

Her voice woke up Sarah.

'Oh,' she said, 'I must have drifted off.'

'Don't you worry about that lass, but what's that in your lap?'

Scrap sidled down and slipped past Jenny and out of the back door.

'Sometimes,' said Jenny, 'I think dogs are smarter than we are.'

'Aye,' said Sarah, 'who knows what goes on inside that head of their's.'

Jenny started to unpack her shopping, distribute it around the place, into the pantry, into different cupboards and drawers…

'Can I help?' asked Sarah.

'Yes, you can, I got a good cauliflower, it needs washing and sorting out.'

Sarah started to shift herself.

'No problem, Ma, there's nothing like a good cauli.'

Jenny laughed.

'I wish everybody thought like you lass,' she said, 'it's all I can do to get George to put it in his mouth.'

The two women slipped effortlessly into their roles, each instinctively knowing how to best help the other. They were a good team. No mother and daughter could have been better.

Chapter 77

Wilkinson Hughes was talking to his class,

'That's the difference between fact and fiction; in fiction there's a story arc, in fact there's only a timeline.'

He could see by the faces that not everyone had grasped his meaning. It had been a long day, an accident in the playground had left a young boy with a bloody nose, and in the afternoon the sunshine had streamed through the windows, replacing the customary chill with an increasing stuffiness despite all the windows being open.

As the afternoon wore on, the fidgeting steadily increased and it was all that Wilkinson Hughes could do to maintain an externally calm demeanour.

When the school day was finally over, he sighed, relaxed his vigilance, and allowed the children to run out of the classroom, desperate to get out into the fresh air.

He caught George on his way out.

'Does your brother Jack still read books?' he asked.

'He's got little time for it now, sir.'

For Wilkinson Hughes this made the day slip from bad into worse.

'He does read when he can though,' said George, 'he's reading a book called "Kidnapped" at the moment.'

Wilkinson Hughes brightened.

'Then please give him this,' he went over to his desk, opened a drawer, took out a book with a blue cover and returned holding it in his outstretched hand.

George took it.

'Can I read it too, sir?'

'Can you read it?'

'Yes sir, I like reading.'

Wilkinson Hughes' day became brighter; a ray of sunshine had pierced the gloom.

'I didn't know you liked reading,' he said.

'Yes, sir, I always enjoyed listening to Jack when he told us about what he'd learnt and the stories he'd heard, and then, when he started reading, he used to tell us about the books, the stories I mean, some of them were really strange.'

Wilkinson beamed inwardly, as a teacher George's words were music to his ears.

'Which one was strange?' he said.

George thought hard.

'I can't remember the name, sir, sorry sir, but it was about a man who got shipwrecked on an island full of little people, he seemed to be very unlucky because he got shipwrecked a few more times, on islands full of giants, or horrible things or talking horses. My father said it didn't make any sense to write a book like that; it was full of nonsense.'

Wilkinson laughed.

'I used to read Jack's books,' said George, 'I'm not sure he knows.'

'Used to?'

'It's more difficult now that he's moved out. He took his books with him.'

'I see,' said Mr Hughes, 'then the answer is yes, you can also read this book, perhaps you should read it first.'

'Read it before Jack,' said George, 'that would be great, I've never read a book before him before. Are you sure, sir?'

'Yes, I'm sure. Now let me tell you a little about it.'

'Yes please, sir.'

'Well, first of all it's a new book not an old one. I have it because the Owner bought it for his son but when his son saw it, he didn't want it, so it was given to the school. Just two weeks ago, in actual fact.'

'Didn't want it?' said George, incredulous that anybody could not want a book, they were so rare, and precious.

'Their loss, our gain Lawley. It is an adventure book called "The Lost World" and it is written by Sir Arthur Conan Doyle, the same person who writes the Sherlock Holmes stories.'

'Jack likes those,' said George.

'This one is about exploration and has dinosaurs in it, so I suppose your father would think it silly!'

'But I think I'll like it, sir,' said George.

Chapter 78

Jack's life was split in two, below ground with Barney, coal and the clammy darkness, and above ground with his home and Sarah and family on the next street. And at the join there was the ritual of leaving with bait and a kiss on the cheek, and the ritual of returning and washing and being made clean, or as clean as possible.

Each time he got home, the bath was already in front of the fire, the water was heating in pans. As he undressed the sight was almost comical, black from the top of his head all the way down to his belt line and then lily white from there to the tips of his toes.

He had now been working in the coal mine for so long that the black on his face and hands could not be completely removed, no matter how much soap, how much lather or how much scrubbing was put to the task.

In the village it was almost a mark of honour to be distinguished by this ingrained dirt and young boys, fresh to the pit, were chided for the lack of it. So strong was the urge to conform that some of these youngsters would rub handfuls of coal dust onto their arms and faces to hasten their process of transformation.

As her pregnancy progressed, Sarah was sickly and often went to bed early after Jack was washed and fed, and when he tried to hug her she winced and pulled away. Jack was alarmed,

'It's alright,' she said, 'it's just that I'm feeling tender at the moment.'

'They're getting bigger as well,' said Jack.

Sarah laughed.

'Men,' she said, 'you're just like little boys.'

Jack was happy to admit it as he nuzzled in closer, more gently this time.

Jack, like his father, would read the daily newspaper and tell Sarah what the latest was on such things as votes for women, the football results, strikes and speeches and she would normally listen attentively, but on this particular evening she said,

'Put your bloody paper down! All it seems to be full of is bad news!'

And then she sat down and started to cry.

Jack had never seen Sarah cry like this before. He was nonplused. He got up, came over to her and knelt at her feet.

'What's wrong?'

Sarah looked at him through teary eyes.

'I don't know, and everything, and I want my mother, and…'

She sagged in the chair and fell silent.

'I'll make a cup of tea.'

'I don't want a bl…'

Sarah stopped in mid-sentence as she saw the concern on her husband's face.

She clenched her fists.

'I'd love a cup of tea,' she said.

As soon as he possibly could Jack was round at his mother's. She was sewing.

He asked her how she was and she said 'fine', he asked her how his father was and she said, 'You see as much of him as I do', he would have asked her how Edward was but he feared the same answer, instead he asked her how George was,

'He's taken to reading,' said Jenny, 'like you. Mr Hughes is encouraging him.'

'That's good,' said Jack.

There was a moment's silence.

'And how are you mother?'

Jenny put down her sewing.

'You've asked me that,' she said, 'so why don't you just tell me what's bothering you.'

Haltingly at first and then in a torrent, Jack told his mother what he was worried about.

'…and I don't know how to help,' he said.

Jenny put her hands in her lap and sighed.

'I should have thought of this. I'm sorry Jack, but Sarah acts like nothing's wrong when I see her, I should have known better. I'll talk to her.'

Jenny was as good as her word and the next day she walked through Sarah's back door and found her resting in a chair by the range. As soon as she saw Jenny she sprang to her feet,

'I was just…' she said.

'Sit down, sit down,' said Jenny, 'what you were doing was the right thing in your condition.'

'But I've got so long to go, I shouldn't be feeling like this.'

'Every pregnancy is different, Sarah, with George I was in bed for a week, couldn't get up, was being sick all the time, I'd never had anything like that with Edward or Jack.'

She didn't mention the miscarriages and her anxiety during her pregnancies. That definitely would not help.

'I just feel so tired and sickly. It's painful to be touched sometimes and I'm sure Jack thinks…'

She started to cry.

'It's alright, Sarah,' said Jenny, 'I'm sure Jack will understand if you tell him.'

'Will he? It sounds so ridiculous. I want him to touch me, then I don't, and I've been angry with him, and I don't know why.'

'You're pregnant, your body's changing… you've got to be gentle on yourself.'

'And,' said Sarah, keen now to get everything off her chest, 'and I've been wishing my mother was here. I'm sorry Jenny, please don't take it wrong, but I've been missing her recently, and I don't know why.'

Jenny took Sarah's hands.

'There's no one like your real mother,' she said, 'you're like a daughter to me, Sarah, and I'll always do my best for you, but I know I'm not your real mother. Alice loved you, still loves you, and I know how difficult it was for her to leave you with us, but she really believed, really believed, it was for the best.'

Sarah collapsed into Jenny's arms.

'I'm really lucky to have you,' she said.

Jenny choked back her own tears, 'Get a grip of yourself!' she thought to herself.

'Why didn't you say anything?'

'I didn't want to worry you. I didn't want you to think I couldn't cope.'

Jenny pulled away and wiped her hands down her apron.

'Right!' she said, 'now, let's be thinking, men are no good when it comes to these things. Let me talk to Elsie Walton and see what she can suggest to settle your stomach, and before that let's get Jack's meal sorted and I'll bring in some water to warm for his bath.'

'But Jenny, you've got your own…'

'Don't you worry about that, you get the kettle on and we can also have a cup of tea, it's good for the digestion you know.'

Meal prepared, water heating in pans, the two women were drinking tea, Sarah warily sipping her's.

'I'm going to tell George to come round here after school every day. He'll fill the buckets and bring in the water. It's a heavy job and he'll be happy to do it, especially if you let him have a look at Jack's books.'

'He has taken to his books, hasn't he? I hear he's just as bad as Jack.'

'Or worse,' said Jenny, 'I'd never have thought it, he's always been such a bundle of energy, but with his nose in a book he's a different lad.'

Chapter 79

Underground Jack kept his concerns about Sarah and her pregnancy to himself. It was not a suitable topic of conversation. To take his mind off things he worked with a fierce focus and talked to David Goodwin about books.

David was reading "A Tale of Two Cities" by Charles Dickens,

'If you skip over the over-romanticised bits,' he said, 'it's a powerful story. The French Revolution must have been a terrible time for those in Paris. The guillotine was in regular use and the image of women sitting, knitting as the heads fell is a powerful one.'

'Didn't do much good did it,' said Jack, 'ended up swapping a King for an Emperor and spilling lots more blood.'

'You know,' said David, 'I was pleased our strike ended when it did, there were more and more flashes of violence, the "haves" versus the "have nots", it's not so different to what caused the French Revolution.'

'I was pleased to get back to work,' said Jack.

'And at least we achieved something,' said David.

Elsie Walton had come up with an ointment whose smell she said would bring calm and a potion to settle the stomach. The potion worked better than the ointment.

The pregnancy was increasingly showing and Sarah wore looser clothes. Her chores were not lessened though and she was pleased with the help she got from George who not only brought in buckets of water but also supplies of coal from the coal shed.

'What would I do without you?' she said.

George felt he was doing something important and beamed at the compliment.

He'd finished reading "The Lost World" long ago and it was now sitting on Jack's bookshelf waiting for another pair of eyes to peer into its adventures and mysteries.

'Could I take one of Jack's books to read?' he said, taking a chance when he was so obviously in Sarah's good books.

She smiled.

'Which one?' she said.

'"The Jungle Book",' said George without hesitation, 'it's full of stories of a boy being brought up by wolves.'

'Sounds scary,' said Sarah, 'but I'm sure that will be alright, you will look after it, won't you?'

'Like gold dust,' said George.

Sarah was sitting in her chair by the fire, chatting to Jenny, when suddenly she let out an exclamation,

'Oh!'

'What's the matter?' said Jenny, immediately concerned.

'I think I felt something,' said Sarah, and put the palms of her hands on her 'bump', moving them in a circular motion.

'Oh, there it is again!'

'The baby's moving,' said Jenny, 'that's always a good sign.'

Jenny was aching to feel the movement for herself but knew it wasn't her place to ask.

'Would you like to feel?' asked Sarah, 'it's like it's doing a roll.'

'If you don't mind,' said Jenny, moving forward quickly in case Sarah should change her mind.

'Do you need that much salt?' asked Jack, as they ate the stew that Sarah had prepared, dipping their bread and butter into the thick gravy.

'I can't taste it without salt,' said Sarah, 'everything tastes bland without salt these days.'

'You seem to use a lot.'

'And do you see a problem with that?'

Alarm bells sounded in Jack's head. It was time for an unconditional retreat.

'No, not at all, have as much as you like.'

Jack had also been allowed to feel the baby move and from that moment everything, for him, had become more real. A living thing was growing inside his wife, and it was their baby! He was so preoccupied with the thought that he hadn't even minded when Sarah told him that George had borrowed one of his books, all he said was,

'Ah, "The Jungle Book", a good choice, it's more a collection of short stories than a proper book.'

'What do you fancy, boy or girl?'

'What?'

David and Jack were sitting eating by the light of their safety lamps, the coal dust adding a gritty texture to their sandwiches.

'For your firstborn,' said David, 'boy or girl?'

'I just hope it's healthy,' said Jack.

'Must be close now.'

'Any day.'

'I always thought I wanted a boy until our Ruth came along, don't know what I'd do without her now… the little scamp.'

He smiled.

'That's the thing about kids, you can't imagine what they're going to be like and when they turn up you can't imagine that they were ever going to be anybody else.'

It was now a waiting game. As births generally happened at home, a bed was set up in the downstairs parlour.

The fire was tested and a grill added so that water could be heated. The aspidistra, much healthier now, looked on.

Elsie Walton agreed to be midwife, with Jenny and Mrs Tindale as helpers. They were all 'on call' awaiting the start of proceedings.

As the day got closer Sarah got larger and more uncomfortable with indigestion and leg cramps adding to her difficulties. She was getting impatient to get it over with, while at the same time being worried about giving birth.

Chapter 80

Traditionally, gynaecological matters had been dealt with by general surgeons, there was resistance amongst the medical profession to recognise midwifery as a specialism.

However, a lecturer in midwifery and the diseases of women and children was appointed to the Newcastle University Medical School in 1899 and this was a welcome sign that things, at last, might be beginning to change. The same man was then appointed consultant gynaecologist in the new Royal Victoria Infirmary that opened in Newcastle in 1906 and, in 1908, became the first professor of obstetrics and gynaecology at the University of Durham.

Ever so slowly the needs of women were being given more credence and more attention and, by this time, Sarah could have gained access to these improved services through Jack's membership of the Permanent Relief Fund.

There was some distrust of hospitals from those in the mining communities however, there were too many stories of people going in and not coming out again. They were unfamiliar institutions and, although Sarah's pregnancy had been awkward at times, no one saw the need to seek help from the outside, especially as there was very little understanding of what that help might involve. Women were used to just getting on with it and looking after themselves.

What was well understood, learned from the raw school of everyday life, was that childbirth was a dangerous business and it was not uncommon for the lives of healthy women to be lost, just as an unexpected roof-fall might claim the life of an otherwise fit and healthy miner. Indeed, at this time, 4 out of every 100 mothers died in, or as a consequence of, childbirth.

Sarah had talked to Jenny about her worries. She was excited at the prospect of being a mother but frightened about giving birth.

Jenny had tried to reassure her,

'It'll be alright, pet,' she had said, 'I'll be right here and Mrs Walton is coming round. She's a sure hand at birthing is Mrs Walton.'

And now the time has come, the biological processes of life creation, the cell division, multiplication and specialisation have taken place and a baby is ready to be born. The oft repeated miracle of birth is due, and Sarah is in labour.

She is lying on the bed that has been prepared for her in the front parlour. The curtains are drawn, and the room is lit by oil lamps and candles. The coal fire is burning in the grate and large pans of water are heating.

Jenny and Elsie Watson are in attendance.

Jack, Edward and Frank are underground.

Grandpa is sitting by the range in the kitchen reading his paper, on hand to run errands if needed.

George is at school.

Down in the pit, Jack is trying to concentrate, and is talking to Barney,

'My wife is having a baby,' he whispers.

Barney whinnies softly.

'I don't want to be down here. I want to be up there, with her, even though I'd be no use at all.'

Time proceeds at a snail's pace. A tub derails, Jack heaves it back on, his body moving with a learned familiarity, his muscles concentrating, his mind elsewhere. He grunts with the effort.

A voice calls from the darkness. It is David Goodwin.

'Jack, you alright? You've been awfully quiet.'

'Yes, David, I'm alright, just thinking, that's all.'

'You know it's not good to think down here, keep your mind on the job, Jack, keep your mind on the job.'

At the start things are progressing well, and Jenny goes into the kitchen to see her father. He immediately looks up from his reading.

'Dad, can you fill a bucket of water and put some coals in this scuttle?'

Grandpa has almost forgotten the word "Dad" and he smiles up at his daughter, proud at the use of it.

'When you're ready just knock on the parlour door. Don't come in! The birthing room is no place for men.'

Grandpa nods and immediately sets about his tasks, waving away questions from neighbours at the communal water tap, all keen to know how things are going. He returns with the water and then takes the empty scuttle to the coal shed and fills it. When the bucket and the scuttle are ready, he carries them to the parlour door and knocks. He tries not to listen to any of the sounds that are emanating from the room. Jenny opens the door and takes in the water, then she returns for the coal.

'Thanks,' she says.

'If you need anything else…'

'I know,' she says, and closes the door behind her.

'I'm going to be a father, I can't believe it,' Jack whispers to Barney, 'Sarah and me, mother and father, what kind of parents will we be?'

A coal tub scrapes against the wall, Jack slows Barney, the tub settles.

'It's only now, when I'm about to be a father, that I think about my own Mum and Dad. And when I do I realise how hard they've worked and how well they've done. I can't even imagine a life without them always being there, keeping me in check, helping me grow.'

He reaches the junction, meets the Driver, swaps full tubs for empty ones and then turns Barney's head back towards the face.

'I wonder what you're thinking?' he says, 'You listen to me prattle on all the time but I don't know what you're thinking.'

Barney shakes his head and then twists his neck around and bares his teeth.

'Oh I see, you know I've got one more apple do you…'

Jack digs deep into a pocket and takes out an apple. He gives it to Barney. The sound of scrunching echoes loud in the confines of the tunnel.

In school, the lesson is Geography and the subject is Wales. George listens attentively, carried along by the teacher's passion for his homeland. Wilkinson Hughes is in full flow and his words have a lyricism that conjures up pictures of mountains and rugged coastlines, the sea breaking white against stubborn rocks, while inland rolling green hills release freshwater streams that tumble into the valleys and feed the lazy rivers where native brown trout swim and otters play.

'And there's good coal in Wales,' he says, changing tack, 'and there are men and families, just like us, bound to its extraction.'

George tries to imagine a land as foreign as Wales, a place that is both different and the same.

'My Wales,' continues Wilkinson Hughes, 'is a land of song, of myth, of legend, and of dragons.'

Eyes open wide at the thought of dragons.

'It has its own language, and in that language, it is not called Wales but Cymru…'

George wonders fleetingly why anyone would want to leave such a place and come here to be a teacher… his young mind is too full of ideas to think about anything else…

Grandpa finds he can't concentrate; he's read the same line in the newspaper several times and he still doesn't know what it says. He stops trying to read and puts his head back. He remembers how Jenny was conceived when he was on leave and that he was half a world away when she was born, finding out by letter 10 weeks after the event.

And there were times when he thought he would never get back to see her, skirmishes that came far too close to finishing him off. He remembered one in particular when he had been wounded and would surely have died if his mate, Private Harold Carpenter, had not dragged him back to the relative safety of their camp.

He hadn't been a good father, he knew that, appearing and disappearing, leaving everything important to his wife to look after. And what a fine job she'd done! And what a fine woman she'd been! And what a fine woman, wife and mother Jenny had grown up to be. Maybe he should tell her that sometime, he shook his head, he was getting sentimental in his old age, and anyway, she probably knew how he felt.

And now… now he is about to become a Great-grandfather, it's hard to believe that he's made it this far.

He smiles to himself, Jack is a fine man, he'll make a better father than he'd ever been.

Sarah's labour is progressing, she is showing signs of distress, Jenny comforts her, Elsie keeps everything clean.

As time goes on, it becomes increasingly obvious that something is not right.

Sarah is bleeding. Jenny is mopping her brow and trying to keep her calm, talking to her gently.

Elsie takes more things out of her bag, some have sharp edges. She beckons to Jenny, who reluctantly moves away from Sarah who is panting.

'Jenny, we need to put these in boiling water to sterilise them.'

Jenny says nothing.

'I'll go into the kitchen and do that, you keep Sarah as calm as you can, try to encourage her.'

Jenny whispers desperately, 'Is there anything else we can do?'

'I'll do what I can, but I think we should get Doctor Milne here if we can.'

Doctor Milne! Elsie bows her head,

'I can only do so much,' she says.

'Tell my father to go,' says Jenny.

Elsie explains the situation as much as she dare,

'Something's not quite right,' she says, 'to be on the safe side, we'd like you to go to get some help. We think it's best to get the doctor in if we can. '

Grandpa reads more into Elsie's face than her words and rushes out the back door. Dashing up the back lane he sees a bicycle and takes it. This is too urgent; he can apologise later.

Elsie gives Sarah an Ergot tea.

Hours pass.

By the time Doctor Milne arrives Sarah is exhausted. As her labour continues there is more bleeding.

Dr Milne and Elsie Walton work together and do what they can.

Jack finishes his shift, unharnesses and feeds Barney, makes his way to the pit bottom. He does not walk home with his father and brother but runs to his parent's house where Jenny has arranged with Mrs Tindale to prepare his bath… he must be clean before he is allowed anywhere near the birthing room.

The water is steaming, the soap, scrubbing brush and flannel are all laid out, clean clothes are waiting for him. For the first time he is first in the family bath. Frank and Edward, unwashed, go to the pub for a drink in order to give Jack some space.

Sarah is flagging after such a long and difficult labour, but nature takes its course and Jenny is thankful when she finally sees the baby's head appear.

And then it happens quickly, the baby is born and gives a cry.

The relief in the room is palpable, but the doctor's work is not done.

Jack is clean, he runs round, full of anticipation, trying to control his heartbeat, his breathing. He crashes through the door off the back lane that gives access to their yard. He stops to steady himself, his boots scrape over the cobbles, he enters their kitchen, the kitchen of the home that Sarah has created for him. The kitchen is empty, he wonders why, Grandpa is not there, perhaps he is fetching water… he hears sounds from the parlour, through the joining door, he hears a baby cry, his heart leaps, the parlour door opens. Elsie Walton enters, he wonders why it isn't his mother…

Elsie is wiping her wet hands on a cloth.

'You have a daughter,' she says looking at Jack, 'the baby looks strong.'

From the look on her face Jack knows there is something else.

Elsie sags a little.

'Jack,' she says, 'there's been bleeding…'

Jack doesn't wait to hear more, he pushes past and into the parlour.

Jenny is sitting in a corner; her hands are in her lap.

Jack ignores her.

The doctor is by Sarah and saying something that Jack doesn't hear.

Sarah is on the bed. She is holding their baby, swaddled in white cotton.

The little face is red; the eyes are closed. But then she sneezes and wriggles and re-settles, wrinkling her nose, opening and closing her mouth.

'Look,' says Sarah, 'our daughter, Jack. Isn't she beautiful.'

The bedclothes are discoloured.

Jack looks and goes down on his knees by the bed. He looks into his wife's face, her hair is plastered to her forehead, her skin flushed.

'How are you?' he asks.

She smiles.

'I'm glad you're here with me,' she says.

She holds out a hand.

Jack takes it in his.

It feels damp, cold, clammy.

'Oh, Sarah,' he says.

'Don't worry, Jack,' she says, 'everything will be alright…'

Author's Note

Whilst having the privilege of access to a University Library archive for the purposes of my own research, I came across a series of lined school exercise books with the name 'George Lawley' written on the front.

When I opened the first one I was astonished to find the beginnings of a manuscript, written in black India Ink and in fine Copperplate handwriting which was still clearly legible and had succumbed to no serious handling or water damage as, unfortunately, can be quite often the case.

I had no intention of reading it but did decide to bring it to the attention of one of the University Librarians.

But "the best laid plans…" as they say, and, as my own research hit a brick wall, I used the time I had on my hands to dip into the manuscript myself.

As I began to read, I got hooked and simply could not stop until I reached the final line.

I tried to then part myself from it, I had too much else going on to allow these old exercise books to distract me. But try as I might, I could not shake the idea that they deserved to be published.

I tried to research what might be known of George Lawley; his background, his life, his academic record and managed to convince myself that his legacy was worth preserving and so, after taking advice, I finally allowed myself the time to attempt the task.

I have to say that the job of compiling, editing, fact checking, and in general getting the entire manuscript into the form needed for publication was a far greater task than I had thought. This was in no small measure due to my decision to incorporate parts of my own research in a way that I thought might increase a modern reader's understanding of the times, without unduly weakening the narrative.

Now, finally, after many long hours spent alone in my study pouring over words that were difficult to decipher, I am happy to say that I have, to the best of my ability, completed the task and now lay the work before you, dear reader, with both trembling hands and a relieved heart.

John S. Langley
The Old Mine Museum

Note:

Shortly before the publication of the current volume a second box of papers has been found, again containing exercise books that appear, on first inspection, to have been written by the same hand.

Unfortunately, there has not been time to do anything other than to make a late note of this discovery.

Looking back at all the books she had written, Agatha Christie said 'the one that satisfied me completely … was written with integrity, with sincerity, it was written as I meant to write it, and that is the proudest joy an author can have.'
("My Autobiography", 1977)